Touching Earth

Also by Rani Manicka

The Rice Mother

Rani Manicka

Touching Earth

SCEPTRE

First published in Great Britain in 2004 by Hodder and Stoughton
A division of Hodder Headline

1 3 5 7 9 10 8 6 4 2

A CIP catalogue record for this title is available from the British Library

ISBN 0 340 82384 4 HB
0 340 82389 5 TPB

Typeset in Sabon by
Phoenix Typesetting, Auldgirth, Dumfriesshire

Printed and bound in Great Britain by
Mackays of Chatham plc, Chatham, Kent

Hodder Headline's policy is to use papers that are natural, renewable and
recyclable products and made from wood grown in sustainable forests. The
logging and manufacturing processes are expected to conform to the
environmental regulations of the country of origin

Hodder and Stoughton
A division of Hodder Headline
338 Euston Road
London NW1 3BH

For
Girolamo Avarello who told me
about a man called Ricky, and
Sue Fletcher who blew her precious breath
into this book and made it live.

Author's Note

Dear Reader

If you have read The Rice Mother *and desire a similar story then I must, in fairness, advise you to leave this book unread, for this is a dreadfully sordid world you seek to enter. But to you, bold reader, who raises your eyes to me light your lamp, and let us venture forth. We must find Beauty, she made a mistake, succumbed to temptation and now lies naked and without a friend, but she endures, because a single glance of admiration from you will rouse her from the ashes of her degradation.*

Rani Manicka -

The woman stretched out her neck and howled like a wolf. She tore at her hair until clumps came out in her clenched fists. With the same fists she beat the dull earth. Alas, alas, the boy was dead. She sprang up suddenly, her eyes wild. 'Do not touch him until I return,' she instructed and ran all the way to the Bodhi tree to fall at Buddha's feet. 'Oh Enlightened One,' she cried, 'my son is dead. If you are indeed the true master, then bring him back to life.' Buddha opened his eyes. Perhaps he wanted to tell her about the inevitability of birth and death for the un-awakened, but he must have seen the dust of dreaming in her eyes, so he told her, 'Go forth and bring me a handful of grain from a home where death has not yet been, and I will return your son to you.' Overwhelmed by gratitude and joy the woman bowed many times before she withdrew to begin her search. She searched, and searched, and searched and . . .

Contents

The Players

Watch them carefully. They are not all to be trusted and one or two might even be ghosts.

The Twins

Nutan

Dawn was breaking over the hills when I opened the miniature wooden doors of our ancestral shrine. Into the exposed niches I placed coconut-leaf containers of fruit, flowers and cakes. In the trees, bushes and vegetation, everything was quiet and still. I lit incense sticks. In the cool fragrant air I closed my eyes and brought my palms to meet – and the world fell away. I could have remained thus for a whole hour, but for a sudden burst of childish laughter beyond the garden walls. In that wisp of sound, just for an instant, she had shimmered. I snapped awake.

It was not her. Of course it was not.

I stood frozen and staring at my clasped hands. The knuckles were white. It couldn't be her . . . but I was tearing across the hardened earth, scrambling up the wall, my feet instinctively finding the familiar crevices in the uneven stones. Over the wall I saw them. Two little girls, no more than four or five years old dazzling in their dancing costumes, great helmets of finely worked gold-leaf bouncing and glittering in the early light. By our entrance gate their bare feet crushed the fruit rind the squirrels had discarded during the night. Then they rounded the corner and were gone.

I heaved myself up onto the wall, and sat, unthinking, my fingers caressing the velvet moss carpeting the stones, my eyes on the tiny creatures scurrying inside a crack in the wall, and suddenly the past returned. Innocent and undefeated by the day I had slumped to a filthy floor in a squalid London flat, and surrounded by uncaring strangers, died.

I stared at it, tantalised. How completely untouched it was by loss. How magnificent we all were. A molten gold sun was setting and my sister and I were dancing to Mother's string instrument, the *sape*. With her deformed right leg tucked under her buttocks and the other drawn up to her slender body Ibu, our mother, attained the grace denied her during the day, standing and walking.

And I saw Father too, his hair long and still black, worn in the knot of a priest, squatting by a row of bell-shaped cages. Lovingly he fed corn kernels to his prize fighting cockerels. He was a puppeteer and a highly skilled ventriloquist. Actually a star of some repute. His shows were in such demand that he was often away for long periods, travelling from village to village performing with his two hundred or so leather-covered puppets. I was terribly proud of him then. Yet, in the shining bubble, it was Nenek, our grandmother, whom I saw most clearly. She sat on the steps of her living compartment, her fathomless black eyes half-obscured but intent and watching through the milky-grey smoke ascending from her clove cigarettes.

Ah, the past, that enchanted harmful fairy tale.

Tears splashed on my arms. I touched them. Fetched from a well of sorrow. If I could only reach out for the past. Catch it. I had smashed it up needlessly. Careless, careless. How vast was my carelessness. See now what is left over from yesterday.

The sun had come up over the hills. A spotted green and grey frog leaped into a cluster of banana trees, and I jumped off the wall restlessly. Yes, I will tell you everything, but not here. Not in this high garden of bright flowers, and trees drooping with clusters of ripe fruit. Here I would be accused of sentimentalising the past. The right home for my story is in the temple of the dead. There I will be forgiven. Transience is expected. It is not far from here, a marvellous place where time ceases. Its gates are intricately carved and guarded day and night by giant volcanic stone figures.

But wait, if I tell all, leave nothing out, and your travels bring you to my paradise island one day will you promise that if you see me, sarong-wrapped, and dusky, you will never call my name? For your glance of recognition will hurt. Like excrement on a flower, it will awaken the pointing finger and shame, oh God, such shame. How people will talk!

You see, in paradise a name come to harm trembles without remedy. One is required to go to great lengths to defend a reputation. Of course, I can hardly bring myself to care any more, but there are other members of my family to think of and protect.

Come, once we go past the open marketplace in the centre of the village, you can see it.

Here we are. Look. Didn't I tell you how fabulous the temple doorway is? Take your shoes off. Even this early in the morning the flagstones will already be warm. A dog will never set foot in here, but cats, they come and go as if it were home. When we were children we came here often, drawn to the eerie silence. Mortals among Gods. Hushed by a certain anxiety we tiptoed down corridors lined with life-size statues of grotesquely leering demons their tongues protruding down to their navels. But now that I am grown they emerge into my mind benign, smiling and genuine. Mortality is a game.

Here. We will sit in this patch of sunlight here, so when the disillusionment becomes too painful, our eyes may rest upon the splendour of the flame tree in full bloom, yonder. As you take my hand to draw closer do not forget your promise.

I was born twenty-four years ago in this tiny remote village. Balinese believe every child is a treasured gift from the heavens, and my sister and I were considered the most cherished treasure of all. Identical twins. So completely adored that for the first few months we were held in permanent bodily contact with either Nenek or Ibu, so our bodies would not touch the sullied earth. Afterwards every effort was made for us to awaken to a wondrous world.

My sister and I roused to lingering kisses in our hair and the nutritious first milk of cows curdled in a pan with rock sugar. We drank lemonade made with rainwater and limes that Nenek, to soften and heighten their flavour, had rolled under her broad feet. And because it is also our belief that a child's connection to its body and this material world is tenuous, never was there an occasion when we were beaten, or even scolded.

Why then in this season of delight did I stir from confused dreams, to confront a reality that existed only with the scurrilous laughter of night animals, and the sound of tree roots stretching for water? A ridiculous insistent whisper moving from room to room, 'It's all lies . . . It's all lies . . .' Why did it sometimes seem as if my sister and I were guests of benevolent strangers? That Nenek, Ibu and Father were owners of a secret they all conspired to conceal. Shame they didn't know that a lie must never be kept in paradise. That it will wreck everything in its desire for release.

I suppose I should start my story with Father, the puppet master. A shadow maker of incomparable talent, and fingers like moving snakes. He would lower himself onto a mat set in front of a coconut oil lamp and, with a wooden hammer clutched between the toes of his right foot, strike a rhythm, tock-tock. It was the signal the orchestra waited for. A delicate sound would fill the air as he picked up a flat dead puppet from a coffin-shaped box. On the screen a lacy silhouette would tremble, then distort as he threw it in and out of focus behind the flickering flame. Then it stopped suddenly, motionless in the middle of the screen.

By the time he had recited his magic mantras and began manipulating their articulated limbs a beautiful spell had been cast and all the little puppets had come to life. Their fantastic adventures never ended before dawn. How proud we were sitting in the audience, our bellies aching with laughter, or helpless tears running down our faces. Afterwards we went to kneel before him. To bless us with magical protection he sprinkled holy water on us, and pressed damp rice grains onto our foreheads, temples and throats.

Oh Father, Father . . . how could you?

Unbeknownst to us the puppet master had fitted invisible strings to our bodies, and on the sly threw his voice into our mouths as he pulled us this way and that. It was he who first brought grief into our home.

In my mind my father remains truly handsome with long sweeping eyelashes and a high nose bridge, but also mysterious, veiled and remote. Under his thin moustache the edges of his lips rose cautiously in a polite dignified smile. In all his movements he was measured and thoughtful. Except for the huge black and yellow orchid he sometimes wore behind one ear he dressed plainly, always in black. Mild mannered, yes, but behind the mask?

'He loves you both dearly,' Ibu said to my sister and me.

But I knew a secret she didn't. My father loved only my sister. Perhaps because he had guessed that my sister required his regard more. Or more likely because with my jaw clenched I was too much like Nenek. Too fierce and too bold for his liking. I sensed the barely disguised rejection in his whole being, in the tightly drawn-up knees, the implacable curve of his narrow neck, the wincing thin-lipped smiles he turned in my direction, and in his beautiful, purposely hiding eyes. But that's not the secret. The real secret was that I didn't care. The only person I ever wanted love from was Ibu. The one thing in the world I craved was for her eyes to descend upon me, bright and adoring. Filled with that same caressing light with which they rested upon my father. I thought her the most amazing, most beautiful and cleverest soul on earth. I wanted to be just like her. In my memory are perfectly preserved snatches of conversation where she appears brilliantly witty.

In fact, my memory serves me wrong. In reality she was a withdrawn, frail, crippled creature. Not by any standards could she be considered beautiful, but she did own two remarkable assets. One was a spectacular mane of thick, knee-length, jet-black hair that sat in a perfumed, sleek bun at the nape of her neck. The other was an unusually pale complexion. Her ghostly skin came from never having set foot outside the house on account of her easily tiring heart.

A hole-in-the-heart baby, she had lain in Nenek's lap and taken all of six hours to empty a bottle of milk. The doctors shook their heads, and warned that she would not make it past childhood. But Nenek gathered my mother to her breasts, spat on the disinfected floor, and cursed, 'What your cruel mouths have flung at me, may your children suffer.' She returned home rigid with resolution. Was she not descended from a long and illustrious line of medicine men?

Her daughter would live. There was nothing she would not dare, no sacrifice too great for the puny life she had brought into the world.

I remember well many bad nights while I was growing up, when the dark winds howled down the valley, only to turn around restlessly and like wolves dart up the mountain slopes again, wanting to take. Impatient for my mother to cease her rasping breaths. I wanted to stroke Ibu, comfort her, but I dared not. She lay on her thin mattress on the floor, a crumpled figure, too delicate to be helped.

That is how I remember Fear. A small dimly lit room dense with slowly smoking herbs and seeds. In the middle a woman's desperate fight for breath. The feral, haunted look in my sister's eyes as we passed each other noiselessly bearing countless braziers of red coals into Ibu's living quarters. And of course the blood pounding in my wrists.

And Hope I remember as another figure, crouched beside Ibu's prone body. Oh, so powerful that her force radiated from her palms, soaked her clothes and swirled around her. I wish you could have seen Nenek then. Slowly, rhythmically, she rubbed her home-made ointments onto her daughter's chest all the while singing to the spirits, her native hill-tribe dialect begging, wheedling, and now and again threatening. She made promises of offerings and sacrifices. Quickly I became an apostle of those strange half-commanding, half-plaintive songs. With every flare of lightning that struck the drenched sky, I too implored again and again,

> *Do not call her name at night, not at night.*
> *Oh Powerful spirits, I welcomed you to my home.*
> *If I have harmed you, forgive me, be kind.*
> *Accept my offerings, Oh powerful ones.*
> *Do not take what is not yours.*
> *Do not show your wrath.*
> *Oh you, leave me the child.*
> *Consent that she lives another day.*
> *Do not call her name, not at night,*
> *NOT TONIGHT.*

In the face of her mother's ferocious purpose Ibu's small hennaed hands lay still, her silent enduring eyes hopeless. Then it seemed she was a beautiful, fragile child already lost to us. Sometimes the child was moved to kiss her mother's broad feet, splayed like a fan. Gently she laid her cheek on them as if they were a pillow. In truth, she was weary. Softly, breathlessly she soothed her mother, 'It is only a garment I will discard, Mother. Let my soul go.'

The reasonable words only stung Nenek into beseeching the spirits so wretchedly that they listened. From our outposts in the shadowy doorway, my sister and I sat excluded and awed by the immensity of love in that tiny room, conscious of the night outside straining for what belonged to us. Suppose we lost Ibu to the night? Suppose in a moment of weakness we lost the battle? Outside, the inexhaustible wind bayed.

By the time Father's cockerels crowed in the dawn, my sister had long since curled up against the wall in exhausted sleep and my voice was hoarse or completely lost from relentless bargaining. Only then did I know relief. Only then through the solid smoke did Nenek's eyes, savage and triumphant, swing around to meet mine, her accomplice.

Even in the dark we had cheated death of his quarry. Again. He was not strong enough, not against the combined strength of Nenek and me. We had planted another day for Ibu to hobble into. Nenek stood up, taking with her Ibu's spittoon, half a coconut shell; inside, a mix of ashes and Ibu's yellow-green phlegm. Dizzy with exhilaration I stood up and went to claim the victor's seat, the place Nenek had vacated. Softly I touched Ibu's hand and it curled weak and pale around mine. She shut her eyes and opened her mouth, perhaps to say thank you, but I forestalled her. 'Sshh,' I whispered, 'sshhh,' and all the tenderness in the world trembled upon my lips. I remember it now like it was yesterday. How warm it was. That special space vacated by Nenek. Beside Ibu. And Ibu, poor thing, she smiled sadly, bravely, and endured another daybreak.

Painfully shy and reclusive, Ibu often passed most of her days in silence, her expression rapt, as her nimble clever hands, dyed red with plant juices, effortlessly twisted a single palm leaf into a work of art fit for a God, or created pretty umbrellas from the lacy stomach of a pig. She did these things as offerings for us to carry to the shrines.

Under her charge even the humble pale yellow feathers of an immature coconut leaf aspired to be a delightful vessel, held together by its own central spine.

One year during the *Galungan*, a great Hindu celebration, Ibu made the most beautiful offering I have ever seen, a two-meter-tall tower, so skilfully constructed that not even a hint of the wooden skewers nor the supporting banana stem showed through the cluster of whole roast chickens, sweetmeats, fruits, vegetables, cakes and flowers. Nenek carried the majestic thing on her head to the temple. At the inner temple entrance she bent low enough for the men waiting on the other side to receive the soaring tower.

The other women circled my mother's magnificent creation again and again. They stared at the wild sago-palm fruit, green satin balls quilted with red silk and jungle purple pitcher flowers. I saw their eyes changing: surprise, envy and, without fail, passion for my mother's skill. How long they stood studying the technique that managed clusters of waxy pink berries with scarlet bark, or vermilion chilli peppers with the crimson bracts and yellow petals of a mangosteen bloom. But in their hearts they knew they would never reach Ibu's perfection. No one could.

We rushed home to tell her. Smiling gently she gave us permission to decorate her hair.

I will never forget that first tantalising waft of coconut oil in my nostrils and the feeling of silk, released and uncoiling in my hands. Together we set about pinning it into a large smooth shape called *susuk konde*. While we surrounded it with jewelled combs and delicate pins worked in gold, Ibu chewed dates wrapped in betel nut leaves. Afterwards she traced our eyes, noses and mouths with her callused fingers saying, 'It is a good thing that both of you were given your father's face. Eyes like shimmering morning stars. You are the most beautiful children I have ever seen.'

Then she placed bougainvilleas in our hair. She wanted us

to be famous Balinese dancers. Gently she cupped our chins in her hands drawing us so close that we smelt the scent of dates and betel nut leaves on her breath, but I pushed my face nearer still yearning for a fiercer embrace, wanting those calluses deeper in my skin, because even with her fingers inquisitive on our faces, I felt her pushing us away. As if we did not belong to her.

As a result of her frailty we were never allowed to sleep with her, so those indolent afternoons when we lay quietly beside her were precious beyond words. Thrilled by her attention we took turns begging for more stories, wanting glimpses of her childhood in the hills with Nenek. But Ibu's memory was poor or her tongue lazy. All she cared to recount was still being hungry after a meagre meal of baked rice from the night before and sitting at the door of an improvised one-room hut waiting for Nenek to come up the hill slope. And when Nenek came, it was with her neck moving from side to side like a classical Indian dancer, in an effort to balance the enormous container of water on her head.

In her right hand she carried more water in a blue pail, and in the left she held the hand of my uncle, long dead. He was a blur in my mother's memory. A thin boy who broke Nenek's heart when he died in childhood.

Once Ibu told us of the moment of his passing. 'There were brown rats running along the walls of the hospital corridor when a white-coated man came to tell Nenek her son was dead. For a moment she stood utterly still. Then she sagged to the ground, sitting awkwardly, her head crooked, her mouth slobbering, and her breath rasping like some great felled beast; in terrible agony, but unable to die. Sometimes I think she should have.'

We did not ask why. Hypnotised by Ibu's voice, we absently stroked the odd, toeless stump that she usually curled up and concealed under her sarong. It was smooth bright pink and utterly useless. Only with the help of a walking stick could Ibu limp around. Though she thought it important that not even her good foot had sunk into the brown ooze of the rice fields her defect was not a cause for revulsion. We had not yet learned shame and we accepted things as they were, and if anything loved her all the more for her imperfection.

As a rule, when Ibu was well, she worked all day, every day on a simple loom. For though we lived in paradise we were very poor and each of us did our share to fill the rice bins; my father made his puppets talk, Nenek cured the ill and made the cakes that my sister and I sold after school, and Ibu wove luscious glorious lengths of *songket,* gold or silver thread embroideries on silk dyed in rich deep tones of indigo, ochre, turquoise, lime, black or cinnamon. Patterns so intricate and complex that they took her many months to finish. Each brought into existence to adorn the pampered curves of wealthy women. Even now it is a cause of sadness to me that not a single one was born destined to rest on my mother's body. Ibu would never wear anything but the simplest batik sarongs. 'It would be a waste to wear them in the house,' she always said.

On our tenth birthday, on two lengths of chocolate cloth, she began to make our heirlooms, pieces so exquisite that they took her two years to complete to her satisfaction. Fantastic forests of birds, animals, flowers and dancing girls. It is no lie to say they were the most beautiful things she ever made. It was another time, but if I close my eyes now, I can hear the bells on her loom tinkling as her industrious fingers worked swiftly, incessantly. It is the sound of Ibu, her work, her worth, and her beauty.

It was Nenek who carefully folded the beautiful pieces and took them to the expensive, air-conditioned boutiques in Seminyak. Now how do I describe Nenek to you? To start with she looked like nobody's grandmother. I remember many a time when strangers mistook her for our older sister. By Balinese standards she was considered a great beauty, and whenever we were out with her, *always* on our path stood staring men, tourists, their armpits sticky with sweat, and their eyes like licking tongues, so she must have been beautiful even by your standards. But what words can I use to make the rest of her acceptable to your Western mind? For my grandmother lived in utter simplicity, but accomplished feats that will have you suspecting trickery.

In her universe all of nature was a source of spirituality. She talked to it, it talked back to her. Have you seen a tree smile? I have. When Nenek passed. She acquainted them with her business, and they shared their ancient knowledge. Sometimes they gave her roots that looked like cassava, but when the dark bark-like skin was removed the flesh was as fresh and as sweet as watermelon. Other times they spoke of special roots, which had to be dug out with one's bare hands or their magic would dissipate into the earth. Squatting, she dug deep into the ground; only the thickest roots yield the special healing oils she needed. Sometimes her fingers bled, but no matter, the patient must smile. She needed them to make Ibu's medicine.

The villagers called her *balian*, a healer specialising in curing the ill and setting broken bones, but they sensed that she was more. Much more. And while they had no proof there were whispers all the same, insinuations that Nenek was in reality a *balian uig*, a maker of spells and charms, some dangerous. They pointed to the 'male' papaya tree growing in our compound. According to an old Balinese superstition only witches needed the strangely uneven shadow of such a tree, to congregate under and to indulge in obscene blood-drinking orgies. And so the innocent tree confirmed their ugly suspicions.

Although Nenek had arrived in the village when Ibu was

only nine years old she remained a stranger but accepted she would always be one and didn't care. She carried on making her daily offerings of flowers, fruit and sweet cakes in the temples, and at crossroads, graveyards and accident sites, rotting meat, onions, ginger and alcohol. Kneeling, she chanted, '*Rang, ring, tah.*' Born, living, dead. Let them think that she was odd.

She refused even to change her dance, to be like the rest of the women in our village. I saw them watching her when she danced in the temple courtyard, a container full of glowing coals balanced on her head. They kept their expressions neutral, half-interested, but I knew they thought her vulgar.

It was her vigour that they mistook for a fault. I perceived only the amazing energy in her pagan movements. They were, after all, tribal dances. Unsmiling, she craned her neck until its veins were like cords under her skin. Then she lifted her right foot, stiffened it into a weapon, and kicking it sideways, pranced high into the air, her eyebrows in her hairline, her fierce eyes wide and staring. Her mouth screaming a slow peculiar cry. With her wrists arranged in front of her face, she began to whirl, at first with controlled grace, then more and more wildly until she was spinning so fast that her eyes were rivers of black in her face. Spiteful sparks of orange flew around her.

The other women were frightened of her.

And yet their vanity was greater, and they courted her cautiously. They wanted the beauty she brewed inside her cauldron. In her charmed hands roots and leaves turned into potent liquids called *jamu*, capable of beautifying a body and captivating youth to dance a little longer upon a woman's cheek. She and Ibu were the best advertisement for her medicine, for even after Nenek touched fifty, and Ibu thirty, youth tarried. They remained as if in their twenties, with wasp-like waists, jet-black hair and dewy skin. They consumed so many unguents that their skin became fragrant to zigzagging dragonflies that sought camouflage on their colourful clothes.

When my sister and I reached puberty, we too were required to take a handful of the tiny black pellets Nenek rolled once a week. And once a month for two hours, she covered us from head to toe in *lulur*, a yellow paste made with ginger, turmeric, spices, oil, rice powder, and a secret blend of jungle roots. It could not be denied that my sister and I had exceptionally fine skin, finer than all the other girls in the village. It was a source of great envy, for every Balinese girl coveted beautiful skin the colour of gold. And so the women and their daughters came, smiling, their eyes carefully polite. They did this for beautiful skin the colour of gold.

But behind her back the cowards called her *Ratu Gede Mecaling*, after the legendary King of Nusa Penida, a fearful, fanged sorcerer, or simply *leyak*, witch. I even heard her referred to her as *rangda,* widow, but in fact the name is synonymous with a dreadful witch who tears children apart with her long fingernails and eats their innards.

'*Leyak geseng, teka geseng.*' Burn the witch, burn them all, their children chanted at the crossroads.

I rushed up to them and pushed the gang leader so hard he fell backwards into a ditch. My hands on my hips and breathing hard, I challenged them all to fight me. Nobody dared. I was the granddaughter of a witch. Instead they mumbled that they had seen her alone at midnight, meditating in the cemetery.

I laughed. 'I do not believe you. None of you has the nerve to go there in the first place,' I mocked.

They alleged that inside her locked cupboard was the smoked, dried corpse of my uncle, but I crossed my arms over my chest and retorted that I *had* looked, and her cupboard was completely innocent. Scornfully I advised them not to talk of that which they did not understand.

But here's the real truth.

They were right. Their tiny insignificant hearts were right to fear my grandmother. Nenek was a witch. A powerful one. She had magic powers, inherited from her father. She could see 'far away'. Things you and I cannot. It was she who taught us about the spirits that reside in each tree, animal and oddly shaped stone. 'Be good to them,' she said, 'they confer power to the respectful.'

But her real power she derived from another source. She secretly nurtured *buta kalas*, invisible treacherous ground spirits. Creatures of harm she bought from another like her. Keeping them was very dangerous, and she had to pass them on to another witch or sorcerer before she died or, unable to cross over to the next world, she would suffer terrible tortures on her deathbed. It was an ugly horrible business, but she could not do without them. She needed them to protect Ibu. Everyone had a purpose in life and my grandmother had only one, to prolong her daughter's life. There was nothing she would not do for Ibu.

In her command was *macan tutul*, a sleek, long-bodied, panther-like creature. He did her every bidding, but required fresh blood and wild boar meat on a regular basis, and sometimes the whole corpse of a dog. She also sought the assistance of another potent spirit, pale snake, who gave her visions and taught her to heal. When first he appeared, he tested her fortitude by coiling his monstrous body around her. She stood in the middle of the immense serpent, unmoving and unafraid, until he recognised her, his new master. Forced into submission he showed her how to listen to the blood rushing inside a man's veins, to know what sickness ailed him.

One moonlit night, I awakened in the early hours of morning and, still not fully awake, thought I saw him in my peripheral vision, enormous, vaporous and resting a few inches above the ground by Nenek's head. I swung my eyes around instantly, but the thick white coils had already returned to darkness. There was nothing left but gloom by Nenek's sleeping face.

Once I asked her, 'What if it ever came to pass that you simply cannot find another to pass your *buta kalas* to?'

She looked at me steadily, her enigmatic eyes bleak. 'I have already seen the face of my heir,' she replied finally. Her voice was alien and sad.

'Who is it?' I whispered, my heart leaping in my chest. I feared her answer.

'You are still too young to meet my successor. Think no more of it. I will not suffer. I will die in peace.' She placed a gentle hand on my forehead. 'Now, go find your sister and play in the fields.' And comforted by the cool sure hand on my skin I went. The world was so full of grown-up secrets then.

And Nenek went back to heating leaves and squeezing the green liquid on wounds and sores. Routinely she spat on her patients. Her spit was powerful. It could cure the sick. Muttering her chants she rubbed a dough ball all over a sick body to draw out the poison. Then she ripped it open and inspected the inside. If she found needles or black seeds then black magic was the source of sickness, and her black eyes would gaze at her patients warily. They left her with secretive eyes and a small square of hair shaved at the back of their heads, a puncture in the middle of it.

One day I saw Nenek, without warning, skilfully stab a man between his fingers. Shocked he tried to pull back but her grip on his hand was mighty. She held his hand over a pot, letting the blood flow into his medicine of tree sap. There was also that woman from Sumatra who came with blinding migraines that the Western doctors could do nothing about. I saw my grandmother reach up and carefully cut a vein in the woman's forehead. It was late afternoon and a whole bowl of blood was caught before the spiteful spirit pinching a nerve in the woman's head finally consented to exit her body.

It was while sitting on a mat sharing our evening meals from a common pot with Nenek that my sister and I glimpsed her secret special world. One that you would never believe. One where night wanderer spirits disguise themselves as black cats, naked women and shiny black crows. Invisible they travel in straight lines, gathering at crossroads, spots of great magic and importance, causing accidents and harm. Sometimes they tarried by the pigpen and Nenek caught and released them into trees and stones.

I was right. Your eyebrows have risen by the smallest fraction. You do not believe me. You think it is hocus-pocus. But remember this, you have your science, and we have our magic. Only when you look into my grand-mother's eyes will you know what I say to be true, will you name her remarkable.

For my grandmother sees out of eyes that are indescrib-able, at once tantalising and terrifying. They are coal black, bottomless and, in flickering lamplight, nearly inhuman. Inside her eyes you begin to understand why the Dutch stopped importing Balinese slaves in favour of more docile captives. It was ferocious women like her who wounded themselves with daggers and, dipping their fingertips in their wounds, painted their foreheads red before they fell into the flames that carried them and their dead husbands to the underworld.

And yet I remember Nenek best as a liquid shadow, moving silently in the gloom of early morning, her gold bracelets glinting. It was her habit to awaken at four in the morning, just as the windows of the rice farmers were beginning to yellow with the light of oil lamps. Softly she entered Ibu's room, and stood silently over her daughter. Satisfied with the gently breathing vision she went out to awaken her songbirds and begin her day. In Bali the sky lightens early. By five in the morning the sun is already in the sky.

She swept the courtyard clean of the lemon-white frangi-pani fallen overnight before hoisting a round bamboo basket onto her back, and setting off unarmed up the bodies of mountains. She was their child. She honoured them and they blessed her. Their jungles of laughing monkeys, beautiful butterflies and screaming birds were her medicine garden.

When we returned from selling cakes we found Nenek sitting at the doorway, eating wild quinces and flossing the coarse fibres caught in her teeth with strands of her own hair, or fanning herself with a woven palm leaf, lamenting for the cool mountain winds. She was descended from those remote tribes that lived in the blue-grey mountains. That much was clear, but the rest was a mystery. There was an abandoned husband and a dead child somewhere, but everything else was not for telling. Her secrets were many and could not be readily divulged. A loss of power or, worse, insanity awaited the loose mouth. Terrible secrets may only be revealed to lizards.

For they are special animals. Nenek said that they understood our language, but had been forbidden to speak of anything but the future. Even then they could not be completely trusted. At certain times of the year Nenek caught them in her bare hands and carefully sewed their mouths shut before whispering her secrets to them. It saddened me to see them scuttling away, their mouth sewn shut for ever. I remember the disloyal thought that she should keep her secrets to herself if they were so intolerable that a lizard must starve to death to protect them.

Still, I loved her deeply and recognised her and not my father as the head and protector of our family. Many a night during the hot seasons when we slept outdoors, my sister and I curled up to her warm body like puppies on the *bale*, platform. And though it was clear that she loved us much less than she did Ibu, she was the most extraordinary figure of my childhood. She took us to do amazing things, like going in search of the rarest flower in the world. Its tiny bud grows for nine months to bloom fleetingly, for four days.

We had to trek all the way up to Sumatra to find it. At the end of our exhausting journey, deep in a rainforest surrounded by the unfamiliar, we stood and stared at the strange flower. Deep red and dotted with velvet yellow warts; it emerged alien and enormous (four feet across), from between the roots of wild vines and the decaying litter on the forest floor. It was immediately apparent why it was called the corpse flower. It stank like a dreadfully rotting corpse. Carrion flies buzzed around it. But once dried and pulverised only a few motes of its dust were required to shrink a womb stretched by pregnancy or restore the sexual potency of an ageing man.

Often Nenek took us to the seaside, to rocky outreaches where tourists do not go. Squatting on the edges of rocks she used a hook to prise away sea urchins hanging on to their submerged undersides. We ran around in the salt spray helping her gather seaweed. On our way back we stopped by the poor village of the fish eaters to buy salt fish. We picked out the fish we wanted from the many carpets of dried fish and from a rattan basket Nenek selected the freshest fish in all of Bali.

With the crimson sun taken by the hills, Nenek began to grill the seafood over coconut husks. Ibu brought out plates of boiled sweet potatoes and the juicy bamboo shoots marinating in vinegar and chillies. We sat in a circle at the doorway of my mother's living quarters, eating fried soybean cake while the bats left the trees to look for food.

Dusk came quickly and Nenek rose to light the brass lanterns while we carried on talking. Soon the courtyard was sprinkled with the soft glow of burning lanterns each with its orbit of countless buzzing insects. And when it grew black the fireflies glowed.

Paradise is unforgettable.

It was with Nenek that we went to the bird market to buy the songbirds that she hung in wood and bamboo birdcages outside every pavilion in our compound. She was unerring in her ability to choose only the ones with exceptional voices. Some she chose for their high sweet voices, keekey, keekey, keekey, and others for that odd round chuckle they made, churr, churr, churr. If they were ill, she grasped them gently in her right hand and, opening their mouths, fed them the rice-sized pellets of medicine she herself prepared. When the moon was full she set them all free, but instead of flying away they came to perch on her shoulders, hands and lap, tame and singing. They filled the whole house with their beautiful song, and my sister and I sat beside Ibu and watched my bird-covered grandmother with awe.

Together we hunted the markets for the flesh of green forest pigeons, wild purple moorhens and cave bats. The bats Nenek bought still alive and chittering. She hung them upside down from the ceiling from where they turned their necks to peer at us. Hours they remained twisted and still, but for their languorously waving claws. Always she apologised to the animals. 'You are a sacred soul and I respect and love you very much, but this day I must invite you to be the fragrant ingredient in our feast.' Then she took their necks to her jaw, and in one quick savage movement they were ready for the pot.

It was also Nenek who sat with us as we practiced the English father taught us, her eyes as always hooded and inscrutable, but her mouth grinning with pride. She would not let us teach her the alien clipped sounds of the white man's language.

'Thorns in my mouth,' she said.

She had amassed an inexplicable loathing of the white race. One I never understood until it was far, far too late. But then I thought they were wonderful, cash-rich and generous. Nenek would have been furious if she knew that in gangs of three or four we used to run up to the German and French tourists who arrived in their minibuses to 'experience' the rice fields. With our thin brown hands stretched out and pitiful expressions borrowed for the occasion we begged. It was easy money. Undisturbed by the intensity of Nenek's hatred we really believed them harmless. Often when we went with her to Denpasar, to meet the Dayak merchants selling black coral and tree sap from Borneo, white men asked us to pose for their cameras. We grinned cheekily remembering the round hard feel of their coins in our clenched palms, but Nenek shook her head rudely and, grasping our hands, quickened her pace.

She glanced at them briefly, discreetly from the corners of her eyes. It was not only that she did not trust the concept of capturing a person's essence on paper; she was also perplexed by their meatiness, for she had tasted their food, so *nyam-nyam*, tasteless, that it made her wonder if their corpulence meant they secretly feasted on human flesh. Then, of course, there was the hygiene issue. She had heard that the white man was dirty beyond imagination.

'They hardly bathe, and use combs to stir their tea,' she said, her head rearing back, the tips of her mouth dipping with disgust.

We thought we knew otherwise. How clean and crisp were the notes that passed from their hands into ours. 'Who told you that?' we chorused immediately.

'The Dayaks,' she said simply. 'White people go to stay in their long houses.'

'Oh, but those are backpackers,' we defended loyally. We had heard about them in school. 'They probably did it for lack of a spoon.'

But Nenek remained unconvinced. 'Would a tiger dine on dates even if it was starving?'

'It would if it was magic,' my twin sister said, waving her hand at Nenek, her little worried face giggling.

My sister loved animals. All animals tugged at her heart. She saved the lives of overtired bees that lay stunned on the ground. She picked up the fatigued bundles of fuzz gently and set them in a spoon of shallow sugar water. She was fascinated by the smoky brown-glass trumpets the insect extended to draw in the liquid. And it pleased her greatly to hear the revived creature hum again.

My sister is the giver, the one who never fails to say, 'Here, you take the bigger one.' Whether it is a piece of *jaja*, rice cake, a kite, or a garland that Ibu has made for us. She always offers me the bigger piece or slips over my head the better garland.

Once we watched a dying monkey that had been run over by a passing motorbike, its pitiful eyes blinking. My sister turned to me. 'What if we are parted?' she asked in a small frightened voice, holding her pink slippers in her hand. She loved them too much to wear them.

'Don't be so silly,' I said. 'Of course we will never part. Nenek will never allow it. We will be two old ladies together. You'll see how utterly inseparable we will be.'

Yes, my sister was an innocent. I have a picture of her in my head – still a child, solemnly making her rounds in the village, on her little head a large tray of cakes, a tall pot filled to the brim with sweet coffee, and a stack of glasses. I might have forgotten to mention it, but my sister is also my heart. She belongs to me. And if my heart ceases to beat, then I will stop breathing and come to an end.

Zeenat

What are you doing here? Where is my sister?

You must be lost for this treacherous path leads only to the graveyard, a dangerous, haunted place at the edge of a deep ravine. No one dares venture into it alone once night falls but fear not, take my hand. Evening is not yet upon us, and the temple of the dead is not so far from here. I will lead you back to my sister before the sun sets. She is too gentle. This portion of the story always makes her cry so I will carry the burden of the tale for a while. Just until she returns.

If you have called my sister Nutan, you may call me Zeenat. They are not our real names, of course, but I too have much to conceal, a great fear of the finger raised to point, and a greater sorrow for the poor flower dipped in excrement. Sad but fitting that we must hide behind the names we once gave to a pair of pigs. Still, they were hand-some and well loved. Their fat bellies sagging to the ground, they used to push their snouts over the low walls of their pens to gape at the ripened papayas. The clever beasts knew the discarded peel was theirs but, utterly spoilt, they forgot their curse; sleek knives waiting to plunge into their chests.

In our greed we too forgot, but never mind that now. Beware, this path is bad. See those enormous dark green trees edging the cemetery? They are magical *kepuh* trees. They shelter ghosts.

Ah, you smile. Politely hiding your superior derision? But I recognise you. Sometimes you speak English, sometimes

Italian and sometimes German or Japanese, your pockets always full of money. Our fingers might even have brushed. You are from that race of migrating humans. Every summer thousands and thousands of you descend upon our beaches seeking the unspoilt under a gently swaying pandanus tree. Hoping to see a prince sitting cross-legged or catch a mysterious maiden bathing without a shirt in a stone pool.

Your parched soul suspects the hidden magic behind the two-dimensional men who pester you, day and night, 'You want room? You want transport? You want girl?' But your pale eyes so bored and indulged by Hollywood get distracted by the unconvincing Sucky sucky girls, the transvestites posing under the neon lights of Hard Rock Café. And so you return to your reality insisting that your camera has caught the exotic – a funeral procession, or a smiling local – but guilty.

Or perhaps guilt has even led you to sit amongst earnest Japanese tourists in a covered theatre, to watch the barong dance listlessly performed in the heat of midday by those whose boredom matched only your desire to be gone. Did you see them pretend to go into a trance and stab themselves with the blunt point of their daggers? And because it was presumed you understood nothing, a beautifully dressed woman came up to the stage, stamped her foot, and clapped to signal that the performance was over. Immediately, dutifully, you applauded and stood to leave.

You knew you had paid too much for too little . . . but what if I told you there is more? What if I showed you what lies behind the meaningless Asian smile in your camera? And showed you mystic rites by lamplight where human blood touches the ground? What if I told you Bali is magic? Each gentle breeze, the breath of Gods and Goddesses.

I must warn you, though, that all I grasp in my hands are crumbs. Moving shadows of when my sister and I were the beautiful twins. Impossible to tell apart. The villagers thought of us as one person. 'Where are the twins?' they asked. No one would have thought to send just one of us to run even the simplest errand.

Of the two of us, my sister was the better dancer. Even eyes lowered and motionless she was breathtakingly hypnotic. Between eyebrows that had been shaved and reshaped into perfectly painted black arcs, she wore *priasan*, a white dot, the dancer's mark of beauty. Effortlessly her small fingers arched back until they touched her forearms, as if they were the delicate, opening petals of a lotus bud. My sister could dance for hours. Like a marionette on a wire, her face as fixed, and as unchangeable, as a mask.

During celebrations she danced the *legong*. Wearing cloth decorated with gold thread, a headdress ornamented with rows of fresh frangipani, and long golden nails on her quivering fingers, she transformed into the lone anguished princess. Wiping her tears, she slapped her thigh with a fan. The crowd, recognising the gesture, sighed. Bottomless grief.

The golden headdress sparkled in the sunlight.

Afterwards we ran past the stone pool where we bathed to Ni Made Wetni's *warung*, the wooden shed from where she sold slices of unripe pineapple in a sauce of red peppers, garlic and salt. We plotted to be her first customers for the day. The first customer must never be refused. A sale must be concluded at any price, or an unlucky precedent would be set. Sighing heavily she took the crumpled notes we held out, folded them in half, length-wise, and slapped them moodily on all her wares all the while muttering for profit.

We ate our fruit under the shade of the tamarind tree.

'Pretend you are me. Do what I do,' Nutan said and instantly I became her mirror. It was a game I was particularly good at. Each movement copied in such a split second it seemed as if we shared one mind. As if we were the same person. The other children were envious, and we smug.

She took care of me unconsciously. I am younger, only by minutes, yet it often seemed to me as if by years. I was shy, and she bold and daring and kind. She tells everyone that I am kind and always rescuing animals, but in fact I am nothing compared to her. She is like Nenek, deep and secretive. Did she tell you that she sobbed over a dying monkey by the roadside? When she was a child she took extra time to carefully build little ledges on her sandcastles for tired birds to rest upon. So they could say, 'Oh lucky me.' And it was always she who organised raids on the boys' crickets. We stole under their houses to free the fighting crickets they had trapped in the dried-out cracks of the harvested paddy fields.

My sister is special, more so than me.

I cannot explain how I feel about Nutan. I love my Nenek and Ibu, but it goes without saying that they are separate and different individuals. My sister is in my bones, a part of me. We belong to each other. What is hers is mine and mine hers. When we were children we even shared dreams, seeing each other in our sleep. I used to pity all the other children in school. How alone and frightened they must be.

When I saw a picture of the first Siamese twins, it shocked me. Surely some wicked fiend had caused such a monstrous abnormality. That night I dreamed my sister and I were joined at the stomach and struggling up a flight of stairs. At the landing we stopped. Together. An ungainly Y, joined at the hips, our bodies twisting away from each other. Stuck for ever. We had three legs between us, two good and one bad. It hung, limp, between us. I looked into my sister's face, and felt no horror at the three-legged creature that we were. We exchanged smiles. She comforts me. She is my heart. We are Siamese twins at heart. How can I explain it to you? It is indescribable.

Two afternoons a week we went to watch old Hindi movies at the temple keeper's house. He possessed a vast collection of old favourites. We sat enthralled as beautiful heroines in saris and their leading men danced down hillsides and played hide and seek behind coconut palms.

'*Laila, oh laila, laila, laila, ho se ho laila,*' we sang as we foraged the waterways by the paddy fields for small fish and frogs.

And when Father returned from his long absences we sat up the whole night through, captivated by all the different voices and beautiful chants he kept inside him. Nutan must have told you, of course, that our father knew more than a hundred stories by heart. Seamlessly he slipped out of the skin of a demon throwing thunderbolts and became a celestial prince speaking archaic Javanese. But among all the stories he told we had our favourite. Eagerly we waited for the evenings when he raised his head from reciting the special mantras to awaken his puppets, and began his tale with the words, 'And Valmiki sat upon a carpet of *kusa* grass, sipped holy water and said, "As long as the mountains endure and the rivers rush to the sea, so long will the epic of Ramayana be repeated upon the lips of mankind . . .".'

Of course you have heard the story of Rama and Sita, but never as my father told it. From his lips it was music. Did you know that Rama and Sita played hide and seek amidst blue lotus flowers in clear moonlit waters? Yes, Rama submerged himself into the dark water until only his blue face sat upon the water. Seeking Sita could not tell the difference between the flowers and Rama until she held each blue flower in her hand and, bending down to smell them, touched her lover's lips.

But in my most secret dreams Rama was not as beautiful as a blue lotus but stood with the flowing yellow hair of the Australian surfers. Men who could dance on waves. From where I stood on the beach they were impossibly beautiful.

Oh, was it already canto fourteen? Rama was to be king. Celebration and joy, but look, look, to the left where all the evil characters surface from; the misshapen hunchback servant, Kuni, with poisonous words. 'Oh foolish one,' Father hissed in her hateful voice to Rama's stepmother. She persuades the young Queen to use the two forgotten boons the Maharajah once granted her to banish Rama from the kingdom and install her own son as king.

You cannot imagine the childish passion with which my sister and I loathed that hunchback, Kuni. At his favourite wife's words the old king's shadow trembled and fell upon the ground, helpless. 'My beautiful queen, a tigress? How easily she accomplishes my ruin,' my father sobbed in the sonorous voice of the old king. All who heard Father wept. Rama was banished to the jungles.

A few verses later Father suddenly struck the gamelan drum and laid his palm flat on its throbbing yellow skin, muffling the sound. It was the breath of the evil demon Ravana, hiding in the bushes watching Sita plucking wild flowers. And on and on went the fantastic adventures of Father's puppets until Rama was returned to the throne.

My sister and I sighed with contentment. Father extinguished his lamp and the screen became dark. His face appeared at the side of the screen, his beautiful eyes sweeping the crowd, looking for us. He smiled. We grinned back at him. As the crowd dispersed my sister and I helped him pack his belongings, and together we walked home. The hills still withheld the sun and in the sea-blue light we saw Ibu sitting at the doorway, waiting, radiant. Her eyes fixed on my father. She loved my father so dearly I sometimes thought she was jealous of my sister and me.

It was a mystery how she came to be married to my Father at all, for not only was she a cripple, she was

descended from the animistic ancient Bali Agas, a fierce
mountain people who not only stridently refused to accept
any form of class, but once filed and blackened their teeth.
Such was their obsession with isolation that they swept the
paths of their village after the visits of strangers, to
obliterate their footprints.

My parents' past was obscure, muddy even, but Ibu
would shed tears when questioned so we learned not to ask.
At different times, I thought my father's beautiful eyes
looked ashamed, even trapped. It seemed certain he had
relinquished some cherished freedom. In my moment of
childhood I assumed his shame was for my mother's flawed
limb, but later, when I was much older, I realised that all
through the years his regard had never faltered once.

It was not revulsion, but a tender, passionless love. A
gentle hand on her bent head as if she were a dear sister.
The secret disgrace nourished itself elsewhere. Perhaps in
the *jong*, the dream bracelet he wore? It represented a
masked memory that was close to his heart. Another
woman? Before Ibu?

Ibu on the other hand was tireless in her adoration of
him. Carefully positioning her body slightly lower than his,
she ministered to his every need, serving him with a quiet
obsession.

Early one morning Ibu suddenly had the idea that we
should bake a cake together for Father. Nenek, Nutan and
I took the bus all the way to Denpasar to buy the ingredients and that afternoon we followed the recipe on the side
of the margarine tin. Ibu laughed and laughed. She was
happy that afternoon. Afterwards my sister and I carried it
to our friend Ketut's house and sat outside while the cake
baked. When it was ready we carried it home, deep chocolate and fragrant. We had beaten it for so long it was like a
cloud in our mouths. But Father did not come home that
evening and the four of us sat on the *bale*, ate, talked and

laughed. How Ibu laughed that wonderful evening.

Far away in the fields, the rice stalks had been tied into round bales of gold, and the left-over straw torched, so their valuable minerals could be returned to the soil. At sundown Nenek went out to put more coconut-leaf containers of food, flowers, money and a smouldering coconut husk in front of the gate so evil spirits would get everything they wanted without entering our home.

Isn't it strange the things you remember? I remember my mother's hands, how pale they were when she suddenly announced that she was tired, and needed to retire to her room. And how Nenek had lifted her up and carried her as if she was a child. I remember going into her bedroom to ask if she wanted some more cake. She lay on her bed, shook her head and said, 'No more cake for this body. As the eagle leaves his nest to soar across the sky, I too must leave this nest to fly free.'

Word was sent to Father. Ibu was very, very ill. She lay in bed, no longer able to weave or spin, her skin papery, her eyes usually closed, but when open, glittering with a strange excitement. Like a child who was waiting to go on some long-promised trip. To my tear-stained, frightened face, she advised only, 'Grieve not. It is only without my limbs that I shall be able to walk a while in the shining mud along the river.' Nutan would not cry. She sat straight backed at the door, addressing the spirits, her voice commanding and powerful. As if she was Nenek. For hours she rasped the same words, again and again. She would not cry. She would not stop. She was like a stranger. It was frightening.

> *Oh you forgive me if I have done wrong*
> *But do not take her.*
> *Do not take what is not yours.*
> *Do not call her name,*
> *Not at night. Not tonight.*

34

From a distant village came the faint but primal call of
drums and singing, preparations for a dance performance.
Tenderly Ibu trailed her weak fingers along Nenek's high
cheekbones consoling, 'Look, how even the years dare not
touch you.' Nenek could hardly hear for the harsh sound of
Nutan's voice pleading with the spirits. Sadly she lowered
her bowed head further, so Ibu's dying hand could rest on
it, as if Nenek was the child, and her daughter the mother.

When Father arrived he hurried to Ibu's bedside. She
turned her face to him and I saw her sigh with contentment.
Her eyes were no longer feverish. Her voice was already no
more than a fragile whisper when she said, 'For so long
now, I have laughed the laughter you planted inside my
mouth, and wept the tears you left in my eyes, but it is time
to burn the frankincense and return me. For I have begun
to long for the feel of your hands in my ashes, as you scatter
me to the seas.'

A day later she extinguished her own weak lamp.

I fell asleep and awakened suddenly in the middle of the
night to see father sitting as still as a stone statue on the
steps of the rice barn, Nutan staring in with shock and
disbelief, at Nenek bent over Ibu's still body. The air was
soft with incense. Nenek, drunk on *arak madu*, palm spirit
with lemon juice and honey, was massaging Ibu's body, the
strokes long and loving. A heartbreaking hymn issued from
her pagan lips.

> *Remain, remain for ever close to me.*
> *Never forget*
> *I grasped your foot,*
> *I stroked your face,*
> *I washed your hair,*
> *I kissed your cold lips.*
> *Fear nothing. Flee not.*
> *Remain, remain for ever close to me.*

When eventually her gaze met mine at the door, she shook her head as if confused or lost. Then she looked at Nutan and in a strangled voice cried, 'I could not keep her. I'm so sorry. You know there is nothing I would not have done to keep her. Nothing. I would have walked into the deepest jungle, and let the animals devour me, or not cared if forced to give my breasts to poisonous fish in the afterlife. She was my life. My life is gone.'

And when Nutan only stared back dumbly, she pressed her cheek against Ibu's and wept copiously. If she rose from Ibu's face it was only to beat her forehead wretchedly with her palm. Her sorrow was such that I went to fall at her feet, helpless. All through the night Nenek wailed her terrible songs. They carried over the silent rice paddies covered in mists, while Father sat unmoving on the steps of the rice barn, and the uncaring world slept on. Just before dawn when all the palm wine was gone, Nenek stood up slowly, unsteadily.

The sky was blood red.

Carefully she opened the petals of many flowers, and scattered their scent on Ibu's still body. As the petals fell she cried bitterly, 'If I lived in the jungle I would cut away my fingers and ears to show the horror of my loss, but in this dishonest land, I must pretend to be happy that my daughter has gone.'

Then she brought all the birdcages into the room where Ibu slept and one by one opened their doors. Standing in the middle of the room she clapped her hands loudly. In a flutter of confused feathers the frightened birds flew out of the open windows. The newly acquired ones made for the sky, but the ones that had belonged to her for a long time sat in the bamboo groves outside the compound, puzzled, singing one last time for her before they too, took to freedom. Covering her face with an old cloth she wept. Afterwards, we watched her smash our sacred shrines. Her deepest prayers had not been heard, so she would build a bigger better one for another divinity.

I remember they held Ibu up, washed and anointed her pale body with oils and flowers. Nenek rubbed fine rice powder onto her skin and decorated her hair for the last time. Her ankles and thumbs, they bound together. Steel on her teeth to make them strong, mirrors on her eyes to make them bright, intaran leaf on her eyebrows to beautify them, and jasmine flowers in her nostrils to perfume her breath. Eventually they were done. And then she was really dead. Until that moment she was alive. Now she was a body of glory. And I remember she was beautiful.

We stayed up all night to guard her body against obnoxious spirits. Every night that she lay in the Eastern pavilion, a lamp was lit to show her wandering soul the way home. In dark corners people huddled to nap. All through the night the *gambang* hummed and boomed.

They doused her with kerosene.

In the shade of a great dark kepuh tree beyond the temple Nenek stood. She looked like a toy, small and misplaced. Nutan clenched my hand, and Nenek turned her head away when the men poked my mother's corpse. They wanted to help it burn. Neither the frightening sight nor the charred smell of her blackened flesh affected them. In a good-natured way they joked with my mother's corpse, advising her to burn fast so they could go home. Do not be shocked. It is our way. A cremation is a happy occasion when friends and relatives send a loved one home.

It was only after her tranquil death that Father came to realise the depth of his loss. He sat alone at the doorway, his head leaning on his arm, the afternoon breeze in his hair, believing himself in a slow dream. Amazed that he had held her bad leg against her. Ashamed he had not let her into his world. Desolate, he would never again be the centre of an angel's life. He stood there tearless and devastated by the loss of his lame deer. Never again would her eyes light up at the sight of his handsome face.

For me the shadow of my mother's death was confusing. Had she not been eager to leave the rags of her life behind? For I truly believed Ibu when she explained, with luminous eyes and utter sincerity, that it was only right that she should be the first to go to heaven, so her missing limb could be returned to her.

'There is a pair of shoes of astonishing beauty waiting for me. We will walk for miles and miles together when you come,' she had promised. And the promise illuminated the house my thoughts lived in, but not a single ray from my lamp would consent to light Nenek's dwelling. She stumbled lost in the pitch black, knocking down furniture and crashing into hard edges. She awakened in the morning with her daughter's name on her lips. Returning from school I felt her inconsolable sadness from the moment we walked through our entrance gate.

Always her wandering led her to daughter's silent loom. Sometimes she sat on the *bale* as if listening for that rhythmic sequence of three sounds, the softly jingling bells, the ruler hitting the hollow bamboo, and the quick double knock on the weave. Other times she stood at the door of Ibu's narrow dim room, staring at the mattress on which Ibu had died.

Unlike my father, Nenek was not acquainted with the ways of the high born. She didn't know how to be disdainful of this life, to mock at its momentary pleasures and sufferings. To view death as a door, or a friend. Death, she always said, was when you saw no path in front of you, and you fell down. Therefore death was barbaric, and its celebration unnatural. No, no, she received every breath with joy. She was a child of mother earth and while her feet remained in contact with the ground, she was home.

She suffered greatly the physical passing of her daughter.

For her, the body could never be simply an impure, temporary container for the soul. The body was full of magic. In the past, my grandmother's ancestors had even been accused of cannibalism. It was not true, of course, but if in some ancient time they did consume human flesh, it was an act of love, to keep their dead alive.

Deep inside Ibu's drawer Nenek found an old black and white picture, curling at the edges, that Father must have taken while Nenek was away on one of her trips. Shocked, Nenek stared at the picture. Why, there it was, Ibu's spirit. Imprisoned. The sight of her daughter undid her. She put her face into the crook of her sleeve and sobbed. Truly she had loved her daughter, but photographs were wrong. They caged the spirit. Nevertheless every time she went to destroy the browning tear-stained thing she found she could not.

For many days she stared at her captive daughter. Then one day she made up her mind. She took it to the Japanese photographer's shop in Denpasar and he restored it. Airbrushed away every single flaw, tinted Ibu's cheeks rose and painted her lips such a delightful pink that she looked like a film star. Inside a gold and black picture frame, she hung in Nenek's living quarters. Often Nenek made offerings of incense to her image.

Nutan

How did you end up in our cemetery?

Come away, it will be night soon and unsafe. This way, and tread carefully. See that hunched sorry figure in that makeshift hut, yonder? That is Father. He is impure, but I have forgiven him. I had to. How to detach the tainted blood of the observed from the observer? It must be full moon tonight, if he is seeking his own company. All night long he will sit, old and forgotten, haunting the silver rice fields with his flute. If he is lucky he will catch sight of a sky snake, a falling star.

For a long time I thought our shameful family secret had something to do with his ancestors. And although you could never have guessed by how poor we were, they were once the powerful rulers of Bali. All that remained of their noble past was a rather astonishing heirloom. Three fine pieces of silver tableware taken – no, looted – from the Dutch shipwrecks, ferociously fought over by rogues, only to be confiscated by kings. I thought the superbly crafted things marvellous, but Ibu saw only their glint. She ran her delicate hands over the polished silver.

'How clever these beautiful things are,' she commented turning them so they caught the glossy light on their smooth bodies. 'Blinded by their glitter we are deceived into the illusion that they are our possessions. We forget we are nothing more than temporary caretakers. They will survive us all. Living for ever, carefully tended by fools.'

And she was right too. So polished, so completely tempting that they decided the demise of my father's proud forefathers. It was the excuse the white man used to take our power, land and wealth. Now my father's people were owners of crumbling palaces they could not afford to repair, lowly puppeteers denuded of land, and silent sweepers at deserted mountain temples.

But watching Ibu carefully polishing them, I began to imagine my simple father in a different light. With an ornate *kris* tucked into the back of long gold and silver robes, standing at the gates of a splendid palace. A Hindu prince. You see my father's ancestry was not Balinese at all. My father was entitled to the royal title, *I Gusti Agung*.

He was one of a handful of survivors of the royal house of Majapahit, the rulers of Java, who watched the Islamisation of their country with horror. The way its arid breath shrivelled and withered all the beauty it passed. They decided to take their decadence elsewhere. To Bali they brought not only their religion, but their finest actors, dancers, artisans, concubines and loyal servants. But to them a happy ending was not given; theirs is a story gory and terrible. In Bali, many years later, they did an insane thing.

They wagered the glory of an entire dynasty in a shocking rite called *puputan*. You must have heard of it. It happened when the Dutch first thought to rule Bali. Armed with superior fire power they advanced, expecting an easy battle over men wielding six-inch knives, and instead came upon a deserted town, smoke rising from the palace, and the chilling sound of pulsating drums within the palace walls. As the Dutch watched bemused, a silent procession emerged from the tall gates.

The Raja, dressed in pure white and heavily adorned in a magnificent array of jewellery, sat proudly inside his palanquin hoisted by four bearers. He wore his ceremonial *kris*. His armed guards, officials of his court, wives, children and servants, all splendidly dressed, followed him, their eyes

41

glazed as if in a trance. One hundred paces from the Dutch the Raja halted his bearers and, stepping down, gave his signal.

At once a high priest approached, bowed low, and with perfect precision plunged his dagger into the Raja's breast. The horrified Dutch watched as all the others in a wild orgy of self-destruction turned their daggers upon themselves or one another. Singing they died. Then the women dressed in their best brocades surged forward, their eyes touched by frenzy, taunting the soldiers and contemptuously flinging their jewellery and gold coins at the frozen army. They offered their breasts, inviting the soldiers to shoot.

The startled Dutch could only stare. Never before had a colonised people behaved in such an unfathomable manner. Where was the automatic display of docility they had encountered everywhere else? How could they even begin to pretend munificence faced with such insanity? Here was irrefutable proof that the Balinese were too fierce, too depraved a sort to be brought to heel or suffer rule under a foe. They were nothing but savages.

Without shame the Dutch opened fire.

The children fell, riddled with bullets. The ones knee high, their dying mothers held up in the air. More and more people, *krises* drawn, rushed blindly out of the palace gates, stumbling over the pile of dead. But the Dutch fired until the butchered made a high hill. Underneath the silent bodies full of angry eyes lay a beautiful dream. They would not be ruled by the enemy.

One of the Raja's wives watched. Not even a whimper escaped her lips. She waited until the soldiers had stripped every corpse of gold and valuables and then she carefully wrapped the bloody body of the Raja in a woven mat. She would have gladly thrown herself into the flames of his funeral pyre but she was pregnant. A gift from the Gods cannot be refused.

She was my great grandmother, Nyang Ratu and in her belly was the holder of the proud name Anak Agung Rai, my grandfather. That is another story, but naturally I am not privy to the puppet master's secrets, and anyway you are in a hurry. So I will quicken my tale. Let the years fly past like wild birds in the evening sky. Let their wings carry you to the moment of our insanity.

Fed on Nenek's potions and herbs we sprouted like bamboo.

With the onset of menstruation, Nenek arranged for the rites of transition to be held. After a three-day period of seclusion, amidst much ceremony, we grasped between our thumb and forefinger the fringe of an undyed cotton cloth decorated with drawings of the Gods of love, and passed it gently over our cheeks. In this way we were given to the Gods of love. They protect but also bring uncertainty and temptation. Neither Zeenat nor I were interested in the village boys. Their eyes lingered as we went about our business but they were terrified of my grandmother and never approached.

When we were ready to have our teeth filed we were put into seclusion. We emerged cleansed, and were led in gold brocades and crowns of flowers to the *bale*, vividly decorated and filled with offerings. A Brahmin priest held our mouths open with small pieces of sugarcane while our front six upper teeth were filed straight to refine and beautify our appearance, and rid us of man's coarse, animal traits: lust, greed, anger, drunkenness, confusion and jealousy. Nenek had never had her teeth filed. She laughed and told us long canines were reserved for animals, demons and witches.

We were eighteen years old when Father came home one day and, in his cultured voice, told us an astonishing thing. He told us that he had sold his silver heirloom so we could go to university in Bandung, but before that, he had another surprise, a treat, something unexpected. His extravagant eyelashes swept down to hide his eyes. We listened in awe. A holiday overseas. Three or even four months in London. What did I know of London? *London Bridge is falling down, falling down . . .* Father told us about an uncle who had found us work as waitresses in his friend's café, very near Victoria Station.

Victoria Station. How foreign and exotic it sounded on my father's tongue.

It was all arranged. We were to stay in a room in a house nearby. Every meticulous detail had been seen to. We gasped, too amazed and excited to say anything. It seemed hardly possible. What a dream! The idea was so wonderful and fantastic we hardly dared respond, but then Nenek, who had been silent all the while, let out a thin, shrill cry. Her face was pale. 'No, don't take them away too,' she cried.

Father did not even turn his head. His beautiful eyes were set far away on the horizon, on the blue shadow of Mount Agung.

'They are my children and I will decide,' he said, using for the first time, not the usual familiar mode of expression we used with each other, but the very fine, formal one used by his people. As if he was a stranger. As if she was a stranger. So polite, so cold that a shiver ran up my spine. He turned to her, and an extraordinary look passed between them. In that surreal moment, without any warning, every foundation that I had taken for granted cracked and crumbled into dust. It was like looking into a mirror and seeing another's face in it. I realised that it was the first time I had seen Nenek actually look directly at Father. For many moments they were locked in a throbbing simmering world of their own. My sister and I had ceased to exist. In my head, as if from far away, I heard a voice, long forgotten. Ida Bagus's.

It was not friendly, her voice. It had long ago known the

taboo the adults in my family cloaked. Why, the gloating ridicule in the voice I had heard while stealing crickets under her house was true. It wasn't more idle gossip about Nenek. It was actually true. Only then it became clear why they called her *janda kembang*. Although the words simply translated mean young widow, their real meaning is derogatory. It means a newly widowed woman of easy morals.

For the first time I really understood. *He had made her look at him*. Finally he had made her look at him. At his terrible power. Of course, if I had only looked a little harder. The secret chase. It was my beautiful grandmother that my father had first and truly loved. And it was Nenek who had first lain with him, until she saw the light of desire in her crippled daughter's eyes. There were two laws my grandmother lived by: she never denied her daughter anything, and she made her own rules. She stepped aside and gave her lover to her daughter.

Ah, silence. The Balinese silence is a clear sign of disagreement or fury.

My father's fingers angrily twisted the *jong* bracelet he wore religiously day and night through all the years I had known him. Nenek had discarded him so easily, yet his crushed heart jealously hoarded her memory. It was startling the passion my gentle father masked. In my head I heard Nenek's voice, that night Ibu died, and the only time I had seen her drunk, '*You know there is nothing I would not have done to keep her. Nothing.*' Her decision had left her without regret. A high-born lover is easily replaced, but never a daughter.

Suddenly it all made perfect sense. No wonder Ibu's love was so despairing, so desperate; and Father, a puppeteer with a suitcase, his ferocious anger tumbling into his puppets. From very far away I saw Nenek's private angst, her legacy. And I pitied her. What had she allowed love to

do to her? Like the paddy sheaf that willingly allows itself
to be led to the threshing floor, to be trodden upon and
defenceless submits to the grinding stones. And her dust?
We scorched it in boiling oil, labelled it rice cake, and
laughed while we ate it. How great and wonderful was her
love for my mother?

But my father saw only that she had sacrificed him. Given
him away to her crippled daughter like an unwanted
possession. How blind my sister and I had been! The
drama the adults in our life had played right before our unsuspecting noses. The uneasy ghosts that had walked
around us.

No wonder. No wonder.

And that day I knew why the oppressive whisper, 'It's all
lies . . . It's all lies . . .' moved restlessly from room to
room. He had never loved us. None of them had. Not Ibu,
not Nenek and certainly not Father. Our existence made
theirs possible, polite, acceptable to the outside world.
What did my father actually offer? What was this treat if
not a bitter brew of thwarted passion simmered down to
revenge. And yet I was willing to eat it, for I wanted his
gift.

Sprung from poison it sat on the floor of our shabby
dwelling like a marvellously winged fox. Just born, its
existence was weak and fragile, but hidden in its shimmering wings, I knew, were the arrows meant for Nenek's
heart. Even knowing that I couldn't help myself, I still
wanted it. And why shouldn't I? Had they not for years
plotted to offend us with their shabby protestations of love?
The fox opened its special mouth – and yawned.

London, how near to me it stood.

Although I remained silent in my heart I had already
abandoned Bali and my dear, dear Nenek. It's only a
holiday, I told the guilt inside my chest.

'Inside every tiger hides a tired old man,' Nenek warned. Her voice was such a thin whisper.

But they made my father's back go rigid, and he stared unseeing at the once colourful woven mats carpeting the walls. She spoke the truth. The haunt of the tiger is always desolate and overgrown with weeds. Friendless, every majestically striped tiger hides a tired old man. I saw him, sitting as erect and proud as a warrior, but only half-alive. He was without doubt not one of us, but from a race old, shattered, and eaten by its own thoughts. His core was not Balinese, like Nenek, my sister and I. My father was a Javanese prince. And he had never forgotten it.

His carefully blank eyes hid a horror of the exuberance with which we embraced the coarse vulgarity of gilt, the baroque and the bright. The Javanese lord imitates so well the art and culture of the Balinese that he becomes a master of them, able even to entertain in the rough and ready Balinese humour, but he can never, never absorb any of it as his own. He was a refined knight, bearing misfortune, even injustice without flinching. The master of his emotions.

Ah Father, you should have clutched your secret better for you seem less beautiful now. Now you seem nothing more than a blind hawk, malicious with frustration and wrath. Over the years we had learned to love his dereliction as beauty. The fallen pillars, the moss-covered statues, the cracked stone steps, and the stagnant-smelling pond, we learned to admire. We purposely overlooked the thing inside him that was worn-out and defeated. Some part of me that still needed his love wanted to reach out and hold the lonely body hunched with years of crouching over his puppets.

'My sorrow is nothing. And if you do not look back you will not even see me fall with my wounds, but is it sweet, the blood of your own children in your mouth?' Nenek asked. Her voice was sad.

'Did you not decide the future of your child? Will you now deny me the privilege?' My father's voice was caustic.

Nenek smiled. It was a Balinese smile. It did not mean she was happy. It was simply an attempt to placate, to turn a disagreeable state of affairs into a more positive one. To show the opposition that one is not a threat.

In the ensuing silence my father rose suddenly and left for the temple. That night, after he had silently fed his cockerels, I hid outside his living quarters and spied on a shocking prayer. It was a prayer to intimidate a witch.

> *Your eyes be blind,*
> *Your hands be paralysed,*
> *Your feet be useless.*
> *The lofty and the learned guard over my sleeping*
> *body.*
> *I shall not die dreaming,*
> *My parasol is yellow, the Gods esteem me.*
> *Not afraid, not afraid.*
> *A thousand witches will bow down to me.*
> *Not afraid, not afraid.*

That night Nenek had a fit. In a trance-like state she began to crawl around the room growling that we must never leave the island. The Gods would forget to protect us, and she would lose control over the evil spirits that schemed to harm us. She cut her wrists and sitting as still as a sculpture let them bleed, feeding the insatiable pale snake and the black cat for so long that my sister hurled herself into Nenek's lap sobbing, 'Enough, enough, enough.'

Later that night my sister's urgent voice shook me awake. 'Quick, it's Nenek.' Together we ran to the *bale*. Nenek was sobbing like a child, the way she had that night she lost my mother. My sister knelt beside her and gently stroked

48

her hair. And I saw Nenek surface as if from a terrible nightmare. 'Sorrow is upon me. I broke the rules. It was a mistake, looking back. Now the black cat will not be still. I am losing my power over him. He is becoming greedy,' she cried, her eyes haunted. When I brought her some water, she grasped my hand and begged, 'Don't go. If I beg your forgiveness will you say you will not go? Say it. Say you will not go.'

But I lowered my face silently. My mind was made up. They did not care for us. When I looked up I saw Nenek's eyes dim and slide away. Right before my gaze she appeared to grow old. Her jet-black hair mocked her suddenly tired face. 'Oh no, have I really left a crow to guard my precious eggs?' she whispered. Her eyes alighted on me again. This time they were terrifying. She understood that I was the head and my sister, the tail.

'Do you really want to go?' she asked at last.

The trip was not a gift, but a bribe; the reward for her loneliness and her frighteningly haggard expression. I tried to think of the two of them in this house. The bitter silence, Nenek's sad footsteps. That was what he wanted. That was why he wanted us away. Poor Nenek.

But that day I too wanted to punish her. Did she not clutch one edge of the blanket of lies? I felt my sister's hand on my arm and when I looked into her face, it was pleading. But the winged fox could not be denied.

'We will do as Father desires,' I said. I wanted to break free of our claustrophobic village where every person knew what we had forgotten to suspect. I wanted to go out into the big wide world. We deserved it. They had cheated us of my mother's love. Now they will not cheat us of this opportunity too.

'They run towards their destinies,' she said feebly. Although her eyes glistened in the night like two black pearls, her face was defeated. For Nenek had never denied

49

us anything. Not once. If it was in her capacity she strove towards it. Once she told me, 'We seek to turn our children into messengers of our own thoughts. But our soul matures and our grandchildren we dare only love.'

For days she busied herself rolling thousands of little black pearls, five months' supply of *jamu* for us. She packed them into two old powdered milk tins. On the day of our departure we went to her dim room to receive her blessing. She sat alone on her narrow bed. By her were strewn the ingredients to make clove medicine to deaden pain. We went to kneel at her feet. 'Even now it is already too late,' she marvelled, and then she turned to me and advised, 'When the puppet master gives you wings of course you must fly away, but remember to beware the predators in the sky.' I did not know that she already saw me beyond the protection of her gaze. Like her, I would hobble with a broken heart. To my sister, she said only, 'Dream of Ibu.'

As we turned the corner I turned back and saw her at the gate, her face a mask of grief. I raised my hand to wave but she immediately fell back, away from sight. Her hand on her mouth. All her earlier outpourings had served only to harden my heart, but this, this dumb sorrow, it moved me. It seemed unfair that such a great woman should be felled by me. 'I am sorry, so sorry, but it must be so,' I whispered. Quite suddenly I remembered my sister and I perched on Father's knees, pretending to be ventriloquist dummies, opening and closing our mouths in perfect measure to his voice. And for first time my feet, following behind Father, hesitated and I felt a twinge of fear for the big wide world and the predators in the sky. Still, Nenek was right. Even then it must have been too late because my father turned around and in his calm disinterested voice said, 'Quickly now or you will miss the plane.' And the fear went and my feet hurried on.

*

I must sift the story very carefully now. Make sure all the gold is washed out of the river.

We arrived in England in January. Father's relative came to pick us up at Heathrow airport. He was a proud handsome man who looked us up and down as if he found us wanting, as if he couldn't believe my father's thoughtless deviation from the purity of their bloodline. For *this* . . . his look said.

'Come,' he instructed briefly and turning around took us through the crowd milling about the arrival gate. Just before we reached the doors he stopped. We put our bags down expectantly. He looked at his watch. He was in a hurry, he said. He had to return to Manchester where he lived with his family. We were not to meet them.

Outside it was freezing cold. Colder than the coldest night on the mountains. We had not dressed appropriately. Quickly we climbed into the back of a black taxi, huddling against each other for warmth. He gave the driver directions. It seemed we were to be taken straight to our room. Over a kebab shop. Unwilling to accompany us into our lodgings he waited in the taxi while a man from the kebab shop came out and, bidding us follow him, went ahead of us up a dark steep staircase. His name was Mustapha. He opened the door of our room. Tiny, squalid. Musty smelling. Two narrow beds pushed together. A window overlooking the street. Black handprints by the light switches. There was some sort of meter to put coins in to heat the place. There was a shower cubicle in one corner of the room and, at the end of the landing a toilet, with a proper flush toilet like the ones they have in Denpasar. The rent for that rat hole was £105 per week. I met my sister's scandalised eyes. It was impossible that such a hovel could cost so much. Why, a palace could be rented in Bali for such a sum.

We left our bags, hurried down the dingy stairs and back

into the waiting taxi. A very short drive away was the café we were to work in. There was condensation on the windows. A brass bell tinkled. Inside the air was thick with the smell of frying. A few customers dotted the chairs, eating huge meals, what I would later learn was called a Full English Breakfast. Fried eggs, sausages, bacon, baked beans, mushrooms and a fried tomato half. Even the bread was fried in that greasy world. My uncle shook hands with the owner, a man with a knife slit for a mouth, then introduced us, not as blood relatives, but as old friends of the family. Afterwards he turned to us and said, 'Well, I'll be leaving then. Since I won't be seeing you again, I might as well bid you goodbye and a safe journey back to Bali now.' We watched him walk out and get into the waiting taxi.

The owner was a cold-hearted man. We were to work six days a week from 6.30 in the morning till 6.30 in the evening with two half-hour breaks. Our take-home wage was £120 per person. He handed us a set of uniforms, white shirts and short black skirts. He would deduct £16 from our first wages to cover their cost. We could eat as much of the left-overs of every fry-up as we liked and there was a 2 litre bottle of lime cordial for our use.

'You can start tomorrow,' he said. 'If anyone official-looking asks, you are relatives on holiday. Just helping out for a couple of days.'

We nodded. In truth we were horribly frightened. We had not expected to be so quickly abandoned in a strange city. So began our wonderful holiday – working six days a week in that grimy depressing place. No matter how hard or how often I cleaned there was always a film of grease on the tables.

Six mornings a week we walked to work in the chilly dawn air, often passing the prostitutes working the morning trains. We waited outside until the cook arrived to open the doors. Very quickly we got used to the trade. First thing in the morning beefy builder types, who tried to pick us up with faultless regularity. There was no harm to them. They did it all in good fun. A little later aggressive, demanding, shapeless women with hard faces and two or three brats in tow burst in, threatening and swearing at their children. Chips and sausages for the little monsters and a full breakfast for them. I found out from the cook that these people did not have to work because the Government supported them and all their children.

At lunchtime some of the office crowd wandered in. Usually men. With pale timid eyes and often with something to read in their hand.

When school was over, more freeloaders on the Social Security system too lazy to cook dinner (they referred to this meal as tea). After them, just before closing time, after our mean-hearted boss had shut his till and left us to finish emptying out the ashtrays and lock up, a crowd of tramps. At first one came in and, carefully counting his change, ordered coffee. I felt so sorry for him that not only didn't I charge him for the coffee but I warmed up some left-over bacon for him. Within a week word had got around and we had seven or eight who became our closing-time regulars. We were no longer just serving left-overs but raiding the fridges.

We knew that if our mean boss found out he would be absolutely livid at the liberties we took with his stock, but we felt no allegiance towards him after we found out that only the two of us and the illegal Macedonian boy doing the washing-up received such pitiful wages. The other English waitress and the Greek cook with the proper papers were paid more than double our wages. It was almost certain he would deduct our wages if he found out.

The tramps' odour suggested dead dog, but was probably a mix of alcohol escaping from their pores and the rotting

bits of food in their pockets. On the pretext of watching out
for the boss, I opened the café doors to let the stench out.
In the meantime I stood looking out at the bus stop across
the road.

I watched the beautiful red double-decker buses roll up. In
the gathering dark the fluorescent interiors made the drivers
seem ephemeral. I gazed wistfully at the people queuing to
enter doors swishing open. They stepped in one by one.
Through the bus windows my eyes followed them paying
the driver and hastening through to find a seat. Once seated
they opened books or simply turned to peer out into the
gloom. Sometimes their searching gazes met mine, and for a
moment there would be surprise at being watched, but then
their eyes would slide away from the watching waitress.
Uninterested. Happy with their lot. I envied them.

Still, not once did I dare join the queue. The bus, I was
afraid, was only a symbol. An illusion dreamed up by a
disenchanted foreigner. An attempt to pretend that
boarding just such a vehicle could spirit us away from the
grinding boredom of our daily toil, our perpetually cold
room, and the ugly reality of our holiday, and magically
transport us to a place of warmth, security and love. If I
allowed the illusion to capture me, where would I have
gone? The bus would have become just a bus, futile, full of
graffiti, splotches of chewing gum stuck on the seats.

The truth was I was miserable with regret. In a moment
of childish pique I had broken my grandmother's heart for
this grey raw place. She had always loved us. Of course she
had.

And I was bitterly disappointed with London. It was not
at all as the shimmering fox had promised. So often ignored
by the sun, the city's gaze had become bitter and damp. In
fact it rained nearly every day, huge freezing drops that
splattered on the window. Even the day left early. By four
in the evening it was already dark. And Victoria Station?

The place that had seemed so splendid, so tantalising was even greyer, even stranger.

We walked for miles in the foreign city, but always with shoes. There was nowhere to walk barefoot. The land was barren of emerald green or gold rice fields. Its people rushed towards you wrapped in thick funereal garments and unhappy faces. No one smiled. No one spoke to us. Once while we were out an old man in a squashed hat met our eyes and declared mournfully, 'Treacherous old day, isn't it?' We were so surprised at being addressed by an English stranger that we nodded and grinned. How starved we were for a little love and warmth.

And where did the Rice Goddess live? They must have chased her away. There was not a single bamboo shrine laden with offerings to be seen at crossroads. How mean the people had to be to deny their God food.

They held festivals for neither God nor demon. In fact they kept their kind-faced God, and they have only one, in very grand, enormous cave-like buildings they called churches and cathedrals. It was very cold inside their temple and the religious passed silently in and out with downcast eyes. They had nervous sombre faces as if they had committed very terrible sins and were in need of forgiveness.

I missed the taste of fern tips, bright green and glorious, served with slivers of the searingly hot chillies that grow wild in the edges of paddy fields. And my tongue remembered the small bright-red pineapples that Nenek gathered in the morning mist while foraging in the forests. Waking up in the chill of the morning, I saw on my closed lids Nenek bending to catch pollen falling from an exotic pink and yellow bloom. Disturbed, an iridescent orange lacewing butterfly as big as a dinner plate flirted away, flashing and fluttering.

'The forest is my mother,' Nenek said, carefully dropping the yellow pollen into a small plastic bag.

Curled close to my sister for warmth in bed I missed the sound of crickets singing in the night, but on Friday and Saturday nights children as young as thirteen and fourteen roamed the streets in groups, drinking cider from plastic bottles. They congregated outside the kebab shop. Intoxicated by their own daring they swore recklessly. I tried the word on my tongue. The 'f' was long and the 'k' salty.

There were no birds to call in the dawn, but in the still air of Sunday morning, on our way to get croissants for break-fast, we saw flocks of crows and pigeons feeding on the children's vomit.

Working six days a week and earning just enough to cover the rent and a few necessities, we didn't get to do much. Everything was so horribly expensive. One Sunday we walked to Trafalgar Square. It made us laugh to see the many pigeons there. How familiar, their grey bodies. The sight of them, moving grey puddles on the ground, reminded me of Bagaswati, a mountain dweller from the Batak highlands who made his money in Kuta Beach at night. He lit his kerosene lamp in the middle of a circle of tourists. When he had everyone's attention he broke a matchstick held between his thumb and forefinger and inside a cage placed on the ground, a pigeon would fall dead. Always a gasp, then silence from the women and theories from the men. Everybody paid.

Bagaswati would make a fortune in Trafalgar Square.

We walked to Piccadilly Circus and there was a thickly wrapped street vendor selling roasted chestnuts for a pound a bag just outside the tube station. Roasted chestnuts have the most amazing perfume. I know it will be the smell I associate with winter in London. We waited by the heat of his fire while his charcoal-blackened hands 'sorted' us with a portion each.

'Here, love,' he said, his voice hoarse, and handed me a small paper cone filled with hot, sweet chestnuts.

Down Shaftesbury Avenue we found Soho. How odd that homosexual men should show such aggressive defiance! In Bali, homosexuality is only an experiment indulged by young boys before they settle down with a woman and have children. Ah well, Bali is paradise, after all.

We had lunch in Chinatown where the smells were familiar.

There too we found durians, which made us long for home. Zeenat did some calculations and pronounced that the fruit cost twenty-two times more than we would pay at home. It would burn a noticeable hole in our meagre budget, nevertheless we were helpless to resist its call. In the tube station people turned to stare at us. The smell that made us salivate revolted them. How extraordinary! In our room we broke the fruit eagerly, but to disappointment. Inside it was not the coppery colour of the jungle fruit Nenek brought home but an insipid yellow. And in our mouth it fell short of the smoky intensely sweet taste we loved. They had harvested it too young. Afterwards, as we had been taught since childhood, we filled the hollow shell with water and drank it. Seven times.

After more than two weeks the letter that Nenek had written on the day we left arrived. It was a sad letter. We had broken her heart for nothing. We sat by the window looking at the grey rain and I whispered, 'Shall we go home?'

My sister nodded eagerly. We decided to leave before the next rent was due. In less than a week we planned to be home. We looked at each other with excitement. How happy Nenek would be to see that we had come to no harm. The next day during break time we went to a telephone box and changed the dates of our tickets. They were valid for a year, Father had paid extra for that, but we didn't care. We just wanted to go home. We meant to hand in our notice at the end of the night. I always look back on that fateful day with something approaching amazement, at how close escape had been.

In minutes our shift would have ended.

If it had not suddenly begun to rain.

But as Zeenat and I watched, the skies opened, water rushed out in sheets, and a man dressed all in black, dashing past, made a right turn. The brass bell tinkled and he slipped through the door of the café.

He was not our usual customer. He was big, tall and deep bronze with flowing yellow hair. His eyes were as blue as the sea, his nose straight and proud, but it was his mouth that I stared at. It was impossibly sensuous. Curling upwards at the edges into a sort of mocking smile. Never before had I seen such a mouth, in either man or woman. He sat down, brushing water droplets off his yellow hair and his expensive leather jacket. I noticed that he did not wear a wedding ring, but when he grinned at one of the slobs the Government paid not to work, he showed the long teeth of a dog.

Still, how I wanted him.

My sister and I looked at each other.

'I'll go,' I said, and I swear, I did not feel the tiger's breath upon my face. Until then we were innocent. Another might have said, babes in the wood, awaiting corruption.

Ricky Delgado

Ricky

Without any warning it began pissing down with rain. Swearing and cursing at the lousy English weather, I slid through the misted glass doors of a coffee shop. Jesus, what a fucking place! Someone had perfumed the joint with industrial-quality air-freshener. As if it was a toilet. Under their layer of grease the tables were probably still in quite good condition, but the chair, when I slunk into one, was a byword in plastic discomfort. A black-and-white-clad waitress approached, unfretted by any concept of haste, but definitely moving. Head erect, shoulders back and swaying very slowly from the hips. All of a sudden I was glad, very glad that the English weather is such a contrary, spoilt bitch.

When eventually the black and white vision stood before me, her eyes secretive and her mouth half smiling, I didn't bother to stop myself; I looked her up and down and whistled. The other customers turned to stare. Fuck them. What do they know about Asian babes with skin like silk? This one was so beautifully exotic, blood sped into my brain. Oh man, you should have seen that smoking body. My hands itched.

Sometime during the slow whistle, the half-smile floundered. Really black eyes stared at me, bemused and a touch unfriendly now, but inside my head I was already running my fingers down that rich honey and cream neck, into the valley of her breasts, resting my palms on the delicate smooth skin of her stomach . . . fucking her.

'What can I get you?' she asked. Deliberately cool. Good tactic. I liked it, hard to get. Rarely fails.

'Espresso, short,' I said, automatically gesturing with my thumb and forefinger.

'Espresso, short,' the voice repeated, the accent so foreign it made me think she had not been long in this country. I suspected her English might be a bit basic. Luckily for her, for what I had in mind, even if she was limited to nothing more than, 'Ooh, aah, Cantona,' we were in business. High-pitched kitten sounds would be an added bonus, of course, but . . . hey, I'm not fussy.

Twisting at the hips, she walked off. Head erect, shoulders back, tight skirt; nice arse. As she passed a large mirror, she turned her head; the blue-black hair in a pony tail high on her head swung far left, and our eyes met. Hers slid away quickly. She slipped behind the bar and busied herself with the coffee machine, speaking very fast in some chinky-sounding language to a sick-looking, miserable, yellow man. I hadn't eaten since lunch the day before and even the crispy-around-the-edges food in the fluorescent-lit glass cabinet looked distinctly edible. Perhaps I could ride out the rain inside the café with the slowly moving Goddess. The Goddess returned with my coffee.

'Thanks, Bella,' I said, my eyes hustling, softening, caressing, my mouth already tasting pussy.

'Anything else?'

I spooned sugar into the coffee. 'Have dinner with me,' I invited, grinning evilly. Contrary to popular belief women find two-legged wolves irresistible.

Teeth that looked as if they had been filed straight with a nail file appeared between her stretching lips. 'Where I come from we have a name for men like you.' She paused, and grinned. 'Land crocodiles.'

I threw my head back, laughed. Great. My kind of girl. Her mischief was infectious. 'And where is it that the rest of my kind live?'

'Bali.'

I knew it. A pagan. 'I've been there,' I said.

'Really,' she cried eagerly. Black eyes started to warm nicely.

'I'm Ricky. What's your name?' Not that it mattered. All girls can usually be trained to answer to Bella.

'Nutan.'

'Come on, Bella, it's only dinner.' I winked and nodded. Just in case you haven't realised by now, I'm Italian. Actually I can do even better than that. I'm Sicilian. She was considering. I could hear the wheels in her brain revolving.

'Bring a friend if you don't trust me,' I offered. This line never fails. If nothing else works, trust me, go with this one.

She laughed. Pretty. 'You are so determined. What must you have done when the ice-cream man came to your village? Okay, if I bring my twin sister?'

Mamma mia, her accent was a bit funny, but did she just say two for the price of one? Surely such completely unlikely offers were found only in supermarkets, not greasy little cafés in Victoria. Another exactly like her. Two. A set all for me. I had never had twins before. I wanted to wallow in the filthy fantasy of two fabulous bodies rubbing against each other, but she had said something that was making my mind race to another time, another place.

The ice-cream man is in the neighbourhood. I can hear his bell.

I am the little boy rushing into a homely farmhouse kitchen. There is a good woman in that kitchen. She is making involtini. Her husband says it is the best in the whole of Sicily.

'Mamma, Mamma, *gelato*,' I shout desperately.

'Not today.' This is her voice at its most decisive.

'Mamma, *gelato*, *gelato*,' I cry harder, racing madly around her.

'No, Ricardo. I said, no,' she says more firmly, louder than my screams.

Nobody calls me Ricardo any more.

I throw myself on the ground and kick my heels against the stone floor. '*Gelato*, Mamma, *gelato*,' I begin sobbing in earnest. Outside the silly tunes are getting louder, but soon they will be fading away.

She shakes her head again. 'No.'

I think this time she means it, but I was born to hustle. My hands rush up to press my temples, as if I am in mortal pain. She must relent or the ice-cream van will be gone. I go crazy. You will call it hysterical. 'My head, my head, help me, someone,' I scream.

'*O Dio Bono*,' she swears. She is giving up, I can tell.

'Mamma, help me, my head, my head,' I yell even louder.

'*Disgraziato*,' she hisses, but a plump floury hand is already reaching into her blouse, and pulling a purse out of her soft chest. I quit the bawling immediately and jump up, my hand outstretched. I snatch the money from her and run out into the yellow light outside.

Oh fuck, you don't really want all this childhood crap, do you?

You do. Okay, baby, I'll tell you what I know, and what I don't . . . well, it's not worth knowing. I'll try to save your blushes, and keep the swearing and cursing to a minimum. *Andiamo*. From the beginning this time.

My mother said that while she was pregnant with me she attended a wedding in Corsica. Now Corsicans have so much African in them that they are a bit odd. They believe in black magic. Anyway, at the wedding some old hag, a black-clad widow complete with a fishnet veil over her ugly mug, called Mamma over to where she sat, under an olive tree.

The old fright laid her gnarled hand on my mother's belly, and prophesised, 'Be triumphant. A beautiful boy will split your legs. And mark my words, he will grow to be a phenomenon.' My mother, who was thirty-six years old, and slightly embarrassed to be pregnant again after a sixteen-year hiatus, was gladdened by the blessings of a Corsican witch. Though in the coming years it made her soft in the face of my wilfulness, and served only to reinforce every contemptible quality in me.

After every misadventure I would set off at a sprint for the land, leaving Mamma, hands on hips, heaving at the doorway. Usually there was a broom or a rolling pin waving in her right hand. '*Disgraziato. Ti faro in pezzi.*'

Disgrace, yeah, but *you* cut *me* into pieces, never. You learn quickly. Italian parenting stipulates, in the unlikely event a child does not manage to leap out of reach, the consequences for bad behaviour must be a tolerable thing. Poor mite and all that. Hours later when the coast was clear I would return to raid the larder. Standing in the middle of the kitchen I'd hear her shuffle down the stairs, a short chunky woman in sensible shoes.

'So, you're hungry then?' she would observe, voice gruff, arms folded across her chest, but she had already forgotten that I was a shocking disgrace. I'd pretend shame, hang my head low and nod. She would expell a long suffering sigh, and set about making me supper. Then she'd sit at the wooden table and watch me eat. Ah, Mamma, pasty fleshy face, gun-metal hair and caramel eyes full of loving indulgence. She scolded and shouted and then gave me everything I wanted.

We lived in an dwindling ghost-like village called Ravanusa. So undeveloped that every fortnight around seven in the morning a lorry came around to supply our domestic water needs. If we finished the water before then, we had to borrow from neighbours. There was a pessimistic air even in the central *piazza*. Too many lean years had depopulated the town to the extent that everybody knew everybody else. Any stranger was the subject of the guarded eyes of the entire village, until he became a part of our secretive village life, or at least until everyone thoroughly knew his business.

Ravanusa boasted a deadbeat bar, a good-sized market, some sad small-town shops, a tiny post office, chained unloved dogs in every yard, and the notorious *circolos*, gambling clubs. Rooms rented along the piazza for use as gambling dens. This was one of the few vices available to the men of this dying village to ruin themselves on. But how can you blame them their bad habits? In a funny way I admired them. They were men running away from intolerable boredom.

When their burnt faces cried, '*O Dio bono*,' it was without resignation. In a drought they alone drank at the fountain of sweet water. They were husbands, brothers, fathers, cousins and even a paraplegic lawyer who came accompanied by a little helper whose only function was to hold his master's cards, and fill out cheques for the huge sums his master called out.

My uncle lost his home in one of these dingy dens. He held up a six, the other pulled out a seven. And then there were the professionals, their eyes glazed and manic, shuffling their cards so fast, the flying cards swished by, tak, tak, tak. They were the ones who were capable of gathering crowds of gawking men. 'Are you completely crazy?' or 'Don't be a fool,' the men whispered excitedly to the brave and absurd men who gambled their unwary wives for a month, or six, or for good if the good woman upon hearing the news hanged herself.

If you didn't gamble chances are you indulged in that other very common vice. Alcohol. My favourite alcoholic was Toto, a funny, correct, little man who walked every day to the bar. Standing, he ordered his three grappas, threw them down in quick succession, and then took a step back, hollering out as if he was still in the army, 'One step back.' He followed that little routine with an, 'About turn' as he turned around smartly and clicked his heels, his back ramrod straight. Nobody took any notice. He walked home, drank a few litres of wine and passed out, usually in his barn. He bought his wine from my father, two barrels of red wine a year, each barrel with a holding capacity of 1,500 litres. My father says that, when Toto was a young boy he used to beg my grandfather for alcohol.

'Come on, *Zio*, give me some wine?'

'*Madonna mia*, not that again,' my exasperated grand-father would say.

Then one day he saw Toto lying on the ground, mouth open, drinking red wine straight from the barrel tap.

My job was to wake Toto up every morning. Spring, summer or winter the ritual was the same. I chucked a pail of water over his head and waited until he turned over. '*Alzati*.' Wake up, I shouted, until his heavy lids came unstuck and bleary eyes squinted up at me. His lips, stained purple by red wine jerked at the corners. He mumbled something that sounded like, 'And good morning to you too.' He sat up and I swear the man creaked. Then his right hand rooted around in his jacket for my wages.

One freezing February morning when the almond trees were frothy with white flowers I tipped a pail of water over Toto's head, and ordered him to wake up but he refused to move, so I rolled him over. His purple lips were twisted into a strange, sly smile, as if he knew something I didn't, but he was stiff and dead at thirty-five.

'Are you dead, Toto?' I asked the corpse.

No answer.

I took a step backwards and knocked the pail over. The noise of its clattering and rolling startled me, and suddenly I was scared witless. Toto smiled his dead smile.

I was alone with a dead body.

'Mamma,' I screamed and, filled with terror, ran. I ran as fast as my nine-year-old legs would carry me, but in those days I could really run. In fact I was famed for speed. Whenever there was a football match, both teams first begged, then resorted to the Italian way, bribery, to tempt me to play on their side. All the time I was running I saw Toto's dead face smiling insolently. Crazy.

By the time I pushed open the heavy wooden door of the house my great-grandfather built, I was shivering uncontrollably. It was cold and dim inside. Pushed against the thick solid walls were lumbering pieces of hideous, teak furniture. Everything had been acquired in my great-grandfather's day. There was a picture of him hanging on the wall. In it he looked like a good, honest, hardworking man, and no matter how hard I tried I could never see him as a murderer.

But he was. He even did time for it. Twenty years for ridding the village of a bullying oppressive gangster. On his release he became a Godfather. Exactly like Mario Puzo's Godfather, except that my great-grandfather had to give up twenty years of his life for the dubious privilege of being so loved and respected that not the smallest thing happened in the village without his blessing.

That was when the word *mafia* actually meant family, and stood for loyalty. When one pricked his finger, smeared the blood on a picture of a saint, and held on to the burning scrap of paper, swearing the *omerta*, 'I will burn this way before I betray the family.' Those were the days when powerful, carefully anonymous men of honour like my grandfather, an illiterate poor shepherd, lived without fuss, collecting favours in exchange for other favours. No one outside the village knew that the simple shepherd living in his hovel on the hill slope was *capo*. That was the way it had always been done in Sicily. Ruled from afar by a succession of mistrusted conquerors, our people learned to solve their own disputes.

If you asked the older people about Don Delgado, they

would first smile with remembered pleasure and then shake their heads forlornly. 'That was then. . .' they lamented. Before the fantastic profits from drugs and prostitution in the seventies and eighties changed it into the feared, cruel, insatiable thing it is today. My father hated the Mafia, what it had become. 'Let them all kill each other,' he spat every time there was a story of another killing in Palermo. 'They are a pack of dogs without blood or honour, killing innocent women and children.'

Once in the heat of summer, Mafia soldiers, five men in city clothes, arrived at the house opposite ours. As we sat spooning minestrone soup, our front door open to let in the evening breezes, they stood at our neighbour's open door and gunned him down. Just like that. Right in front of his wife and two screaming children. The noise was like an explosion. He fell to the ground with his chair, two streams of dark red running away from his body. They turned around to leave and met us, shocked and staring. For a moment no one moved, not them, not us, then Father stood up and closed the front door. 'One less of them,' he said. No one spoke about it afterwards. When the uninterested *carabinieri* arrived, we had not seen or heard anything.

Panting slightly I slammed the heavy door shut, the biting cold and Toto's crazy smile behind me. It was nine in the morning and only Mamma was home. She was standing in front of the huge open fireplace holding a long-handled pan. She turned her head to look at me and the orange and red fire illuminated her face. Quite often in winter she cooked my breakfast in the fireplace. Her cloud omelettes were quite delicious. When Father was home we ate them, sitting in front of the television. Afterwards Father would catch Mamma's eye, stick the forefinger of his right hand into his cheek, and rotate it clockwise on the spot. That meant the food was first-rate.

I ran up to her. Breathlessly I pulled at her skirt, and

delivered my death notice, 'Dead, dead, Toto, Toto, dead.' Her left hand flew to cover her open mouth, but I remember that she did not drop the saucepan. She is a pragmatic Sicilian mother. There is death outside the family circle, and then there is a good meal that does not need to be spoilt.

Yeah, Mamma was no Madonna. She was nosy, interfering, loud, shameless, aggressive, and tight-fisted into the bargain. She dragged me with her to the market and spent hours haggling over a shirt or a pair of shorts. Her strategy was simple. First she insisted that the trader was a rogue to charge such exorbitant prices. He must reduce his price. If that failed and it usually did, she dropped bullying and did begging. She took her purse out and opened it to show how little it held. The next course of action saw her pretending to walk away, so he could shout her back. '*Vieni, vieni, Senora.*' Then she would swagger back, triumphant, and pay the price she called. But sometimes he didn't shout her back. Then she had to back down, return. Apparently, if done in good humour, there is no shame attached to this perfectly legitimate renegotiation device. And so it began again, the entire process right up to the walking away bit. To the best of my knowledge she duplicates this scenario until today. She can't help herself.

She still recollects a time during the war when her family was so poor they wore the same dress for weeks, when they survived on almonds. The only meat to be had was when her father shot a wild rabbit.

The traders understand. They are all from the same generation. They were always nice, never gloated. It was just a game they played. Sometimes they lost and sometimes the loud lady lost. In the end it all evened out.

Toto's funeral was held three days later. It was a very Sicilian affair. The suffocating scent of white lilies, ill-at-ease men in their one good navy blue suit, women in black clutching starched, ironed, white handkerchiefs, rooms crowded with relatives come to shed the obligatory tear, and of course the grieving mother. Let me take a moment to tell you about tragic Sicilian mothers and their uncontrollable grief.

You will find her beside the coffin. It is a key position and much is required of the person who takes on such a role. She must weep for all of Sicily. Flinging her clenched fist into her own chest she howls, 'Oh, the p...a...i...n, oh, the p...a...i...n, ah, the p...a...i...n.' Then she recounts in great detail a boring non-event, an incident when she had refused the deceased some request he made. She sits there berating and cursing herself so much that you begin to imagine it was something of momentous proportions. And then you find out that it was nothing more significant than the refusal to bring a glass of red wine the dead person had asked for, many months back. But the lamenting, moaning and weeping doesn't stop there because the mother then starts to remember and recount other incidents of guilt further back in time. She intersperses them with more cries of 'The p...a...i...n, oh, the p...a...i...n. . .'

Don't forget, all the while there is continuous upper-left breast hammering going on. The men try unsuccessfully to comfort the woman. 'Enough, enough,' they plead unconvincingly. Like the traders in the market everyone knows their roles. It is a game they play.

Toto's mother looks at my father and then wails, 'Ooooh only last week Toto told me how much he liked you . . . The p...a...i...n, ah, the p...a...i...n, oh . . . why, oh why, didn't I . . .' Undaunted by the dismal success rate of convincing a grieving Sicilian *mother* to please just stop, Papa manfully moved forward.

Needless to say my father failed at the task he set himself that day, but in fact Papa is very special. He can smell rain in the air, and tell the time by looking out of the window.

He has never been more than fifteen minutes wrong. We share a special meal in a special way. We drop two anchovies into our mouths, followed immediately by two, or even three green grapes, and then we cram the remaining space with bread. It is our own special combination. We invented it, and we think it unbeatable.

He is a farmer. Sicilian farmers work uncomplainingly, like bulls, every day, even Sundays. Even on the coldest winter morning he is up and on the land by five o'clock. His consuming greed is land, land and more land, and once acquired never sold. He has twenty *tumina* of land. It is an old form of measurement that remains in the rural parts of Italy. 'How big is that?' I asked.

'Big, very big,' he said. The pride was quiet.

'Tell me in kilometres.'

He shrugged. 'Who knows? But it's big. Very big.'

I remember him as strong, hardworking and funny, so funny. He told such stories of life before the war. Times in Paris, more than once mind you, when he 'accidentally' found himself slap bang in the middle of a girlie bar with a drink in one hand and a ravishing blonde in the other. He liked a good blonde in his day. I wish you could have heard him. Even as he was opening his mouth I was already laughing. He was so funny. But if interrupted he became cross, and that was even funnier.

'Don't interrupt. Your grandfather was like that, your uncle was like that and now you are like that.'

'All right, all right, tell your story then.'

'No, now I don't remember any more,' he said sulkily.

Toto's funeral procession itself was a sombre thing, a painfully slow march in the freezing cold through the town, with the wailing women in the middle. As we passed, shopkeepers and other householders shut their windows and pulled down their shutters. I know it sounds like a heartless rejection of the dead and the grieving, and believe me it looks even worse, but it is our custom. They will do it when I die too.

In front of the procession, small children scattered flowers in the path of the hearse. At the back Giuseppe, Lillo, Ignizio and I whispered. We were a gang and we were up to no good. Our hero was Sandokan, *la tigre de Malaysie*. We never missed an episode of the Malaysian tiger on television. We were making plans for the February carnival celebrations. It was a street thing. The full gang that patrolled the streets to protect it from lunatic enemy gangs from other villages was twenty strong. We chased them out with sticks.

But the best times we had were always in summer when it was still warm and bright at eight in the evening. While my mother sat downstairs making a list of my misde-meanours for my father and his belt's attention, I crept into the attic. Lifting craftily loosened boards I climbed out to the ledge and shimmied down the drainpipes.

By the time I got to the main piazza, Giuseppe, Lillo and Ignizio were already there smoking cheap German cigarettes. We pooled our money and joined the queue of people buying *sangonaccio*, blood sausages. There is just nothing in the world to compare to those sausages warming on Don Collogere's small portable coal stove. If one ended up far enough back in the queue, there was a very good chance of leaving with only Don Collogere's regretful smile. He is dead now, but he was an institution in my day. Narrow, ancient, with patent leather hair, he sat on his wooden Peroni beer case, dressed completely in black, from the delicate little cap on his head to the highly polished shoes.

We wolfed the sausages down standing, but once when money was scarce and *sangonaccio* unaffordable, Giuseppe begged his father the fish seller for a box of sardines. Then we sneaked into my father's storeroom and stole some wine. We carried our box of fish and wine to a disused farmhouse, lit a fire with twigs we found on the hillside, and grilled the fish. Mindful of being discovered we ate and drank in the dark. Completely intoxicated, we ate even the heads. The next morning poor Giuseppe vomited when he realised that he had eaten fish eyes. I didn't care. I'm not the squeamish type.

Sometimes we staged sword fights in my father's garage. First we dipped our swords into the oil tank of my brother's Vespa, and then we lit them. One crazy day Lillo dipped his *burning* sword into the petrol tank. Instantly the petrol tank caught fire. In a blind panic we rushed out, only to stop suddenly three yards from the garage door, and run back screaming. Giuseppe grabbed a chair and advanced towards the burning Vespa.

'What are you doing?' I yelled. I saw the whole house going up in flames. We rushed this way and that, looking for water. In a fit of despair Lillo began to batter the mouth of the petrol tank with his sword and, *Grazia Santa Maria*, the fire miraculously went out. We sank to the ground in sheer relief.

Then school broke up for summer.

And I no longer had to leave for school with my father at five in the morning on a torturously slow, one-and-a-half-hour ride on his tractor. I used to dread that trip in winter when it got so bitingly cold on the open tractor that in minutes my teeth were chattering uncontrollably and my fingers were numb. Passing motorists automatically stopped to give 'the poor boy' a lift. But if the Sicilian winter was fierce, the summer was unrelentingly fiery. It got so hot that I could hardly sleep at night. I dragged the mattress out onto the balcony, but by half-four in the morning I was woken up again by farmers on the street below.

'What are you doing outside? Go inside,' crusty, irritatingly cheerful voices shouted up, above the rattling of their tractor engines.

'Too hot inside,' I shouted back.

'*Allora*, go back to sleep, then.' And the noise of their tractors died away.

During the holidays I didn't have the usual bread and milk or cloud omelette for breakfast, but took a lidded container to Tsi Stefano, down the road. In the basement I stood in a queue of clacking housewives and sleepy young boys. Tsi Stefano tended to a huge old iron cauldron of simmering milk over a roaring olive-wood fire. When it was my turn, the cheese maker's knotty, craggy hand dropped into my bowl three, sometimes four, shallow scoops of fluffy ricotta cheese, and some broth. I handed over my two hundred lira, and scuttled home to clean the bowl out with a hunk of bread. Beautiful.

My first job was to feed the pigs. They ate a paste of sawdust, water and leftovers. After the pigs I rushed to my grandmother's. She lived in a dusty house that smelt yeasty, as if she was growing mushrooms under her bed. Like every other grandmother in Sicily, she owned a red bulb and a bunch of fake flowers that she carefully displayed under a picture of the Madonna. I rushed about washing her floor and plates. This I did for money. Sometimes she made me sit in her living room and listen to her drone on about the war, 'Two days and two nights the Germans passed through Ravanusa . . . And when the polite American soldiers came to ask for watermelon, they put sugar on the flesh.' Cackling and chortling with delight. 'Those Americans, ha, ha, sugar on the watermelon. . .'

Summertime was also when my brother and I went olive picking with Papa. With hand rakes we loosened all the fruit onto a net on the ground. Then the bright green olives were gathered, poured into the wheeled container behind Father's tractor, and taken to the mill. Then there were those two crazy summers when my father was still growing white grapes for the supermarkets, and he had me march up and down the rows of grapes banging a spoon on a frying pan to keep the birds away. Seven hours a day that was my job. He was too stingy to invest in one those cannons that exploded noise every now and again.

The year Toto died was also the summer the *zingara*, gypsy children, came to steal our honey, made by bees that took their nectar from chestnut flowers. It was July and we were plucking almonds then. Almonds harvested that young are soft and sour and a local favourite. The gypsies came during siesta when they thought the land was deserted. Silly kids stole the nest and carried it away from the house, but when they opened the hive, the bees swarmed out, irritable with the midday heat and being knocked about. Running around in circles, the children flapped their scrawny brown arms, screaming, 'Get off. Get off.' We ran out into the fields and threw handfuls of dust and soil on them, and the bees flew away.

Up the Saracion hill were Greek ruins. We were always finding broken ceramic plates, cracked terracotta pots, damaged amphore, and bronze cooking utensils. Usually the things we found were crudely made, deserving of little attention, and just tossed away. However one spring when my father and brother were busy spraying the trees with noxious chemicals that kept away the maggots, I stumbled upon a treasure. I found a thing so fine that I, a vandal who took pleasure in killing chickens for fun, thought to keep it. It was some way away from the fallen half-buried limestone pillars, where it was believed a temple once stood.

The entrance to the cave was so narrow that it could be entered only by lying flat on the ground and slowly dragging oneself along for four or five feet into pitch darkness. Then the space widened until you came upon a domed room where it was possible to stand upright. There were niches carved into the walls, and ashes and burnt sticks inside a circular arrangement of stones on the ground. But the funny thing was someone, a long time ago, had gone ape-shit crazy in it. Everything in the room was broken or violently smashed to splinters. Everywhere lay fragments, a fractured male torso, damaged goats' antlers and bits of what must have been fine vases with red figures on black backgrounds.

But it was to the fireplace that I held my candle closer. Two-foot high, half buried, and charred around the edges, was a statue. One half of her marble face was hacked away as if someone had taken an axe to her, leaving an ugly crack that ran all the way from her rounded breast right down to her hips. Her legs were broken off at the thighs and both her hands were missing. I found one later. Someone had flung it against the wall, and it had landed in one of the recesses. Her smile was smashed, and even the one good eye that survived was as sightless as any Greek or Roman carving, but when I turned her sideways in the flickering light of my matches, a thrill ran through me. I recognised her as incredibly, indescribably beautiful. A blood goddess. A treasure. I ran my dirty fingers along the good side of her face and felt initiated in some inexplicable way. She was mine.

Many centuries ago an orgy of destruction had taken place in my secret cave. That much was obvious, but why? Once she must have graced a temple or a fine house. What was she doing, wilfully destroyed and abandoned in this cave? The whole thing was mystifying. As I cleaned the Goddess with the sleeve of my sweater, greed settled into my little heart, and for some reason, mysterious to me, I resolved to keep her away from the eyes of everyone else, even my *own* gang.

Carefully I concealed the cave entrance. Often I ran up into the hills and slid into the cave just to look at my deepest secret. Until one day love made me wrap it carefully and bear it as a gift to a girl.

That was the year the olives were too small to pick and turn into oil, and the farmers had simply left them on the trees. We had too much in store anyway. I was sitting in a tree waiting to discover the entrance to a rabbit's burrow, when I saw her coming from the adjacent fields of wild flowers. Her head was a glorious puff of honey-brown curls. She was quite the sweetest thing I had seen with a tiny mouth the colour of a half-ripe cherry.

Unaware of my presence she came to sit under the tree. Big blue dragonflies flirted around her. From a pocket in her skirt she took out a margherita bloom and began plucking the petals out one by one, chanting, 'He loves me, he loves me not, he loves me, he loves me not . . .' and the last petal . . . 'he loves me.' Instantly she sprang up and, laughing joyfully, began to whirl around, her small feet going faster and faster, the cloud of hair bouncing and flying as she spun around. What a curious delightful toy she was.

After a moment she sat down again and turned to another margherita. Once more she pulled out the petals, 'He loves me, he loves me not, he loves me. . .' and the last petal . . . 'he loves me not.'

'No,' she gasped. Incredible. Was it possible that her dismay was genuine?

That empty stalk was flung backwards. Another bloom was whipped out and the ceremony repeated. That stalk was immediately dispensed with, and another consulted. Why, that one gave exactly the same result too. She was not loved. Without warning she dumped her face in her hands and burst into tears, sobbing as if her heart was breaking. Watching her from above, I was intrigued.

That such a little thing could cry with such ardour was a novel and satisfying idea. I experienced a flash of resentment for the unknown *amore*, for the passion wasted. Quite without warning the strangest sensation coursed through me. Competition. The thought to win her love. The thought to possess her. Not in a sexual way. I was innocent then. I just wanted to own her. Like a toy. To be able to say to my friends, 'Look, look at this splendid creature. It is mine.' That was what I thought I felt, but perhaps I was already in love with her flying curls and the generosity with which she could love.

I dropped out of the tree beside her and her startled face flew up. What do I remember? Eyes. Soft, brown, wet. As I watched, that first open-mouthed flash of fear turned to horror as the realisation of what I had witnessed dawned upon her. And the blush? I have to tell you about it. A charming endearing bright crimson. But before her humiliation could develop into lasting awkwardness I stood and pulled her up by the hand, as if she was an old friend. Already determined that she would be mine one day.

'Come, I'll show you the caves' – not my secret one – 'and then we'll have ice cream.' It was while we were eating our ice creams sandwiched inside brioches that I learned all about Francesca Sabella.

Like so many other Sicilian farmers struggling with high taxes Francesca's father had migrated to foreign lands to better his family's lot. They returned every summer to spend the holidays with their relatives and swell the population of the town. She told me about this faraway land they lived in, England. Enviously I listened to her describe a place filled with hundreds of shops, houses, cinemas, dancing places, restaurants and big cars.

When the holidays were over we said goodbye sitting under the olive tree. I held out my clumsy newspaper-wrapped package. She opened it eagerly enough, but recoiled from its contents as if my present was a live snake. She stared in horror at my beautiful blood Goddess.

'It's horrible,' she uttered, hugging her body.

I had made a mistake, wasted my most beautiful possession. I should have given her a sweet, a cake, or a trinket stolen from the village shop. It is a huge blow when a loved one cannot appreciate the sacrifice endured in the giving. Then, meeting the confusion in my eyes, she lied. 'No, in fact, it is too beautiful . . . unusual . . . stupendous.' She bit her impulsive lip. 'A work of art. Yes, yes, the more I look at it, the more I like it,' she added. But the damage was done. I had given away my most precious thing, and she did not want it.

'I'll come to join you. Give me your address,' I said.

Quickly she wrote it down. I squashed it in my hand.

'Ti amo, Francesca.'

She beamed. There was a soft breeze in her hair, and I bent to kiss her young plump mouth. It was strange that first kiss. It was my first taste of innocence, no teeth, no tongue, no passion and no technique. Yet it was the most beautiful thing. Why, I remember it now. Ah, the past. The incredible softness of Francesca.

'One day we'll get married,' I promised. Well, you say things like that when you are thirteen.

'I'll be waiting for you,' she promised sincerely.

Many years later I stood at her front door. Francesca of the sweet letters, her curls exactly as I remembered them. The big brown eyes full of light. Politely I bid her parents goodbye, we were going to the cinema. I walked her down the path sedately enough, but as soon as we turned the corner, I pulled her into my arms and kissed her. I had learned a great deal since our last kiss. I kissed her long and hard. By the time I lifted my face, I was ecstatically happy and she had merited the title of my girlfriend, future wife and mother of my children. She had learned nothing since our last kiss. She still didn't know how to kiss.

I remember I once slept for a week. It happened when my mother and aunt took me to Caltanissetta to remove a

small growth on my hand. I remember lying on an operating table looking at the big bright overhead light, and
waking up to my father peering worriedly down at me.
Then the world became black again. They had screwed up
a simple operation. My neck and chest were swelling up.
Later my mother told me my father ran down the corridor
screaming blue murder, pushed a doctor up a wall, and
swore to kill everyone in the hospital if anything, anything
at all happened to me. I woke up a week later to a room
wallpapered with all my relatives: distant aunts, uncles who
had not seen me since I was a baby, cousins I did not recognise, second cousins I did not know I had.

They said only the big hospital in Palermo could puncture
my enormous chest and draw out the air. I didn't know
what was wrong with me, but I wasn't afraid until I was in
the ambulance, all alone, and then I was convinced I was
dying.

In Palermo, the doctor decided on local anaesthetic. I saw
him coming towards me, in his hand a sharp knife, and I
began to scream, 'I am dying, I am dying.' He was a man
with a sadistic sense of humour. 'Ahhh, die then,' he
suggested. 'Come on then, die. What? Still not dead?' he
taunted, laughing.

For a month I could not move, a tube ran out of my chest
into a pyramid-shaped bottle full of water. My breath
showed as rising bubbles in the water. My leg muscles had
become so weak I had to be supported when I first tried to
walk. Then Rocco moved into the next bed. We were
instant friends. He was older and from Palermo.

At night after we had been fed, and the last round of
medicine had been dispensed, we climbed out of the
window, Rocco, me, and my triangular bottle safe in a
plastic shopping bag. Palermo waited in the dark. Usually
we just hung around the bars drinking coffee and smoking.
Then came the day Rocco suggested getting laid. We went

to the train station and I stood by an iron pillar and sang the old Neapolitan love songs from the 1950s that my father used to sing. Although they were songs normally hung on male voices made raspy with years of grappa swigging, they didn't sound too bad on my high unbroken voice.

Women responded immediately. 'Poor little boy,' they said, their eyes slipping on the tube running into the plastic bag, and each one with a dewy expression threw a coin into Rocco's hat. Women probably respond to children the way men respond to a beautiful woman. Instinctively, instantly and without justification. Soon there was enough in the hat.

By a side street we found her, leaning against a lamp post, using a folded newspaper to fan the hot night into her face. She wore a pair of black, very, very high heels. Wedged between the sharp stilettos and the black leather straps, the skin of her feet was as smooth as the eggs of a bird, but reddened with the weight of her. I stared, fascinated by her bulging calves. No woman in Ravanusa would ever dare wear such a thing.

Rocco did the negotiations.

She wanted to know how much he had, and he tried to lie, to keep back the price of a little celebratory drink and cigarettes afterwards. Eventually a price was struck. She led us down a short walk, up a narrow staircase, and opened the door to a grimy room.

'No, no, not together,' she said, when I tried to enter too.

Rocco was to have his turn first. I stood with my ear at the door listening intently. For perhaps five minutes the springs on her bed creaked. Then Rocco groaned as if in great pain. I heard the chink of a belt and had only time enough to take a step back before the door opened. I looked past Rocco's smirking face.

She sat on a filthy bed crooking her finger at me. I picked up my plastic shopping bag and went inside. I closed the door. Outside I hadn't seen her properly, but in the harsh light of a naked light bulb, I could see she was a proper slapper. The black lacy bra, the red suspenders, the heavy blue eye-shadow and a crimson mouth to clash with her crazy flame hair. She wore no knickers. All in all, cheap and foul.

Holding on tightly to my plastic bag, I walked my walk towards her. I put the bottle down. She unbuttoned and unzipped my baggy trousers. They fell around my feet. I felt the brush of her long curving nails. And suddenly, up close, the flaming hair that didn't match the unruly jungle of black pubic hair, the bored mouth, the garish make-up, and the copious amounts of flaccid breast were all too much.

I came.

The hard eyes were amused, but she only shrugged carelessly. Turning away from me, she began to dress.

'Hey,' I cried.

'*Bello*,' she explained, laughing openly now, 'for this price you only get to come once.' She dressed very, very quickly and stood with her arms crossed looking grimly at my trousers. I was not the man to get the better of her. I pulled my trousers up and zipped them. She opened the door. I followed her out. Rocco was lounging against the opposite wall. I did not meet his eyes. She locked the door and we walked down the stairs together.

'*Ciao*, go straight home now, boys,' she advised, in what I thought was a rather kind voice. Then she took a right turn down the street and disappeared from sight.

'What happened?' Rocco asked.

'It was great,' I said, my face flaming.

We went and had a slice of pizza each. I had Pizza Napolitana. Couldn't finish it. Sometimes I wonder where she is now, that pseudo-sincere, damaged creature who, in an irrelevant moment, for ever associated pizza with the taste of humiliation.

I returned to Ravanusa soon after and all the people in the street said,' Aah! But I heard you were dead.'

It was late summer, but the days were still sizzling and the wind was just a blast of scorching air. All of Sicily had turned into one giant oven. And on the hill slopes where the soil was chalky white it was dazzling to the eye. There were even water mirages on the roads. Behind the houses children were sneaking into the troughs the animals drank from. Stupid with heat I stretched on the shady veranda and baked. Some insect buzzed near my ear, but I was too sluggish even to flap it away.

The air was so still I could actually hear straw-hatted Tsi Stefano, creaking in his rickety rocking chair down the street. I ignored my mother calling from the kitchen for the fifth time. In that unrelenting heat I felt as if my life was slowly seeping out of my pores.

And it occurred to my lethargic brain, that if I was frozen evermore in that moment, it would be my description of hell. To be stuck for all eternity in that mind-numbing, merciless monotony. That was the first time I thought of running away.

Then it was autumn again, and the air was warm and drunk with the smell of grapes fermenting on the vines. Clouds of midges descended on us as we plucked the fruit. I sat in a cart lazily removing the leaves from the grapes. The mouldy grapes Father put aside for making wine. Only when the seeds have turned from bitter green to brown will a grape make a wine of full smoky flavour. And afterwards it must be stored in wooden barrels so as not to shock the grape. Papa made the best wine in the village. Red, of course. A true Sicilian's drink.

Ignizio, Giuseppe and I ate and fought with grapes, splattering bunches at each other. We jumped off mules, whistling and dancing our mad dances. Ignizio had learned a little trick. He kicked his mule in the mouth and it jumped into the air with pain. This he found hilarious. I laughed loudly too, but I was no longer one of the gang. I was dying in that small-town mentality. I needed to get out. I was hungry for a taste of what I had never had, for the arrogant wide world outside. And then, of course, there was the crumpled piece of paper with Francesca's address. The gleaners were under the almond tree carefully sifting through debris for almonds my father had missed, and I was making plans to leave.

My father had just begun to lay the foundations to my house when I stole some money and ran away. To Florence.

In Florence I worked in a market stall for Signor Rivoli. Helping him carry boxes of produce, carefully arranging the fruit into neat pyramids, and calling out to the women customers. I began to learn English. Language, unlike maths I found, came easy to me. I waited for the American and British tourists to come to the stall, so I could practise my English. I was cute then, and they had a lot of time for me. And so, it seemed, did the priests and friars who strolled by in their cassocks, stopping to buy fruit. It appeared they had a great weakness for fruit. They came often, masking their illicit desires with delicate humble gestures that thoroughly deceived Signor Rivoli. Their sexuality blazed in their pasty faces when their dark furtive eyes encountered my blond hair in the sunlight and flirted with my blue eyes.

Their voices were soft, but their breath was hot on my forehead as they made their orders, always a bag of peaches, as if it was some secret password that I might understand. Once one of them lightly ran his fingernail up my forearm. '*Che biondi*,' he murmured. Both of us for different reasons stared mesmerised at the blond hairs on my arm as they lifted and fell under his passing fingernail. A manipulative streak in me reacted instantly, producing sexually provocative behaviour in exchange for the money that they pressed into my palm. For ice cream. For Francesca. I glanced at them, always sideways, always innocent.

I was in a hurry to get to Francesca and to save money I lived in the train wagons. A lot of poor destitutes did at that time. We sneaked in when they came to rest for the night in the station. In the morning the guards came around shouting at the top of their voices, 'Oooo wake up – get out.' I washed myself in the toilet, locked my little bag of belongings in a locker at the train station, and went to work. At night I slept with my little bag underneath my head. One night I regained consciousness with a throbbing pain at the side of my head, my pillow with all the money I had in the world had been taken. Robbed clean I sat in that train carriage and wept with defeat. In front of me I saw Francesca's father sneering, the relief on my mother's simple face, and my father, all is forgiven, my son, holding out the keys to that damn tractor. Under my feet the baked Sicilian ground burnt. Francesca was lost.

Curled tightly into a ball I cried myself to sleep. And I dreamed. In my dream I saw a mist gathering in the empty carriage. The steel under my feet became the pale chalky earth I had run upon as a child, and the air turned so wintry I began to shiver. The mist formed itself into a man. Slowly his edges stopped wavering. Once solid he was tall and beautiful, but foreign with that flat lean face of an Aztec warrior, chiselled cheekbones and thin cruel lips. But what was extraordinary about him was the enormous spider that sat on his chest. In my dream the spider spoke in a smooth, slightly ironic, female voice, 'Had enough, Ricky?'

I was robbed of speech because I could see that the spider had made a hole in the man's breast and was suckling red milk out of it.

'Had enough yet, Ricky?' the spider asked again. 'Had enough of your pathetic life? Come, Ricky, build me a temple once more.'

86

Once more? In my dream I couldn't speak. I was cold, so cold.

'Hecate, my little temple keeper does not recognise me.' The spider laughed, a private mocking chuckle. And as I watched, strangely unafraid, the spider grew bigger and blacker, its eyes glowing bright green in the dark. It changed its shape and then turned to show me her profile. I recognised her immediately.

My broken statue dressed in long flowing robes, the edges embroidered with gold. She was so beautiful I stared spell-bound, intoxicated.

She smiled a long slow smile. A woman had never smiled so knowingly, so seductively before. 'I have waited an age for you, Ricky. Will you build my temple? To herd the lost and wounded, who walk the earth like sheep, to my altar. Bring me their poor little souls. Offer me equal amounts of lust, decay and ruin. . .' She paused, her eyes cunning. Her mouth elongated like a trumpet, a poisonous datura. 'Like before. . .' All around her the air crackled. 'And you will marvel at what rewards pour into your hands.' Her voice dropped to a whisper. 'All your heart desires – fame, fortune, love. . .'

I knew without being told that I had served her before. And that it was *I* who had once destroyed her temple in an uncontrollable fit of fury. Her watching eyes blazed with desire and deceit, and her alabaster skin, soaked so long in corruption, glowed a greenish hue. She stood before me, a monster. And I felt her evil deep in my freezing body, and yet in my dream I was a man, and when she moved and her robes parted I knew such a hunger it was irresistible. I was shivering.

'Say yes.'

'Yes,' I said.

And her eyes glittered like a fox's. After it had killed every chicken in the coop. I touched my stomach. Heat was glowing from the centre of me, and coursing through my veins. The black despair I experienced earlier had fluttered away and I felt as if I was soaring high with this new-found heat. The future beckoned heady and glamorous. In front of me the mysterious mist beings were slowly vaporising leaving behind only the spider woman's laughter, a low, cruel, idle sound.

I awoke suddenly alone in the cold empty carriage. It was just a dream, but it had left me strong and powerful. The path in front of me shone brightly.

I slid open the carriage door and a manic smile came to my lips. Unbelievable, but the entire world was covered in that magic mist of my dream. When you can see with your eyes closed. When the image your open eyes perceive is similar to the one you have seen on your closed lids . . . I touched the bump on my head. It was hot and throbbing to the touch, but I felt nothing. Perhaps the Corsican witch was right after all. *He will grow to be a phenomenon.* I was going to build a temple, a spider's temple of power, wealth and pleasure.

A friend told me about a room in a house. I moved in. Bloody hell, my landlady was so tight she would not eat for fear she would have to shit and use toilet paper. Nine-thirty sharp and the old bag switched off the electricity at source. I brought home a little portable television, and found it outside my room when I came back from work. 'No television,' the crack in her face warned bleakly.

I found work as a plasterer. It was hard work, six coats before we could call it *finito*. The plaster in Italy is different. It is completely different from the matt grey one used in England. Ours had a finish like pink marble. New plaster was a source of joy in Italy. People lived with the plastered surfaces for years, until the walls got so dirty that they cried for a coat of paint.

One summer we plastered a new block for a school.

During recess the giggling teenage girls lined up in a row and, emboldened by their numbers and the separating wall, openly stared at and commented on my shirtless body. For me it was the first time I came face to face with the availability of the opposite sex. Every day their comments became more risqué and it's a wonder how my head fitted through the door of my little room.

I bought a hair dryer, spent some money on an expensive leather jacket and some boldly coloured shirts and I was in style. When I walked the streets women and men turned to look at me. But I was dissatisfied; my wages were hardly going to make me rich. When was I going to be rich and powerful? I had to make it to England, where pots of money and Francesca waited to be mine.

I was seventeen when I hitched a ride to Paris in a French woman's car. She offered me her house for the night. That night she came to share the sofa. Maybe for one second my sleep-addled brain was confused by the sensation of a naked body next to mine, but when she began to kiss my back I turned myself over to the unexpected encounter. And what an encounter it was. It's left me with a soft spot for all French women.

I stayed in her home for three months, an addict. Sex, sex, and more sex. I surprised her at least three times a night, no words just suddenly something hot and hard inside her. At dawn I woke her warm body with more friction. When she went to work I spent the day just waiting for her to return, so I could pounce on her all over again the minute she came through the door. How mad I was for the newly found experience! Then one day I had enough of her, and I left.

I went to work in a restaurant, washing dishes; lunch and dinner. At night the boss, not a bad guy actually, locked me in the storeroom with a single mattress in the corner. All night long I listened to my little stereo blasting Pink Floyd and Cat Stevens. Soon I was trying the tunes on an old guitar my boss gave me. I found I already had the music in my head. Music came easy to me. I learned the chords and then the words. Getting the pronunciation right. To know all the words I bought an English/Italian dictionary.

There were rats living in the storeroom but it was cool. Very quickly we learned not to bother each other. They are funny creatures. I do not dislike them. Furry and half ugly. They were as hungry as I was. Those were the days I was crazy for cake and they kept cake in the storeroom. So some nights we got through a whole cake, the rats and I. But it was no life, and after a month the rats and I parted company. Now when I think back, it was the most blameless, uncomplicated time of my life. Hours strumming the guitar, learning to love the naivety of Cat Stevens and the idealism of Floyd.

I left to be a barman. Someone taught me to serve a warmed cognac, the glass resting on its side over a cup of boiling water, and someone else taught me about the ways waiters cheat their employers. They bring their own gin, keep the bottles in their sleeves and ask for the mix off the bar. They pay the bar for the mix and charge the customer the full whack. It was a great racket. The best stock-keeping system could never catch them. They cut me in too. Have to keep the barman sweet. He could squeal. Spoil a good thing.

And when the shift was over I went out with the waiters, the chefs were too dangerously unstable to contemplate a night out with. We went in search of tourists in the night clubs. 'Gosh, look at his eyes!' they cried as I passed. 'Are they coloured contact lenses?' Sometimes I said yes, sometimes no. What did it matter? They wouldn't see me in the morning. In my own way I was being faithful to Francesca. The faces and bodies I no longer remember, but I know they were many. Many. I was working my way to England.

The French taught me a great deal, but my favourite is the effortless way they manage to look and smell clean with one bath a week and the right mix of deodorant and perfume.

Finally I was in England. The weather was lousy, but it didn't matter, this was where I was meant to be. This was home. I knew a man from Sicily who had opened a restaurant in London. Don Calabrese's restaurant was more like a pirate's trove, stuffed to distraction with all kinds of crazy junk. He came to embrace me, he was so happy to see me. I nearly cried to hear someone speaking Sicilian to me. He knew my grandfather. 'Your great-grandfather was a hero,' he said. We sat down to a plate of spaghetti vongole.

He liked giving the impression that he was an eccentric, harmless, gently ageing man. He even had a mynah that ate dog food. He had trained it to screech, 'Oh no, not you again,' when customers walked in through the door; call out, 'Where's my dinner, then?' when customers were being served their food; and demand, 'Have you paid your bill?' to the ones departing. The customers lapped it all up, not knowing that most of the time the 'pretty, delightful' bird was screaming abuse at them in Sicilian. 'Bunch of *Inglese* pigs, they know nothing. Give them dog food.' It was that lunatic bird with its horrible smoker's cough that taught me to wolf whistle in response to a moving skirt.

In the kitchen Don Calabrese kept on his payroll a crazy chef who threw vats of boiling water, screaming, 'You are a shit,' at the poor Polish lad who jumped out of the way, pronto, with the agility of a cat. 'Piece of shit.' He was so crazy he stroked raw pieces of meat and fish cooing, 'Look, as beautiful as a Prada bag . . . a Gucci belt . . .' But when he came out in his white apron at the request of customers he was utterly charming. Unbelievably so.

'Don Calabrese, I need work.'

He stopped being the eccentric, harmless, gently ageing character for a minute and looked at me with sharp shrewd eyes. Yes, *this* was the man who dredged the lemon slices out of the bottom of the sink to reuse in the next day's drinks, and had his waiters go around the restaurant at the end of the night collecting all the left-over wine in the customers' glasses on the tables for the kitchen to use.

'What kind of work?'

'The kind that pays well.'

He downed his grappa. 'Do you want to carry packages? It's good money and it's not very dangerous because you're still a kid. They can't touch you.'

'*Si*,' I said.

'Come back Friday.'

'Can I work as a live-in waiter, do the washing up, or be a kitchen help?' I asked.

He grinned. 'Sure, but I warn now, the money is shit.'

'That's okay.'

I went to live upstairs, and when I was not pouring drinks, waiting on tables, or helping the Polish boy wash up I was running errands. Picking up packages and dropping them off, usually in pubs. After a while I was taking packages in sports bags, to France. It paid a lot more, up to £3,000 a go. When I had saved up about £30,000 I asked Don Calabrese if that was enough for me to buy something with. He raised his bushy eyebrows, nodding with admiration, 'Bravo'. A few days later he told me about a restaurant, La Giocanda, the Joker. A leasehold, of course, but still cheap considering the location. 'VAT problems,' he said sadly. Apparently he too was afraid of these people called the Customs and Excise. 'The curse of all restaurants,' he spat viciously.

The restaurant was a little hole in Jermyn Street, but it was my hole and as holes came it was a very nice hole indeed. In fact, its price was not £30,000, but £90,000. In the time-honoured traditional Italian way £30,000 was the official, Inland Revenue-declared, subject-to-capital-gains-tax price. Under the table, over the next eighteen months, the rest was to be spread as cash payments. That'll do me, I thought.

I got the key late one Saturday night. The previous owner left with his Saturday night takings, and I stood at the doorway. I looked into the half-lit restaurant at the glasses gleaming under the spot lights, the empty bar, the tables closest to the till still unlaid, and in that blessed silence it was all magic.

For the longest time I simply pottered around the place, touching this, rearranging that, examining that. Carefully I turned all the bottles in the fridge so their labels faced out. I emptied all the ashtrays. Then I wiped down and polished the bar until it shone. By the time I looked up it was five in the morning. I crossed the street and stood looking into the lighted interior of the restaurant. I almost couldn't believe it. I closed my eyes and imagined it full, noisy with well-dressed people and the deserted street full of parked cars. Years later my greatest pleasure was walking slowly along that street, seeing the expensive cars tightly parked and knowing they were there because of my restaurant.

After a while I put out my cigarette and went to lock up. I was only eighteen years old.

At the beginning I worked hard and long. The first weekend after everyone had gone, I went out back and brought in every single black bin bag of rubbish my staff had thrown away. I emptied them all on the kitchen floor. On my hands and knees I went through every single one. I have told you before, haven't I, I am not squeamish. The wastage was unbelievable. I collected every reusable thing and cooked a beautiful meal with it. The next day I fed it to my staff. After they had eaten I told them where the food had come from. One of the girls vomited and gave her notice immediately, but the ones that remained, they learned that once in a while the garbage still got checked.

Four months into trading, and I received a letter asking me to prepare for a visit from a VAT inspector. The dreaded VAT man turned out to be a woman. She arrived at ten o'clock on the said morning. Poor woman. She had paid too dear a price for the privilege of brains. Exactly as I had with the friars, when under threat or for monetary gain, I automatically switched into flirt, seduce mode. I gave her the look.

I wasn't called wolf in Paris for nothing. I had learned my craft well. I let my eyes travel from top to bottom, lingering on her saggy breasts, back to her eyes and then stopping on her narrow lips. For those sixty seconds she was the most beautiful woman on earth.

I raised an eyebrow. She blushed.

I offered cappuccino. She licked her lips uncertainly and nodded.

I winked. She touched her mousy hair.

I reached for a pot of sugar and brushed her arm. 'Sorry,' I apologised, my eyes on her mouth. Would she have dinner with me? I saw her hesitate.

'No,' she said, but both of us knew she was lost. She moved to a table in a corner of the restaurant and, going through my books, sipped my coffee. Fucking bitch. I went to offer cake. I smiled. I flirted.

'No,' she demurred, and instead approached my till. She tapped in a combination of numbers, and to my complete horror, my machine began spewing out a roll of information. Without looking at me she returned to her table, to pore over the incriminating till roll.

I began to sweat. I should have gone to see Don Calabrese's accountant. Now I was really in the shit. How was I to know that these tills were programmed to hold information even after the Z reading had been done?

She called me to the table. She looked into my eyes and said very clearly, 'Your figures don't match.' Blood rushed into my head. I felt the heat in my cheeks. Something alien grabbed my insides. Shit. Damn the bitch. Over the rim of her third cup of cappuccino her watching eyes were level. *She knew.* She let the silence ride. The fucking fat ugly bitch was letting me stew.

'I suppose someone in the restaurant could be stealing from you.' Her voice was like her eyes.

I stared at her. It was not blood she wanted. It was a power trip. Not so much for the flawlessness of my earlier performance, but because she had been tempted even though she knew it was her inspector's badge that I was flirting with. I couldn't speak for the relief that coursed through my body. Fat bitch had been playing with me.

And then she actually proceeded to teach me how one would go about catching such a culprit, what figures to look for and where. The things my thief could do in the future to hide his crimes, and the undetectable methods other criminals have employed before. When she was finished she packed her things. 'Good luck,' she wished and was gone.

She knew I was up to no good, but had just taught me how to conceal my tracks better so they were invisible to prying eyes. Was it a trap? I walked to the phone and made an appointment to see Don Calabrese's accountant.

'A Jew, but an irreplaceable marvel,' Don Calabrese had said.

I drove to Hounslow, rang the bell of a green door on a back street. His assistant was an ugly woman with a speech impediment. I mean, I'm all for hiring the disabled and all that, but it took her the best part of five minutes just to say, 'Please wait. Mr Fass is on the phone.'

She showed me to a closet-sized waiting room with tattered curtains. I was beginning to have serious doubts about Mr Fass. I mean, you should have seen that waiting room, the peeling paint, the mud sofas, that back door entrance. From behind the wall came the sounds of two children. One screamed. The sound of footsteps. A hard smack. The screaming moved away with the footsteps. The troublemaker, reduced to sniffles, remained. The walls were that thin. His assistant returned, this time to offer me coffee. It took so long for her to get the words out I finished her question for her and answered it. I smiled broadly. 'No offence. I'm just not used to disabled people.'

When she came in again she just used her finger to point upwards. I ran up the bare wooden stairs and knocked on the only door.

'Come,' someone called out.

I opened the door and it was wall to wall stacked with brown files. Always a good sign. In the middle of a table littered with papers sat a tiny man with a major black and grey moustache.

'Sit, sit,' he invited, half rising, pointing to a chair with a broken seat in front of his desk. His left eye moved but his right remained staring. Jesus, they had been serious when they'd joked that he was one-eyed because he had closed it so many times it went out of business. I sat, and for the next hour he talked, and I knew then why he was the darling of every Italian and Chinese restaurant as far away as Birmingham. He just knew everything there was to know, every tax dodge, every shady method.

'The Inland Revenue and the dreaded Customs and Excise . . . they know you cheat. If you didn't, they know you'd go bust. They've seen the figures. They've been in the business so long they've got to know all the scams, but they close one eye.' He pointed to his own unmoving eye. 'But it is when you get too greedy that they swoop down on you. Even then, it is not to close you down, but to squeeze you for as much as they can get. And they have the powers to do it. They can even come into your home. You must never play with them.'

In minutes he taught me everything I know today. Buy black (in cash without invoices) to keep the margins consistent. The walls have ears. Destroy everything, anything incriminating instantly. Split the linen supplier. They count it. Same with pizza boxes. Never ever declare your true wage bill to the Inland Revenue. They don't understand about Italian cooks who jump you for money day and night while flatly refusing to even consider paying their own national insurance or taxes. And very, very important, never let your profit margin drop below 30 per cent. That will keep the computers from throwing your figures out. Remember, the minute you open a restaurant in this country you are forced to inherit a silent greedy partner who does nothing, gives nothing, but wants almost half of your profit.

But VAT is 17.5 per cent.

Yes, 17.5 per cent of sales. Restaurants, unlike accountants, don't invoice the 17.5 per cent on top of the value of the bill. They have to eat it as a cost. When you work it into your final profit figures 17.5 per cent of sales does equate to half.

After that Mr Fass brought his trick box out. All kinds of schemes to keep the bastards out of my honey pot. I would have been a fool not to hire such a raving genius on the spot.

He nodded approvingly, modestly.

Before I was twenty the lease was transferred to my name. When I was twenty-one I married Francesca. I was in love and the world was perfect. Two years later I had my second restaurant and my first child. Good man that he was, Mr Fass sent one of his minions four times a year to work out the VAT and play around with the figures, to ensure the profit margin would be acceptable to the

Customs and Excise central computer. And once a year he did the year-end figures.

My parents came one Christmas. I went to pick them up from Heathrow. They looked like refugees. My mother was wearing the full-length fur coat I had sent for her birthday. It looked a lot better on the hanger in the store. She looked like every Italian middle-aged woman who wore such things, short and dumpy. My father, white with anxiety, almost sagged with relief when he spotted me. Poor things, they had never got on a plane before. The stopover and change in Milan had confused and frightened them. Francesca greeted us at the door. I stood back and watched her clap her hands, kiss her in-laws and hug them, as if she did not completely detest them.

Mamma unzipped her bulky hand luggage and pulled out three 1.5 litre bottles of Primera Aranciata filled to the brim with homemade red wine. And then like a magician conjuring a rabbit out of a hat, she extracted a whole suckling pig, dead and raw. She smiled proudly.

'Bravo,' I cried fondly. I have always liked pigs, dead or alive. What she would have done if Customs had made her open her bags remains a mystery. I turned to my wife and I saw her eyes wide with disbelief and a hint of disgust. I must make her watch Bernado Bertolucci's movie, the one about the killing of a pig, so she will know the significance of Mamma's gift. Why was she not moved by the sight of a pink pig waiting to be roasted? She hurled herself too deeply into the task of being English. That was what was wrong with her. She was not a romantic. She had forgotten to be Italian. She made chicken souffles and served them in ramekins. Without a pig there is no feast, Francesca.

The children were thrilled with the pig on the table. Luca grabbed its trotters and Maria wanted to examine its mouth, but Francesca's strangled croak stopped them dead. 'Stop touching that pig and go and wash your hands.'

That's the shame about Francesca. She has not the hardiness of village folk. She had succumbed to the great Italian preoccupation, a neurotic obsession with hygiene. That need to clear the 'air' in a room every few hours by opening all the windows, even in the dead of winter, to dress children in designer clothes that they are forbidden to soil, and to call the doctor to the house every time a child has a cold.

Mamma folded her hands across her chest. She disapproved of the fact that her grandchildren had been taught to eat spaghetti with a fork *and a spoon*. She never got over the discovery of a spaghetti measurer in one of Francesca's drawers. Papa was tapping the partition wall. He turned to me and pronounced it as thin as cardboard. Ahh! Another Christmas to look forward to.

The restaurant was doing very well. So I made another. One, two, three, then four and five until I arrived at ten.

To pay for it all I ran a sort of drug ring. I got the ounces in and cut them into halves and quarters and distributed them around the managers of the different restaurants and night clubs. The Italian waiters in Tramp did an absolutely roaring trade. There was a time when just one of them was selling up to three ounces a week. Everybody it seemed was on it. Even the managers of my restaurants. After a while I started supplying them with coke in lieu of wages. Much cheaper.

It was brilliant. Money poured in. I had two gold Rolexes, bespoke shoes, Savile Row suits, piles of cashmere sweaters and an expensive address, 181 Chevening Road. My hero Cat Stevens had once lived in that road. The spider woman had kept her word. It was time to build her a temple and fill it with damaged people. A place purely for sin.

I decided on a flat. Anyway I wanted to say goodbye to humping waitresses in uncomfortable places, toilets, over kitchen sinks, on cutting boards, in walk-in fridges and inside pizza ovens! The couch in the office was lumpy. Besides, drunk and horny female customers were not as frequent as I liked. I wanted a place stacked with porn where I could throw massive orgies. Call prostitutes by the dozen. I would supply the coke and make even more money.

So I began to look for a flat. A place to offer equal amounts of sin, lust and decay. Through all this I loved Francesca. My *mater dolorosa*. Impeachable, virginal and pure. An essential part of me.

I found the flat, paid for it in cash, and registered it in my brother's name. Inland Revenue was not going to get me on that one. The flat was simple, open plan downstairs and two bedrooms upstairs. It was over a pub and you had to climb a set of stairs where someone had painted in purple, Stairway to Heaven. I found it quite appropriate. So started the craziest time of my life. Day and night people, often strange and troubled, came in and out. Prostitutes were a phone call away. All-night parties.

Up until then I had never touched a single grain of coke and then one day I thought, I'll have one; and poof, just like that, I saw the spider's web. Before I sprinkled it white, it had been invisible. But there it was, a perfect orb made of thousands upon thousands of delicately intersecting, catching angles. To the unwary, a dangerous trip wire, to the wary, an opportunity for endless sin.

Things were going well. I phoned my mother to tell her Francesca was pregnant again. There was silence for a split second, and then she fell over herself to congratulate me. But eventually she couldn't pretend any more, it was that other great Italian anxiety, and she inquired suddenly, 'Can you afford another child? You know you have to feed, clothe, educate and then build them houses, don't you?'

Jacked up on coke, I laughed. '*Si* Mamma. I can afford ten children now.'

'As you want,' she said doubtfully.

The parties became crazier, the prostitutes wilder. The money poured in.

All black, as they say in Italian, cash, and under the table.

Francesca Sabella

Francesca

When Ricky dropped out of the olive tree that afternoon in Sicily, I nearly died. I thought my heart would burst. There I was, crying over him in a deserted field, and suddenly he appears, his eyes so blue they were like the Sicilian sky on the clearest summer day. For as long as I could remember I had loved Ricky, from afar, of course. It seemed to me as if he rubbed sunshine on his skin and hair until he glowed. A burnished sun god running barefoot upon the earth. I stared at him blankly, a complete fool. I thought I had humiliated myself so spectacularly that it was irreversible, but he gave me his strong hand and took me to see the caves.

He asked me who I had been crying over, but once I over-heard my grandmother counsel my mother, 'The more you love them, the less they love you. The best way is to always pretend to be the hunted. All men prefer it so.' I looked into his eyes. Let him be the hunter. Let him always be the hunter. So I told him it was an English boy. His blue eyes turned nearly purple with the jealous storm in his heart. My grandmother was right. I never forgot that lesson. I took it with me when my father replanted our family in England.

My father used to say, 'My vice is my work.' And he viced obsessively. I always remember Papa by his absences. He worked day and night to save enough to open his deli-catessen in England. Of course it is closed now. You know how it is . . . the supermarkets . . . But for years he worked all the hours God sent, breaking off only to eat a piece of bread and a few tinned sardines, so one day he could afford his dream.

Before we came to England, he worked in Germany, building roads and houses. Living in large cold bunkers, cooking his food on makeshift stoves made from stones and firewood, and sleeping on mattresses of hay laid on bricks. When the roof leaked his mattress grew moss. Every mark he earned he sent home. I cried when he told me of the day he was so broke he had to eat bread and shoe polish. '*Fa niente*, it did no harm,' he said, 'after all, polish is made of lard.'

For the first couple of years after we left Sicily, my family and I lived in a mobile home on an isolated field in Egham. My father was a waiter and my mother a chambermaid in a beautiful old hotel nearby called Great Fosters. My father could hardly speak English then, but he worked in the tea rooms and he got by for almost a year knowing only how to say, 'Black or white, madam?' We didn't even have access to a tap. Every day I walked down a footpath to a well owned by a Sicilian farmer called Mario. He grew acres of vegetables, and let me pick whatever I wanted. Since we didn't have to buy our vegetables my mother pinched little things like soaps, washing-up liquid, bleach and polish and gave them to Mario, to show our appreciation.

Life was very hard in those first few years when my parents were putting every penny away. I was very lonely. I had never wanted to leave. In school I was a stranger. I spoke English with a funny accent. Sometimes I stood alone and tried to figure out what the other children were saying. They spoke so fast I found it hard to understand them. How I missed my friends in Ravanusa. So close to me that I never had to knock when I went through their front door.

It seemed as if girls grew up faster in England, wearing make-up, mini skirts and stilettos, drinking alcohol and making out with boys. My mother would never allow me such freedom. Not that I wanted it, of course. In fact, I often cried wondering how I could have left Ricky and Sicily for this.

In Sicily they said the English were cold, but the beef was good and there were lots of horses walking in the streets. I was fifteen years old, the English were a cold, unfriendly race, I didn't like beef, and there were no horses walking in the streets.

I decided to save money and go back to Sicily. Sometimes I wonder what would have happened if I had never left Sicily. Married Ricky and lived in that house his father had built for him. When you listen to me talk, or look at me, I may seem like any other European woman, but in blood and bone I am Sicilian. Sicily is only three hours away but it's like a different planet. Everything is utterly different, the weather, the people, the vegetation, the soil, the air, the buildings, the taste of the water. . .

'Marry me anyway,' Ricky said when we parted. How inconsolable I was! How ecstatic! How young! So young I waited. Then one day he came, his gold hair clean and his shoulders broad and strong. I was frightened that he would speak in the way my parents did, embarrassing me while I was growing up. But no, he spoke like a God. He even spoke French. He called me *cherie*. I was so proud of him. He asked my father for my hand. My father offered him grappa and my mother cried with happiness.

'Thatsa nice,' she sobbed.

We went to Bali for our honeymoon. I had never ever been outside Europe, let alone somewhere as exotic as South East Asia. For the first few days, I thought I was in paradise. They kept wild jungle cockerel in the hotel grounds so we awakened in the morning to their crowing. Everywhere there were gorgeous palm trees, their leaves swaying in the breeze. I stood on the balcony of our hotel room and ate a whole mango with both hands, the way the brown children on the beach did, sucking the stone until it was bare. In the sea below, the men on their inflatable banana boats waved. I waved back, the mango still in my hands, like a child.

Ricky came to embrace me. 'Here's my wife. Jeans, T-shirt and no underwear.'

I pressed my back into him. 'Here's your wife. Jeans, T-shirt and no underwear.'

And the sunsets. Unbelievable. So breathtaking they looked fake. Every day we stood holding hands on the beach to watch them. Swallows skimmed the water. In the pink light we stood staring, marvelling at the crazy insatiable craving we saw mirrored in the other's eyes. I pinched myself. Am I really in this paradise? We left our clothes on the beach and glided into the water, aflame with gold and copper glints. Warm and silky it swirled around us, as our young bodies, slipping against each other, found love in the sea.

I remember it like yesterday, when the world ceased to exist, and all that mattered was the warm sea and Ricky's skin. We came out of the water and walking along the beach waited for night. We watched the little children racing and diving into the sea shouting, 'Baywatch.' Then the sea turned as black as the sky, and in the distance the lights of the ships and boats looked like twinkling stars.

Alas we should not have left the hotel grounds.

Drive a little away from the touristy area and there are large open drains clogged with stinking rubbish. Take any road that does not lead to the airport, and you will see that their Government has not cunningly commissioned enormous, beautifully carved monuments at every roundabout. Keep going and you will eventually fall upon a horribly squalid Bali.

Even where the tourists gather, its commerce is insulting. There is nowhere you can go, nothing you can see without having to pay for it first. As for Kuta beach it is a polluted armpit full of hustling natives greedy for tourist dollars. If I was left alone for a minute, a gigolo – usually short with flat, unappealing features – would slide up to me with the offer of his company. None of the natives seem to understand the concept of a dustbin. They simply discharge their rubbish to the ground even when there is a bin next to them.

And their ridiculous dance performances, where a man dressed as a wild boar gets his long pink penis pulled off and carried away amidst laughter. And to top everything, there is not a single God-fearing person on that island. They all believe in some weird pagan religion, apparently a mutation of Hinduism.

The whole population would at different times come and throw, in a purposely disdainful manner, a disgusting mess of half-decayed food at crossroads, because crossroads, they believe, are dangerous places, infested with malign ghouls. As if that is not repulsive enough, they then pour alcohol on the mess and throw pieces of raw and rotting meat that are instantly covered in green flies and then pounced upon by the numerous stray dogs on the island.

Many times I just avoided stepping into that half-consumed superstitious nonsense on the ground. Apparently all these putrefying muddles are offerings intended for evil spirits, but even the little roadside temples meant for their gods are filthy.

But the thing that frightened me most was how fascinated Ricky was by their godless practices. How much he wanted to be part of their dangerous evil. One night while walking along Kuta beach we came upon a black magician and his pigeons. He was old and dressed in rags. He claimed that every time he snapped the matchstick he held between his forefinger and thumb, one of the pigeons in the cage a few feet away would fall dead. Ricky, convinced that it was a mere trick, watched him unblinkingly for an hour, and he must have moved a dozen times to see the trick from a different, more revealing angle but the mystery remained intact.

After the performance Ricky approached the old man, gave him some money, and asked him to show us the real Bali. In the man's considering face I saw something that night. A sort of recognition. As if my husband had spoken to him in a secret language. One I would never understand. He nodded and led us in the light of his lantern down narrow back lanes. He hailed a taxi, and we drove out along bad unlit roads for perhaps an hour. When the taxi came to rest, we were in some highland. The air was cooler, the ground soft.

Then we were going over a wooden bridge, underneath was the sound of trickling water. Even before we reached the bamboo groves I heard the primitive beat of drums, and smelt the incense. Bamboos creaked in the dark. An unhappy sound. We were going through the thicket.

Beyond, I could see a clearing lit with burning torches, and further in the distance the dim outline of a thatched temple. On either side in the half shadows were natives, their faces arranged into a wall of waiting. They stared at us curiously. The devil's work was afoot, but Ricky strode forward eagerly to join them.

There was a dark and malevolent presence in the air. May God strike me dead if I am lying, but the thing caressed my skin as if with a fingernail, until all my hair stood on end, and I shivered in the warm night. And then I heard it very close to my ears. A soft mocking laugh.

The savages stood around, alert, but unafraid. After all, it had left whatever dark pit it lived in because they had called it. This horrible unnatural presence was what they had travelled miles on foot to gawk at. This was their theatre.

In the middle of the clearing about a hundred and fifty bare-chested men, each with a single hibiscus tucked behind his left ear, sat cross-legged, in expanding circles, like some horribly massive, meat-eating jungle flower. In the flickering light their faces were fiendish. They appeared as if in a trance, their eyes unseeing and glazed, as they swayed in unison to the pulsating beat of the drums. In a bizarre way the drums were affecting me too. As if they were a force working together to hypnotise and control me against my will. Under my feet the ground began to vibrate. Suddenly I heard monkeys in the dark, screaming.

'Yes, yes, Ketchak, the monkey dance,' Ricky whispered excitedly. 'Let the battle begin.'

Men guised as demons rushed in, shrieking and triumphant. In the shadows the squatting swaying bodies, scenting danger, became rigid. They split the night with a single united clap and a great yell. Their bewildered swaying grew and their mouths began jabbering, and hissing a hypnotic rhythm, chak-a-chak, chak-a-chak, chak-a-chak. It was the chattering of monkeys.

'The performers have eaten the spirit of the monkeys they disturbed in the forest,' the old man whispered.

Three hundred perfectly coordinated hands waved in the air, fingers strumming, and the heaving bodies, like petals, shuddered and with a roar burst open. The air was full of clouds of dust and incense smoke. For a suspenseful moment the squawking stopped, and all was still. Then the wild chattering faces with their hair flying wildly swelled again. The demons were in a panic. The hot damp air lingered.

There was a piercing scream. It chilled me to the bone.

Magnified and made impossibly grotesque by the flickering flames, a sorcerer balanced in utter stillness on one toe. In my worst nightmares I still see him poised to strike. He tossed his long flowing hair, glared at the cowering bodies on the ground and began his magic. And what magic it was, wailing spells emitted in a falsetto scream. The night became eerily still with his satanic frenzy and silence prevailed in the surrounding bushes and paddy fields. Where were the animal and insect sounds? Slowly he began to dance with jerky, yet strangely graceful movements.

The demons attempted to fight him, writhing and rising up with fingers clawed as if to scratch his face, but the master's magic was too powerful. He reared up, glaring balefully, his hands curved and high over his head, hissing dangerously. And while I was still holding my breath it was over.

The flames were put out, and the exhausted men stole away into the black night. Ricky and I stood amazed. Something had happened. Something dangerous. The air . . . the way it had vibrated around us.

In the glow of the torches Ricky's face was unrecognisable. He stared as if in a trance. I had ceased to exist for him. I felt confused and frightened. As if I had caught a tiger by the tail and had just noticed the reason for its teeth. The pigeon murderer appeared once more beside us. My newly caught tiger handed him more money from his wallet. The man did not count the money, but led us away. He bade us goodbye at the beach where we had found him.

We walked in silence, each lost in our own thoughts. There was a dreamy moon in the sky, and waves broke on the beach softly. Into a beachfront hotel microphone someone was singing 'Killing Me Softly with His Song', and tears came into my eyes. I felt numb inside. Everything had changed. Perhaps I knew even then that my husband was not mine to keep.

On the dark water a lone fisherman lit his lamp. It shone yellow, and threw a beautiful reflection on the black water. The thought of fishermen eking a living from the sea has always moved me, and that lonely man seemed even dearer to my heart.

That night I awakened suddenly. The sorcerer had come

to touch my cheek. His hand was freezing. He was smiling. He had come to take my husband away. The air-conditioner hummed steadily and Ricky was fast asleep. Quietly I slipped out of bed and went onto the balcony. Out on the sea my fisherman had extinguished his lamp and gone home. Strange how acutely I felt his absence in my heart. I tried to imagine him in his wooden home with a simple supper of fish and rice, his five children and his wife around him. But I could not. He was another world away and yet . . . he belonged to me.

I went back in, sat on the edge of the bed, and watched Ricky. He slept like a baby while I was racked with fear. It was as if the island had tried to tell me something, a little warning. He too will disappear like my lone fisherman.

'The fisherman you may take back, but my husband I will keep for ever,' I said aloud. Against the crisp white sheets his tanned skin gleamed like polished copper. I knelt on the bed and licked the salt off it, savouring the sleepy warm taste of him, and was suddenly swept away by some name-less need. I bit him so ruthlessly that his golden head jerked, and swearing brutally his hard body possessed me. He is mine. See, he is mine. Curled inside his strong arms I slept. I forgot the sorcerer waited nearby.

My husband had asked him to.

The day we were leaving we sat at a nearby café drinking coffee, when a man selling wood carvings stopped at our table. Amongst the coffee drinking paraphernalia he spread out his wares, one by one. One I liked, an old bearded fisherman carrying a basket of fish.

'How much?' I asked in English, but surprisingly he spoke Italian, with a curious accent. So many Italians went to Bali that he had learned our language and learned to recognise us by sight. 'Italians appreciate elaborate handi-work,' he explained. 'The Germans are too mechanical. In paradise they just want to drink beer, but Italians have style. Americans are the best customers.' He rubbed his thumb and forefinger together. 'American *troppo denaro*, too much money.' Ricky went to reach for his wallet, but the old man smiled knowingly and asked, 'Wouldn't you like a *penunggu*, a watcher, to go with your carving?'

Instantly Ricky's hands stilled, but how his eyes stirred. He was uncurling his long brown body. 'What?'

'Into this carving I will cast a spirit, and when you return to your own land you will awaken it with a piece of music that I will give you. Afterwards it will sit on your shoulder, invisible and watchful. Its only aim will be to protect you. Day and night, your *penunggu* need never rest. Whenever your enemies try to harm you it will destroy them.'

'How much?' Ricky asked. His voice was so cold and precise.

'No,' I cried, my heart beating fast inside my chest. 'No, go away,' I shouted harshly to the man, but he did not budge. People were looking at us. The man watched Ricky. His black eyes were knowing and contemptuous. I grabbed Ricky's hands and pulled his face towards mine.

He wore a stranger's eyes.

'No, please don't play with things we don't understand,' I said desperately, and after too long he nodded reluctantly, and told the man to go away.

'Don't hurt us,' I begged. He smiled regretfully, and absently stroked my cheek. And in my heart I wondered what it was about my husband that made these Balinese hustlers seek him out to buy their magic even in the streets.

Another inexplicable thing happened while we were there. One evening while watching a performance about a contest of might, between a hideously masked child-devouring witch called Rangda, and a very large lion-like animal called Barong, I spotted in the audience a delightful pair of twins. They were richly dressed in traditional

costume and long golden nails attached to their little
fingers. I think they were waiting to perform in a bit. I
walked up to the girls and offered them sweets. They smiled
shyly. Their older sister, a truly stunning beauty, stood over
them.

When I looked up to meet her magnificant eyes, they
were black as the night, and at once remote and hypnotic.
An effect that made me want to shiver, but I could not look
away. They held mine cautiously without warmth or
hostility. She was obviously the guardian or parent of those
beautiful children. Then Ricky, who had been taking
photographs of the dancers, being sprinkled with holy
water to bring them out of their trance, appeared at my
side.

'*Che bellina*,' he said, and put a hand out to stroke the
cheek of one of the girls, and suddenly that strange and
beautiful woman hissed like a striking snake and, jerking
forward, snatched the two girls away, as if his touch could
harm them.

Startled, I looked into her black and forbidding eyes and
found uncontrollable fury in them. Ricky froze, and the
strange woman with one last look of, I thought then, hate,
pulled the girls away, and quickly disappeared into the
crowd of onlookers. For many years I couldn't understand
what had happened. I thought perhaps she had misunderstood Ricky's intention towards the little girls, or some
custom forbade those children to be touched by a man, a
foreigner . . . and then one day I awakened from a fantastic
nightmare, shivering in my own sweat, and suddenly, in the
dark, I knew. I saw the woman's real face. So inappropriate
to her nature she had to disguise it with fury. The hair on
my arms stood on end.

It was fear. She was terrified of Ricky. Terrified of his
hand on her charges. As if my beautiful blond husband was
an evil spirit who would contaminate them for ever.

I was pregnant. Ricky swung me around in a savage dance. It was our first Christmas together. My in-laws came to visit and I understood we would not get on as soon as I opened my present and found, inside an old shoe box, a peach negligee made from some synthetic scratchy material with bits of white lace around a deeply scooped neckline. It was unapologetically hideous. She had bought that revolting, cheap scrap of nylon in a Sicilian market, and brought it all the way to England as a Christmas present for her new daughter-in-law.

What did she mean to achieve? Perk up my sex life?

'It's beautiful. Thank you, Mamma,' I said, fighting not to show my hurt. And my mother-in-law sat there holding the beautiful Louis Vuitton handbag that I had given her, smiling. Actually proud of her nasty present.

Another year the woman pulled a pig, a whole dead pig, out of her bag. From snout to tail that piglet must have been about two feet long. I couldn't believe my eyes. She was like some African mamma bringing bits of bush meat illegally through customs. Then I looked up and caught Ricky's blue eyes. They were amused. I had never thought of him as a cruel man before.

When did I find out my husband was faithless?

That like a dog in heat he wanders without shame along dark alleyways and, finding the dirty bitches, ruts with them by stinking dustbins? The usual way. Through a close and poisonous friend. It was through Rosella I learned about my husband's search for mysteries new.

When I knew her she was the proprietor of an upmarket boutique, *Momi Intimi*. Soft pink carpets, one or two exclusive evening dresses and a very risqué line of Italian underwear. She played *Astor Pizzaola* but so softly that you had to strain to hear. We used to sit for hours just talking.

She was Italian too, but from Naples. I thought she was my best friend.

Then one day she opened a small box file of cheques, and suddenly remembered something that needed doing urgently. 'Watch this,' she instructed as she rushed to the back of the shop. Naturally my eyes fell upon the box and the very first cheque on the pile bore Ricky's bold untidy scrawl. I reached out to take that cheque, and stared at it in shocked disbelief. A hundred and ninety-five pounds he had spent. Buying underwear. Not for me: I was four months pregnant. For a moment I couldn't move. Then I flipped the cheque over.

It was blank. I picked up my bag and walked out of the shop.

I went home and sat down on the bottom step. I did not feel pain. I was in shock. Little things came into my head and, still unfinished, left. Soon I would have to pick the children up from school. I walked to the kitchen, opened the fridge. There were skate wings that, if I did not cook that day, would begin to smell of ammonia. The flesh tenderised, but the odour pungent. It would need a stronger stomach than mine to eat it.

I went into Ricky's study. I saw myself in the mirror over the fireplace. The area around my mouth was white, white with fury. I was so furious; my nose was running, and my hands shaking. I opened drawers and slammed them shut so hard the photographs on the surface of the desk toppled over.

It was the end of April. I smelt the hyacinths dying, leaving their last papery breath in the conservatory. How dare he? How dare the bastard? Buy my body and sell my soul. And a small voice said, 'How could he?' And why Rosella's boutique of all places? That really hurt. Finally I understood the reason for her sneering eyes whenever I talked of Ricky, his successes, his love, his devotion to his daughter. How she must have hated me! What a blind prize idiot I had been!

No wonder she had taken such pleasure in ensuring my discovery. She was so jealous she wanted to turn my prize unworthy. What a bitch! I hated her and I hated him. My eye fell upon a rabbit carved out of water agate, beautiful brown swirling in smoky grey. A Christmas present from Ricky. An expression of love during the season of indulgence. Or a fucking joke. A rabbit jumping in and out of holes.

I picked the thing up. It felt heavy in my hand. I swung around and hurled it into the fireplace. It shattered in a satisfying explosion of noise and flying shattered glass. There was an ugly ashtray, a present from his mother, bizarrely dear to him. That followed the rabbit.

The urge to destroy, I cannot tell you how it fought to take over, and after a while I let it. Afterwards I stood in its mess cold, my anger spent. I put my coat on and went to pick Luca up. After I had fed her and put her to bed, I called Ricky on the telephone.

'*Si, amore*, be home as soon as the restaurant shuts,' he said.

'I'll be waiting.'

From eleven to three that night I lay awake. Every time I closed my eyes I saw myself hit him with a lamp. I saw his shocked face, his hands rush up instinctively to cover his face, and the flash of pain in his eyes when the lamp hit his head. Even as I hit him I died inside. Oh God, he's the father of my baby, my stomach screamed, but I could not stop my body. It moved forward, hit, and, pushing him down the stairs, rained deodorant cans and perfume bottles at him until he staggered out of the front door.

I sat on the bed waiting for him to come home.

He tried to lie at first, deny history, the slimy snake, but I was prepared, I lied too. 'Rosella has told me everything, about all the other times, all the other women.' His jaw dropped. He had never for a moment suspected such a betrayal.

Kill two birds with one stone, they always say. That will take care of that bitch's further business with my husband. And then, oh God, this was not the first time. In my pain I asked the wrong question.

'Don't you love me any more?' I asked, crying.

'Francesca, please, you know I love you with all my heart. She was nothing. A mistake.'

'Don't lie to me, Ricky.'

He switched to Italian. He knew I could never resist that. '*Amore mio*, I have loved you for years. I have been bringing you flowers since I was a kid. Through all my travels I did not forget you. You're the only one I have ever loved, or wanted to marry. You are the mother of my children. We will grow old together. We will return to Sicily and sit in the evening on the balcony of the house myfather built for us, drinking the red wine from the grapes that we have picked together. Our bones will be old and our faces will be like the unattended grapes that fall forgotten to the ground and shrivel, but still I will say to you, "Let me look at you once more." And this, because you will always be the most beautiful woman in the world to me. I love you, Francesca. These women, they are nothing. Do you understand? Nothing. *Putanas*, all of them.'

It was a mountain that he asked me to swallow, but when I opened my mouth I was surprised to find it fit nicely. What he sold I wanted to buy. Be careful not to be too scornful of me. Wanting to hold fast when people are moving away is an instinctive reaction. Only now I can see how pathetic I was. Then I couldn't. My heart was young, and like an innocent child it longed for the sweet fruit of his words. I believed in my battle.

'Why do you need them then?' I sobbed.

His face crumpled and his hands went to hold the sides of his head. 'Because I am weak. Because I am a man. Because they tempt me, these *putanas*. But you are the only one in my heart.'

'So who is this woman?'

'She is not important. I'll give her up now,' he declared instantly, although I knew even then he wouldn't. Why should he?

I remembered the time he had brought me that grotesque statue hacked so brutally it made my flesh crawl. Yet his shining eager eyes had told me it was the most precious object he owned. He did love me once in the land of my father. Before these immoral women, who needed under-wear from a shop owned by a viper, obscured the path he walked.

'What does she have that I don't?'

'Nothing. She is only young.'

I know he said it to console me, to tell me that she was only a cold-hearted fuck, but I crumpled. He had hit too hard. No more kidding around. He didn't know it, but there was nothing worse the crazy bastard could have said. Until he said it I had never felt the passing of time. It was out, the essential truth. I was ancient and unattractive. If he had said that she was good in bed, or a better cook, or more understanding, I could have competed, but how could I compete with youth?

I had given birth to two childdren and carried another. My body had changed. I was no longer attractive to him. What did he know of bearing a child? He had never had his body shared, stretched, and finally torn. Of course, there were bits of me that sagged and wobbled now. I had regis-tered them only with the corners of my eyes, but he, he had seen them and judged them.

He reached out his hand as if to physically stop me from crumbling. I looked into those sky-blue eyes and I could not see through them. Once I knew what he was thinking. Once I knew what he liked. He liked pears and pecorino cheese drizzled with honey after his Sunday dinner of lamb cutlets. Once I even thought he was mine and only mine.

That night after he had gone to bed I went to look at his mobile phone. The last call to it, at midnight, was from Gina. I knew her. That very young, impeccably polite wait-ress who had served me at the restaurant before. She called me *senora*. '*Si, senora, no, senora, per favore, senora, grazia, senora, arriverderci, senora*, I am fucking your husband, *senora*.' Fucking slut. Where did they do it? On the couch in his office or in the toilets downstairs? No, in all probability on table nine, when all the others had gone home, with all the lights turned off except for the one at the bar. He likes it there. I know from experience.

How I hated her! Still I decided she had only the novelty of her firm body. I had the children, the ring, the house, the history and half of everything. I would play my game and she would look up from digging her grave and call me dangerous.

'Pretend to be the hunted. Let him be the hunter.'

In the morning when Ricky came downstairs he looked wary, but essentially unshaken. He found breakfast waiting on the table and his suitcase packed by the door. He begged, he cajoled, but I stood unmoving, as cold as marble.

'Go to her,' I said. 'If you want her so badly, have her. There must be something lacking in our relationship if you need her body.' And when he would not stop his pleading, I said, 'Just go.' When finally he was gone I cried.

My plan was simple and brilliant. If I made him get rid of her she would be that forbidden thing. The fruit he must savour secretly. If I gave her to him on a plate her perfume would no longer be so alluring, her flesh too would sour. *The more you love them, the less they love you. . . Pretend*

121

to be the hunted. And he would return on his knees and I would have him for ever. I was taking a chance, but not a big one. I was resting on the assumption that Sicilian blood ran in his veins.

The children and I were family.

It worked. He returned on his knees. Given so freely she lost her value. Sex on table nine became a bore. He gave her up willingly, but now that he and Rosella had taught me what to watch out for, it didn't take me long to figure out that women, and there were too many to count, made themselves available to him regularly. I saw them in his tousled hair, smelt them on his skin, understood them in his ripped buttons and gently touched them in the scratches their coloured nails left on his back.

But I had grown weary, lost the nerve for battle. I affected a sophisticated amusement at the thought of his furtive grubby affairs. When I thought the battle was won, was when it was lost. I was to blame. I had shown him clearly that I would take him back. That I not only knew how, but desperately wanted, to forgive. There was nothing left to do, but grow a little colder and harder. I was, as Maya Angelou said on *Oprah*, 'being pecked to death by ducks, by ducks for heaven sakes'.

And then I began to look at younger women. I sat in the middle of shopping malls staring at teenage girls, and weighing the difference between them and me. At first I didn't really understand, I knew the difference was there but couldn't put my finger on it. I went into changing rooms in swimming pools and surreptitiously observed their unaware bodies. I stood beside them in night-club toilets pretending to reapply my lipstick or flick back my hair and compared.

And slowly I saw the difference. I learned about the obvious ones like fashion; their clothes were cheap, but the height of trend, fun. Everything I put on my body was expensive, superbly tailored and understated. My skin was always wonderfully tanned and my lipstick pale. I looked like a million dollars. Exactly like those first wives of very rich men that you meet while shopping in Knightsbridge or Bond Street. The young, they just wore charming peacock feather chokers and little bead bracelets.

I, of course, wore a very large solitaire diamond ring.

And then the difference that made the difference; fat. In the places where it counted, face, derriere, hands. I learned to recognise them even from the back. They hardly felt the cold, so they preferred thin cheap materials that clung to their unripe rears. They pranced ahead, not mushy or dimpled but just learning to curve. I noted how redness concentrated on the inside middle of their lips. Of course, what is fresh meat if not red? Everywhere I looked my envious eyes met gorgeous skin stretching from jaw to chin in one smooth line.

I was terrified of the mirror and the judgement I saw there. When would I experience that bittersweet wonder and gentle resignation that Mother claimed was hers?

I took to shopping at night, at the weekends, when Ricky was at work. It is a lonely life for the wife of a successful restaurateur. The weekends were the worst. While everyone else was out getting drunk, having fun, I walked along the deserted aisles of the supermarkets. In a way the brightly lit interior of Sainsbury's comforted me. Among ready cooked meals and toilet paper I browsed filling my shopping trolley with their top of the range, premium, organic, better tasting, better, better, better . . .

At the checkout I glanced askance at the women who had bought store brands or items with the 'reduced' red sticker on the packaging. For a little while I would feel superior reaching for my gold card, and then I would look up and see across in the next aisle a couple flirting over their miserable bits of shopping, and I would realise again how much

I had given away to be able to hand over a gold card.

Because it always came back to that. The truth is love doesn't survive in an unfaithful home. It is only practical considerations that rule. It was always with a tinge of sadness that I wheeled my trolley out into the darkness. It was over. The night for me was over. After that I would put away the shopping, watch TV alone for a while and go to bed.

In bed I would toss and turn for I was a wretch. Ever since youth showed me to the door, my husband honoured me with the shell of faded affection. His wedding ring he fidgeted with unconsciously, and the fidelity that I wore as if a crown of precious gems, he gave away numerous times in dark and secret places.

One morning I went out to take in the post, and saw that some lovesick girl had drawn a lipstick love heart on the windscreen of Ricky's car. I came back in and made his breakfast. I told myself quietly that I desired only continuity from Ricky. He promised me that and I would have it. He was going to watch me grow old. We would be two shrivelled, forgotten grapes together. The others, he would only use disrespectfully and discard. Momentary pleasures. Bitches.

Ricky and I turned an aisle in a supermarket in St John's Wood and came face to face with a woman so coldly beautiful she reminded me of a mannequin. A platinum blonde. Tall and flawless in a white billowing top with Mexican stitches and stretch jeans – she was everything I wasn't. Ricky had no option but introduce us. Even though he tried hard to hide it, I heard it, respect. *For her.* And in Elizabeth Miller's frozen grey eyes I saw pity. *For me.*

Elizabeth Miller

Elizabeth

I stared at the half-eaten slice of toast that the man had left behind on his plate, the blobs of yellow butter too thick to melt. No matter how many times I saw such a sight it never failed to bring back the same picture. My sister's small red hands, nails bitten to the quick, meticulously wiping the butter off a triangle of toast with her napkin. The man returned to the breakfast room and the picture tilted a little.

'Like it?' he queried, his hands slightly raised at his sides.

Of course he looked as he always did. A fat bulldog in a suit he had paid an obscene amount of money for, but I made my face light up.

'Very nice,' I replied in Arabic. 'You must get another, in the same blue, definitely your colour.'

He moved away to admire himself in the mirror over the mantelpiece. He could afford to ignore me because I belonged to him in the truest sense of the word. Bought and paid for. One morning he woke up and decided he quite fancied a grey-eyed Irish witch in his collection, and I fulfilled the criteria. Once he even said it, that I was a fairy, a gay creature, having no soul, nothing in my bright body but a mouthful of sweet air, and, of course, silly negligible secrets. Yes, he chose to think of me as a body full of nothing. I was a function, a pleasure. I fulfilled a desire in him to be captivated, and amused. For a little while.

He looked down at me and I smiled.

Was I really that good an actress? Was it possible that I had managed to completely mask my horror of him? It amazed me that he saw nothing malevolent in his 'grey-eyed Irish witch'. Even now when I had become foolish for another man. It must be the blessing of the 'off' switch I found in my head long ago. It is a brilliant thing to switch off and feel nothing, no fear, pain, hate, sorrow, or joy. Once in a while the repressed emotions rise up as a paralysing panic attack, but all said and done, the switch works pretty well.

In the beginning it used to shock me the way he thought he could get away with it, the way he so effortlessly assumed I would never retaliate. I concluded that it could be three things. His culture that made him assume a woman could only be docile and powerless, the arrogance that came of his boundless wealth, or more likely the cynical pact we had made: a substantial lump sum when he tired of me.

He looked into my eyes. I knew he wanted them sad so I turned them the right amount of mournful. It was one of a fairy's functions, to mourn his absences. He was going away again.

'Ready?' he asked.

I nodded.

Outside the door beefy watchful men took over. They surrounded us. Beyond the lift another two waited. The teamwork was always flawless. We walked together through the opulent hotel lobby. Someone had already perfumed the path ahead of us so it smelt like a flower garden. A man held open the door of a perfectly vulgar white limo. We got in and it slipped away immediately. In front the guards, behind a procession of cars. Inside it was pleasantly warm. His fat hand settled on my thigh. And suddenly I had an unbidden memory of the fat hand.

I swung my head away and felt myself begin to sweat. Not now. If he knew about the suffocating anxiety, the unquiet waves . . . Please not now. He would be gone soon. I breathed deeply. Slowly. Come, come don't be such a sissy, Elizabeth.

I felt his fingers absently in my hair. He twisted a lock of it around his forefinger. It was what attracted him to me first. 'What fabulous hair. I have never seen anything like it before,' he said, staring. I had left the bleach in too long that night. It was a mistake, but now he insisted on this tasteless soul-destroying platinum. Softly, softly I brought myself back to normal. Back to frozen. The switch still worked. I turned around to face him. I could even look at the fat hand without emotion. He brought the twist to his lips. Obligingly I moved my head closer. Before he could tug.

At the airport I stood facing him, smiling softly. Ah well . . .

His eyes were on my mouth. He once said I reminded him of pink and white bone china. If he only knew what this mouth has seen and done. Suddenly he asked a shocking thing, something he had never asked before.

'Do you love me?' he asked. Oh there it was, he wanted to own everything. Was I wrong about him? Did his selfish, shrivelled, ugly heart want even more? He was watching me closely, his hard eyes sharp. Perhaps I wasn't such a good actress, after all. Perhaps he had begun to suspect about the other. I had to be careful. He was dangerous.

'Yes,' I said.

'How easily she lies,' he murmured. The black rat eyes glittered, but he was smiling. He was only playing. It was only a test. A meaty hand fumbled around in his pocket and found a box. He made me open it. A diamond ring. Ah, sweet baby Jesus, he was closing the exits. He was half playing just now. A ring this size is never given freely, but lent out for as long as you belong to the borrower, in payment for good behaviour. The ring was not mine. It simply meant escape was going to be harder. Run, Elizabeth, run. Run now.

He slipped the ring on my finger. It was a perfect fit. I

stared at the enormous stone. He never did things by half, always the biggest, the best, the most expensive. My sister's fingers, bloody and raw, were busy. The toast had to be cleaned. I was frightened of him. Of the fat hand. The cold black eyes. How pitiless had I seen them once before?

He was right about one thing. I am a fairy, but he is wrong about everything else. I am not one of those iridescent creatures dreamed up by Enid Blyton, carrying gossamer wings on my back, and living at the bottom of his garden. I don't stay with him because of the substantial lump sum at the end of the nightmare. No, I live with him because it's all I deserve.

You see, I am an Irish fairy and Irish fairies are angels, who sat indecisively on the fence during the great rebellion in heaven. Since they had proven themselves neither good enough to be saved, nor bad enough to be lost, they were sent to earth and given dark and remote places to dwell in. This is my dark and remote place. Once I too had sat on the fence and watched a little rebellion. Did nothing at all. And because of my dangerous hesitancy, I was exiled.

Under my palm, inside his new suit his heart beat, regular, unwary. He pulled me towards him and kissed me. Then he turned away, and was lost in a mob of body-guards, and secretaries.

I turned away, took a handkerchief out of my handbag, and wiped my lips. I hated being kissed. It was like a phys-ical harm. He was gone. I tried hard not to run to the waiting limo.

'I want to do some shopping. Just drop me in Knightsbridge,' I told the driver. I leaned back and stared at the unreal rock on my finger. What did I feel? Nothing. I entered Harrods and walked quickly past a smiling woman who stepped up and tried to offer a perfumed envelope. They cannot resist me, these perfume sellers. I was a magnet to them. I sidestepped her neatly and, quickening my pace, exited through the next double doors, back onto the street. I hailed a black cab.

'Swiss Cottage, and hurry please.'

The cab dropped me outside the Newt and Cabbage pub. From inside the barman waved at me. Once he ran out and said he always watched my legs run up the stairs until even the tip of my stiletto was gone from sight. At the top of the stairs I wrenched the ring off my finger and dropped it into my purse. A worthless bauble.

There was a doorbell but I did not ring it. I had a key. We all did. Ricky had given us all one. He wanted us to think of this flat as ours. I closed the door behind me and for an instant, leaned against it. This was another of the dark places I had been banished to. There was an assortment of people lounging about on the battered sofas, and from the kitchen came the smell of Ricky's famous *arrabiatta* sauce and singing. Soon he would be coming through the door, carrying a huge bowl of pasta.

I was home. Back where I belonged, in the Spider's Temple. The twins stood up, hand in hand and utterly beautiful, they came to greet me. Perhaps you have already met them. They are Balinese. I like them. They are from one of those pagan societies where sex has not yet been un-ravelled by Freud, and desire is not a bloated slut, but a beautiful barefoot nymph wanting to step into thresholds new.

In Nutan's outstretched palm lay a short length of straw.

I promise to tell you everything if you are patient. I will take you past the old-fashioned candy shop where they sold aniseed balls, blind mice, toff-o-mints, bulls eyes, and bright pink Galway Rock, up to where the road split into two narrow roads, into a land so wild and beautiful it will make you gasp. They call it Connemara. But first let me have a line. A neat row of white powder brought all the way from Colombia. Hurry with the straw, Nutan, these good people wait to know when I decided that I would be no better than I should be.

Only last year I returned to it, the land of my childhood, and it was exactly as I remembered it. I got off the bus at Clifden. The town was busy getting itself organised for the pony show as I took the Lower Sky road. I followed it slowly winding around the seashore. On my left the ground fell away fairly steeply into the sea, quiet and lazy that day, and rising on my right the untamed beauty of the Irish countryside. Still higher up, bracken and furze.

It was late August and the days were still long. The hedgerows were ablaze with purple loosestrife, montbretia and meadowsweet, and the ground was a carpet of blue with harebells, scabious and tufted vetch. There were children on the beach. Ah yes, I too was a happy child of the sea once, picking cockles and mussels barefoot, shrimping knee deep in rock pools, my dress tucked into my knickers. Now and again shading my eyes with my hands to watch the mackerel break.

I walked further up the road and everything was as it should be, until I turned onto a flint path. Until I stood before my old home, shocked.

The thatched roof of our cottage under the blue netting was still intact, but the half-doors that my father had painted bright red were missing and so were the window shutters. The walls were choked with wild woodbine tendrils, and Mother's red and purple fuchsias were woody with neglect. Inside, the floor was thick with dirt and debris and in one corner, a discarded flour bag. Did *we* consume its contents?

And when I looked up, the beams, smoke-stained from all those years ago, brought a dull ache to my chest. I stood for a long time with my back to the sea, staring at the ruin. Some cycling tourists wheeled past. I turned away from the great wild hill and walked towards the shore of the sheltered bay. A gust of cold sea wind buffeted me. There must have been a storm the night before. The beach was full of black and yellow seaweed.

I began to climb, sure and familiar, up, up, to the high cliffs where the great grey rocks wear their dangerously slippery yellow moss. Therein lay the past. Up, up high above the sea. If you stand at the edge during a storm, the soaring winds will fetch the salt spray to your face. I knew that place well. Awake, the sea was so beautiful, untameable, and wholly wild. I could almost hear it then, roaring, mighty.

Raging and wanting.

When I was a child, the storms that terrified my mother and sister and had the dogs cringing and whimpering under the bed, never frightened me. In fact, I loved them. The storm lantern swinging madly from the roof shed, the shrieking gales, the flashes of white lightning ripping open the sky, and those great claps of thunder that crashed nearer and nearer. Louder and louder, until the windows shook and it seemed our dear little house would smash to smithereens. In front of the fire, my mother gathered together my sister, my brother and me to her. Snug and warm we smelt dinner on her breath as she sang in her high, lilting voice haunting Irish songs.

Outside, the fierce winds, having circled the house, reappeared, only this time to talk in a human voice. 'Ach, it's only the ropes of the thatch rubbing against the walls,' my father dismissed, but I was convinced that the wind spoke.

Some bitter nights, I donned my father's oilskin and crept out while my family slept. Leaning against the wind, my teeth bared, eyes narrowed to slits and a lamp in my hand I made for the cliffs. Sometimes a bolt of lightning struck so close that my skin bristled with electricity, and my heart beat like crazy. From my high vantage point, I could see the entire countryside illuminated, the winding road shining white, and our little thatched cottage luminous against the hillside, an enchanted magical sanctuary.

Freezing rain lashed sharp and biting on my bare legs as I crawled right to the edge of the furthermost cliff. I wanted to watch the hungry sea smash against the rocks, frenzied, black and frothing, and catch the smell of wet seaweed rising from it. Before I left I always pulled from my pocket a bunch of wild flowers, a button, a feather or a dead butterfly to hurl into its seething turbulence. Roaring and hissing with mad delight, a huge white claw came up to seize my offerings. I owed the sea. From the time I was child I knew it wanted me. I felt it calling, but I refused to go. So I fed it. Little things so it would be content, but I had not fed it enough, so it reached out for something more precious. Too precious.

That late August I stood on my old perch, but without flowers, my best pebble/or a dead insect, so I took off my little silver bracelet and flung it into the water. My offering. Do not take me yet. Further ahead the sea sucked up to the beach, calm, friendly, lobster pots dancing in the water. So calm it made me sure that if only I turned left, the way of the rocks, I would see a jam jar full of shrimps.

A mob of seagulls flew overhead screaming harshly, and suddenly I remembered that day when my mother turned her unseeing face to the sea, her black cotton shawl limp around her waist, and grieved. But no, let me start before that.

Let me start with my father. My father is the most Irish Englishman you could ever meet. He had a bouncing shock of brown curls, eyes stolen from a child, a smile that urged you to mischief, and a great desire to laugh. Often he tumbled to the ground with laughing. He first came to Connemara in answer to an advertisement by the Ardagh Hotel for a piano player. My mother who was working there as the chef, was sitting at the bar after her shift, when he sauntered in, smelling like a brewery. 'You could tell straight away he was a rogue,' she said.

'Taxi needs paying,' he said to the manager, propping himself against the bar. Of course they went out to pay the 'taxi driver', although it was well known there was no taxi service from Galway to Clifden. It was just another of my father's hitch-hiking scams. *You get the drinks and I'll figure out something for you.*

But if my father was telling the story, he skipped that part, and started history with the day Mother and he first acquired our little house. How they came upon it on a stony hillside during the soft month of April. How it was raining and the sea was moaning quietly when Mother stood in front of the house and burst into tears of love.

Having been abandoned during the great famine only the thatched roof under the blue netting was still intact. A rotted green half-door, blown off its hinge, lay on the cracked stone floors. Successive storms had kicked away huge portions of the grey walls. Mother wanted to make right its painful dereliction. She ran to the shed that stood beside the house.

'And this here will be your studio,' she sobbed happily, for my father's real passion was painting. He only pounded the piano to pay the bills. So my father restored the house and the shed. He gathered the stones scattered on the hillsides, and built her a dry stone wall so her Arum lilies and potatoes would be enclosed. My mother said fairies' fingers couldn't have done better. On the iron gate outside he hung up a simple black and white sign that said, Paintings For Sale.

On the day they moved in a farmer from across the hill came to welcome them. He was rosy about the cheeks and had in his hands home-churned butter wrapped in a piece of white muslin. My father invited him inside, and offered him a share of the whiskey bottle. They had a right old time, my mother on the spoons, my father on the fiddle and Seamus dancing and singing 'The Blackbird'. When he was leaving he said, 'Aye, good neighbour, yer know, this land here is mine. Would yer be wanting to pay some rent, like?'

I used to sit in my father's shed posing on a three-legged stool with a Kerry cream biscuit or an apple in my hand. Afterwards when I went to peek at his work he would have turned me into a frog in a pink dress or a strange lizard with long curly locks. He was not successful, my father. His work was too strange for the rural art shop. It lacked refinement. The tourists didn't want it.

When he was not painting he was a gardener, though it must be said he was incredibly unsuccessful at that too. He tried growing cherries and gooseberries, but in the unyielding soil they never made it past their first shoots. His vegetables were another sorry sight. Still it was certainly not for lack of trying. Whenever there was a storm he shook us awake at six, sometimes five in the morning, to rush us into rubber boots so we could collect the seaweed that the Atlantic sea had hurled at our shores and that he used as fertiliser. In the freezing cold our hands turned bright red and stiff and when I screamed with pain my brother, Jack, would stuff my hands into his armpits. Inevitably armed with tin cups we resorted to the ditches for wild strawberries and blackberries hiding like jewels among the green leaves, for Mother's kitchen and pantry.

If my mother had been born a French man, she would have been a world-renowned chef, for she could do amazing things with the simplest ingredients. Even the humble potato could be transformed with mustard or orange peel into something grand and magnificent. Newly married girls came to her to learn how a dollop of sour milk could make plain-boiled green and white cabbage taste exceptional. With plainly cooked fish she taught them to serve burnt fennel relish, and with roast pork a russet-coloured apple pickle.

And her preserves, by God, they were legendary. Elderberry jam with cloves, cherry in orange marmalade, and gooseberry with candied lemon. It was a happy day indeed in our household when Millars in Clifden agreed to stock her pickles. We went with Father to the kitchen of Ardagh Hotel, where we sat on the steps and ate the gorgeous honey, orange and lavender ice creams she made. On The Day Of The Well-Buttered Piece Of Bread, or The Day of The Big Portion she made ragouts of oysters and fricasees of artichokes and figs.

Discarded as a baby on the steps of a Christian Orphanage my mother told incredible, hair-raising stories of the cruelties endured at the hands of nuns. But she was not bitter. She threw away a solicitor's letter urging her to join a group of victims seeking compensation. 'What goes around comes around,' she simply said, wooden clothes pegs in her mouth as she filled the washing lines with clean clothes. She liked wearing a hat in the kitchen, a rather sad affair that she was very proud of. Even though my last memory of her was her mouth stretched sideways in the belief that she was smiling, I still remember her contented; a big pot bubbling on the traditional black stove behind her, a rough wooden table full of pickle jars before her. Above her a fading picture of Our Mother Mary.

My brother Jack was seven and I five when my sister Margaret was born. I remember the first day she came home, an ugly wizened, ill-tempered thing with thin lank hair. She had very dark eyes that followed you about gravely and spindly limbs that reached out, needy and clinging.

All the while she was growing she sat in corners screaming her screech, until my mother came to pick her up. My brother and I watched, surprised by her single-minded tenacity for attention. I couldn't understand her screaming rages. Why she was so needy of my parents' notice. Still it did not bother me, and it was Jack who first thought that the new baby might be a changeling that the wee people had left behind, when they stole away our real sister. He whispered that she would wreak ill in our home, and when she was done with her mischief, she would simply be gone, and no one would know where. He felt certain that only when the changeling was driven away would our real sister be returned, unharmed.

'Watch her appetite,' he said, 'changelings have abnormal appetites. They eat all that is set before them. They can eat a larder bare.' We took her clothes off to check if she was covered with the light downy hair of changelings. She had none. 'It might sprout later,' my brother muttered darkly.

Sitting on the three-legged stool I told my father about my brother's suspicions. For a moment his startled eyes left his canvas and settled on me. He tried to look earnest, but his eyes were twinkling. 'A duckling is ugly to protect it,' my father said, and set about telling me the story of the ugly duckling that became a swan.

'Aye, fairies have to be treated with respect or they will turn nasty,' Father said later, throwing Margaret, tears and all, high up into the air, 'oops' and catching her with a laugh. Jack said nothing. Despite all the attention I remember her only as a sullen round face at dinner.

It was late autumn, the sun was hazy in the sky and plump bees were buzzing in the hedges that day we took the warm footpaths to hook lobsters by the rocks. Jack put Margaret on a smooth boulder. 'Don't move now. Be a good girl and watch the seagulls for a bit,' he told her. The seagulls were sitting on the rocks like fat ducks. It was a good day and Jack's bag was almost full when I looked up and saw Margaret gone. My brother went white. I looked out to the sea and saw her head bobbing in the water.

'Look,' I cried. 'She's doing Father's trick.' Father had

taught us all that we would never sink as long as we kept our ears in the water. 'Will I go and get her, Jack?' I said immediately, but Jack was already running into the water. He was a strong swimmer. His arms moved powerfully towards the black head as he swam further and further out to sea. I never thought she was that far.

I felt a cold horror in my stomach when I heard a happy voice call my name. I turned around, and there she was, the little changeling.

'You couldn't find me,' she sang proudly.

Dear God, she was playing hide and seek. I started screaming out to Jack to turn back, but the strong winds coming from the northwest mountains simply snatched my voice and threw it back at me. Until suddenly I couldn't see my brother any more, only the black head floating further and further away. I had not fed the sea enough.

For a long time, I sat on the beach, waiting, shocked, numb, disbelieving, a vice-grip around the changeling's wrist. I think she might have screamed, but I did not hear. It was impossible. Impossible that the boy who could thrust his hand into a burrow and pull out a fine bit of rabbit wouldn't resurface. In the sky the seagulls were swerving, twisting and calling.

'Oh, God of all evil,' my father cried, anguished, when my sister and I went to tell him what the greedy sea had done. My mother ran out of the door straight into the green prickly gorse, scrambling down the cliff, cruel black gravel slicing her hands open, shouting, 'My jewel, my jewel of a son, do not leave. Do not leave me.' Who could blame her for her limitless grief? I thought of him eating periwinkles, his eyes twinkling. Who could blame the sea for wanting him?

That evening my father was so drunk he fell backwards, landing on his backside, his legs straight out in front of him. He looked around him in confusion. My mother just sat facing the window staring silently at the sea, her black shawl bunched around her waist. She would not speak. She would not cry. She was waiting for his body, but he was so precious, you understand, that the sea refused to return him, even lifeless. My mother was heartbroken that she could not even scratch a hole in the ground to lay her lost child. How could she go on living where her son had died in such a hurry? Within a month we had left Connemara. We moved to England. A horrid place called Kilburn.

I won't bore you by trying to explain just how sordid Kilburn was, how hideous our two-bedroom council flat was, or how my father forgot he was a great painter whose time had not yet arrived, and went off to become an ordinary employee in a courier company. No, I'll just tell you about the changeling.

She ate without stopping. Late one night I switched on the kitchen light, and found her sitting on the floor with her back to the refrigerator, hurriedly stuffing raw sausages into her big white face. I stared at her, shocked. 'What in God's name are you doing, Margaret?' She looked like a leprechaun hugging its pot of gold.

Our changeling. *They can eat a larder bare.*

'Get out. Get out. Stop spying on me,' she snarled, pulling her lips back from her teeth like a cur.

'I only came to get a glass of milk,' I defended, stunned.

She looked at me with hate and dashed out of the kitchen, still clutching the string of pink sausage in her hand.

It was only when she reached puberty that she suddenly became a total stranger, hiding inside huge woollen jumpers, layer upon layer of clothes, and a curtain of long hair. One morning she announced that she had become a vegetarian. It was the most insidious form of rebellion. It was not meat that she was cutting away. It was our way of life, the warmth that made our family. While the rest of us tucked heartily into roast duck and green beans glistening in a sauce so transparent it was like maroon glass, she reluctantly trudged through a meal of five beans, two boiled cauliflower florets and one new potato. She suffered one plain flat boxty while we had ours rich to bursting with the most delicious stuffing. And yet I caught her looking at the shining juices on our plates from the corners of her eyes. Fascinated and yet horrified. She had become a vegetarian in a bid to leave behind the calories, but I could never forget the sight of her greed. Pushing raw sausages down her throat.

It took mother to realise her cheekbones were sticking out of her face.

Then came the day she was being force-fed in a hospital. Her potassium level had fallen to dangerous levels. 'It is not a food thing,' the doctor explained.

'Oh God, save her soul. She is at war with herself,' Mother said.

'Ah well, anorexia,' Father sighed aloud, relieved. One of them new-fangled diseases then. Nothing serious. Just a little bit of attention seeking. But the same vein of determination that had made my sister scream for as long as it took to be picked up, took over the five-and-a-half-stone bag of bones that she had become. She turned meal times into a meeting of hunched, brooding strangers, each carefully watching the other. The silence we endured as we sat in front of our empty plates, and watched her cut her food into impossibly tiny pieces, and slowly, slowly, with the greatest reluctance, chew each tiny morsel.

To give the impression she had eaten already she emptied out the crumbs from the toaster into her unused plate. Cunningly she kneaded pieces of bread in the palms of her hands until they were lumps of dough that could be pushed up her sleeves. But the war was fought on both sides. While she filled the pockets of her baggy trousers with food from her plate my parents surreptitiously concealed double cream and butter in her mashed potatoes. As she obsessively wiped the butter off her toast with a napkin, my parents spilled sugar on the sly into her custard. Outside their tight circle I watched the cat and mouse game, an intricate contest of many rules and forfeits. Only the initiated may partake.

No matter how much love they poured into her, it simply wasn't enough.

I looked at her hooked nose, and understood her warrior blood. In a Turkish Sultan's turban she would die trying. It was the city of Constantinople itself that she wanted. Even if it was empty, all its inhabitants dead. Many times when we went to visit her in the hospital, she turned her head away, ignoring us, to glare defiantly at the tubes that carried nourishment into her starving body.

I remember her standing in front of the mirror. Lifting her blouse she complained, 'Look how fat I am,' but when I met her eyes in the mirror I found a proud liar. Of course she could see how pitifully thin she was, but she simply would not admit it. To admit it would ruin everything. Would turn her from a helpless victim, unable to stop herself from nibbling on wads of tissues to stave off the hunger pangs, into a conniving, selfish person.

I knew she did not want to die. So what did she want? She would go so far, but when she was near enough to see the edge, she would pretend to resist as my parents carried her back one step, or two if they were lucky.

And then she was back at the table strumming her fingers, fidgeting . . . refusing to eat. That was when I began to hate her. I recognised the cunning with which she kept my parents on the hook. Day and night. They thought she was sick, but I knew better. You see, I had seen the real Margaret in the mirror, as she turned this way and that and announced, 'Look how fat I am.' I had seen through her thin manipulative face and her long clinging fingers. The way she was tearing apart my family. The way she'd killed my brother.

I watched my parents patiently waiting for her to take the next mouthful and felt a surge of violence. Can't you just relax and fucking eat? Why do you have to be such a hog for attention? And then I lay on my bed and heard her in the toilet, throwing up. She came back, her eyes watery, but challenging. I hated her.

She was turning my mother into a hag, whose sobs came through the bedroom wall. In the dark of our bedroom I waited until I heard her breathing evenly, sleeping, and then I whispered my foul secret as loud as I dared, 'I hate you. I hate you, Margaret. I wish you were dead. Do you hear me? DEAD.'

One day I walked into our room and my sister was stretched out on her bed, her eyes staring at the ceiling, a bunch of flowers pressed to her chest.

'What are you doing?' I asked, shocked.

She looked at me, amused. 'Just pretending,' she explained serenely. 'Death, steal away my breath. Death, take my hand. Death smile on me. Death, don't wait too long . . .' and closing her eyes, she feigned death. Had she heard me whispering my hate in the dark? I decided no. She was just being a drama queen.

One day a big black raven nesting in the chimney flapped into our living room, its feathers badly scorched, and its poor body suffering. The poor creature shat the entire room before landing dazed and trembling on the dresser. Margaret couldn't watch my father kill it, but I did. I saw how quickly its spirit left its burnt body. Death was not so repulsive after all. In fact, a welcome release from pain. We buried it by the railway lines. One day Margaret too will be inside the earth, I thought. I will smell her in the brown fragrance of the earth.

She died, peaceful as an angel, in her sleep.

I remember that night coming upon her, not yet dead, and yet so close to it that I should have run to alert my parents about her gravelly breathing, but I climbed instead into my own bed. That was my moment of fence sitting, when I did nothing. That is why I was banished to dwell in dark and remote places.

It seemed for ever that I lay awake in the dark listening to the torturous breathing die away, until finally a great silence fell upon the room. Then I turned my head and watched the day break through the window. How beautifully the sun came up. For just a few moments the sky was white and gold. I could see it would be a fine day. The great silence was wonderful.

Then Mother came into the room and I closed my burning eyes.

I felt her move towards Margaret's bed. I heard her gasp. I heard that pallid woman panic. 'Margaret, Margaret,' she called, but of course Margaret was long gone. Isn't it quickly she went from us in the end?

'Steven, Steven,' my mother shouted for my father.

'Elizabeth, Elizabeth,' my mother shouted for me.

I opened my eyes and met her shocked, widened ones. We looked at each other and in that instant she knew.

Sabotage.

Pale as death she drew back, shaking her head violently. She turned her back on me and went to hug her dead child. But for one incredible moment, I had seen not the condemnation of her turned back, but gratitude glimmer in her eyes. I had cut away the source of her greatest torment. Done what she had not the guts to do. Dispatched my sister off into the night. And then the moment was gone and she was asking me to help her, although she knew there was nothing to be done. I stood up to look at my sister's corpse. Her still face was turned in my direction and her eyes were open and unforgiving. Why, those hard eyes had watched me all night.

Who knows what the dead see?

'Did you not hear me call? I did not want to die. Did you not hear the unpeaceful sound?' the staring eyes accused. 'The sound of me dying, those gasping desperate whispers calling your name?'

So now you know. I lied to you before when I said the breathing died away into silence. 'The unpeaceful sound.' Yes, I heard it. Horrible it was, too. A right bloody torment. Once the gasping voice even tried to trick me: 'Quickly, call Mother,' it begged weakly, 'I am already dead and I must say goodbye.' My sister, as I had always suspected, did not have the nerve to face death. In the end she did not want to die, but she cried his name so often in jest, *Bean śi*, the messenger of death, came. He swallowed her into his enormous mouth, sucked her soul clean, and spat her lifeless body out.

My mother closed my sister's eyes. The first time they sprang open again defiantly, but she managed the second time. Then she carefully wrapped my sister's cold body in blankets, and cradled her precious head. Once the blanket fell away and we saw it then, the fine hair that had sprouted all over her stomach. My mother ran the tips of her fingers wonderingly over the gold velvet. 'She was cold. So cold her body grew her a blanket of fur,' my mother crooned. She shook her head and her mouth twisted on one side.

And I thought to myself, why, Jack had been right all along. She really was a changeling. For a long time Mother would not let my father call the ambulance. She sat there rocking, and singing the song of the dying swan. I understood that my mother was singing peace into her daughter's chest, but it was not the beautiful haunting voice I remembered, from the times she had gathered our little heads together, and sang to keep the terrible storms outside from frightening us. No, this one was a raw and tuneless screech, to accompany the grotesque dance of her rocking body.

I stood over my sister and decided that with her accusing eyes shut there was beauty in death after all. Good old Margaret, she made a nice corpse.

That evening the cat carried a dead blackbird into the house and placed the corpse reverently at Mother's feet. It was meant to be a gift, to console and comfort the grieving. Father erected a stone angel over Margaret's grave. Draped in stone garments the angel mourned with downcast eyes. Sometimes I went to lie on the grass over the quiet earth she lay in. I did not mean it. It was a mistake.

I was the snake child. I saw it in my mother's eyes.

The glue that bound my parents was gone and they drifted apart. Father left on St Patrick's Day with a secretary from his workplace. I thought of him in Connemara, flying around the room, unspeakably funny, on pointed toes and a tall hat. When he scooped my laughing mother up by the waist and called her *ma chroidhe*, my heart, and sometimes shortening it to a beautiful sound, *machree*. Afterwards, full of bright cheer, we roasted eggs on the open fire, and Father smoked a pipe.

Mother and I moved back to Ireland. We lived in squalor in Dublin.

Mother stood by the kitchen window in her dressing gown, an empty carton of milk in her hand. 'There's no more milk,' she said, bewildered.

'No,' I agreed. 'There is no more anything in the cupboards, Mother.'

I wanted her to ask, 'Why did you let her go?' but she wouldn't.

Mother's guilt was like an eight-inch kitchen knife that had approached from the side, when she wasn't looking, and embedded itself deep in her. I watched her try to draw it out, but it only made her bleed all the more. From this moment on she must always wear the blade. She used to say in a befuddled voice, 'Wait a little bit for me. Just a little bit and I promise I will be better.' So I waited and I waited, but Mother recovered into a stranger. She could not meet my eyes. She had forgiven the nuns, but she couldn't bring herself to forgive me. I knew her secret shame was so terrible we had to become strangers. We could not comfort each other. We were murderers. Both of us. We could not indulge in the comfort of sorrow.

I went to visit Father, and his secretary girlfriend sat on his lap and whispered things to him. Little secrets so I would know that I was the stranger, the third person. The man she wanted, his offspring she had no place for.

I have never found a place to put Margaret in, so I am forced to keep her inside me. Sometimes she slips into my dreams, her eyes demanding, 'Why? Why didn't you help me? I should be there, but I am not, because of you. Therefore you are responsible for my well-being.' Other times in the night she comes to sit in a corner of my bedroom, staring balefully at me. Her blank eyes are able to see in the dark without a torch. She is making a necklace of rats' teeth, and when she is finished my time will be up. 'Say my name and I will live,' she says.

Of course I have always refused. I did not deserve to heal, for in the mirror I had begun to see what my mother saw, a murderer hiding inside my skin. Like those fish that pretend to be coral, or floating seaweed, so they may survive on a diet of the unsuspecting. If you saw the murderer inside me you too might try to destroy her.

By the time I was sixteen I hated the monster inside me. Now every time I looked in the mirror I did not see the pretty girl that men declared undying love for. Just that cold monster that ignored a dying girl's plea.

So I ran.

Back to London.

I got off the train pale and lost. How busy everyone looked. Rushing, rushing, rushing. The world spread out, big and full of exciting adventures. One stepped out of the shadows in the form of a man. He was extremely good-looking in a polished, smooth style. He wore a nice blue suit and said, 'Would you like to be a model?' Instinctively my heart knew he was not to be trusted, and yet my mouth answered, 'Yes.'

He produced a card. It was plain and proclaimed him a talent scout for a modelling agency. Not Elite but Elites. Very similar. I was fooled. I wanted to be fooled.

The dangerous man took me to a flat. There were other girls there. All beautiful. One so beautiful I could not help staring. She wore ballet shoes and had curly brown hair and blue eyes. She was Irish and as familiar as soda bread. She smiled at me. 'Oh,' my heart whispered, 'she will be my friend.'

'Come,' Maggie invited. 'You will share my room.'

It took me no time to become a prostitute. It's very similar to pouring a Guinness. A two-step process. You pour some, you wait and then you pour some more. But you wouldn't understand if you haven't been through it. It's something like this anyway: 'You are my woman. Mine. No one else must even look. I don't share. Do you understand? Mine and only mine . . . But wouldn't you like to help me, if you could? You'll do it, if you really love me. Come on, it's only sex. It doesn't mean a thing. I'll love you more, you'll see. It's just another job for Christ sake. . .'

Like a butterfly on offer to every flower. Fluttering indiscriminately until it is snatched away by birds and the cruel cats next door. Your soul to the devil.

Men, I will tell you now, are despicable creatures. Ahh, I can see your secret smile. You think your man is better than those I have known. No, no, you poor misguided thing.

Elizabeth

While you are me in my land I will be you in yours.

Your man is my man on the dark nights he wants it rough, or quick or different. Ultimately they all seek the same thing. They seek to try all, no, reveal all, without fear of dissension, or censure. It is there day and night, the desire to prove what despicable creatures they really are. You do not believe me. Perhaps it is better that you don't. Yes, heed the warning of the fairy crones, 'Too much knowledge can make a person old too soon.' Wring it this way and it establishes the bed barren, the sheets soulless. Look what it has done to me. Once an innocence is stolen it can never be given back.

Was it not you that I saw quickening your pace, grabbing the man you thought was yours alone, all the while glaring at me, as I leaned with another girl in a sleazy Soho doorway calling out to the passing men? We laughed at you when your back, indignant and offended, had passed. That wasn't prostitution. It was just a scam then. They paid dearly for my 'champagne cocktails', beautifully decorated glasses of highly coloured cordials. There was no such thing as regulars in that business. They slithered down the darkened staircase, got fleeced, and even the ones that didn't leave disgruntled and shouting blue murder never came back.

But did you notice the way your man's eyes slid over to me? The way he was helpless in the face of the bare-arsed curiosity that stole into his mind. But because you have labelled yourself pure, you are no longer free to explore your own sexuality, so you have to pretend condemnation and loathing to mask your secret envy of illicit little me, of all the things I will do for a price. You wish all of my kind annihilated, don't you? We are natural enemies since time immemorial, aren't we?

And then a young man, a client, a small-time drug dealer decided to save me from my profession. He installed me in

149

his flat. Proudly he called me his girlfriend. He took me out on his arm. A sort of decoration, I suppose, for his mates and colleagues to admire. Until one day he misconstrued a glance exchanged between his mate and me. It made the young man insecure. The thought troubled him until he found the solution late one night in a bottle of gin. It was a brilliant plan. Why he had not thought of it before was a mystery. That night he lifted the square cut away from the false ceiling and brought down his stash, a hunk of white rock. It fell away into white powder with magical ease.

'Try it,' he invited. Until then he had never tried the stuff himself.

So we tried it. It was brilliant. We kept trying it late into the night, every night. Time turned me into a thief. I began to yearn for it. From the time I woke up I wanted a line. So I learned to pinch his stash during the day. Not so he'd notice. Slowly we changed. Right before each other's eyes we became monsters. Moody, greedy, unscrupulous. Turned me from grateful to desperate. At first he didn't notice, but eventually he saw his white rock dwindling in its hiding place. His eyes turned mean. He screamed at me and called me a prostitute. In the end they all seek to show their real nature, despicable creatures, but I stayed, as he knew I would. He held the power. He held the white stuff.

Once I had been snorting all day, stuff that I had stolen the night before while he was up there, high as a kite. That evening when he came home he decided to be mean, he decided he wanted to party at a friend's place. Without me. No doubt another woman waited. It did not bother me until I saw him take his white rock from its resting place and carefully pack it. He was taking the white rock.

I had a little money. I'd wait until he was gone and go out too. Buy some from another of his friends, but outside the door I heard the deadlock turn. The bastard was locking me in. I banged the door and shouted at him, but all I heard was his heavy boots fading away down the stairs. I was so furious I did not think at all. I acted instinctively, as an animal does. I opened the window and jumped out.

The air was cool and fresh, and flying, I can tell you, is glorious. I felt no fear, not even when I landed on the soft grass outside, flat on my back with total numbness along the length of my body. I heard his footsteps on the last step of the stairs.

I had reached ground level before him.

Unable to move I called out to him. For a moment he stood on the last step, confused by my voice. Then he came forward and stood over me, his face comical. Slowly he bent down to look closer at my face. We stared at each other for a while.

'Stupid bitch,' he swore, and slapped me hard. It did not hurt. Then he walked away. The sky was not black it was the most amazing midnight blue. So beautiful it made tears run down my face. He had a party to go to, but he must have called an ambulance on his way there. Sirens screaming, they came.

They trussed me up in a corset that ended beneath my breasts. I was lucky, they said. Could have broken my neck, died, and gone to heaven. They thought I had been pushed. They did not believe someone so young and beautiful could ever jump of her own free will. They looked for bruises and found none. Surprised and disturbed they hurried away back to their two children and their two-up two-down, glad they had no role in such a strange, strange world.

He came to the hospital to see me, weighed down with a truly enormous bunch of flowers, a heart-shaped box of chocolates, and a sorry face. I turned away when he gently put his hand in mine. And by and by I felt a neatly folded paper package slip into my hand. I turned to look at him. He looked steadily into my eyes. It was a test. How far would I let him go?

Watching him carefully I curled my fingers over the offering. His eyes flashed, triumphant. He had won. Now it was clear to both of us that I always was and always would be no more than a prostitute. With a price. I could be bought and sold at will. At such a silly price too. I shall never forget the moment of that dishonour. That unplanned moment when I had permitted an arbitrary value to be placed upon me. That moment when I invited the world to use me.

I am really one of those sin-eating cormorants. In my belly are my sister's sins. That is why my sister waits, unfinished in the dark, glaring angrily, making her rats' teeth necklace. I have to unform before she can claim back what I have eaten, and become whole again. She wants me to unform, to die.

The only time I forgot about death was when I was invited to Jamaica by a client who didn't like nut-brown lasses. Some golf tournament. For three days he disappeared at seven in the morning and came back drunk late at night, but the whole day was mine. Near the hotel was a little beach bar and the woman running it had a child, the loveliest thing you ever saw. Brown and fat.

She let me take the baby to the beach where she could still see us. For hours I lay on the sand playing with the baby. He ate a mash of potatoes, peas and chicken. He had hair like a black cloud, unbelievably soft. In the afternoons he slept under the bar in a basket and I went to swim in the warm water. When the baby awakened I went to collect him. Oh it was heaven. Then I forgot my death sentence. And at night, strolling on the beach on my own, the moon permitted itself to shine even on a whore.

It lay on my path, on my last day – a tiny dead baby bird. I had the brown baby in my hands. I stopped for a second to look at its corpse, no bigger than my little finger, naked and purplish. 'Poor thing,' I said, and the baby boy and I looked curiously at the still bird. At that moment I was like him, like all other men who live their lives on this earth, see death all around them, and yet hardly believe it will happen to them. With that child in my arms I was invincible. I thought I could be different. I thought to start again. Return to England, adopt a little brown baby. All for me.

I was different when I came back. The sin I bore didn't feel so heavy. I knew what to do. No more drugs. I wanted to belong to someone, wear his ring, carry his name. And when there were no more than a few teeth left in his head let him be heartbroken if I died. I wanted a baby, a family and my own kitchen that smelt of baking bread. All for me. I registered on the waiting list for a council flat, and went and got a job in a night club as a receptionist. A week later a girl in the queue screamed my name with delicious delight. Oh! Elizabeth. Oh! Maggie.

We became friends again and she told me that she too wanted to give up prostituting. She invited me to move into her top-floor apartment in Maida Vale until my flat came through. It seemed like a good idea.

Her flat was a shabby little place where great big cats suddenly landed in your lap and everywhere you cared to look were dozens upon dozens of second-hand books on philosophy, history, art and culture. They were piled into towers, arranged in book shelves, lying on top of tables, supporting tables, well just everywhere really. Cobwebs swayed from the ceiling, and all the cushions had been shredded to bits of fluff by the cats. The kitchen reeked of stale cat food, and the fridge was empty, but for cartons of milk and beer cans. Running free and untroubled on her kitchen window sill were millions of ants.

'Have you never heard of insecticide?' I asked, looking at the black swarm.

'They're just hungry. If I leave a spoon of jam on the window sill they don't roam around the rest of the place.'

Then she took me to her bedroom and I gasped. It was like being in a different house. There was not the least trace of cat smell or fur. It was spotless, but the most amazing thing was the walls. Every wall was covered with oil paintings.

'You?' I asked.

She nodded and smiled.

Ah, so that's what you really are, an artist, I thought. What a priceless thing to give up, for an easier life. They reminded me a little of my father's work, but better, much, much better and charged in some extraordinary way with terrible sadness or loss.

'They are grand, Maggie. Will you sell them?'

'No one wants them.' I thought of my dad struggling to sell his work and the soul-destroying knowledge that no one wanted them. Poor, poor Maggie.

To me she was everything a prostitute wasn't supposed to be. Some nights on my way to the toilet I was greeted by the shining sight of Maggie in a ruffled nightgown sitting in front of the fire, her feet up on a tattered padded stool, one hand gently stroking a cat in her lap, and a book in the other. It was from her that I learned about the gentle joy of reading. The trouble a book took to transport me into a world that was not mine, and could never be.

She got a job as a waitress in the night club I worked in. We had such fun together. We were invited to all the best parties and were the belles of the ball. We had no money to speak of, but we bought the latest fashions from Top Shop and updated them, gave them a zing of our own with buttons, pockets, laces, and velvet trims we cut out of the clothes we bought for a few pounds from charity shops. That was the greatest fun I ever had.

Some nights Maggie and I partied so hard we emptied out the last bottle of alcohol in the flat. At six in the morning we hurried past the milk cart and threw pebbles at the upstairs window of the corner shop. After a while the curtains parted and a brown face peered down. We waved brightly. We knew the routine. First the face would withdraw and the curtains would twitch again, but this time barely a flash of brown would show. That would be Mr Dulip Singh's wife. Soon the locked door would be unlocked and kept slightly ajar, just long enough for us to slip in quickly. At that time of the morning Mr D would be without his turban. His greying hair was wild and bushy.

'Vodka,' we said, pretending to gasp desperately.

'Ah you naughty, naughty girls.' His thickly accented voice was stern, but his wagging finger limitless in its indulgence. While wrapping the bottle with green tissue paper he warned us with touching paternal concern about the cold and the dangerous men in the streets. Then he would open the door and furtively peer out into the street, quickly looking left and right. Hurriedly he ushered us out. 'Don't forget, if the coppers ask, you're borrowing a bottle to return later.'

'Of course Mr D. Thanks Mr D.'

'Join us one day,' Maggie would invite. His eyes would gleam. He had long guessed her for a night walker, but in his black avaricious eyes I saw that he was devoted to sweet little Maggie.

One day I came upon Maggie cleaning her paint brushes in the kitchen. 'We need a new start,' she said.'Let's start with the hair. Let's bleach it.' We left the bleach on too long in mine. 'Oops,' she said, laughing. But then she looked again and said, 'No, actually I like it. Looks all the rage.' We had a party to go to, but on the way, not far from Park Lane, a white stretch limo stopped alongside us. An olive-complexioned man got out of the driver's seat. 'You girls want to party?' he said, in a thick ugly accent. I shook my head.

'Yeah, sure,' Maggie squealed, and clambered in.

I stood outside. 'What in God's name do you think you're doing?' I hissed. 'This is how they audition actresses for snuff movies.'

'Don't be such a child,' she said impatiently. 'He's obviously just the driver. It's a party for loaded men. Come on, get in.'

I couldn't make her come out and I couldn't let her go on alone. 'A fine friend you are,' I said, and got in too.

Two things happened to me at that party. I met a tall blond man called Ricky, not an invited guest; he had only come to drop off the drugs. He sauntered up to me and slipped a key into my hand. 'When you get bored here, make your way to the best party in town,' he said, and walked away. The address was on the key ring. Has that ever happened to you before? Has anyone ever come up to you and given you a key that you know is forbidden? I felt like Bluebeard's wife.

I slipped the key into my purse, and looked up into the eyes of a stocky intense man who wasn't drinking or snorting. In his country he was a religious leader. The others at the party referred to him respectfully as Mullah. He was also the billionaire host. He put his hand out to touch my bleached hair and said in perfect English, 'What fabulous hair. I have never seen anything like it before.' He smiled. 'Also it is good that you take no drugs. It is a disgusting habit.'

He was a physically unattractive man, but exquisitely educated in England, and of course, his foreignness was intriguing. At the end of a game of chess he wouldn't cry out, 'Checkmate,' but shout, '*Shah mat*.' The king is dead. And he knew how to woo a woman. He showered me with gifts, set up expense accounts in designer boutiques, took me to the best places, and generally treated me like a queen. My slightest whim was his pleasure to fulfil. All I had to do anywhere was say his name and magically all things were

156

mine. And in return he wanted to install me in an inordinately opulent apartment in Mayfair, so he could visit me whenever he was in town, and expected me to spend the winter in Saudi Arabia.

Do you know how irresistible is temptation? It sounded like so little for so much. So in the end, even though I didn't love him, I became his mistress. The months passed in decadent luxury. In winter I flew to Saudi Arabia. And right in the middle of the desert, the helicopter landed above a magnificent palace surrounded by acres of immaculate lawns and gardens greener and more luscious than any you could find in England. But in my heart, even while bathing in water that had flowed out of solid gold taps, I still felt like a prostitute. It was not what I wanted and when the council wrote to say my flat was ready, I knew it was time to leave. A sign from God. So I told him I was leaving. I was gentle. He had been good to me.

First he laughed, the laugh of a man who wanted for nothing. And then without warning, for I never perceived danger, and so fast that he must have been prepared for the eventuality of my request for freedom, he taught me all about the 'off' switch inside my head. It locked me in a cold dark place where I felt nothing. No fear, no pain, no hate, no sorrow, no joy. No hope.

Afterwards he kissed my forehead gently, stroked my hair and said, 'Why do you play these games with me, *habibi*? My temper is such a terrible thing. Maybe next time I should be the one to decide if it is time for you to go, hmmm.'

For days I paced the floors. Furious. Incredulous. Vengeful. I made plans. I thought of knives, poisons, hired assassins. I would not be the captured creature of such a predator. Maggie could only look on in disbelief.

Then one night I dreamed my sister had finished making her rats' teeth necklace. She opened her mouth and terrible things came out of the black hole. I awakened sobbing. I lost all hope then. No one could help. In the end I was only a prostitute. I felt hate towards the whole world. It had nothing for me but contempt. Always waiting to knock me down. My only defence was never to allow it to touch me again. I would be impregnable to its advances, its coy invitations to play by its inequitable rules.

Suddenly there was no need to punish my aggressor. I would remain purposely within his reach, but only to use him. To make him pay for what was worthless anyway. All the while keeping only disgust in my heart. As an act of defensive anger I froze. This way I could never be out-manoeuvred.

I knew only one way to keep my sister quiet. Scrambling out of bed I began searching in my cupboards, my drawers, my bags until finally I found it in a jar with all my forgotten odds and ends. The blond man's key. It was not the man I was looking for, it was what he promised. In my hand Bluebeard's key was already weeping blood. Arterial blood. It ran through my fingers and soaked my clothes. Had I not already been in that secret room, seen the headless corpses of all his other wives? But there was nothing else. All hope had been ruined. I was damaged. The key wept and wept in my hand as I left my Mayfair flat and made my way to the Spider's Temple . . . but here comes Anis now. You must meet him. I never know whether to admire or pity him.

Anis Ramji

Anis

I suppose you could say that I loved my father until I opened a 'not to be read until after my death' file on his computer. He was out managing my grandfather's business empire. It wasn't easy breaking his secret password, but it fell apart when I inserted his shoe size into the equation. I remember it was an exciting moment when the screen flashed 'God Bless' in bold letters and took me into his secret world. Gosh I was so young, then. What a horrid shock it was.

I still remember reading every word with disbelief and utter disgust. My wonderful father was a gay pervert. Every repulsive detail described with brutal relish or clinical detail. Every anonymous encounter lingered over. Apparently men of all shapes and sizes entered him. And all the times he sneaked into this room and locked the door it was to pore over these explicit diaries for sexual gratification. Such was the power of his words that in my mind I became a spectator of every nasty scene.

In the kitchen my mother was dry-roasting the shells and heads of prawns. I sat there so long staring out of the window at nothing that I heard her go outside to grind them on the stone grinder, and even smelt the finished curry she had thickened with the ground powder.

When he returned home, I looked at him and saw him on his knees, in a stinking toilet, before the large black man he had referred to as 'the dark angel'. I saw my father with impatient hands unzip the angel's trousers and suck him greedily. Ugly, ugly, ugly.

'What's the matter, Anis?' my father asked. He had changed into traditional clothes. From this flesh I had been fashioned. The thought sickened me.

'Nothing,' I said.

'Food's ready. Come to the table,' my mother called.

Silently we went to the table. My mother spooned food onto my father's plate. Rice, green dahl and my father's favourite, prawn curry. As she passed him, she tenderly smoothed a lock of hair off his forehead. It made me want to slap her. How could she? How could she not know about him? How could she be so blind? How could she touch such filth so lovingly? Well, I blamed her. I stood up suddenly and left the table.

'What's the matter, Anis?' my mother called. Her voice surprised and hurt. Her heart was too gentle. She could never be told.

'Nothing,' I shouted, running out of the door. I hated them both. I ran to my grandfather's house.

When my father came to look for me he had to leave without me, because my grandfather, a big powerful figure, said, 'Leave the boy here for a few days.' From a window I watched my father leave, subservient and defeated. Even as a small boy I understood. My father compromised himself, living a lie in exchange for his father's love and approval. Acceptance precluded homosexuality. There could never be permission for such unnatural perversions.

From that day onwards I lived with my grandfather.

My grandfather had fled from India to Kenya looking for gold, but living by the lake he had seen how very rapidly the fishermen's catch decomposed. So he brought in salt, and made his fortune in salt fish. He bought land and the family moved to the hills where the air was cool and roses the size of children's heads could be coaxed to flower. He built a huge bungalow and surrounded it with wide wooden verandas. It made the house so inviting and cool, that often the postman, or the labourers repairing the roads around the hill, came up to lie in the shady veranda. It was a wonderful house.

There was a set of white stone steps that led down to a cellar where my grandfather leaned back, fat Cuban cigars clenched between his teeth, and listened to the blues. Those songs have a special place in my heart. Lonely songs sung by the most blameless and misfortune-prone bunch of people that ever walked the earth. Got no money, the wife just walked out, the girlfriend's a slut, the rent's not paid, even the damn dog's gone and died. It was a strange choice of music, considering the red-blooded, robust, never say die, shrewd, tough entrepreneur that was my grandfather. Once, after consuming a great deal of wild boar meat and whiskey, he jokingly told me something that surprised me.

He told me he had never looked at another woman since he married my grandmother. He said it was because my grandmother had played a trick on him. She had never once completely disrobed. Always she sought the half light, so some part still remained an exciting mystery. And in this way she taught him never to tire of her. One day he would discover all of her, but until then he was content to let the illusion drive him crazy.

In seeking to explain away his deep love I think he did my grandmother a great disservice. She was far, far more than a partially robed body. She was an enigma. She spent most of her day in silence. When it rained outside she went for a walk without an umbrella. She thought the joyful sound of the temple bell the most desolate sound in the whole world. She could never bear its lonely, piercing clanging.

She had no friends to speak of, and if someone had taken her to a hospital they might even have labelled her insane, but I knew that behind my grandmother's serene face a whole different world ate, slept and talked. One she preferred and returned to under the cover of darkness. My grandfather said the night was an occasion for the enlightened, who meditated, the worldly, who plundered it, the sick, who suffered it, and my grandmother, who sat up listening to it as if it belonged only to her.

At night she became special. Night dew covered her and dripped from her skin. When she walked in the long grass by the green pond, frogs hopped every which way out of her path. Her travelling feet were noiseless. Only she knew where she was going. Madness is private, a velvet secret. Like a moss garden that refuses to be coaxed or persuaded into being, but once it finds its rare corner it spreads its beautiful magic and makes alive every stone and surface it spies. It must not be trampled on by the curious, or it will be destroyed for ever. Its secrets may only be whispered in the darkness of the night into the lonely ears of young boys. Sometimes I went to sit beside her. Hers was a still, gentle presence.

Her face softly illuminated by the pale light of moon she asked, 'Did you hear that, Anis?'

'What? That frog croaking in the pond at the end of the garden?'

Her eyes were set in the dark distance. As if she could see the ripples in the pond, the gentle wind that bent the reeds, the sleeping white lilies.

'How deep his craving to relinquish his coat of slime, sprout wings and soar into the blue of the forest yonder. In his dream he is no longer the soft prey of the snake he hears searching in the long grass. But listen . . . listen, he dare not. He fears he will lose his nerve, tumble from his freedom and plunge to his death, or find a new enemy in the beak and claws of the eagle.'

Sometimes she asked, 'Did you see that?'

That firefly that flickered into light so we could see a single leaf fall.

When I was younger I used to wonder about that
enchanted world inside her head, the power it had to reach
out and change the one inside mine. In the silvery night air
I too began to hear the huge old trees cry for the treachery
of man. For ever, every frog will be the risk-averse, self-
doubting, wanting creature that one night long ago, for fear
of what could happen, dared not its greatest dream. And
what of the earth? A farmer fattening humans to dine on
them when the time is right. Maggots? The earth's teeth.
Listen . . . Do you hear that?

What did I really see and what was her imagination?

She drew me into her dreamworld and blurred the edges
of mine. One day she handed me a velvet pouch. 'It will be
good if you could use the contents one day.' Now I only
remember her for the silent tea ritual she observed. Every
day, once at ten in the morning, and again at four in the
afternoon, she sat alone on the veranda in complete silence,
drinking a cup of tea, eating exactly half a chocolate mint
biscuit.

My grandfather knew he could never enter my grandmother's moss garden. He was content to wait outside the
stone gates, guarding. None other may enter. And if he was
not listening to the blues, he returned to the memory of his
other passion, hunting. He told thrilling stories of lions that
turned hunter in the dark, circling and recircling his camp,
growling, their eyes luminous in the firelight. And how
once the big cats stole away a man in their jaws. The entire
cellar was lined with pictures of him standing over game he
had killed, usually with one foot resting on the carcass. He
loved his meat. My grandfather had never gone a day
without eating meat. Even on holy days he waited until my
grandmother had gone into the kitchen to get something
before he took a piece of fish or meat from a Tupperware
hidden inside his clothes and slipped it under a mound of
rice. And then slowly, surreptitiously, he consumed the

meat with rice, yoghurt, and the one vegetable that he would concede to eat, aubergine.

Then at a high society party in Canada he saw a Buddhist lama in a wet tunic step onto a snowy patio to meditate. While he sat in the freezing cold the incredible heat his body emitted dried his clothes.

My grandfather was so impressed by the feat that, in a shocking turn-around, he became a vegetarian. He sat unmoving for hours chanting, '*Om Mani Padme Hum.*' Om Jewel in the Lotus.

'Who are you? Sit very still and suddenly see yourself looking down at yourself. If you do it really fast, and without warning, you will catch yourself unwittingly. You will see what the knower, your soul, observes. A stranger.'

Many months later he felt a flaming sensation in his loins and pelvic region. For a few days the terrible burning persisted, but when it was gone, my grandfather could see people in a very special way, with colours around them.

'*Satchitananda,* God exists,' he told me. 'He will dilute himself into any soup you care to drink.'

As if his eyes were suddenly opened he saw me with my troubles, with the wrong colours swirling hatefully around me. Until then he had taken me into his room and encouraged me to meditate with him, but now he said, 'That which is coiled can strike back if awakened. First the boy must throw away his rage.' He wanted to know why I was so furious with my father, but I would not, could not tell him.

And then the political troubles of Kenya started and our entire family fled to London. So much land and so many valuables had to be left behind, but my father with great acumen invested everything he had managed to bring over into the hotel industry. He had a good business head and the business prospered. Soon he had acquired three for the family chain.

I found insidious rebellion came easy to me. I turned away from the subjects that my parents were especially proud of, maths, biology, physics and chemistry. I let them drop by the wayside, and found new interest in art and poetry. If you could have seen the disappointment in my father's face, you would have understood the pleasure I derived in giving up my best subjects. So I began to sculpt. First I simply sculpted blocks with holes in them. I did it to annoy, to be banal, unoriginal and useless, but they thought my efforts were logical attempts to understand form. So I took to painting. Here my rage found its outlet.

I painted my father. I disguised him sometimes with masks, sometimes using only one feature of his face. I painted him in a variety of demeaning poses. Unsatisfied, I slapped an apron on his ageing body. And then I began to pile bodies on him. My paintings were waterfalls of nudes, each a study of agonised faces. Some were downright obscene, and the critics were quick to rip my art to bits, but help came from an unexpected source. The agony in my faces was mistaken for pleasure.

I was knocking on the same door my father had knocked on. My paintings were selling as fast as porn on the gay market. How laughable! At parties gay men began to proposition me openly, those that did not, sent silent smouldering appeals. I noticed something weird, that gay men, *all of them*, had very beautiful eyes, often with long thick eyelashes. 'Try me,' their beautiful eyes said. 'Hey, it's dark in the closet. Come out, you know you're one of us.'

I stared back at them boldly, smiling mysteriously. I did not say yes, but I was careful not to say no. I even went to some of their parties. Rooms full of plotting, screaming sluts and Kylie Minogue blaring in the background. Did they imagine I did not know what they did? Filthy pigs. I knew about the towel soaking with brown slime. Sometimes I was even tempted to give the more persistent ones my father's number, but no, I did not succumb. I was very, very careful never to let them see my disgust for their kind.

With the money I inherited from my grandfather I bought a house in South Kensington. The living room with its beautiful tall bay windows I turned into my studio. I was picking up something of a cult status. I couldn't paint fast enough, but in my heart I knew I was a fraud. I was no painter. I was only a child trying to punish his parents. Secretly I agreed with the critics. My work was no good.

One day my father came to see my work. He had developed a nervous habit of biting the inside of his left cheek. He pushed his cheek against his teeth and ground it. It was the physical manifestation of his guilt. So many years of hiding such a turbulent secret, leading his double life. Dodging disgust. He stood brooding before each one, silent, his teeth grinding furiously, and when he was finished he turned to me, not ashamed and sorry as I had intended him to be, but in utter anguish.

'Some children we are given for our good deeds, and some for our sins,' he whispered hoarsely.

Then he walked out of my house, his feet dragging on the wooden floor, his head bent; a dirty old man with a collapsed cheek. He had seen in the jigsaw of my work pieces of himself. Now he knew, but he saw with the eyes of a philistine. Do the people in an art gallery filing past a glass case with a calf sawn in half and pickled in brine really believe that they are the shocked witnesses to brutality? They are only fools titillated for an instant by what they imagine is violence. Like my father. They see what they want to.

My father saw the violence and the mockery he wanted to see, but not the unspeakable agony of my soul. For one second, watching him walk out of my door, I wanted to call him back, take him by the hand and show him the difference. Teach him the unspoken language of art. It is a secret known only to the artist, sometimes his harshest critic, but almost never to the buyer.

That real violence is usually hidden inside a painting of a naked virgin waiting on a stretch of grass, a basket of beautiful white tulips by her side. In that delicate innocent smear of soft pink, therein lies danger. It must have been chilly if tulips were in season. There are other clues. Picasso was not violent he was simply selfish, greedy and ugly, the mad thick strokes of Goya, that's just frustration, the encrustations of Van Gogh, yes that's madness, the grinning false teeth of Bacon, that's unspeakable soul pain. For real insidious violence, you have to take another look into the paintings done by the repressed gentlemen of the Victorian age. If you don't find the cold, cold menace I speak of, knock on my door one day, and I will take you by the hand to any art gallery, and show you the face of real violence.

I didn't call out to the departing back.

I just carried on wasting my life painting those vulgar pieces of despair.

Then I met Swathi.

'Swathi means star,' she informed me with a laugh, but I already knew that. Like me, she was of Indian extraction, but unlike me she was HIV positive. I met her in Tramp just as I was getting ready to leave. Dressed in a minuscule black dress and lacy hold-up stockings that did not meet the hem of her dress, she was sitting cross-legged on a table under a pool of red light, regaling the group seated around with some anecdote.

Arrested by something in her I moved closer.

Saw the group break into laughter, saw her grab a man's head and pour champagne from a bottle straight down his throat. Saw the group hoot with more laughter. I stared at her, until she turned her head, and met me in the reddish light. She smiled the saddest smile I ever saw. I walked up to her, helped her down from the table and, pulling her close, came to two conclusions. She was very tall, and slight, too slight. Against my body I felt all the tiny protruding bones in hers. I took her home and we sat in the kitchen, drinking coffee and talking. She was full of life and dying. 'I married an American, a closet homosexual,' she said.

Ah, betrayal.

The next morning I put her on the window sill of my studio. She reminded me of the rich shades of autumn, from her burnt-sugar eyes, and riverweed, russet skin, to the clever yellow-leaf streaks her hairdresser had slipped into her hair. With the sun glinting on her rust coloured fingernails, I slipped my thumb through my wooden pallette and for the first time in my life began to paint a woman, a beautiful woman.

I painted her charcoal eyelashes so long that sad shadows fell upon her cheeks. It made her look gaunt, the way she was, and other-worldly, the way she soon would be. And I painted as I never had. When I stood back and looked at my work I could not recognise it. The chance to be a mediocre painter was gone, denied. Something brown and beautiful slept upon my canvas. I had found my muse. Melpomene, the muse of tragedy.

My pink period was over.

Slowly, slowly, one by one I took her clothes off. Unaccustomed to passionless nakedness she clutched at her breasts defensively. But I kissed her closed eyelids, and whispered that every single inch of her was beautiful to my eyes. Could she not see that she would be sheer magic on my canvas?

'Look at me,' I begged. She opened her eyes and they were wide with her inner world. How complex and intriguing. I kissed her shoulder and removed her skirt. She did not resist. Afterwards I let my lips rest on the curve of her hips. She lay naked on the wooden floor unmoving.

'Oh, Swathi,' I sighed. The disease is inside you. I must hurry.

Swathi the star. In a drawer I found the old velvet pouch my grandmother had given me. Did that amazing woman know all those years ago I would need a bag of silver stars one day? I emptied the tiny silver stars by Swathi's naked body. They made a glittering heap. When I looked into her eyes they were gleaming with wonder.

'Look how long they've waited to touch a real star,' I whispered. One by one I put the stars in her hair. Many times I kissed her gently. 'Beautiful,' I murmured absently, but all the time her nakedness reminded me of when I had hidden in the cupboard choking with the reek of moth balls to peep out of a tiny crack between the doors, at a group of women washing my grandmother's still corpse. In complete silence they rubbed lime halves on her body. They rubbed so hard I was terrified her skin would come off. It was so long ago. Who knows why I keep such an ugly memory so fresh. Be gone.

'My own very beautiful Swathi.' Now it is your turn.

I painted her with the stars in her hair and a hand still covering her desolate breasts. One morning while I was painting I told her about my father. For the first time my secret was out.

'Do you not feel grateful that he spared your mother?' she asked. Apparently since she had adopted a saintly attitude towards her husband's betrayal, I was expected to do the same. I wondered where her fury was. I did not completely believe that sweet sad smile buried nothing. Unless hers was not a complete deception. Perhaps Swathi had married for a green card.

'It is society's fault that you and I suffer. If we didn't pros-ecute, discriminate and show our utter contempt for the way they are made, for what they cannot help, they wouldn't have to hide, lie and pretend, would they? Your father wouldn't have hurt you, and my husband wouldn't have married me. They would have done what their heart really wanted. What if it was the other way around? What if you were considered the one with the odd sexual preference? What if society forced you to have sex with a man?'

I stopped painting in mid-stroke. I felt betrayed. She had taken his side. Quietly I fetched another canvas and I painted her like an adder hiding in the sand, only her eyes visible, watching and waiting to strike, to murder. I had spoken once more, using the language of my art. But she only smiled. Angry, I painted her, mouth red and wanton, copulating sinuously with an enormous purple and green python. Still she smiled.

So I refused to paint her any more. I put my brushes away and sulked. Until one day I saw her, still without rage, her eyes open, her thin legs stretched in front of her, begin to die. The leaves were falling off my autumn tree. She was dying from a disease that only affects pigeons. It was her deficient immune system that allowed it. It was me. I had wanted to see Melpomene with a sword in one hand, and a pigeon in the other.

Oh, that disease ravaged her quickly. In a month her delicate body was so wasted she could not even sit on the window seat. I brought my canvases upstairs to the bedroom to paint her dying in my bed. I only stopped to feed us, and give her her medication. One day she began to talk, first about her grandmother, then her mother and poor father. I knew then she was giving herself away, piece by piece.

I learned of a rich and fierce woman who married her ugly, downtrodden son to the most beautiful girl in the village. I learned about the dutiful daughter-in-law who had to keep her eyes downcast at all times. Until one day the fierce mother-in-law died, and the beautiful woman raised her head, and showed her own fierce and terrible eyes. She will be the new power in the house. The husband was sent to pick coconuts like a servant. He may no longer enter the house through the front door. And the little daughter they shared, once she was slapped so hard she flew across a room.

The daughter ran away and married a gay dancer in an American dance troupe. She had never returned since. Now there was a longing in her sunken eyes. To see once more the hunched figure of her father, to call once more that beautiful fierce woman, Ama. I saw it in her eyes. Unspoken. But I could not let her go. Not now. Not when I was so inspired.

I remembered seeing a painting by Pierre Bonnard. He painted his wife as she died. The colours and the strokes slowly becoming hysterical. Remember the secret language of art. The price was high but the opportunity was price-less. Yes, in his terrible excitement, he began to use blue in her skin. Never taking his gaze off her dulling eyes, the downward pull of her mouth; he recorded everything. More than sadness he was filled with the most intense curiosity, to watch her dying. Record it on his canvas. Now I too was filled with the terrible desire to watch a star die. More and more she resembled death.

A sleeping skeleton.

Sometimes I looked at her sleeping, so still, so thoroughly embalmed, that I was surprised when she opened her eyes. Once I gently parted her clothes, and stood looking at her breasts. They were shrunken, unused, unloved, the areoles blackened and ugly with dying. Suddenly she opened her eyes, and we stared at each other until I couldn't face her gaze any more. I had broken something irreplaceable. I slunk away, ashamed.

One morning I found her standing in front of my canvas, staring at my painting.

'Do you like it?' I asked.

She placed her palm on her face in the painting and, very deliberately, slid her hand down the wet paint.

'Why?' I asked. Shocked. I thought it very good.

'I don't look like that. I am not dead yet, Anis. Remember it is nothing before you join me.' She turned around to look at me. Her eyes were resentful. The days had aged her. It occurred to me then that she loved me. And that she did look 'like that'. Exactly like that. What would this room be without her? I closed my eyes. I saw the sun streaming from the window and the dust particles suspended in its beam. The sheets, the way they crumpled on the empty bed, and my eyes snapped open.

'What's the matter?' she asked.

'Nothing,' I said furiously. I wanted to miss nothing. I must miss nothing. There was death. Coming to fetch you wherever you are.

When she realised I would never willingly let her go, these words seeped out of her cracked mouth: 'Take me back to my mother's bed. Don't let me die here. You never wanted me anyway.'

I took her back to the wooden shack in Kerala. Her father ran out from a field of coconut trees to greet us. He was a tiny, bow-legged, ugly man in a dirty loincloth. Once the weak son of a rich woman, now a coconut picker. Bowing and scraping, tears running down his face, he stood bleak before his fading daughter.

'Ama,' he croaked in the most pitiful voice.

His shaking hands moved towards her, but they did not dare touch her. Then her mother came out. She was decked in gold. Her brilliant blue sari shimmered as she walked towards us. Around her she had gathered the essence of crushed roses, but no one had told her that her once exquisite beauty was obscured by the worldly dust that had settled over her face. Wordlessly her hennaed hands took over, and helped her daughter in.

The father stood outside, his chocolate arms crossed over his jutting rib bones, and looked longingly into the house, as if he were an untouchable. A villager came running with water caught in a bottle from the Ganges River, procured at source, high up on the Himalayan mountain.

'The holy water will cure the child,' he said respectfully, his sun-blackened hands holding forth the sacred gift.

Then there was some mention of black lentil samosas, but when I saw her on her mother's bed, and heard her say, 'Ahh, my dear, dear Anis, don't you know every separation is a new opportunity,' it made me feel sick. I stumbled away and almost collided into her mother.

The woman's eyes were narrow with accusation. 'Have you taken too much from my daughter?' she asked quietly. The worldly dust shifted as if teased by a breeze and some fell to the ground.

I stared at her.

'When my daughter was little, she once went into a sweet shop and tried to give away her gold bangle in exchange for a piece of candy. That was probably the only man who ever refused her generosity.'

I felt the blood rush into my face. Ah, the shame . . .

I made some feeble excuse and returned to England to paint her day and night from memory. Big ambitious canvases that I covered feverishly, impatiently. The head is very important for scale. I made hers huge. She reclined, unconnected to the landscape, grotesque. I painted those terrible shrunken breasts. Those bits of her that I had promised with my eyes I would never paint. It was cruel to attack a dying creature, and yet the impulse was impossible to ignore. I was furious with her. How dare she accuse me of selfishness? How dare she blame me for her destruction?

You never wanted me anyway. I applied thick paint quickly with a chisel. I found that exact shade of her skin by adding a touch of French ultramarine to cadmium red, titanium white, yellow ochre and burnt sienna. It was revenge. Every separation is a new opportunity. How dare you? The shadows under her cheeks worked best with sap green. Ahh, my dear, dear Anis. No, you will not. I painted her in the jaws of a lion. Her skin-and-bone body in a slinky red dress. Offering flowers. With her back to me. Her wings spread out.

I cursed the light as it went out but I did not stop.

Until one day there was a reverse-charge call from India. It was one of her aunts. Her niece had died with my name on her lips, the last thing the child had called for was me. I had never called or written to her. Not once. She lay heavy in my arms. So heavy I longed to put her down, but there was nowhere to lay her. I cleaned my brushes. I was done.

A week later a letter arrived from her. But she was dead. I tore it open. It was dated from three weeks back. She wrote that she was feeling very good. Perhaps I will come to see you, she had written. If not for this tiredness, I feel as if I don't have this virus. Maybe not. Please God. Maybe not. Write soon, please, she begged. My only job is to wait for the mail.

The letter crumpled in my closing fist.

I exhibited in the Serpentine. It seemed I had arrived, with my paintings of Swathi. I was the critics' darling. The toast of the art world. Serious New York collectors thought my work beautiful.

I saw only the merciless cruelty. So did the critics. Remember, the secret language. I had thought I was angry with her, but in truth I had begun to loathe myself. For the first time I stood back from my creations and saw what she had seen when she smeared that painting and said, 'I am not dead yet.' I had abused her. I was a brute.

There was a chill wind blowing when I fell into a drinking spell.

I sent a large cheque to the father, and although I received by return a pathetically grateful letter I still exhibited the painting of his daughter copulating with the green and purple python, titled, 'Remember It Is Nothing Before You Join Me'. They slapped a ridiculous price on it, but it was the first to sell.

I felt more a fraud than ever, but I drank the champagne they served, and kept an appropriately enigmatic expression. The smear of my guilt went unnoticed. Drink in hand, I turned away from one gushing face, towards another congratulatory voice, my cheek muscles moved, and I smiled. I had learned well the only lesson my father taught me, grin and bear it.

When I was fourteen it had been impossible to express my shock, and now it was uncool to express my sorrow. Caged, it turned on me and began to eat my insides. When all was quiet at night, I heard it feeding voraciously, but I could not feel it. Sometimes I jerked awake, my fists clenched.

I couldn't bear to paint any more. I took up poetry. I drank a whole bottle of wine, and held my pen poised over a clean sheet of paper. Nothing. I dropped the pen and abandoned poetry writing. It felt odd not to want to pick up a paint brush, but it did not hurt. No one knew about my painter's block. I was the toast of my field. An enigma that intrigued men and women alike. I wore the perfume of success, and everywhere I went a great many people raised their eyes, seduced by my heady scent. I spent my days sleeping and my nights partying. There was always something happening, a new restaurant or club opening, a book launch, an art exhibition.

During one glittering event a sly man told me about a very special courtesan. 'There is nothing she will not do to give pleasure. Her refinement must be seen to be believed. None of that undressing straight away to speed up the erection business. Her name is Chandni and she is a disciple of Vatsyayana's *Kamasutra*. As a greeting the wonderful creature curls herself until her fingers can part her own buttocks,' he paused and looked at me gleefully, 'this she does so she can respectfully kiss her own anus, to show her client that no part of the body is disgusting or dirty. Everything and everything is permissible. . .'

He slipped a matt silver card into my shirt pocket. 'And then the goddess will, if asked, bend forward and kiss your arse too. But let me warn you. She is dangerous. She performs a dance called the enticement of the lotus. That alone will turn you into the most miserable addict. Mind you,' he said, 'the slut costs her weight in gold.'

I was angry with his familiarity and yet a dusky, sloe-eyed vision kept me still and silent.

Chandni, moonlight.

My grandmother had left a lingering enchantment for moonlight. 'Listen, listen to the moonlight. Its light will turn your limbs to fluid, and your head, your arms, your legs will dance in time with her voice.' I thought of cheeks smooth and curving, hair as black as the night. When she raised downcast eyes they would be huge with unspoken whispers. Yes, I decided to help myself to a little moonlight. I arranged an assignment with my Indian vision.

She opened the door and my heart sank.

I stared at the blonde, blue-eyed, almost plain woman. How dare she call herself moonlight? There was nothing of her that was mysterious or enchanted. When she told me I was early but enter anyway I realised that she was American to boot. She had applied too much black eyeliner and her eyes, like her accent, stood out, false and separate from her beautiful mystical name. She nodded and indicated with a tiny move-ment of her fingers that I should follow her. As she led the way down the narrow hallway I caught glimpses of her naked body through the long diaphanous blue gown she wore.

She turned her head slightly towards me, 'It can happen that in pursuing profit one tastes loss.' In her nasal accent I recognised Vatsyayana's words, and became uneasy, but she was pointing towards a tray arranged with interwoven betel nut leaves. I placed the agreed price on top of the leaves. She opened the door and I entered. 'I will only be a moment,' she said.

The door closed with a gentle click.

There was a sound of a sitar playing gently in the background. I looked around me. Painted in shades of the darkest green, fragranced with sandalwood essence and lit with many clay lamps, the room transposed one into a completely different world. By the side of an elaborately carved four-poster bed stood a lifesize statue of an Indian dancer. A lazy fan made the gossamer pink and white drapes flutter gently onto the figure. There was a dark green rug in the middle of the room. All the window shutters were closed, but beyond must have been a garden; from it came the tinkling of metal wind chimes.

There was someone else in the house. I could smell roasting coconut.

The door opened and she slipped in. And in that magical room she too was transformed. We travelled back in time. We were in the secret bedroom of a Raja's daughter. In the flicker of the many oil lamps her face glowed a warm gold. She came closer to stand on the green mat. An old-fashioned, nearly familiar fragrance drifted around her.

She wore a *chudamani*, a head ornament made of fine filigree leaves and butterflies. There were huge velvety red flowers in her hair. Around her neck a *harsaka*, a serpent-shaped choker. Two strings of the biggest *rudraksh* beads I have ever seen held up a gold breastplate. *Hestali* bangles encircled her forearms and bracelets of carved elephants moved on her wrists. There were rings a-plenty on her fingers and toes. From a thick belt of dull gold, engraved with fornicating couples, a fabulous curtain of silver beads dropped until the ground was attained. Adorned from head to toe in metal she whispered, '*Takht ya takhta?*' Throne or coffin.

'*Takhta,*' I replied. Coffin.

Surprised by her appearance and the strange query, I had answered without thinking. She was offering the law that had once ruled the behaviour of the ruthless Mogul dynasty. I should have said throne – for unlimited pleasure.

An eyebrow rose quietly but she only smiled. Everything is interesting, permissible.

'Mmm . . . could be what you deserve, but not here. Not now. Not when the throne is paid for,' she said and opened her fists. Petals fell to the ground. She was right. The throne was paid for, long before she even set eyes on me. My hands were as bloody as the most hideous Mogul emperor. In my court, I cruelly tortured and killed a beautiful star. I deserved this.

Chandni lay down on the rug in front of me. Hundreds of silver beads parted and pooled around her naked legs. It was a beautiful sight. She raised her waist and legs gracefully, until they were perpendicular to her body. I had not noticed before that her hands and feet were dyed a deep red. She let the soles of her feet touch so the dye on her feet joined to make a beautiful red circle.

Then she curled her torso up, until her head was touching her thighs. As I watched she parted her legs wide, and bent her head into her spread buttocks. Slowly, lingeringly, she kissed her own anus. When she straightened, strands of blonde hair curtained her heated face. She looked at me through the fair hair. And I had thought she was not beautiful!

Flushed, she was utterly beautiful, with eyes that coaxed the sullen. I was suddenly aroused in a way never before. A large and beautiful dog came into the room. She knelt by the dog's face, and watched me carefully. Everything and everything is permissible. I stayed silent.

I was not there for that. 'Go,' she said and the dog padded away noiselessly. She turned her back to me and began to fill an antique, copper instrument with hot water. She dried it with a cloth, her strokes long, smooth and deliberate, until it glowed in her hand. She left the smooth object on the ground, to wait. Useless until it is five degrees above body temperature. Then she turned around to stare at me. I stared back. Her plans were secret.

She was the mistress of the sixty-four methods of love.

She released a little knot in the *rudraksh* bead chain that held her breastplate and it came apart in her hand. She opened a small tub of some perfumed cream and started to rub her breasts. They were small but perfect. Indeed everything about her was flawlessly concentrated towards a secret purpose. I understood. She was a mirror. She reflected back everything she saw. Her nails were dangerously long, burnished gold, and sharpened not just to a point, but two, and sometimes even three.

I watched, mesmerised, as the razor-sharp points skimmed, touched and lightly scratched the pink and white skin. I saw her lift her chin and shut her eyes, and when she opened them I was travelling on the glinting waters of a canal. Inside a window, in the distance, two gorgeous Murano chandeliers blazed. How beautiful was this place of exile she offered! It conspired with the aspects of me that needed rehabilitation.

She reached out her left hand and pulled at the nail of her middle finger. It came off easily. It was false. There was just enough professional pride in her eyes to excite a desire for her skilled paid touch. She was a body any man could enter, and yet there was something completely inaccessible about her. Wordlessly she dipped the blunt finger into a tiny crystal jar. Coconut oil. Dripping oil on the wooden floor, she glided towards me, a certain violence in her eyes. I froze. Inside me was revolt. Horrible shame and uncontrollable excitement.

Oh, she knew me. How well she knew me, what I had come for. In her glittering eyes I saw that I was no better than my father.

I took to walking in the worst storms. When the winds howled outside and freezing rain lashed angrily, I walked into it. As if its fury would move some numb part of me. I knew I was damaged. Beyond repair.

One night while I was slowly and with utter dedication getting drunk in Tramp, I saw a man on his back on the dance floor, making a spectacle of himself, pretending to be a dying bug. He was blond, good-looking, and dressed in the colours of the eighties, a black top, a bright green jacket, jeans and a pair of black and white shoes. I decided he could only be Italian. The other dancers had stopped to watch him. At a table in a corner a group of beautiful people were clapping and cheering him on, 'Go, Ricky, go.'

Their table was a mess of champagne bottles, cocktail jugs and too many glasses. It was perfectly obvious they were an exclusive sneaky lot. They had invested in an utterly clever plan, they wore a second skin of sin to disguise the grossness of their rotting wounds. It was Alice in Wonderland, *rats in the coffee and mice in the tea. Baked me too brown? Just sugar my hair*. To my desperate soul they looked like they were brewing up a wild and wonderful storm.

My artist eye studied them, intoxicated. What lay behind the untroubled laughter?

The most stunning of them all was an aloof platinum blonde. She was beautiful in a flawless way, though you could tell by her quick eyes, that she was no bimbo. I knew her type, cold to the core and high maintenance. They were the women who demanded clothes, jewellery, cars, houses, properties and got them.

Beside her was another very beautiful girl, very fair skin and a cascade of brown curls. She tilted her head back and laughed, but she was really somewhere else, somewhere quite sad. I felt it instantly; she sold her body for bread.

Next to her was a hard, tough, obviously successful businessman. He wanted the platinum blonde, but she was having none of it.

On the next two stools sat what can only be described as a fantasy, Oceanic twins, each with the rounded face of those beautiful Indian statues. They were both dressed in black, and identical in every way. But one dazzled, and the other was transparent. As if she was the shadow, or the residue of her twin.

The shadow's almond eyes met mine and quickly darted away. How interesting. In that split second her dark, dark eyes told me she was completely without knowledge. An innocent. I was intrigued. How did innocence hold its ground mixed in with corrupt blood? After nearly a year of not even being able to pick up a paint brush I itched to paint her. Actually it was more than that. I wanted the transparent one for myself. I had not wanted Swathi. I had only wanted to paint her. This non-person I wanted to keep for myself.

Her skin beckoned; so absolutely without flaw or blemish, it was as if she belonged in a Gustav Boucher oil painting. Not the beautiful odalisque, but the slave holding up the mirror, her native eyes turned away from yours.

The reptilian bit of my brain took over, and I became excited by the prospect of the rest of my night.

So I followed the rabbit and fell into the hole, into the riot, never once considering how in the world I was to get out again. I went to introduce myself. The platinum beauty was Elizabeth, the sad-eyed girl Maggie, the dazzling laughing twin was Nutan, and the quiet shadow Zeenat. Little Zeenat. You will be mine.

The black and white shoes prowled towards me. He had dangerous wolf eyes. When he smiled they crinkled at the corners. Each feature considered separately could describe ugly, but arranged together they gained some crazy synergy and made a face of irresistible sensuality. It had been a long while since I had come face to face with such blatant sexuality in a straight man. He grinned and said something about a spider's temper.

At first I thought I had misheard, but the hard, tough, obviously successful businessman stepped forward, his hand outstretched and said, 'Bruce Arnold. Yeah, come with us to The Spider's Temple. You never know, you might even like it.'

Bruce Arnold

Bruce

Earliest memories?

That would be a toss up between a wet dream featuring the three Supremes in their heyday (oh the barefaced hussies) or standing on a chair using half a bottle of Fairy Liquid to obsessively wash and re-wash my plate, knife and fork *before* using them. My mother reckoned I was a troubled kid and packed me off to a psychiatrist. A fat lot of good it did me. He made it too easy – let me know the answers he wanted to hear – and now, at thirty-one nothing has changed. I'm still undressing them in threes, and as squeamish as ever at the least sign of filth or imperfection.

We lived in a humble terrace block around the corner from a council estate in the East End. My mother, originally from leafy Surrey, loathed her new address and was the object of much ridicule amongst the gossip mongers in the Laundromat. I suppose you couldn't really blame them, she did ask for it by referring to them as 'the locals'. To give her her due, she *was* different. She spoke different, kept her figure incredibly well, wore light dresses with little sleeves in summer, owned a real china tea set, and knew milk came after tea.

Her real interest was in befriending the old rich widows who lived in the houses on the tree-lined streets a few minutes up, but she soon discovered that her small-town snobbery was nothing compared to theirs. The sly bags wormed it out of my sister that my mother was an impostor. Her posh accent was only borrowed from the masters my grandmother cleaned or kept house for.

God, how utterly ferocious they were in their efforts to keep their pathetic circle pure. If they admitted the outsider to their little tea parties, where finger sandwiches were served on three-tiered plates lined with doilies, and cakes on glass stands, it was only so their thin condescending mouths could talk down to her, patronise her, and make her run errands like a servant. Why, I hated the stuck-up bitches.

I still remember on the chance of better pickings standing at the end of their street with my sister's rag doll in a wheelbarrow, when Prunella Woolridge's shapeless figure stomped to a halt in front of me. Her face was like a brick wall.

'Penny for the Guy?' I chanced, smiling sweetly. Most people would have thought it was cute, but not her. She glowered down from a great height and employing her fruitiest, most pompous voice said, 'Certainly not. Is your mother aware you are begging for money in the streets?'

'Yeah,' I shot back without missing a beat, lying through my teeth.

She sniffed huffily and marched off. Although I mouthed, 'Miserable old bag,' to the departing back, and resumed my begging, I never really forgot the way she made me feel for those few moments when she looked at me with such contempt. As if she was talking to my mother. I sometimes think that was the beginning of the nagging mixture of shame and pity I felt for my mother. Too often I viewed her less with affection than with curiosity. What made her tick? Why did she put herself through such torture? Why did she stay with my surly father? Not that he ever hit her of course.

When I remember my father, I remember only his eyes. Black, slightly narrowed, sometimes glazed, but always flinty. He was a huge, solidly built man with a deft hand at a belt. I suppose now you would call it abuse, but then he was just 'very strict'. Especially with my sister. Still he did it with the best intention. He didn't want her knocked up like all the other teenage girls in the estate. 'Babies pushing babies,' he used to mutter whenever he saw one of them behind a pram.

It would be easy to knock the man down, betray him in a moment, but if it wasn't for him I wouldn't have even the little education I have. I'd just have dropped out at fifteen like all the other kids on the block, doomed to failure even before they started. When he became ill, and half blind with diabetes, by unspoken consent we made a pact to 'forget' the past. I went to sit with him by the fireside in the evenings. I adjusted the blankets over his knees, and read to him. Funny, isn't it? That we who claimed to love him best should prefer him in his diminished state. The beast without teeth deserved a closer inspection. Through it all we had each nourished a secret fascination to pet the beast.

When I was very young I remember staying at Nan's whenever she wasn't mansion-keeping for Lord Haslem, or cleaning Sir Humphrey's manor. My grandparents lived in a small terraced house in Staines. I don't remember much about Grandad, except he was cheap. He sat on the best chair in the front room, hogging the fire and the television. And because he never thought to move away from the news or sports programmes, Nan saved for years, and bought a little portable for the top of her kitchen counter. Every time he heard me going to the downstairs toilet he called out, 'Don't be using more than two squares now, Junior.' That was toilet paper he was referring to. If he was being generous it wasn't a pack of mints that he handed out, but a single one.

Nan told my mother that the very first time he had taken her on a date he had made her pay for her own bus fare. I could never understand why she didn't just cut and run then because my nan was the best. She tidied other people's mess, cleaned their bathrooms, polished their banisters and emptied their bins, but there was something special inside her head. If she had been born in my time she could have been the CEO of a Fortune 500 company. My mother told me that Nan had once opened her front door to two small-time thieves. Jittery drug addicts with short knives in their hands. She immediately threw herself to the ground and screamed, 'Herbert, quick, let the Alsatians out.' And the two nervous robbers panicked and ran for their dear lives, but there was no Herbert and no Alsatians, just my mother and her in the house.

From a giant bag she poured a pint glass full of penny sweets each for my sister and me. Humming under her breath she went about her business while we sat at the kitchen table watching cartoons on her portable, and working through our pints. Yes, I remember the old bird well.

I remember, too, first day at school. Bawling my eyes out, screaming blue murder with all the other kids, but my mother was a lot smarter than other mums. 'I'll get dinner ready for when I come to pick you up.'

'All right then. See you soon.'

But Mum's Laundromat was my schoolyard. The cultivated accent that my mother was so proud of set me apart. The other kids were vicious. They wanted blood. 'Ooo, pass the butter, please,' they aped, exaggerating each vowel. They wanted the 't's out. B-er not butter. Ga-eau not gateau. More than a pint of blood was lost in the war of the 't's before genetics kicked in, and my father's barrel-chested frame became mine. Suddenly I was bigger than all the rest of the lads. I could beat anybody. Inside my solid fists, butter remained butter, and gateau kept its 't', East End not withstanding.

Glaring out of narrow black eyes and my nose broken in so many places I looked like an old convict, I picked up street cred. Suddenly it was cool to talk posh and I gained a bunch of followers: Paddy, Bonehead, George, Dwayne and Jelly. Jelly is not his real name, but the Chinese girl serving at the local chippy couldn't pronounce 'r'. In our time we took no prisoners. And when you are young and tough, the girls are for the taking. And that's what we did. Had a bit of whatever we fancied.

It feels like an age ago, though. I suppose I recall it with a kind of sad affection. My friends have all become what you would probably call losers. It seems they are always one or the other serving time for petty crimes, or getting right royally screwed in deals too big for their shoes. But in them days we were inseparable companions; rough and fiercely loyal. Oh! The fights we got into, getting home shit-faced from the Turks Arms. I can still remember Paddy shirtless on the sidewalk, loose at the knees, the muscles in his neck straining like wire, oozing blood from his forehead and snarling, 'Come on then, afraid are ya?' while two huge thugs circled him, spewing obscenities, and swinging broken bottles. That was Paddy for you. Crazy bastard.

I tended to fight a cold fight. Catch them unaware.

One by one my mates were dropping out of school and, to be friendly, I joined them after my O levels. There was nothing my father could say or do, his downward slide was already in progress. My grades were bad anyway. Fighting and whoring are not conducive to good grades. Even the idea of a nine-to-five bored me stiff. For a while I messed about with the guys as they tried different scams, but the good deals were thin on the ground. And inevitably the guys started running with small-time crooks, shifting drags, driving cars in from Europe, the tyres crammed with all kinds. Their garages were full of slashed tyres. I knew it was dangerous, and the risks they took didn't sit well with me, but after a while I went along with it. It was good money.

One time I was driving through Earls Court with Paddy when he muttered under his breath, 'Oh shit, pigs.' I looked up and ahead was a police road block. The boot was packed with drums of illegal chemicals. No, they didn't get us that time. They let our car through without checking, but that was it for me. No more runs, it was too high a price to pay.

Then one morning I woke up grey, with the most God-awful hangover, and knew without a shadow of a doubt what I really wanted. I wanted to be a hairdresser. The guys looked at me in disbelief. Had I gone soft in the head? Was I taking the first tentative steps towards a life of pillow biting? I sure took a lot of stick. But I didn't care. It was the only thing that had ever held any real fascination for me. From the time I was a child when Nan first took me with her to the hairdresser's, I had been in awe of that secret wonderful world that men hadn't a clue about.

She pushed open a glass door and suddenly we were in this divine-smelling garden of women. There were no men there, just all kinds of women stopping by to be pruned and trimmed. The soothing chatter of the blue-rinse brigade, the comforting warmth and drone of hair dryers, and the trans-formations. I sat big-eyed and watched one woman until, after one last preening, delighted glance into the mirror, she sailed out of the door, and then I let my eye rest on the next pretty one. And so it went. It was like being in a sweet shop. I saw the quiet pride with which Nan gently patted her immaculate white helmet and asked, 'What do you think, Buba?' I wanted to be responsible for that.

Also I thought I might have a knack for it. I would look at a woman on the street, and know instinctively if her hair-style didn't complement her face.

The diploma was a piece of cake. I started work with a local hairdresser, Mr Wong, a paunchy Chinese man with spiky black hair. I was nineteen when my fighting fists unclenched for a bit of clean wet hair, and I found myself asking, 'Going anywhere nice tonight?' It was a bit of a shock to realise that I could actually reach out and help myself to the merchandise in the sweet shop. I rushed back with news for the guys; it was an amazing pick-up joint. I came on to the best lookers, and tried to fix up the ones that didn't quite make my grade with the rest of the guys. We did a lot of double-dating then.

Very quickly I learned what worked and what didn't. Most girls needed romance and cuddles before they would consent to grace my bed, but more and more I was finding exquisite dames who knew better; who wanted to skip the boring lies. I had my weaknesses. Like the length of a leg, a shoulder that didn't slope, slanting green eyes, a mole around the mouth, and yes, oh yes, long hair. Every time a girl with really long hair came through the door my temperature went up. I had a theory. Any woman who aspired to emphasise the difference between her sex and mine had to have no 'off' switch. No red button worth obeying. Green all the way. She had what the Zen masters termed a fox problem. Something I knew all about. Unless of course she was of Indian extraction, then the opposite could well be true.

So there I was going through Mr Wong's customers at a nice pace, when he exploded into the salon one day. 'What you think you doing, eh? Jigi Jigi with all my customer? Who you think you are? Bruce Lee. No more woman. You understand. Stupid. Shit where you eat.'

I was smoking a cigarette in the back and I didn't even break my stride. I took one last drag, killed it under the toe of my shoe, shrugged into my jacket and left with a two-fingered salute. Poor Mr Wong, his mouth fell open, but I was nineteen and so too cool to be anything other than a short fuse. I bummed around with my mates, and lost more hairdressing jobs for the same reason, until I was twenty-four years old.

By some dint of luck the guys started working on

something real for a change. They had hooked on to a proper con, operated very professionally by nameless drug kings in Amsterdam and linked to the Russian Mafia. They needed front men, stooges to take the fall if things went wrong. It was to do with importing curtain materials, a shipload of it that didn't actually exist from Russia and a lot of money. On the table for us was two per cent. The stakes were high, but the sting looked and smelt good. Only the insurance company would get ripped off. I called in.

Six months later we were walking away with more money than we had ever seen in our lifetime. A hundred thousand between the five of us. The other guys set about blowing their share. I found a run-down, empty shop lot and converted it into a hairdressing joint. I sort of fancied a small old-fashioned place with posters of glossy fifties movie stars on the walls, and a glass jar of candy by the till, just like the one of my childhood, but a smart PR girl I was dating widened my concept of decor and I went with pseudo Italian. As a finishing touch we plonked a stone bust of a scowling Caesar in the window.

On opening night the gang descended with one of those wooden barrels of Guinness. By the time we were finished, we were lurching over the railings of Bermondsey bridge at dawn, wondering why the Caesar bust was refusing to float down the Thames like the empty barrel. Two days later the guys drew up in a white van and from the back of it sheepishly offloaded a six-foot statue of the Duke of Wellington. They carried it into my salon and stood it by the till. I never asked, but I can only imagine it was lifted off some toffs garden. If ever you've sat in a salon in Bermondsey with a statue in a flat hat and long coat that nearly fills the entire frontage then you have been in my shop.

The shop was a roaring success and it was where I honed my skill to a fine art. I didn't want to date the customers any more and became all heart for poor Mr Wong. There's nothing like standing in a man's shoes to see clearly where he's coming from. The girls were the bread and butter. If any of my hairstylists had tried to use my place as a meat market, I'd have done my nut too. A few times an arresting face would meet me in the mirror, smiling. Then I simply slid my fingers down small sections of hair from either side of her face to check they were completely level and reminded myself again, you don't shit where you eat and you're not Bruce Lee.

And the money, WOW. Every time a woman walked in, it was five pounds towards costs, and everything else, pure profit. If she took to colour, a cool fifty quid profit. It was incredible. I couldn't understand why everybody wasn't in hairdressing. Every evening I cleaned the till of at least half the cash. Spending money. What the Government didn't know about didn't hurt it.

I opened another salon closer to London, entered a competition and was given the privilege of displaying a plaque that read 'Hairdresser of the Year, 1999'. It was a nice gold one. Then somebody approached me about lending my name to their hair care range. The Bruce Arnold range. Twenty pence for every product sold. Brilliant. But I took another look at the figures and said, sod off. Found me a chemist who came up with a complete line of hair products. Each item cost me a pound to manufacture, and I sold them in the shops for six pounds upwards.

At this stage I took a gamble and opened a salon in the middle of pricey London. And boy, was that a whole different ball game or what. Except for the rent, rates and slightly higher wages all my other operating costs remained the same, but my prices, you should have seen them go.

'Well, well,' said the boy from the arse end address. 'Who would have thought?' Delicious, snooty, upmarket girls in cat whiskers' jeans slinging ninety-eight pounds on to Daddy's charge card for a haircut. Poor Daddy, once every six weeks he shelled out another cool half a grand for highlights and treatments. It was crazy, it was brilliant. I learned gratitude, to God. Nice touch, giving the majority of English girls hair in tedious variations of mice. I hired a brilliant hair colourist, a real specialist. He arrived at their chair, his comb at an angle, a swagger in his leather trousers, a silver ring on his thumb; officially gay but flirting outrageously. And the cream thought he was a scream. I might have overpaid him. The guy was high the whole time.

There is so much drug-taking in the hairdressing world. And all at the top where the money is. I went for competitions where celebrity hairdressers you saw on the Sky channels were bent over, snorting cocaine. Don't just believe me. Watch them. Sometimes the bastards can't help themselves; there they are on TV and their lips are stuck to their gums, and their mouths twisted into a neurotic tic. The whole industry is so full of noses crying out for relining with some durable metal you could be mistaken for thinking it was all legal. Can't name names obviously, but watch the ones with the fancy foreign-sounding surnames. They're the cuties.

I never really got into the drug scene. My game had always been to get wasted at the pub with the guys. Nevertheless I had started carrying the gear around because more and more girls were asking for it. Cocaine, I found, had become the greatest babe magnet around. It had the miraculous 'open sesame' effect, third base, first night. Once the offer of a wedding ring might have had the same effect. Then again, perhaps not with quite the same ferocity. I have seen girls kneel in men's toilets and tear open zips in their hurry for a line. Disgusting really, but I was hardly going to complain seeing it was often my zip.

As time went on, I found I too was taking more and more but, oddly enough, without the crazy excitement of everyone else at the party. More with a sense of inevitability. That time of the night again. I did it almost from a growing sense of boredom. There was nothing else better to do.

Quite soon after I opened my fancy salon one of those women I call the St Tropez wives, too brown and too thin in white trousers, came in to the shop. She took off her designer sunglasses and her eyes were the colour of fading bruises. Odd how I felt it, a stranger's sadness, but then she smiled a cool confident smile and the impression was gone.

'Francesca Delgado. I have an eleven-thirty appointment with the head hairstylist,' she said.

'Bruce Arnold,' I said, smiling and holding out my hand. Hers was small and soft. For some time I had wanted to try out a new colour system and I saw that her brown heart-shaped face and long straight hair were perfect. I told her my plan. She nodded. Just make me look beautiful, the two sad bruises in her face said. It was only when her hair was washed that I realised that it was naturally curly. I held the wet curls in my hand. 'Jesus,' I said. 'How long does it take you to blow dry this lot straight?'

'Nearly an hour every other day.' A St Tropez wife with plenty of time to waste.

Very few women actually have the ability to look their best in curls, but I felt if she couldn't then nobody could. I set to work. I coloured it four shades of gold. As they dried the carefully waxed curls became a glorious golden riot. When I was finished I saw her blink in the mirror. She did not turn her head this way and that, like the other women. She simply stared at herself. Why, she didn't look like a hard cold neglected wife any more. She looked breath-takingly young and innocent again. Our eyes met in the mirror and she said, 'No, I don't like it. Redo it straight.'

'You *don't* like it!' I was incredulous. I couldn't convince her. In the end one of the girls straightened her hair to her satisfaction. When it was done she turned her head this way and that like the other women, smiled and thanked me politely.

'You must drop in on my husband. He owns the Italian restaurant along this same street. Villa Ricci.'

No shit, I had been going there for years.

So the next time I went to dinner at Villa Ricci, I asked to speak to the owner, and this huge lion of a man bounded out of the back office grinning sheepishly. It was immediately obvious that he was completely hammered. He explained that he hadn't stopped drinking since the wee hours of the night before. He pulled out a chair, and at the same time ordered aspirins and grappas. He said he had a party to go to in some hotel outside London. The problem was he had lost his licence on a drink-driving charge a month ago. 'It's a Jacuzzi thing. Plenty of bikini honeys high on coke. Can you drive?'

'Sure,' I said and he (bear in mind that that was the first time I had ever laid eyes on the bloke) clapped his hands on either side of my face, pulled me towards him, and deposited a noisy smacker right in the middle of my forehead, crying gaily, 'What luck, what good fortune.'

I was immediately struck by two things: his palm was a sight more callused than mine and that I had no defences against such a foreign display of warmth and exuberance. Right there and then I was lost. You just don't find too many like him walking around. His light shone bigger and brighter than mine.

'Wanna come?' he asked.

Was he kidding? After that? 'Yeah, I'm there,' I said, and we've been hanging around since.

I know he's selfish, obnoxious, vulgar, and doesn't give a shit for anyone else, but I can't help liking the guy. He's a human dynamo. A lurid, restless, jacked-up, big-spending, party animal, fucking his way through the London night scene. Somebody plugged him in many years ago, and he hasn't stopped since. One day we found him unconscious on the floor, and rushed him to hospital. The doctor ran a brain scan and pronounced that there was nothing really wrong with him, just that his brain had shut down to get some rest. The guy hadn't slept for four days.

'Go home and get some sleep,' the doctor advised.

'Nah, I slept inside your scanner,' he said. I thought he was joking until I saw him pop a handful of uppers — he was dead greedy like that — and beg space in a car heading for a rave in Southampton.

You see him under the flashing neon light of a club, dancing on top of a massive speaker, giving it all he's got, and shouting at the top of his voice, 'Oi, Oi'. And you want to label him shallow, but then the crazy fucker picks up his guitar and sings Pink Floyd's 'Hello, Is There Anybody Out There' in that weird throbbing voice of his, and goose pimples will scatter your skin. You will swear then that a beautiful distraught soul haunts his barely civilised body.

And then there is his wicked sense of humour. The jokes he tells. Sometimes I laugh so much I am banging the table with my fists, and dying with the stitch in my stomach. They are all in bad taste, but really funny, and unless you are an Italian restaurateur, you'll never have heard them.

And then, of course, there is his phenomenal ability to pull. I mean, I'm not exactly short of a good-looking bird to hang on my arm, with the hairdressing salon and every-thing, but this guy hauls them in by the truckloads. He is ruthlessly effective.

Although, to be fair to my record, I am a lot fussier than he is. He would bed anything once. He even said, 'The ugly fat ones are the best.' Apparently they try harder. I couldn't. Some of the women that ended up in his bed, ugh, I couldn't even bring myself to touch. I'm afraid we are back to that obsessive use of Fairy Liquid again, washing and re-washing.

Even the slightest suggestion of dirt was enough to send me sprinting in the opposite direction. Why, just looking at crutches made my gut ache. It sounds terrible, but just like they couldn't help their affliction I can't help mine. It was the way I was made. Squeamish. Some things I couldn't do and some I could. I could just about do dandruff. My tolerance certainly didn't extend to scars, crooked bits, amputated limbs, unhealed wounds, and bodily fluids not belonging to me.

But blood I could always do. Even as a child I was okay with that. My mother never tired of telling the story of when I walked away from a game gone wrong into her kitchen, a fork sticking out of my foot, announcing, 'Mum, I've got a fork in my foot.' But there were also other things that I was neurotic about, like watching people brushing their teeth. That actually made me want to be sick. When they did it on TV I had to turn away from the screen.

The Spider's Temple? You think it's some special place, don't you? Well it's not. It's just a depressingly dirty little flat in the middle of London where sad people gather to take drugs. Sometimes when I am filled with the queasy knowledge that I am wasting away my life in a rat hole, I can actually smell the cockroaches that infest the place, and yet I go. I go because every good party eventually ends up there. So many faces come and go, but there are a few 'regulars' that you see almost every time you are there.

One is a dazzling jam pot called Haylee. Masses of blonde hair, not out of a bottle, dream breasts, a bottom to peel your eyes, and the sort of instinctive sexual awareness that turns the job of retrieving something from the floor into a strip show; bending from the hips, nicely padded rear sticking out, body arched forward. All in all a truly tasty package, but she's playing for higher stakes. I believe she has pinned her hopes on bagging a first division footballer. Ricky's had her, though. A long time ago when she was drunk.

Then there is little Maggie, an Irish prostitute who always wears ballet shoes. Once she must have been a stunning beauty, but by the time I met her the body was still smoking, but too much wine and song had worn her face out, and touched her eyes with ugly desperation. When Harold Robbins writes about heroines who screw their way through armies of men, abuse alcohol and drugs at every opportunity and still look good, it is pure fiction. Still I like her. She is funny and warm.

Once we got high and ended up in bed. She undressed me and then ruined it all by sobbing her heart out. 'Love me a little, Bruce,' she begged but my ardour didn't run to it. I couldn't be the next in line to use her. Even I couldn't be that basic. I understood that sex for her was currency and every time she gave it away she was that little bit poorer. So I dried her tears and we drank ourselves silly. I was drunk enough to ask why she wore ballet shoes all the time and she told me the saddest thing. She said that, when she was five years old her grandfather told her only princesses wore ballet shoes.

Then, of course, Ricky met the Balinese twins. Lovely creatures. He started going out with the bold one, and I wouldn't have minded the other, but she made it clear she wasn't playing.

The other really interesting person is the artist, Anis. A slight, brown-skinned, brown-eyed man. Sometimes when he had been up all night, the dark circles under his eyes made his irises seem lighter, almost unreal. In a funny sort of way I am almost envious of him. He hadn't spent his school days drinking stolen gin by the bicycle sheds. He'd had a proper education so when he opened his mouth to talk it was never bullshit.

I was told about another Irish girl called Elizabeth, an Arab billionaire's whore, but I didn't get to meet her straight away. She was away in Saudi Arabia, and was, to quote Ricky at his melodramatic best, 'too beautiful'. His wild praise had the opposite effect on me. It put me off. I didn't do girls who were 'too beautiful'. They all seemed to step out of a *Vogue* magazine cover for the express intention of relieving me of my cash. I don't want to labour the point or anything, but I can't stand the mercenary bitches. And this one I imagined to be the mother of them all; but to be honest I was very curious about her, just to know the kind of girl it took to bag an Arab billionaire. Finally one day, just as we were entering a party, Ricky said, 'Oh, by the way, Elizabeth's back.'

I went looking for a juicy young thing bursting out of a non-existent, pink top, so I was totally unprepared for the face that regarded me. Actually that line from Lobo's song, *when I saw you standing there . . . the blood went to my feet,* came to mind.

God, she was dangerous in her perfection; porcelain complexion, the flawless features of a mannequin, snake hips and long, long legs. Except, of course, for the hair. Some idiot had bleached it a ghastly shade of platinum. Still, never could I have imagined one so coldly aloof as her. From the dead straight hair to the unsmiling frosty pink lips she was unreservedly icy. Did the ice sculpture feel it? That sudden tightening in the stomach. That frozen stillness of desire.

Her blood pooling in her feet.

The shock of her made me stupid. '. . . Ricky wasn't exaggerating. You actually are too beautiful,' I murmured, making sense to some slow-moving part of my brain, but wanting to kick myself even as the disastrous words left me. She had heard them a million times before. If she was part of Ricky's crowd she wanted intrigue not boredom.

'Thank you,' she dismissed politely, and turned away.

The platinum curtain parted, and I saw her nape. Tiny bones pressing against her skin. Pathetic or touching, depending how you looked at it.

'What's he like?' I asked.

'Sorry?' Her voice had that cold sound of a Scandinavian fiddle. A disturbing shimmer from the second string underneath that remained unmoving.

'The Arab. What's he like?'

Her eyes flashed, light grey and malicious. Good, I had meant to offend; but her only reaction was to sip at her champagne. I noticed she wore an alchemist's bracelet like the princesses in the legends of King Arthur. Each symbol standing for the secret ingredients for making gold, mercury, aqua fortis, copper, fire, earth, salt. . .

But suddenly she smiled. A trick smile that.

She said something, but I don't remember what. The smile was working its curious magic on me. No shooting stars or music flooding into my head, not even a struggle against strong winds, but I can remember it, in its entirety, today. Perfumed, pink, beautiful and indisputably disdainful. God, you should have seen it. Watching her looking down at me from her impregnable tower had an infuriating effect on me. It made me want the cold bitch so bad, I itched. The need, I soon found out, was blind, naked and apparently shameless.

THE SPIDER'S TEMPLE

The Games They Played

Forgive them their sins

April 2000

Nutan

The light was fading and all the other tramps were gone. Only Martin still lingered in the café, finishing the dregs of his coffee, and sucking the last bits of goodness from his collection of discarded cigarette ends. I watched the bus stop across the road. It was the same station, the same routine, people climbing in, hurrying to a seat, arranging their belongings around them, and avoiding the eyes of the watching waitress. And I was the envious waitress, of little significance, who had stood at that very spot three months ago, but on that spring evening everything was different. Now I knew for sure the bus went nowhere special, and I clearly saw the passengers for what they really were. Bored, and weary with their cheap lives. Certainly unworthy of envy. They did not know about the tantalising smell in the interior of a Rolls Royce.

I did.

Someone passing laughed. A nice civilised sound. Never had I suspected that London could be this beautiful. It was spring that made the air gentle, and naked branches reach for robes of luscious green. In the streets people did not huddle deeper into their thick coats to scurry away like rats. The pub across the road had put its tables out, and customers were sitting with their drinks, and hanging on to the dying evening. Night had a different feel, more dangerous.

Behind me I heard Martin shuffling to his feet, dirty,

ragged, and wearing the stink of stale piss. I stepped aside to let him pass.

'See you tomorrow, Martin,' I said.

He raised his right hand carelessly up to somewhere by his ear as he passed. Once, feeling sorry for him as any who comes upon a fallen tree would, I asked, 'If you could live your life again, what would you change?' He brought his black eyes up to mine and suddenly unveiled them. How fiercely they blazed. 'Not a single thing. Not one damn thing,' he hissed. As I stared in shock, his ruin forgotten, he smiled; for a life of coarse salt on Chateaubriand, the pout of a mistress dressed only in a string of pearls, a black Havana between his teeth, and a Maserati around a bend. Oh, just for a life wonderfully used. To life. Now. Without a thought for hungry ghosts. Unrepentant and uncompromising.

And it was true. He was not grateful for my benevolence. Give, don't give, he couldn't care less. He would dine in the dustbins out back. His smile told me so. Charity was only a euphemism for pity, and, in my case, disgust. There was, and should be, no regret, or apology given for a life lived gloriously fast. Better still, thoughtlessly. Three months ago, I would have been bewildered, even disorientated, by his attitude. A tramp pretending riches beyond me. I would have shaken my head with pity, and feeling superior, would have offered prayers for him.

But that was before, before a sun God sheltered from the rain in our humble café. You see, until he touched me I was unfinished. Didn't know better. Had only days before clapped eyes upon and been amazed by a moving staircase called an escalator. But Ricky was the ferryman. No charge. Just get in, love. He arranged it, so I wouldn't sink. So I would see that sin was only a grape. To be intoxicated all one had to do was squeeze it. And that is what I did, squeezed it.

Suddenly I was different.

And so different I was ready to be infected, dazzled, by the light I saw in the tramp's eyes. What an accomplishment to be able to die grinning from ear to ear, a well used, badly shrivelled crone at ninety. Utterly content with the sin I had consumed.

In a funny way the tramp reminded me of Ricky. Not because I thought he would end up as a bum, far from it, but it was that same reckless defiance in his eyes, the voracity with which he toasted life, the wine sloshing over his glass, dripping down his fingers. They were geniuses for taboos, rogues risking eternal damnation on a toehold. The exuberance of their religion obliterated the instinct for consequences, or the long fall below.

I had intended my own wickedness, so I was hardly alarmed when Ricky took me to a flat over a pub. The Spider's Temple. We Balinese learn from a very early age not to fear the spider. The wolf spider lurks at the base of rice plants, and devours the many pests of the plant. Without him the harvest would be a poor one. So you see, at no time did I experience fear.

In fact, I thought it a fascinating place filled with night people. Each intriguing, but in some provocative way flawed. They thought day was night and night was day. All of them wore the same wound-up expressions, gimme more. There were no provisions being made for tomorrow, and those dirty words 'for the future' never passed their lips. They were having fun.

The wolf spider sniffed and licked at my armpits. Midstride he grabbed me by the hips, and flipped me over. He was not only blond and handsome, but as strong as a water buffalo. He denied me permission to wear anything not made of Lycra, so he could have access to all of me in the dark corners of night clubs. Sometimes he pulled me into deserted stairwells. The sex was quick and furious.

Afterwards I went into the toilet, and in the many mirrors my eyes would glitter back, triumphant. A long time ago, I had run out into the dusty road with the other children to gape at the foreigners, their eyes blue, their skin pink, and their pockets rich. We gave them high fives, *chiu* as we called them. They were always delighted to see us running behind their coaches, wanting them. If it is true, that everything we receive is the fulfilment of our own secret wishes, then running barefoot I must have dreamed of this day when they occupied the spaces in the same mirror as me.

Ricky showed me a world so fantastic it could exist only at night after all the good people had climbed down from the red buses and hopped into their beds. And only if you were prepared to spend enormous amounts of cash. Ricky was. We donned our glad rags and went through dingy entrances guarded by large men in black suits. These places had wonderful names, Tramp, The Fridge, China White, Cloud Nine . . . A narrow flight of stairs led underground . . . into the earth. In these hot, dimly lit spaces people were not dressed in their customary colours of black and navy. No, no, in these secret places, shimmering fabrics and a bubbly drink called champagne reigned. I found what the winged fox had promised there. Gold dust in the hair of bronze strangers. People sampling the illicit.

Both Zeenat and I indulged in the forbidden. Colourless liquids that you mixed with your soft drink. But only in clubs where the beat is played very loud and strong. Or the liquid doesn't work properly. Oh, it was a wonderful thing. Then there was a white powder, so shockingly priced I did not dare convert a single gram into Indonesian currency. It went by a pretty name. Cocaine. A girl's name. Ricky used to call her Coca. Have you ever met her? She pulls an exciting trick in your head. My classmates were cutting grass to feed the cows. To think there was no one in my village who had experienced what I had.

'Coca,' Ricky shouted, tipping a whole bag on top of the TV. Spellbound, I stared at the white hill. Sometimes he made a line from one end of the bar to the other, and got on his hands and knees to snort the river of white. I was not in love with him but he was the ferryman, impossible to resist. In his right hand he swung a chain, at the end of it, the keys to outrageous pleasures. 'It is only a gate and I have the keys.' The ferryman winked.

In restaurants, he grabbed my ankle and, while I squealed with laughter, yanked it unceremoniously on the table. With his dinner knife he hacked off my stocking and tossed it away, to land in other people's soups. Deliberately he brought my foot to his mouth, and sucked my toes. I looked around at the unprepared audience, the bemused waiters, the shocked manager, the scandalised diners, and I wriggled my toes and laughed uproariously. When the white hill was high everything was funny.

Zeenat disapproved, but I knew she was just jealous, as I would have been if it had been she who had found Ricky. To reassure her, I repeated, 'You are mine and I am yours. None may step between.' But she would not believe me. She chose to sulk. She complained that he was a wild animal, too loud, too contemptible. Ugly, in fact. She guessed him faithless.

'You are a banana leaf to him. When he is finished with you he will throw you away,' she warned. But I didn't care. I *wanted* to be used. I wanted my meat to be a sieve for all experiences. To die with the tramp's words in my mouth, 'Not a single thing. Not one damn thing.' So I forgave Ricky everything. Why wouldn't I? The man carried excitement in his pocket.

Whenever I went anywhere with him, envious women stared. He was so handsome. He talked with his hands, his eyes twinkling. I watched him, blond and beautiful, and felt a surge of pride inside me that the ferryman should want me.

'*Amore mio.*' But I knew neither of us loved. We were only squeezing the grape. I felt guilty leaving Zeenat behind, but she didn't enjoy his company. She came to help demolish Ricky's coca hill, but all the time her sullen eyes never left Ricky and me.

'You are mine and I am yours. Ricky is married, after all,' I comforted her. 'It is just good fun. He is one of those gold-headed gods dancing on the surf that I always wanted. Don't you remember? Soon we will return to our little paradise, but isn't this spider's lair so much fun, for now?'

The smell of the tramps was gone by the time I put away the salt and pepper pots. The coffee machine was hissing out its cloud of steam. Zeenat was washing the removable parts in the sink. When she was finished she started switching off the lights. Turning up her coat collar she waited beside me as I double-locked the door. We walked back silently. The nights were still cold.

In the room she sat on the bed and took off her shoes. I opened our wardrobe doors.

'You're going out again,' she accused.

'Well, you can come if you want. Actually, why don't you? It's Sunday tomorrow. We don't have to work,' I said. But she didn't want to. I was getting a little impatient with her, hanging around my neck, clinging without any sense of adventure. I wished she would find someone. Have some fun for a change. Discard her worried expression for a while. We could be boring when we went back to our little village. She stared at me as I washed before the mirror.

I painted my lips a deep red. 'Don't you think that Bruce is really sexy, then? You know, if I wasn't going out with Ricky, I would go for him. I think he is lovely. What's there not to like? Intense black eyes, a film star dimple in his chin, and those shoulders!'

In the mirror her face was impolite. 'You have him, then,' she said.

214

I swung around and faced her. 'Fine, what about Anis, then? Of everybody that we have met you have to admit that he is special. He's kind, gentle, educated, and he's crazy about you.'

For a moment she simply looked at me, at the truth I had uttered, but then she shook her head. 'Please, stop. I don't want any of them. I just want to go home. I hate it here.' Her voice became shrewd. 'Anyway we'll have to go home soon, like it or not. Don't forget, they only stamped our passports for six months. Our visas are nearly expired.'

'Not really,' I said, carelessly. 'Ricky says that most of his workers are without the right papers even to remain in this country, let alone work. They run out through the back at the first sign of an immigration officer. As long as we don't do anything illegal, they'll never catch us.'

'Haven't you had enough? When are you planning to go home?'

I bit my tongue then. What have we imagined, Zeenat and I? That we would be two old ladies together. More and more they seemed unlikely, our girlish promises to each other. I was beginning to consider the prospect of never returning.

'I'll be at Ricky's restaurant, if you change your mind.' I picked up my purse and left our room.

I was on the stairs when I heard Zeenat shout down, 'Don't you miss Nenek at all?' Her voice broke halfway.

Ricky

It was Saturday night at Villa Ricci. From my position at the bar, I could see into the kitchen every time someone went through the swing doors. And what I saw made my breast swell: an assembly of drunks, thieves, compulsive liars, substance abusers, whore-mongering, shifty bastards preparing wonderful dishes. Each a fugitive of the straight and narrow preferring *my* kitchen as the place to lie low. Their aggressive snarls of 'Is table five ready?' and 'Can somebody pick up table nine, fucking now?' was song to my ears.

A woman by table seven was alleging her food contained meat. God preserve me. It was not long ago that I couldn't tell the vegetarians from the lesbians. Why, this one was almost attractive. The waiter footed it back to the kitchen, a sick expression on his face. The bearers of such messages were naked victims in the explosions they triggered. The lad cowered three feet from Franco who was red-faced and bubbling with rage. Remember him? The madcap genius from La Strega.

'Which fucking bitch is it now?' he screamed.

He was scornful of vegetarians. They offended his method. He believed that vegetarians should stay at home nibbling carrots. 'Why the fuck do they come to restaurants? Just to bother us, and force us to produce tasteless food? Illogical fools. Food without animal stock?' he would implore dramatically.

Me, I unrolled the red carpet. For a few pennies of mashed beans in the shape of a beef burger I charged the price of an excellent cut of meat. I saw Franco charge towards the doors. On the way he stopped to raise a starched spotless hat to his head. The doors swung open to a smiling vision. Even I could have been persuaded it was all genuine.

'*Allora, a tavola,*' he cried genially.

He examined the plate so closely I feared he was, in fact, surreptitiously spitting into it.

' Ahh . . .' he diagnosed knowingly. He replaced the plate on the table. 'Madam, you are wrong. Completely wrong. That is –' he paused, his right hand, the fingertips touching rose upwards to jab the air and arc back to his lips for a nippy kiss – '*Scamorzza*, smoked cheese.' With a quirky smile, he sympathised with her error '*Delicioso* like meat, no?' Shame-faced, the woman agreed. The fault was hers. Satisfied that he had set the record straight and redeemed his credibility, he gave a theatrical bow. '*Buon appetito, signora.*' The doors swallowed him, straight-backed and correct. Behind the doors, I knew what he was doing. He was taking his hat off scowling and cursing, 'These fucking vegetarians. Why don't they fucking stay at home?'

The most menacing black man imaginable filled the entrance. He had to stoop to clear the door, but I'll tell you now, Cosmos was sweet – like a piece of bread. Couldn't hurt a fly. Fucking guy was so laid back it took him an hour to get from my flat to the newsagent, ten minutes down the road.

'Yeah, yeah, man, leaving now,' the bastard says, and walks through my door an hour later. One hour . . . If speed was tasteless I would have spiked his tea just to watch.

On one arm a drop-dead-gorgeous chocolate chick purred. Cosmos was my coca supplier, but he also provided party girls. Maybe he could leave this one behind. She gave the impression she managed authentic cat sounds. Something about a good yowl that goes a long way with me. We had to pass the kitchen to reach the office and every single one of the crafty sluts in my kitchen watched our progress from the corner of his eye. They would be knocking at my door in a little bit. I locked the door and Cosmos pulled a block of five kilos out of the girl's handbag. He spread himself over the entire couch like a Sultan. Cosmos never touched the stuff. He always said, 'Touch the shit and you're dead.'

After I had said a sad goodbye to Chocolate – she was unavailable, promised to a party of American boys – and ushered them out, I began the task of reconstituting the coca. Cut a kilo for my own needs, crushed the rest with pain-killers, and put the lot into a press. Solidity returned after thirty-six hours.

I drew myself a fat line. So generous that my mouth was already numb by the time I came through the swing doors. I saw Nutan, sitting at the bar, eight tequila slammers lined up in front of her. My manager leered.

Taking a deep breath she picked up the first glass. Tequila, salt, lemon. Tequila, salt, lemon. The barman was clapping and yelling encouragement while the waiters lined up to drum the bar top. Four tequila glasses were empty. '*Brava,* Nutan, *Brava,*' someone roared. Five, six, seven. Tequila, salt, lemon. She threw her head back and slammed the final glass down. The restaurant erupted cheering. She had downed them without a break, her lipstick unsmudged. Her eyes caught mine smiling and nicely impressed. *Brava,* Nutan. *Brava.* Next time we'll try for ten, huh?

Anis

Why do we always desire the thing that does not want to be ours? I could feel myself gently falling for Zeenat. How not to? Even her walk was an uninterrupted, majestic delight. Shoulders level, head upright. As if there was a huge bronze jar on her head. It was through carrying things on her head from the time she was a child. It changed her gait. I watched her progress towards me, eyes burning. An afterglow of a fallen empire.

And her skin was fragrant! Every inch of her scented. At first, I thought it was some diligently rubbed ointment, but she blushed and said, 'It is my grandmother. She fed my sister and me with special herbs from the time we were tiny.' I stared, amazed.

'Do you like it?' she asked shyly. I took her hand to my lips. So that was crushed flowers and herbs. The thought made my head rush. She showed me the small black beads. An old woman's magic. I once had a magic grandmother.

Zeenat spoke of her homeland, a place so forgotten there were still women who had not been disgraced by a white man's eyes into covering their breasts. And they told stories of a time gone by when only prostitutes wore jackets, to signal their impure profession. In this remote place magic was an everyday occurrence.

Because it was so far away this magic that she spoke of, or perhaps because I wanted so much for it to be true, I believed. Perhaps too, if this weird and wonderful woman she called Nenek stood in front of me, I might have doubted, used the logical part of my brain, but the distance got me. Surley if magic did exist it would seek just such a faraway paradise. But, first let me tell you how I got this close to this intriguing creature.

At first, I could only meet her at Ricky's Temple. A strange place that I am not certain I could properly describe to you. At first sight it will seem seedy, but innocuous enough: an open-plan flat, one half bearing worn sofas, and the other a long glass-topped dining table. By the wall some stairs leading up to two rooms, one a fairly large bedroom and the other a dark box room. In the kitchen you could, if you went at the right time, find Ricky expertly chopping garlic with a huge cleaver, or, wooden spoon in hand, presiding over enormous vats of boiling pasta. In the vapour his baritone voice rang with reasonably convincing versions of *The Barber of Seville*.

And if you hung around some more you would see him carrying steaming bowls of food to the dining table. Still singing he set them around bottles of rough red wine, and baskets of crusty bread, purloined from one of his restaurants. People would drift over from the nest of sofas still laughing and joking, to eat and drink. Afterwards with coffee made in an espresso machine, there was always a bottle of something to burn the back of your throat being passed around. Then somebody comes in with a few grams of coke. And the party begins again.

All night long people will make merry downstairs and love upstairs. But I'll tell you now, it was all vile, vile, vile. If not for Zeenat I would never have gone back after the first time. Once I went there alone. The place was deserted and I swear, I couldn't get past the coat rack. My skin prickled and my toes clawed into the soles of my shoes.

Empty, the place was a sinister waiting presence. Instinctively, I sensed it was something to do with the fresco stretching over the back wall. The open-plan nature of the flat meant there was no escape from the painting. It too, at first sight, seemed harmless enough. In fact, it was not in any way special, if anything it was crude in technique and flawed in execution. Its brush strokes told of an exhausted Greek temple, the pillars cracked, and overgrown with creepers, the floor littered with broken things; red and black amphorae; plates, cooking utensils, goats' antlers.

In the middle of this ruin, a bright fire and a woman dressed in long white robes looking into the flames. Her back was to the viewer. Her hair was black, so black it appeared not to reflect light. She held a crying mask. At the end of the wall where the painting stopped it sawed off a man's leg, lifted in the act of running away. But he wouldn't have got far, anyway. A metal chain shackled his ankle. The funny thing was the chain was not rigid metal, but was elongated and elastic like a Dali timepiece.

Here was violence of a kind I had never encountered. Some ominous spirit had infected the artist's brush. Menace lay in the greenish hue of the woman's white hands and bare feet, the face you couldn't see, the anguished mask, the desperate man's leg.

No, it is impossible to explain. You have to see it for yourself. But it was not only the painting. It was the whole sordid place. Underneath the laughter and the grunts of sexual ecstasy, something horrible was happening. People came in dented and left destroyed.

The temple keeper was, of course, Ricky. Indeed he is that rare man, intelligent, humorous, exciting, energetic and utterly charismatic. Why, I couldn't think of a man alive who could boast to have slept with more women, consumed more drugs, drunk more champagne, told more smutty jokes or knew more friends and yet . . . yet . . . how could a man who slipped so effortlessly into the black and white shoes of a pimp, and went about *acquiring* damaged people be anything but sleazy.

He bribed the wounded into his unsavoury temple, preyed on them if they were women, and afterwards watched curiously as others he had initiated into corruption further tainted and exploited his collection of victims. In the end he was as his face suggested; unpleasant features slyly arranged to give the illusion of beauty. The face showed no signs of suffering or remorse, but a truly nauseating joy to behold the vices its owner had inspired in others. Corruption seemed to lift his heart, the way a car passing you on the street, its stereo turned up too loud to dance music, might. Even the way he loved was an insult; so coldly, his blue eyes always contemptuous of the easy surrender. He had so little use for women.

Sometimes I think the only woman Ricky did not entirely despise was Elizabeth. He had never tasted the pleasure of her bed. He looked at the platinum hair, the cold eyes, the exquisite mouth smiling its cruel smile, and imagined that they were two of a kind. That they spent the same currency. She knew how it worked. Her eyes said she had learned the real truth about men, that they were pathetic. How easily they were caught in the net of beauty. She knew what they wanted, what went through their shallow heads. So she played her little games.

Looking into their sinful faces, she smiled and coolly told them what she wanted. And like servants they ran to do her bidding. She gave nothing of herself away and never encouraged confidences. Even where she lived was a mystery. And that was what Ricky enjoyed. A cold display of arrogance. A willingness to use, abuse, take, and in the following wake of destruction to be beautifully unmoved. And although I suspected her coldness was only a defence mechanism, it didn't change the charge against Ricky. He sat back and took pleasure.

But nothing was as despicable as when Ricky lured innocents like the twins and carelessly proceeded to contaminate them. Once he came downstairs from his bedroom where he had been with Nutan, and his eyes alighted upon Zeenat asleep on a sofa. I saw it in his narrowed gaze, a moment of cynical consideration. Oh God, he wanted her too. The very next day I offered the girl five hundred pounds to come and sit for me. Too much, I know, but Ricky spoiling the child was so offensive a thought, I'm afraid it drove me to responsible action. She must have been exchanging the money into Indonesian currency, it took so long before her mouth dropped open, and her hand came to hide it. She nodded eagerly. So began our association.

I arranged her in the pose I required. In the daylight her skin was her glory. It was flawless, shining from within as if she was not a container for flesh, blood and bones, but a rare and luminous oil.

'It's the herbs,' she said shyly.

'Perhaps I should start taking some of these magic pills of yours,' I teased.

'Oh no,' she cautioned seriously. 'They are for women. There are other things for men . . .'

'Really? Like what?'

'Yes, if you can't . . . you know?' She hid her mouth and giggled.

'Ah well, maybe when I am a little older.'

She nodded agreement. Even in paradise it was quite in order for older men to need help with impotence.

Another lifetime ago Swathi had sat in that same window seat with the sun slanting into her face. For a moment I remembered her, thin, gaunt . . . but she was gone, departed with the words, 'Every separation is an opportunity.' My new opportunity smiled uncertainly at me. I walked away from her. 'Think of someone you love. Go where you are loved,' I instructed. She was not so different. Has not every race in its own way learned to turn flour into a dough ball and that into bread?

I looked up from my sketch pad and she was gazing through the window, lost in an encouraging memory, a tender secret joy in her eyes. I thought of a bird. Small, dull-coloured and so extremely delicate that it must be nervous and jerky when watched, but when safe in the air, it became a supreme beauty, the wonder that nature intended it to be. How incredibly beautiful the mysterious eyes full of longing were.

'Who are you thinking of?'

'My mother.'

I asked her about her mother.

'She died because she wanted new feet,' she said.

Smiling, I began to paint the delightful creature before me. She could disappear into thin air or fly away. Before that I had to paint, paint and paint. I had to paint while the light was good. While her skin glowed like a house lit with hundreds of candles, its long French windows billowing with transparent veils.

The doorbell rang and I went to answer it.

'Can I come in, Anis?' Zeenat said.

Arms folded I leaned against the wall watching her taking her shoes off. Her feet were wide and splayed from walking barefoot. She told me once that she walked without shoes until the age of seven and then only to school.

'I'm hungry. How about you?' I said.

'Me too. I can cook,' she offered.

She had just spent all day on her feet serving customers, and then to save money had walked from Victoria to South Kensington, and now she was offering to cook. 'No, let's get a video and a take-out,' I suggested.

She nodded, beaming.

'Indonesian?'

'Exactly,' she said, nodding even more vigorously.

'What would you like to watch?'

'*Pretty Woman*.' She did not have to think at all.

'Hmm!' I said. Why did every girl I know reserve such a special place in her heart for that vomit-inducing Hollywood lie about a man who falls in love with a street walker. As if it could happen in real life.

I opened a bottle of wine.

Halfway through the food she said, 'This is terrible. Very pitiful food. You must come to Bali with me. For you I will cook baby bamboo shoots and pork with special herbs and red chillies. And you can meet my grandmother. You will fall in love with her immediately.'

She pronounced pork as poerk. She thrilled the 'r' and stressed the 'k'. It made me protective of her. I said, 'Look, why don't you come and model full time for me. I'm sure I can double whatever you're getting in that dump you work in.'

'Oh no, no, I cannot leave my sister. She will be very sad alone. But thank you. Thank you for taking so much trouble, Anis.' She spoke solemnly, the palms of her hands meeting in front of her chest, bowing her head. It didn't look to me as if Nutan cared either way, but I didn't say anything.

We walked out together for the video, and I sat gamely

enough through Julia Roberts' transformation from big hearted hooker to classy lady. Ten minutes into *The English Patient* Zeenat dozed off on the couch. I watched her for a while. She slept like a child, a thumb in her mouth, her gentle chest rising and falling. I wanted to kiss that angel mouth. How little had it known? She was a page, unwritten.

I loved her, but I knew how hopeless it was. She was not even remotely interested in me. She came to me only because she was lonely and homesick. All she wanted to do was return to her little village and her grandmother. She once said to me, 'We are simple people, dirt people. We must go back before the city air makes us sick. Before we fall.'

In my head a sneaky strategy my grandfather had taught me played a tune. 'Anis, there isn't a woman born who can resist a prolonged assault of attention. Shower her with attention, day after day, even in the face of rejection and scorn. Then one day simply stop. And if she is not yours in less than a month, come and see me. Even if I am in the grave. We'll discuss stage two, which I warn you is very extreme, hardly to be undertaken by the faint hearted.' Laughter rumbled inside his chest.

But I refused to be so cynical. This time it was my turn to love unrequited. Love, there might be only two yards of it to go around, but all of it must be irreproachable. I had behaved like a cad with Swathi, yet she had understood, forgiven freely, and then taught me that a noble love does not belong to the professor, but to the professed. This was my chance to redeem myself. If I failed now, her coming would have been in vain.

In the uncertain light of the television screen, I promised to protect that sleeping child. So delicate and so near the wolf's jaws. I alone stood between her and Ricky. He must not be allowed to soil this clean page. I don't how long I sketched her or how long I watched her afterwards in the bluish light, but I must have fallen asleep propped up against the cushions.

She woke me up in the morning by blowing gently onto my eyelids. 'This is how my grandmother wakes us up,' she said as I stared blearily at her, my mouth sour from last night's wine. She held up a milk bottle. 'Look. Somebody made a hole in the top,' she announced.

'That will be the neighbourhood blue tits.'

'Blue tits?'

'They are birds that have learned to stick their beaks through the silver foil and drink the cream that rises to the top.'

She laughed, delighted. 'Really? A bird so clever. I will come every Sunday morning, and hide behind the curtains to see this bird.'

It's a deal.

Francesca

I slept badly again. Ricky did not come home even last night. Ever since he lost his driver's licence on a drink-driving charge, he found it more convenient to sleep over in his office than mess about with taxis. I thought for a while about that narrow couch in his office. Another thought intruded. I pushed it aside quickly. I could hear Rosa downstairs, hoovering. The faint hum bothered me. I rolled over to Ricky's side of the bed and buried my face in his pillows. It was cool and still smelt faintly of perfume, mine. He was not home often enough to leave his scent behind. I threw the bedclothes off and sat up.

Soon Rosa would be upstairs, wanting to do my bedroom too. I pulled my body out of bed, let my nightgown drop on the carpet and, naked, went to stand on the weighing machine. I could look down fearlessly. I skipped dinner last night. The needle remained where it had been yesterday morning, even when I shifted my weight around.

Pleased, I went to stand in front of the long mirror. You could never be too rich or too thin. Standing sideways I took a good hard look for sag, paying special attention to the breasts and the buttocks. Good. Nothing had changed. Yet. Quickly I pulled on a purple leotard and went into the next room for my workout. Forty-five minutes later, a light film of perspiration on my skin, I ran my bath. While I lay in the scented bubbles I didn't allow myself to think. I simply allowed my mind to float. As usual to a field in Sicily. When the water started to cool I got out. In the hot damp air some tendrils of hair had begun to curl. I switched on the hot plates and quickly ironed out the offending curls.

Then I sat in front of the dressing-table mirror in my dressing gown and began to do my face. But before that I peered closely for lines. New lines. None today. Good. Moving close to the mirror I stared at my lips. They were still almost as swollen as the first day I had them injected with collagen, still as unfamiliar, and a painful reminder of how little I understood the ground upon which I stood.

Lost for direction I had defined myself by the women who frequented the same shops as me. I had taken to calling them 'the first wives club'. I suspected I wasn't rich enough to be a card-carrying member; there were over-heard conversations about holidays spent on yachts, and clues that their bronze tans were acquired by different means, on privately owned islands in the Caribbean. Nevertheless I thought of myself as an honorary member. We bled from the same crown of thorns.

These women were my role models. Slowly, by observation alone, for I dared not befriend them, I learned all the unwritten laws that governed their style, and without being told, unravelled the thoughts that went behind each and every purchase.

As I had understood it, rich women spent all their time desexualising themselves. Only the palest lipsticks were deemed suitable because red is a turn-on, a sexual come-on of the highest order. And because only flesh is sexy – it gives shape, moves, jiggles, invites, nods and calls – they were bone thin. It was the same thing with their hair, and clothes. No wind-tossed or déshabillé look for them. They needed immaculate helmets of cleverly tinted hair and clothes that were all about cut.

They did this because they knew it was impossible to compete with the mistresses and lovers their husbands kept. Had I not spent years, helplessly following groups of giggling girls in shopping malls, envious of their firm flesh, and skin yet to coarsen? But that was time wasted. There was simply no remedy for youth gone by. So I understood what made those women spurn as vulgar all that was practised by their rivals. All that was lively and impulsive. They strove instead to distinguish themselves by looking expensive and unattainable.

When I first noticed their bloated lips, I simply didn't know what to make of them. I actually experienced a touch of hysteria. Suddenly I felt insecure as if I was losing touch, for I had truly never expected them to adopt such an overtly sexual advertisement. It was going to be harder to tell the wives from the mistresses.

I tried a pout in the mirror. Secretly I found it all rather grotesque. Like a baboon on heat. For all to see. Blood-engorged genitals on your face. At first I was so ashamed of my inflated lips that I stayed in my bedroom for the whole weekend. Then Ricky came home on Sunday with dark circles under his eyes, utterly exhausted but when he saw what I had done an oddly amused, half-curious expression came onto his face. Sliding his hand around the back of my neck he bent his head and licked my lips. He tasted of brandy. 'I love this,' he said, and suddenly we were rushing up the stairs to make love.

When we were finished I saw his lashes flutter down, but he snapped them open and shook his head. 'My dolls are outside the door,' he said, dragging himself out of the bed. And even though I told him that the children could wait for a bit more, he dragged himself off the bed and went into the bathroom. I heard taps opening, the clink of perfume bottles replaced on the marble tiles, the toilet flushing. When he came out his eyes were alive and glittering. He rubbed his hands together and cried out, 'Where are they, those children of mine? Francesca, what have you done with them?'

He opened the door and the children fell through, screaming, 'Here we are, Daddy. Here we are.' But he pretended he could not hear, see or feel the two younger ones going mad around his legs. He craned his neck looking left and right, and left again, calling out, 'Where are those children. But where are they? *You* haven't given them away, have you, Francesca?'

Lucca was already too scornful of such games. 'Stop being so silly, Dad,' she admonished in her best grown-up voice. So he grabbed her, and began to tickle her until she was breathless with laughter and begging him to stop. Then I lay in bed, enveloped in langour, hearing them squealing with happiness in their father's company and wished it could always be like that. But that would have been completely unrealistic. It is not possible to have everything in life, is it?

I unscrewed the top off my cleanser and applied its contents with gentle upward strokes, followed by toner and afterwards the most expensive moisturiser money could buy. Then I started my make-up routine. First Touche Eclat concealer for the lavender circles under my eyes.

Satin-finish foundation was followed by a fine layer of compact powder. The blank canvas was ready for colour. Black liquid eyeliner, grey eye-shadow, three coats of mascara, highlighter, blusher, and finally a pale apricot lipstick.

I had to be thorough. Everything had to be flawless because I was certain there was much wrong with me. There were even bits that were already dead inside me. I got dressed in the dressing room. A grey Prada suit and soft grey pumps. I stood before the mirror. And I looked exactly how I wanted to look. A very rich man's wife. An honorary member of The First Wives Club.

As I was changing handbags Rosa came in. I did not look up. She greeted me cheerily. 'Hello, Rosa,' I said, my voice deliberately cool. I knew it made me seem like an ignorant stuck-up bitch, but I did not want to encourage conversation. Truth was I hated her in my house. Her bustle, her purpose, her womanly curves . . . she diminished me, made me feel even more deficient. *I wanted to be cleaning my own house*. I heard her footsteps head towards the bathroom.

I opened my wardrobe and took out the clothes I had selected for resale at a dress agency in Knightsbridge. Although I had worn them only once, they were evening dresses and too many people had seen me in them. The agency might even have a cheque for me. I walked down the stairs thinking of Ricky. I wanted to call him, but I knew he hated being awakened before lunch.

On my way to the car after I had dropped the clothes off, Tonino, the owner of Montpelliano Restaurant, a round, genial man, called out to me, 'Ah Senora Delgaldo, what a beautiful day. Come, come, have a coffee with me.' It was a cold crisp morning but he was sitting at one of the tables outside his restaurant having a coffee and a cigarette. Smiling, I refused his offer. I couldn't help feeling they all laughed and pitied me. Still, I told myself, it didn't matter. What did they know? They did not know that Ricky had promised, '*Tutta la vita.*' And that I was holding him to it. We would finish our days in Sicily, in the house his father built for him. From our balcony we would look down and see the vineyard, the olive groves, the white sand . . .

I banked the cheque the agency had given me, did my hair, had a cup of black coffee for lunch in a smart little café and shopped until it was time to pick up the kids. It was the au pair's day off. One day a week I picked my own children up from school.

You could see with one look that I was totally different from all the other mothers. They looked at me without friendship. I thought they might be jealous, or perhaps they had simply picked up that I didn't want to be friends. I didn't want to be part of their pathetic little chats over coffee, exchanging amusing anecdotes about our husbands.

The children came out from their respective classes. Other kids waited a minute to chat or say goodbye to their classmates, but mine rushed out of the gates towards me. Unembarrassed they flung their arms around my waist. The other mothers looked on enviously. They wondered what I had done to make my children so devoted to me. I wanted to tell them it was simple, rudimentary really. Needy, clinging kids are not the result of good parenting, but secured through neglect.

'Come,' I tell my children. 'It's Monday. Daddy's restaurants are closed today and he might come home for dinner.'

Elizabeth

I was on my way to the hairdressers when Maggie called me. She sounded all in a dither, wanted us to meet up at Ricky's. Said she had something to show me. I arrived before her. Haylee, a hard-faced prostitute called Angel, and two men I had never seen before were on the sofas, drunk and high. They offered me some, but I refused. I had to meet some of the Mullah's Arabic friends for dinner, and those bastards could smell alcohol a mile off.

I sat beside one of the men and caught Haylee, at once kitten and tiger, looking at me. Narrow and sneering. She didn't like me. Behind my back she called me a plastic mannequin. Her hostility was a surprise to me. I had never offended her at any time. But Ricky said it was just the competition she couldn't stand. I had never understood why she should be so insecure. Surely she must be one of the sexiest women alive. It made her insecurity all the more surprising.

Once, while the three of us were out shopping, she tried to persuade me to buy a silver dress. A colour that distrusts pale complexions. I had to keep mine pale for the mullah. I smiled then. I understood the venom in the vulnerable mouth. So I bought the dress, rubbed fake tan on my skin until it glowed bronze, and just like that the silver dress was good again. How Haylee hid behind her baby face and fumed.

I saw her do the same to others. When they tried on something really beautiful that suited them, she said, 'Are those stretch marks on your breasts? Never mind you can cover them with some foundation, can't you?' All the while smiling in an unconvinced way. Or she would say, 'I think I preferred you in the green one.' And the green one would have been the worst of the lot. Sometimes we caught her at parties wearing the dresses she persuaded us against.

Maggie came in, breathless. She sat next to me and taking a deep breath placed her hand on my leg. I looked at her face, it was shining. I looked at her hand. 'Oh, Maggie . . .' I said. 'It's beautiful.' Blue sapphire set in diamonds. Please God, please, I prayed, let there be no cruel black rocks underneath her. Let not promises be cheap.

'Where did you get the rock from?' Haylee shrieked, grabbing Maggie's hand from mine, and pulling it towards her face. 'Look, everybody. Look,' she announced, holding Maggie's hand up for everyone to admire. 'Someone wants to. . .' she paused dramatically '. . . marry Maggie.'

Angel leaned forward to behold the ring. 'Ooo result.'

'Congratulations,' the men I did not know said politely.

But Angel suddenly thrust her tough face towards Maggie and said, 'Sell the thing fast, and say you lost it. He's still in love so you won't get beaten up. Besides, it's bound to be insured.'

Haylee's beautiful face was taunting. 'Why do you always have to be such a heartless bitch? It wouldn't be because you aren't capable of getting a man to buy you an engagement ring, would it?' she asked.

Angel shrugged carelessly. 'Trust me, Maggie', she said. 'Sell the fuckin' thing. See how much you get in the little Jewish shop by Edgware Road. See how many grams of coke it is worth.' Then she laughed, a throaty uncouth sound.

'And fuck you too,' Haylee said.

I know what it must seem like to you, but remember, only the most dangerous and venomous species are brightly coloured. Haylee is brightly coloured.

'Come to the kitchen, Maggie,' I said.

She got up and followed me. 'Do you love him, Maggie?'

'Ach Beth, you know I do.'

'Then promise me you will never set foot in this flat again.'

'Wild horses wouldn't drag me back to this horrible place and its horrible people. I love him, Beth. I really do. He knows everything and yet he wants me.'

I pulled her to me and kissed her quickly.

'Don't cry, Beth.'

She sniffed in my hair. 'It's going to happen to you too. You wait. One of these days I'll be putting on a hat to come to your wedding.'

Why did I cry? I thought I was beyond tears. 'Be happy, Maggie. Be happy for me,' I said. Then I heard Bruce's voice at the door and immediately I tensed and itched to leave. 'I've got to go now. Will you come with me?'

'Yes, I'll come with you. I've got nothing here.'

We walked out of the kitchen together. Bruce turned to look at me. 'What's the hurry?' he asked.

'Just got to meet some friends,' I said coldly and walked away. I knew I was being a coward but if I did not let him near he would not break my heart. He was far more dangerous than the Mullah. And look what the Mullah did.

Bruce

I sat opposite Haylee. The two city types on either side of her smiled vaguely. They had obviously paid for all the booze and drugs, their eyes were sticky for a bit of Haylee but surely destined to make do with the old scrubber.

'Where's Elizabeth going?' I asked Haylee.

'A really good hairdresser, I think. Big night tonight. She's entertaining Arab clients.' My head snapped up. Her face was innocent and completely without guile, but there were at least two insults in that little piece of cheek. What really irked me was the bit where she made Elizabeth sound like a hooker in front of those strangers. It made me burn to defend Elizabeth to the two drips who couldn't give a hoot anyway, and that, in turn, irritated me. Why should I care if they thought Elizabeth was a hooker? She was, in a roundabout way.

I got up to leave and Haylee said, 'Send my love to Elizabeth when you see her in Momo's.' What was this thing she had going with Elizabeth? Momo's, huh?

I spent some time at the shop and then made my way down to Soho. I used think of Soho with a sense of exhilaration. Mysterious red-lit doorways where a half-dressed woman or two posed, as they waited to lure you with indecent suggestions, and strip bars where frankly hideous strippers, if they thought you were up for it, ground their sweaty crotches into your face. But Soho has changed.

About the same moment homosexuals decided to hijack the word 'gay' for their exclusive use, they also laid claim on Soho. The place belongs to them now. Powered by alcohol and experimental class A drugs they sit in gossipy groups inside slick designer bars and restaurants, being served high-rise towers of food. For a touch of the Orient they watch the staff. Armies of young boys and girls wearing long, shapeless Mandarin smocks.

The only thing left of the old days are the prostitutes in the first-floor back-street walk-ups. Behind every door that says *models*. Still selling the same product and still in demand.

I walked up Greek Street into a smoky saloon bar where a group of self-absorbed writers were employing their brittle, carefully rehearsed wit to annihilate each other. My friend Ashley greeted me, worse for wear.

'Give us something for the pain?' I said to him.

'A welsh rabbit and a blow job,' he said, 'and I am your man.'

'Will you take just the welsh rabbit?' I said.

He laughed his attractive laugh, his teeth wonderfully white, his eyes crinkling at the corners, 'Okay, rain check on the blow job.' He put a drink in front of me, opened his palm and showed me some interesting-looking blue pills. God only knew what effect they'd give.

'Nah, I'm on liquids today.'

I nursed a few beers before taking a cab to Momo's. It

was ridiculous, of course, but I couldn't help myself. It surprised me. I never burnt shoe leather running after skirt before.

Elizabeth's inexcusable hair stood out like a beacon in that dimly lit place. She was sitting at a corner table with a group of Arabs and suddenly I was unwilling to show myself. I wanted to stay hidden in the dark and watch her in her world. So different from mine. So far away. Her eyes so still and relentlessly pale grey that they reminded me of a walrus hunter I had once seen on TV. That she was a hunter was no doubt. Perfectly camouflaged and waiting. Hidden away was a necklace she had made. Polished walrus ivory. Little animal carvings with their names initialled on their underbelly. 'Don't come this way,' the animals called to me. 'You haven't got a prayer,' they cried.

There was even a polar bear, once twelve-foot tall standing on his hind legs, now no more than a souvenir on her necklace. 'Beware this huntress. She is cold hearted and hungry,' it warned. But the polar bear was large and foolish. It was careless. Sometimes it is the hunter who is watched.

I saw her leave her table and head for the toilets. Immediately I sprinted downstairs so that as she reached the bottom of the stairs and looked up, I was there waiting.

'Hello, Elizabeth,' I said, smiling.

She looked mighty fine in a short white dress and a black pearl choker, but she couldn't have looked more displeased. 'Hello, Bruce,' she said shortly, and would have passed me by without so much as an answering smile, if I hadn't caught her hand. 'Have a drink with me later?'

I saw her thinking. 'All right,' she agreed. 'Where?'

Suddenly I didn't trust her. 'Do you know the Mezzanine Bar in Soho?' I asked, naming a fictitious place.

'Oh yes, I do know it. Shall we meet there about twelve?'

'Sounds good to me. Don't be late,' I said, releasing her hand. She walked away. I took the steps up two at a time. What a bitch. She was going to stand me up. I went back to Ashley's to cool my heels, make my plans. I nursed a few more bottles of beer and thought up punishments. Little bitch. Still I couldn't help smiling at the prospect. At nearly eleven I took a cab to Momo's. 'Keep the meter running, mate,' I told the driver, but in minutes she was already making her escape. And guess what, trying to hail my taxi! I opened the door.

'I changed my mind about the venue so I came back to tell you.' I was dying to laugh but I said it perfectly seriously.

To give her her due some sort of Irish sense of fairness glimmered in her eyes as she got in, saying, 'Good. I was just coming to get you too. Where to?'

I wanted to test her, punish her, so I took her to meet my old mates, rough and ready as I knew they would be. They were celebrating Jelly getting out of prison for kiting, forging cheques. Our cab drove past the river to the East End and stopped outside an unfashionable ramshackle pub. I saw her glance down quickly at her finery, but when she met my eyes, hers were expressionless; fuck you, Elizabeth-style.

Everybody turned to stare at Elizabeth. Paddy was coming towards us, more than halfway plastered and probably already forcibly ejected from at least three pubs.

'My, my, aren't we in fine company?' he said.

'This is Elizabeth. She's Irish too,' I said.

'There you are. Didn't I tell you? Your bachelor days are numbered,' Paddy said.

Elizabeth didn't say anything. Neither did I.

'Don't mind him, Beth,' Paddy said, leading her away by the arm. 'Let me introduce you to the rest of the scoundrels.'

We started playing an old game, Loser's Toast, a comfortingly juvenile game where the loser made a toast and drank like a fish, and everybody else clapped and cheered. I winked at Paddy: load the game so that Elizabeth is toasting most of the time. He winked back: it's in the bank, boy. But it quickly became apparent that the double-crossing little shit had no intention of doing any such thing.

I stood and toasted Paddy, Bonehead, George, Jelly, Elizabeth, my career in hairdressing, England, Ireland, the Queen, Anna Nicole Smith's millions, all the miserable melon-breasted bitches Paddy had lain with, Bonehead's motorbike. I had given up throwing dirty looks at Paddy by the time I was down to Mickey Mouse, or was it Donald Duck, I can't remember now, and then I was back to toasting Paddy and Bonehead and George and Jelly. I was nearly toast.

The room had begun to whirl. My head, my head. The next one I could have drunk for all the wonderful girls blessed with nine-inch tongues whose acquaintance I had been denied. I had to lean against the wall for support to make the next one for the little maggots I had mistaken for friends. Only when the seat behind me checked my backward fall, did my luck suddenly change. The coin started arriving in Elizabeth's corner.

Finally the test of endurance. She drank like a trooper. In her designer dress and her black pearls she almost drank the boys under the table. Everyone was for her. They liked the Ice Queen. Paddy had tears of pride in his eyes. 'This one's too good to give away, eh Bruce,' he said slapping his thigh. Jelly was banging the table, Bonehead was cuddling his head in his hands and Elizabeth, Elizabeth was laughing. God, she knew how to laugh.

To focus better I tried to reach out and touch the gleaming black pearls, and ended up collapsing on the table. By the time I straightened Paddy was talking about going to another mate's pub for a cure, but I was too far gone. If only the table would stop spinning on its legs.

A man across the room was making eyes at Elizabeth. Using the logical form of reasoning inspired by alcohol it was Elizabeth I lost my rag with. Little selfish bitch. If she would only consent to sleep with me, just once, then that guy wouldn't have bothered me. The gnawing in my gut would go away. Of that I was sure. No doubt a purely physical reaction. Only lust unjustly excited by a shade of inaccessibility. Since her armour seemed impenetrable, a surrender had to be arranged for. Paid for. She had a price. Everyone did.

I was so sensationally drunk there was hardly any point in asking, but I did anyway. 'Shall we go to bed?'

That made even her chuckle. Then she sobered up. 'Your bed looks like a busy place. I need peace,' she told me. I stared at her. She must have been rotten stinking drunk too. Her voice was slurred and, Jesus Christ, honest.

'When peace looks in the mirror what does it see?' I asked. I thought I was being profound.

Her answer was immediate and shocking. 'Sadness,' she said.

'Why?' My voice was strange, far away.

'Because of the excitement lost.'

I looked into her face, oddly vulnerable, and I panicked. From high atop her impregnable tower she sent a bizarre message. But I only wanted her gaudy, quickly, without involvement. Not strictly true, a little voice said. Somewhere inside me a warning bell went off. The ground felt shaky. I had never been in that place before. It rocked me a little.

I opened my mouth to protest, but she had turned away and was asking the barman to call her a taxi. Paddy bundled her off into a cab. Dawn was just breaking over a grey high-rise council block. The cold morning air hurt my lungs. Paddy slapped me heartily on the back. I felt as if a sledgehammer had landed on my head.

'Be gentle,' I begged. 'It's been an awful long time since I've done this.'

In front of a wreck precariously balanced on four tyres he said, 'Jump in.'

He slipped into the driver's seat. I was too ill to argue. On the way back he was extraordinarily maudlin. 'There isn't a better or more beautiful girl than Elizabeth in all of Ireland and England,' he waxed, his eyes warm. 'And if I see you take up with another woman, I'll kick your goddamn head in,' he declared hotly. *Paddy* kick my head in? I wanted to laugh, but since my head already felt as if it had been kicked in, I didn't even try.

I collapsed on Paddy's couch. My last thought was if the ice princess was made of tears. The white I saw, salt crystals? From far away Sherlock Holmes accused, 'You see, but you do not observe.' It could turn out bad. It worried me . . . a little.

May 2000

Anis

It was Sunday. I awakened early and with a light step made for the living room, but Zeenat was not hiding behind the curtains waiting for the blue tits. I found her in the kitchen standing in front of the fridge with her hands in the freezer compartment.

'What are you doing?'

She took her hands out, peered closely at her nails and, satisfied with what she saw, held them out for me to inspect. 'Look,' she said. 'Do you like this colour?'

It was a sort of cinnamon. Dull, I'm afraid, but I had noticed that she didn't seem to favour bright colours. 'Mmm, very pretty,' I said. 'Nutan is always wearing red. How come you never do?'

'Red shocks me. Sometimes, when I catch my fingernails or my mouth in the mirror, I am frightened. I think I am bleeding.'

'Really?' I laughed. She was so funny, so foreign.

I watched her making coffee. She was touching everything carefully with the pads of her fingers and I became conscious of how beautiful and delicate this meticulous awareness of her surroundings was. Inconvenienced by her still wet nails she became compellingly feminine. And I thought how attractive if she was always so. Then I wondered if that was where the fashion for foot-binding started. By men who thought forcing women into disability was beautiful.

'Come, try Balinese coffee. I found it in Camden Town. Sooo nice.

I tried it. The Balinese coffee 'sooo nice', was strong and so sweet it was undrinkable.

'You don't like it?' she asked incredulously.

I looked into her astonished face and considered lying. 'Maybe with less sugar . . .'

'It's sooo good like this. Never mind, I drink,' she said and, smiling, drank mine too.

We ate breakfast. I, some delicious banana cake and black glutinous rice that she had woken up at five in the morning to make, and she, toast and marmalade. 'I love this very much,' she said. 'Sooo, how do you say again – errr, delicious.'

We went to Portobello market.

Excitedly she pointed to a mangy old woven-bamboo basket, about two-foot high, in the shape of an overturned bell. In Bali such a basket was used to keep cockerels in the family compound, so that any evil spirit wandering into the home would get so distracted counting the holes in the basket it would have no time to do the family harm. We bought it to keep my house safe from the demons and evil spirits.

Ricky

I remember the day they came, 3rd May 2000. It was bright and sunny. The manager had put two small tables outside and a couple were sitting out having garlic bread and a glass of wine. I should have called Fass as soon as I saw them in the restaurant, but I didn't.

There were three. None of the fuckers smiling. Three cheap suits and two briefcases between them. That should have alerted me because they would have been full of vengeance for the gold Rolex watch that slanted out of the left sleeve of my Armani suit. Any fool could have seen them for what they were – jackals come to steal the lion's dinner. But I hadn't slept for three whole days and was a wreck in a high place. And cocaine annihilates intuition. Makes every problem appear as an occasion to act with perfect confidence, to succeed. It sure fooled me. Nothing could go wrong. Nothing would. I didn't see the precise teamwork, the determination, the way they had me completely surrounded.

'Mr Delgado,' the leader of the pack greeted.

'Yes,' I said, smiling.

His mouth jerked. Fuck me, that was him smiling. 'Victor Bremner, VAT inspection unit. My colleagues, Colin Cahill and Peter Blather. We are here to look over your books.' Their watchful eyes were a far cry from the woman inspector who had blushed when I flirted with her, who had taught me to cheat. Two more mouths jerked. I was just about getting used to their version of a smile when they all stopped simultaneously. As if they had rehearsed it.

I should have called Fass then. But like I said before I'd just had a big hit. Dopamine running riot in my brain. I could have wrestled giant grizzlies, outrun cheetahs . . .

'No problem,' I said, and led the way to the office. I knew all about their vast powers. They can even come into your home. You must never play with them. So in the office, I said, 'Just give me a minute while I make a quick call.'

I telephoned Francesca. 'Bin all the papers in all the drawers on the left-hand side of my desk,' I said in Italian.

As I put the receiver down, Mr Colin Cahill reached into his jacket pocket for his mobile phone. His eyes were cold and hard. Into the phone he clipped, 'The house, in the bin.'

Fucking bastard could understand Italian. Too late I remembered Fass's warning that they often sent someone who could speak the native language of the restaurant they are investigating.

The cardinal rule. I had broken it. *The walls have ears. Destroy everything, anything incriminating instantly.* I had a year's worth of incriminating evidence of the worst kind, sales receipts and black invoices carelessly stuffed into my drawers.

Shit, shit, shit.

I called Fass, but the jackals, snarling and triumphant, were already dragging away my dinner.

Bruce

We met for lunch in a Thai restaurant along Fulham Road.

She was wearing a cream silky blouse and a neat black skirt. For some reason I was nervous. I ordered a double gin and tonic.

'I'll have the same,' she said to the waitress. She raised her eyebrows.

Shit, I had been staring idiotically at her. Where were my famed bedside manners? 'Would you like me to do your hair?' I asked.

'What would you do with it?'

I reached forward, took the ghastly platinum in my hand, and let it flow through my fingers. Under the spotlight it was almost white. I had plans for it. Other plans. 'Why this colour?' I asked.

'It's just the Middle Eastern fantasy, white skin, blonde hair.'

'Who is this man who would change what is already perfect?'

She looked at me strangely and, I thought, sadly. 'Perfection? How terrible.'

'Don't you like being so perfectly beautiful?'

'Don't you know how natural it is for a human being to ruin what is perfect? To want that which is fallen. How charmed we are to find the imperfect, the broken, the ruins hidden by creepers? It comforts our own imperfection to know that invisible to the naked eye, known only to us and the restorer, is the mend line.'

'I will not break you.'

She looked at me, astonished. 'You will *not* have the chance. I saw you coming when you were a speck on the horizon.'

She had been hurt before.

The waitress arrived with our drinks. Were we were ready to order? 'Give us a couple more minutes,' I told her.

'What did you see when you saw me coming?'

She picked up her glass. 'A stiff-legged tom out on the tiles.'

'Ouch.'

'Look, I agreed to lunch today to tell you to lay off. I'm just not interested. You're not my type. I already have a lover. I don't need another.' Her clear grey eyes were totally without expression, as if she had rehearsed it, and said it a thousand times before. She raised her hand for the waitress.

The waitress came and she said, 'I'll have sticky rice, green chicken curry, fish with ginger and the stir-fried vegetables.' She looked at me 'And what will you have?'

Ricky

Fuck, fuck, fuck. What a shit month it was turning out to be. Cosmos's brother came around to say that Cosmos had gone down. He went to the eye of the cops, driving the latest cars, splashing his money around. He is finished, the bastards got him with the stuff and the money. The guy had a safety deposit box in St John's Wood. He used to do his shopping at Europa and then go into the deposit cubicle and do the switch there. Fucking fool used to come out carrying Europa shopping bags filled with six, seven kilos of coke.

The day the pigs got him, they blocked off all of St John's Wood. The thing was he knew as soon as he saw them coming towards him; he tried to slap his forehead as if he'd forgotten something and turn around to walk back. But it was already too late. They surrounded him with screeching police cars and tens of policemen. Slapped him to the ground. The bastards got everything. Poor fucker's down for a long time. Left me in the shit. Had to find a new supplier. Had to use the greedy Portuguese bastard in Chelsea in the meantime.

Bruce

Ricky and I went to score some Charlie. There was a new guy down from Edinburgh. He had a tattoo of a huge dragon breathing fire on his face and throat. He was coolly sitting by a window in a restaurant, selling coke under the table. We sat opposite him.

A girl passed. Something sluttish about her. Ricky couldn't help himself. He had to show off. 'Fur coat and dirty knickers,' he said.

A look of hard amusement came into the dealer's eyes.

'Faer coat and naer knickers,' he corrected. It was a classic moment.

I laughed and the ice was broken. In the end he gave us some ecstasy pills on the house, his grandmother had made them in her garage. Fuck me. The stuff blew our heads off.

May 2000

Ricky

Found a new supplier. He asked me to meet him in an alleyway. Fucking hell, you should have seen him. He was Italian, couldn't speak a word of English, and looked just like a tramp with a large dirty knapsack on his back, but when we reached his flat he emptied out his shabby knapsack, and ounces of coke, hundreds of different Es, Viagra, packets of marijuana and streams of acid tabs poured out. There must have been a street value of at least £50,000 on that table. Some massively tattooed people sat around watching TV, uninterested. They collected payments for him and he kept them in drugs.

Bruce

I met Elizabeth's eyes, cat-like and impenetrable, in the mirror.

'Like it?' I asked, aware of a creeping need to please her. The alien sentiment horrified me. To be like all the other suckers she hustled. String puppets jerking around like fools for her pleasure. She would not have obedience from me. I hatched a plan. A rather cunning strategy. She was not so clever.

'Yes, it's lovely,' she said, smiling a cold professional smile.

I smiled back, and as a final touch, feathered more wisps of hair around her cheeks and chin with waxed fingertips. Unfortunately there was absolutely nothing she would allow me to do about the revolting colour. But even so, I was pleased with my effort. It was a job well done. I wasn't hairdresser of the year for nothing.

I moved my face so it was alongside hers. So close our cheeks nearly touched. Her hair smelt of shampoo, wax and hair spray. Now why would a hairdresser suddenly find such a smell dizzying? She stared steadily at me in the mirror, trying to see behind my eyes, but I had concealed the plans I was making. Oh, the pleasure, the pleasure of taking without asking. 'Want a line?' I asked.

The pale grey eyes seemed pleased.

'Wait here,' I instructed.

It was five-thirty on a Monday evening. There were no more appointments in the book. I went to the back of the shop and told the gossiping shampoo girls they could go home. They looked at each other, eyebrows raised. Such behaviour by me was unknown, but they gave me no cheek. Gladly they packed their little transparent plastic handbags and exited by the back. I locked the door behind them. Their girlish laughter faded. Then I went out front to call Elizabeth.

She swung out of her chair and followed me into my parlour. Here customers had their hair washed and greedy little girls received their justice. I opened a tiny envelope and Elizabeth sat at the edge of a chair. She was very quiet. That was another reason I liked the girl. I never had to dread the moment the wag would start. She understood the value of silence.

I drew two white lines on the fake granite top and keeping my eye on her rolled a note and handed it over. The silver curtain fell forward as she bent to the line.

She handed the note back to me. Not even our fingers had met. I cleaned the top. We sat back in the black leather chairs facing each other, smiling adversaries. I smiled to hide my plan and she, her thoughts. I liked that she had not done what every other woman felt compelled to do when the coke was free, comment on how 'good' the stuff was.

'So tell me about yourself?' I invited. It was incredible how truly curious I was about her. She closed her eyes. She was like an aborigine painting. Abstract and shallow to the casual tourist yet a minefield of hidden messages. Around her eyes I traced white dots. They suited her. She made a good painting. Then she opened her eyes, and caught me watching. Her lips twitched, marginally amused. This was the thing she good at, emotional violence. Pure contempt. Surely once I had had her she would fade and no longer pound in my veins at night.

'What do you want to know?' One eyebrow rose.

'Everything,' I said. We were playing a game.

'I wouldn't know where to start.'

'What about, "Come up and see me some time"?' I suggested.

'Aah, Mae West and her one-liners. Do you know that that line doesn't work if you take away the word 'up'?'

I tried it. She was right. When the stairs ceased to exist, so did the stranger going up them, and the glamorous gal in the negligee waiting behind the closed door.

Then she said something odd, 'I'm going to give you a little inside information – I'm going to leave you the first chance I get.'

I glanced at her quickly.

She laughed at my expression, the sound loud in the tiled room. I smiled back. 'Just another gem from Ms West.'

Being alone with Elizabeth in the back of my hairdressing salon was strangely exhilarating. It emboldened me. Ricky's new supplier was good. Mother of Pearl, he called it. I just about managed to get my hands on it before Ricky could cut it. It was speeding along my veins nicely, making me feel invincible.

I disappeared into the kitchenette. Now for the plan. From a tiny vial at the back of the heater I extracted two white pills, ecstasy tablets. I crushed them quickly and mixed them in with the coke. I returned holding what looked like another bag of coke. 'More,' I said.

It took some nifty doing, but only Elizabeth inhaled the adulterated stuff.

'This is not the same stuff, is it?' she asked.

'Yes, it's exactly the same stuff,' I said, meeting her questioning eyes head on. I am a good liar. 'Why?' I asked innocently.

'It just feels different. Sharper on the nose and slightly more bitter,' she explained.

'It's just you,' I dismissed, running a finger down her cheek. Soon, very soon her pupils should be enormous, her skin extra sensitive to the touch. Soon, soon . . .

When the second packet was all gone . . .

'I feel as if I have known you for ever,' she said laying her cheek against my hand.

'Me too,' I agreed smugly.

'This stuff is really good, but I feel a bit funny.'

Then she lifted her hair away from her nape and held it pressed to the back of her head with both hands. Gotcha! That was without doubt an explicit come-on invitation. There was only thing left to do. The trick never failed to work, even with strangers in clubs. First couple of grams on the house, the rest back in my place. I held three packets up like a fan in my right hand. 'I'm going to take the rest home. Wanna come?'

'No, call me a taxi,' she said. The face was empty.

I'm going to give you a little inside information – I'm going to leave you the first chance I get. I stared at her in disbelief. She was incredible. The woman was incredible. Even the coldest, most mercenary of whores will let you sleep with her after she's consumed as much of your coke as Elizabeth had. But this woman would give nothing back. It was absolutely inconceivable. How did she do it? We really were puppets on a string with her. She pulled and we danced.

I was livid, but I could hardly complain. I kept my face

neutral, called her a taxi and fucking paid for it too.

The possibility of screwing Elizabeth was turning out be as hopeless as stealing our next-door neighbour's, fat Mary's, fish. I can still hear her strident voice. 'Are you stealing my fish, Bruce?' I ducked behind the bushes, jumped over the low garden wall and on the other side my mother was waiting for me, hands crossed over her bony chest. 'Put those fish back now.' And I would climb back over the wall and release the fish as fat Mary's round white face watched through the window.

As her taxi departed the woman had the nerve to wave.

'Bitch.' Fed up, I opened my packets. One after the other. Time passed. The phone rang. I considered ignoring it but it rang so many times I picked it up. It was Elizabeth.

'Bruce,' she gasped into the phone. 'What is this stuff we took? I feel so bad. I think I'm going be sick. My God all the edges of the room are blacking out. Jesus! . . .'

I heard a dull thud and the phone went dead. I held the phone away from my ear and looked at it stupidly. And then it hit me. Shit. I was frantic. I did not even know where she lived. In a panic I phoned Ricky, but he had turned his mobile off, and wasn't at any of his restaurants. I paged him and, grabbing a jacket, rushed out into the night. Ricky's flat was deserted. Everyone was out. I was really scared, but there was nothing I could do. All I could do was wait, wait for someone who knew where she lived to return. But it was Monday and nobody really came by on Mondays.

There was a bottle of dark rum on the table. I picked it up distractedly, automatically. There was absolutely nothing I could do. It was incredible, but not one person knew where Elizabeth lived. The rum was sweet and sickly, but I carried on pacing and drinking. All the while hearing her voice, *All the edges of the room are blacking out. Jesus!* And that terrible thud.

'Fuck, what have I done?' There were people who died bloated and bleeding from taking a single ecstasy tablet. My hands were shaking. 'Fuck, fuck, fuck'. I couldn't believe I had done something that stupid. How could I have done that to Elizabeth? My God, if anything at all happened to her . . .

In my fear I consumed the whole bottle. An hour passed. I lay on the couch, turned my head and saw a bottle of vodka rolling under the table. An hour passed with agonising slowness. I drank it all. I raided Ricky's whiskey stash. I lined up the bottles and began to drink. This time seriously. I must have passed out halfway through a bottle of cooking brandy.

Ricky shook me awake violently.

'What did you want? Why did you page me?'

'Fucking bastard, I paged you hours ago.' I croaked groggily. And I had said it was urgent as well.

'I never answer unless it's my supplier or a great fuck calling.'

'Quick, we have to go to Elizabeth's place now. I gave her some ecstasy tablets and I think they didn't agree with her. We've got to get to her.'

'I just left Elizabeth,' Ricky said, laughing. 'High as a fucking kite sitting at a table full of posh Swedish businessmen. Corny bastards stand every time she leaves the table to go to the toilet. And you know how many times Elizabeth goes to the toilet.'

'The tablets . . .'

'Didn't you know she can do fifteen tablets in one night? No flies on her.'

I stared at him foolishly. 'But she called me . . .'

'Serves you right,' he said, carelessly and pulling off his jacket, started up the stairs. 'I'm bushed, man.'

I looked at my hands. They were hanging limp. My God, I was in love with a complete bitch.

Elizabeth

I called Maggie, but she couldn't talk. She said there was a spider as big as her hand in her bathtub, and she was trying to get it into a container without harming it. I put the phone down and laughed. She sounded happy, and, as usual, terrible for exaggerating. If she said a man in Park Lane had tried to murder her it probably meant he had stopped to ask for directions. I was wondering exactly how big the spider really was when Bruce called.

'Oh, the hero,' I said.

For a while there was only silence, a mixture of embarrassment and rage, but then he burst into laughter and said, 'Oh, what the heck, I'll admit it, I was wrong. I could have killed you last night. Will you forgive me?'

I laughed. What was I faulting him for? I nearly gave him a heart attack. All that frantic paging and calling. It had surprised us, Ricky and me. We never thought he had that much of a conscience.

'Next time try rat poison. It works better,' I said, and that made him laugh.

He invited me to dinner. He said it was to make up for being such a lunatic.

I was feeling really rough from the night before so I did what I shouldn't have done. I said yes. Perhaps that's a lie. Perhaps I had started to long for the sight of him, those big broad shoulders, that gloriously intense stare. Mmm, that dimple. Yes, definitely that dimple. I don't know where the feeling came from but when I was near him I felt secure. As if for the first time ever I was safe. I wanted to say yes, so I did. But some part of my brain was already regretting my impulsiveness.

The man had the power to hurt me. He didn't want me. Not the real me. He was only a shallow creature seeking physical perfection. He imagined me as a gorgeous sprite, and for a little while he wanted to be powerless in the lure of such magic. I was not that gorgeous sprite he was looking for. I couldn't let him get to me. He was not the man for me. He would be the first to walk away if he saw the real me. When he knew the secret I carried. I had learned my lesson well. Men were not to be trusted.

June 2000

Nutan

I awoke shivering. It was still dark. I switched on the light. There was only me and Zeenat in the bed, but pale snake had come to visit earlier. I knew for certain it was him. I had felt him, resting heavily on my back, his forked tongue moving in my ear, but I couldn't understand the language he spoke.

I listened to my sister breathing beside me as the sky turned light. The visit I knew to be a warning, or perhaps I was just coming down with something. There was a throbbing pain in my head.

Unable to go back to sleep I sat and wrote to Nenek. Told her about the pain. The post took so long it could be two months before I heard back from her. By the time Zeenat awakened the pain was so bad I told her to go into work without me.

'Do you want to go to hospital?' Zeenat asked.

'No,' I said. 'I think I have just partied too much for too long. Post this letter for me and after work could you drop by Ricky's flat and get my earrings, the gold ones. I forgot them in the bedroom upstairs. I think I left them in the drawer, or by the bedside. If you don't go and get them today someone is bound to steal them.'

'All right. I'll try to come back during break time to see if you are feeling better, but the boss might not allow me. We will be short staffed without you.'

'That's all right. I don't think it is anything serious anyway.'

But by two o'clock that afternoon the pain was so terrible I started crying.

Ricky

It was two o'clock. I don't where it came from, but in the stillness of my study I felt it suddenly, clearly, that downward tug. Things were going badly wrong. Presentiments of disaster? Fuck that for a lark. I pulled myself up sharp. No way I was going down that road. I opened a drawer restlessly. There were some acid tabs inside. Their strength had been described as 'crazy/brilliant'. I knocked back two aspirins and four tabs, and lay back.

When I opened my eyes, beautiful pink flamingos were flying across the sky. They made me smile. Inside the room, in a tiny rip in the wallpaper, a small doorway was opening. It was dark, mysterious and beckoning. Without a doubt I knew that it was the doorway to a secret world. I could enter it only with my mind, only with a clear unfettered mind. There was a noise and when I looked away from the widening doorway, I saw my two younger girls standing by the desk.

'Papa, what are you doing?' they asked.

They were beautiful creatures, my girls. You should have seen them that day. Fucking angels. So beautiful they were like little bright lights in the room. When one of them was three she was so convinced that butterfly-shaped pasta was made from butterflies that for years she wouldn't eat them. In a perfect moment of lucidity I recognised them as a part of me. I wanted to see, so I saw – through their skin to the blood rushing in their veins. It was mine. Flesh of my flesh. A warm wave of protective emotion lapped over me. I'd give up my life for them and without a second thought. It was then that I decided to share my discovery. I told them about the doorway and their bright faces turned to the rip in the wallpaper.

'There's nothing there, Papa,' they cried in unison.

I looked at the wall. The opening was still growing. A man could nearly squeeze through. We had to hurry or we would miss the unique opportunity. Of course, to make the journey they would need acid tabs too. Hurry, children. They had to stand where I was standing.

Oh, what fun! Just the three of us.

Together we would explore the secret in that other world. I opened the drawer. I split two and told my girls to open their mouths. Immediately their pretty mouths opened like pink flowers. Inside very red and very deep. Full of bits of me. I positioned my hands above their mouths.

'Ready?' I asked.

'Ready,' they cried, excited by the new game.

'Ricky,' a woman was shouting. Her voice was far away, but shrill and full of urgency. My hands stilled. The pink flowers closed. My daughters turned towards their mother.

'Go upstairs, girls,' she told them.

'But . . .' they cried in disappointed voices.

'I said, GO UPSTAIRS.' When have I heard her so firm? Never.

They went, shoulders hunched, bottom lips out.

Slowly I turned my head. I knew I had done wrong.

I felt the blood wash away and something begin to claw frantically inside my head. Fuck, what have I done? Then just as suddenly my brain lost its sharpness and began to drift. Quite pleasantly. The room was suddenly a giant kindergarten. And she was wearing blue ottoman silk and her long curls were damp from the shower. Soon she would iron them straight. I thought then I preferred her curls. She hated them. That much I knew for certain. In her wooden Japanese sandals she stood frozen, shocked, simply staring at me. A gentle breeze coming in from the open french windows lifted and then dropped the almost dry curls by her cheeks.

I stared at her, trying hard to concentrate on her face. I had to remember what I had forgotten. In a funny way I was more shocked than she was. My brain, it just refused to work. I saw her as a beautiful statue. Her skin glowing smooth and perfectly desirable. Was it her I rescued in that abandoned cave temple? I became confused. 'Is it you?' I asked.

But as if awakening from a long dream she opened her mouth. I did not hear the words, but I knew then it was not my spider goddess. She had a different voice. Sweeter, much sweeter. This woman was different. She reminded me of someone I knew quite well. I stared at her harder. I knew her. Why, she was the mother of those gorgeous children.

'Francesca?'

In a few more years, I thought idly, she would look like her mother, heavy and resigned with numerous dimples scattering her thighs, ugly things that can be seen even through the thick material of her dresses, but at that moment she was Da Vinci's *Gioconda*, Mona Lisa.

With her lost and found smile. So dazzlingly elusive even a gay genius had to paint her. Her medieval eyes glimmered with unshed tears and her hands hung limp at her sides. No, not a statue, perhaps more of a corpse. But the mouth was ambivalent, moving, saying something. She was alive then. I tried to focus on her voice. Let it teach me things.

'Under the olive tree it was you I was crying for,' it said.

Even through the fantastic grip of the drugs I immediately knew why she had told me that. It was the end. No more need for games. She wanted to walk away free. It was a shock, actually losing her. After all those years and all the lies she had unwillingly forced herself to eat she was finally ready to call it a day.

She turned and walked away. Her chin was firm, her step

sure. I had lost her for good. This time I'd really gone too far. I looked at the wall.

C...R...A...Z...Y.... There *was* a door in the wall when I came in . . . .

I rushed out of the house.

It was not possible. It was not possible. My head was spinning. I looked at my feet in shock. I was barefoot. I blinked and looked again. My shoes were back on.

C...R...A...Z...Y....

God, I was tripping and badly. I walked. And I walked. I imagined I walked for hours. Down dark narrow alley-ways. As if I was not in London, but Singapore or Bombay, or the Bronx. Sometimes I had to step over huge rats and the greasy coiled ropes one finds in harbours. Once I passed a man standing by an old-fashioned lamp post who was jiggling coins in his pocket. He tipped his hat at me. In another pool of light I saw a beautiful woman with long black hair. She was wearing the same red lacquer jacket worn by a Chinese empress in my history book. When I stumbled over to her, she smiled and opened the jacket. She wore nothing underneath, and her body was long, narrow and perfect, but I was suddenly overcome by a mysterious terror. I jerked away and ran. I heard her mocking laugh follow me into the dark.

Finally it seemed I was returned to this century. I passed a pub and every single person drinking at the tables outside turned to stare with cold unfriendly eyes at me. Shocked, I staggered away. It was only paranoia. My own. I was a mess. I knew I was a mess.

Shit, I had to get to the flat. Two hours I searched for the flat. Walking in circles. Still, it seemed the acid was slinking away. The moments of lucidity were getting more frequent. I opened my eyes and I was sitting in the bus station at Victoria. I hailed a taxi to the flat.

Francesca

I heard him leave. In his shame he ran. Let him go. He was not mine, not the beautiful Adonis I once hopelessly worshipped. I looked at him well today. Running to fat, vulgar. Sneaky blue eyes festering in a face gone squalid. I wanted him as we were when we first met, but my Ricky died many years ago. Who was this vile monster? *Tutta la vita*, Ricky? It had turned dark in the canals. The waters gleamed black. It was time I bid the gondolier cease his rowing. It was time.

Perhaps, too, I should have left a long time ago. Possibly that day I found the neatly folded packet in his trouser pocket. Then I was child, and like a child I touched my finger to the white powder inside, and placed it on the tip of my tongue. It tasted of pain-killer tablets, but immediately it began its numbing effect. And the numbness? Been spreading ever since. I sat on the bed feeling nothing that evening. Not sadness, not bitterness, not even anger. Absolutely, completely, covered in nothing.

The children came in. They were upset with me. 'You made Papa leave,' they accused. Of course they loved him. How not to love a man who kissed you at the door as he was leaving for work, and told you, with twinkling eyes, not to be as good as possible, but as naughty as you possibly could. He was their hero.

How could he? How was it possible he would try to poison his own flesh and blood? What was wrong with him?

Be careful what you wish. You may get it.

It was true a long time ago I wished Ricky for my husband. How could I have imagined my wish would bring me here? But a small voice in my head, said, 'stop pretending.' If the real truth be known my heart, so desperate with wanting, dulled to nothing my instinct to flee and pretended all was well, but my head, lacking greed, always knew this day was coming.

If it didn't then why did I secretly begin saving money? 'My fuck off fund' I jokingly called it. Ricky was so bad with money he never even noticed. Not that he would have cared if he had. Over the years I slowly increased the house-keeping money over and above the inflation rate and salted it away into my fund. I did the same with what I made at the dress agency. It all mounted up.

From the very first when he had cheated and my head caught a glimpse of that waitress's hips, lean as a wolf's, it had known fear for the future. It seemed like for ever that I have been surrounded by wolves. Even though I was completely bewildered, and my head was spinning reck-lessly, I moved automatically. Round and round, replacing my defenceless back with my snarling face. Such a relief to stop the mad waltzing.

'Well, you know Daddy has to go to work,' I told their unhappy faces. It was incredible how calm my voice was. It really was a good thing finally to wake up from my night-mare.

'Daddy said that there's a door in his wall.'

'Did he? I have a wonderful idea. Let us go on a little holiday. Let's go and stay at Grandma's house.'

'Yeah, let's go to Nonna in Sicily.'

'We can do that too, but first let's go and stay with Nonna in Egham.'

I had another wish. I wished for it a long, long time ago. A dream really. I think I might even have stayed with Ricky because of it. He always promised me that we would end our days in Sicily. That was what I wished for. I wanted to feel the Sicilian sun over my head and the white soil of my childhood under my feet. I wanted to return to a time when I was truly happy. Where peaches and cherries were not sterile things trapped between plastic and Styrofoam, but alive and beautiful on trees. I wanted the children to be as brown as berries.

In fact, my dream of returning was connected with another shimmering childhood dream that I always thought was impossible to achieve. Funnily enough it was Ricky who made it impossible. Now that he was gone . . .

My vision started in my father's delicatessen when I tasted a drop of Tuscan olive oil. A drop of oil, you say. But I cannot tell you how that drop transported me to a different place. How it opened a window for me. I saw my future. It was green. It was exciting. Wonderfully so. In Tuscany they pick the olives when they are still green. They lay the unripe olives on presses and scatter olive leaves on top. The result is the most exciting peppery olive oil you can imagine. With a hunk of crusty bread, it is a meal in itself.

In Sicily, very often, when the olives are small, or when there is still oil in the family's drums, the olives are simply left on the trees. No one knows what to do with them. There is certainly no commercial demand for it. Now if I could make such an olive oil in Sicily . . . I could buy the olives from the farmers, make a good quality home-made variety with them and export it to England. I knew all my father's old suppliers. Did I dare do it on my own? I needed to buy some land, just a little. Just enough for us to be self-sufficient. If I could plan to be there after Christmas. January in Sicily. The black grapes would be covered in sheets of plastic. For the late harvest.

But what if I failed? Perhaps there was already too much olive oil on the market. What if I lost a lifetime of savings chasing a ridiculous illusion? How would I bring up the children? I needed time to think. It was too big a decision to take without careful consideration.

Not at such a moment anyway. First I needed refuge at my father's home. Just for a little while, until I regained my strength. The initial numbness seemed to have slipped a little, and I realised that in fact I was badly wounded. The pain was sickening. It was the shock that made me think I was not. I was mortally damaged.

He was my life, you see. I gave up my dream for him. You thought it was the gold credit cards, didn't you? But it was not. It was my heart. It refused to let go. There is a Russian saying, *the fish rots from the head*. Quite right, the rot started in my head. The terrible pain started there. Now it was spreading, spreading inside my body, my arms, my legs, my fingers, poisonous and foul.

And the children hugged me and asked, 'Why are you crying, Mummy?'

Ricky

It was eight o'clock by the time I let myself into the flat. I finally made it. My head felt horrible. I lurched upstairs, and in my bedroom who should I find standing by my bed, but Nutan's little sister. She opened her eyes wide. Well, well, this was a turn up for the books. An unexpected offering from the Spider Goddess. The girl smiled. Warm, open, trusting. She spoke then. I didn't hear the words, something about a pair of earrings. As I watched her back nervously away I was suddenly crazy for the feel of her skin.

She pretended to hate me, but I had seen the lovesick expressions she threw in my direction. The girl was in love with me, had been from day one. In love with her sister's lover. What little secrets the meek hide. I could have had her a long time ago, but I was saving her, until now . . . Would she smell like Nutan? I could already feel her underneath me. The little bones snapping. Breaking in my hands. That she would break was no doubt.

And so fucking what if she broke? I was broken. Her warm eyes were like a balm. I needed that. Somewhere deep inside me was unbearable pain. So raw even the memory could kill and therefore must be killed. Oh fuck the children's faces. So trusting. God, to think I had nearly . . . And if this little one was to perish in my arms? Let her perish.

I smiled softly. '*Com'e va, Bella?*'

For a moment she froze. Difficult to describe the expressions fleeing across her face, and then she half smiled and said the most intriguing thing. 'Pretend you are me. Do what I do.'

'Come. It's warm over here,' I said, holding my hand out.

She ignored my hand and, reaching behind her, grasped the guitar leaning against the wall. And without warning I glimpsed her sister. Fun, gregarious and adventurous. *Pretend you are me. Do what I do.* I knew what she was doing. She was pretending to be her sister.

'Play. Play John Lennon's "Imagine",' she said.

My hands were shaking with the drugs. The guitar felt awkward, the strings, sharp as blades. I didn't want to play. I wanted to drag her to bed. I was craving to forget. Even for a few moments, to be lost in a sexual wilderness. I had done something terrible, unforgivable.

I dropped on the bed and my fingers began strumming. Not John Lennon but Cat Stevens, his voice was in my head, and slipping out of my mouth, enigmatic, searching. And not finding.

My lady D'banville

I am sure it was all in my head, but I tell you my fingers were bleeding. I looked up and I saw Francesca. Standing as still as a statue. Cold as ice. Is it you? My lady D'banville. Lips like winter.

I loved you, my lady

Francesca touched my cheek. Her hands were warm. I looked up into her face.

Oh no, it's not my lady D'banville. She sleeps.

'You are crying,' Zeenat said, crouching like a cat at my feet, stroking my face. 'What is wrong?' Ahh, Francesca. It's not you.

I'll wake you tomorrow. La, la, la, la, la, la, la

Why I put her to sleep was a mystery.

Zeenat, I knew already, would be nothing like her sister. She would be soft and gentle and eager to please. She would want it to last for ever.

'There was once a man who slept with a snake disguised as a woman,' she said.

You, a snake? You are barely an earthworm. I nearly said it, but I did not. Now if she really had been a snake in disguise it might even be fun. An experience to boast about. But she was only the quiet sister.

Still, by pretending to be her sister, she was strangely intriguing. I must ask the fate of the man that lay with the serpent. But later. First I had to bed the woman who pretended to be my lover. At the very least I would have had what Anis wanted so badly. And that couldn't be all bad.

Hell, why not? 'Come, Bella.'

I pulled her up by the arms, but as my mouth reached hers, she began to struggle. You started this, sweetheart. If you catch the tiger by the tail you must be prepared to be eaten. I pinned her on the bed. It excited me, her puny useless struggles, her soft, open, shocked, helpless, stupid mouth. I had learned from Nutan, the Balinese do not kiss. They simply rub noses, smelling each other's scent. To be perfectly honest, virgins are boring as shit, but they are alluring in spite of their lack of skills. To be the first man. That's twice now in the same family.

I was rough. Something tore; a slip, underwear, and the sound made her struggles cease abruptly. The tightness left her limbs. She relaxed out, unfolded, opened like a sea creature opening its tentacles, her eyes huge and frightened.

Underneath me her bones were tiny, passive. It was un-believable to think she was exactly the same size as Nutan. Why, Nutan was like a cloudy leopard in bed, exciting, mysterious and dangerous. This one was small, listless, spread open and suffering quietly. She sure was doing a bad job of pretending to be her sister. It was like fucking a pillow with a hole in. I hated it. Thrusting into her. She had no power over the pain inside me. Even slamming into her so hard I heard the dull thump of our flesh hitting did not help. It was no good. I could not forget. The statue, the children . . .

I gasped suddenly. It was Francesca under me.

She looked at me scornfully. 'You are a vain, heartless rodent. You should have left the girls alone,' she said.

'Fuck,' I swore and my confused eyes met Zeenat's startled frightened face. And suddenly I was repulsed by the simple goodness, the schoolgirl innocence shining in her face. To think I had coveted this! I saw the young, beautiful body under me as a clinging vine. Needy. Repugnant. I knew her type. She would be looking for cuddles and love next. I sprang away from the body and the blood between her legs. Suddenly I was angry. I didn't have to think. My mouth was cunning. It made a club. It had always taken a delight in killing.

'Look, Zeenat, I'm having a bad trip. Too fucked to fuck.'

Now she knew that I knew; that I had always known. The rejection was complete. She was not good enough. Her sister was better. Her shocked eyes filled with tears. Oh no, not that too. Already I was bored. She was better in my fantasies when there were two of them. It was a mistake. An honest mistake. You understand, don't you? I must bear no blame in the event. She lied. It was she who came into the wolf's den, pretended to be its lover.

Still the Goddess of goodness, a statue called Francesca,

different you will understand from the Spider Goddess, accused, her lips pulled back from her teeth, 'You are a vain, heartless rodent.'

To appease the angry Goddess I could have done what the Incas did, sacrificed snakes, butterflies, birds or offered jade, incense and tortillas, but instead I muttered, 'Why don't you stay a while, stand and watch, learn something,' with such indifference that Francesca fell away into the deep gorges inside my head. Goodbye, my angel. No hard feelings. It's only decimation, a Roman Emperor's power, every tenth soldier must die or I will not be the absolute master of all I survey.

Never again would I awaken the statue called Francesca. A hundred curls and wrapped in blue ottoman silk. My head was ringing. It was the acid. As I left the flat I heard Zeenat's muffled sobs, but I was busy. I had things to do, places to go and people to see. No time for a silly little girl. No, no time at all. Would I always wake up the same? A risk seeker.

Nutan

I opened the door and Zeenat was putting on her make-up. Our eyes met in the mirror but hers slid away.

'Are you going out?' I asked.

'Yes,' she replied shortly. Silently she carried on applying blusher. Too much, I thought. What was the matter with her?

'Where are you going?' I asked her curiously, sitting on the bed to take my shoes off. She didn't wear make-up just to go and see Anis.

She turned on me then, without warning, utterly furious. 'What's it to you where I go? Did I ask you where you disappeared to?'

I stared at her blankly. 'I went out to get some pain killers,' I said.

'Oh, and when you stay out all night with that . . . that . . . that Italian dog.'

She had not asked how I was. 'What's the matter with you?'

'What's the matter with me? Nothing. Absolutely nothing.'

She turned back to the mirror and continued putting on her make-up. I watched her colour her mouth as red as the kasoomba flower that my mother used to make dye.

'Did you get my earrings?' I asked.

'Yes, they are by the bed.' Then still fuming silently (I could tell by the jerky movements she made), she yanked a short black dress off our bed, one of mine in fact, and put it over her head. While her head was still inside the dress she said, 'You're just a selfish cow.'

Selfish cow. Where did she learn that from? Cows were good helpful animals. I didn't know how to react. We had never before spoken to each other in such a vicious manner.

Her head emerged from the neckline of the dress, her face tight with fury, and something else. I had never seen her like this. She tugged my dress over her hips. Only then I realised it was too tight, and too short. Combined with the gaudy make up she looked like a prostitute. Did I look like that in it?

I did something silly then. I clapped my hands and said sarcastically in English, the way Ricky might have done, 'Oh, way to go baby.'

The blood drained out of her face then. She closed her eyes for a second. When she opened them, she said, 'Yes, that's right, make me feel small. You think your new friends are special, don't you? They are scorpions. All of them. You will only know when they sting you. Only when your flesh is blue and rotting with poison will you choose to return home. Well, I'm not waiting around until then. I am going home to Nenek next week.'

'You're jealous,' I accused.

She barked out a short incredulous laugh. 'What? Of you? You have no idea,' she sneered. 'Nenek was right. We should never have come. Look how blind you have become.' Then she brushed past me and tottered down the steps in her stilettos. It was so warm outside she had left jacketless, her hair still wet from the shower.

After she had gone I stood there bewildered. I couldn't understand why we had fought – we never fought – and so spitefully too. Why? Had we not filed our teeth at puberty? Were we not then safe from the six evil qualities of human nature, passion, greed, anger, intoxication, stupidity and jealousy? I sat by the window, hugging my knees to my body, waiting for her. She would return soon. She would feel as bad as me. My head still throbbed, but only slightly.

It was nine o'clock, and yet wonderfully light outside. In fact it was such a warm summer's day that the milk on the window sill had gone sour. In the street below people were coming out of the kebab shop carrying white packages. Sitting at the window sill I ate some bread and cheese. *I needed a line.* I lay on the bed to wait, fell asleep and wrenched awake suddenly at five in the morning. She was still not back.

I began to worry. Where could she have gone dressed like that? I looked out of the window. It was dark outside and the air was chilly. I slipped on a night shirt and thick woollen socks and went to sit by the window. The road was deserted. By six in the morning I was sick with fear. The sky was light. Where was she? She had never done this before. Disappeared into the night on her own.

I called in sick and waited all day by the window for her. All day.

By seven that night I was almost hysterical with worry.

Had she found a man, gone home with him? My stomach churned with horrible possibilities. She was a gentle creature. Not like me. And there were so many strange perverted people in this country. I should never have said the unforgivable things I did. But why, why did we fight in the first place? In this country that was not ours anything could happen.

Eight-forty. I called Anis from a phone box down the street. Immediately I heard the worry slide into his voice. By nine o'clock Anis was in our room. I could see he was upset, but he tried to hold it back. It made me feel worse.

I felt so bad I sobbed like a fool in his arms. We sat together listening for the least sound on the stairs. After a while he went down to the kebab shop for some food but I could not eat. The smell of the meat made me feel dizzy. I asked Anis for some coke. He didn't have any, but called someone from his mobile phone. In less than half an hour someone was at the door. I took a line, and instantly went crazy with paranoia. I couldn't sit still. I was convinced something horrible had happened. I paced. Up and down, back and forth, to the window and back. I wanted to go out and look for her. Pointless, Anis said, staring out of the window, his shoulders tensed.

Over twenty-four hours had passed. It was ten o'clock and Anis had just suggested we go to the police when I heard her spiky shoes on the stairs. I ran to open the door and froze. It *was* Zeenat coming up the stairs and yet . . . oh, I cannot explain the change in her. I looked into her glittering eyes and saw the strangest expression: was it furtive or triumphant? I cannot say for sure. But the moment passed and we were running into each other's arms, the expressions we first found in each other's faces forgotten. I looked at my sister's tears, and saw her remorseful, but I knew. Something had changed. There was a distance between us. A secret.

'Where have you been?'

'At Anna's house.'

Anna was the English waitress at the café.

After a while Anis went home. He looked inconsolable. I touched his face. 'What?' I asked. He shook his head and smiled sadly. Then he said goodbye and left. As if Zeenat had not come home safe and sound. As if she had sustained some permanent damage.

We were lying in bed talking, holding hands, and pretending the distance was not between us when I fell asleep. I was so tired. I thought I dreamed that she was kissing my face, stroking my hair, and repeating over and over again, 'I'm sorry. I'm sorry. Do you forgive me?' In my sleep, I answered her, 'Of course I forgive you.'

I awakened suddenly in the cold bluish light of dawn. The witching hour. Nenek said twilight is a crack between the worlds. Only the dead or those who can see with their eyes closed may go forth, pass through the crack into the other. Cold, I reached for my sister. Her shape was familiar. I had always slept with her. I remembered another time. Our small bodies curled and snugly moulded into Nenek's safe shape. I touched my head gingerly. It was only slightly sore.

I didn't like Anna. There was something about her I didn't like. Suddenly I was scared for Zeenat.

Anis

I first made love to Zeenat in a dream, when I found her at dusk, lying half-hidden in a natural depression under a mango tree. And I did it without her permission. Falling upon her curving form I entered her. Still asleep her body arched to receive me. A flock of ducks returning to the village from the rice fields passed us, their flapping wings barely brushing our naked bodies, the vibration of their webbed feet in our ears. When I shuddered to a stop, Zeenat woke up, and tapped the base of her wrists all over my body. Full of exquisite pleasure I closed my eyes.

'Didn't I tell you? You're not like your father. You are not gay at all,' she said, and I opened my eyes, suddenly awake. I could see that Zeenat was different now. I saw it in her eyes. Somehow she had been ruined. She was no longer a page unwritten. Someone had soiled her. I had failed to protect her. She never came around any more. Not even on Sundays. Not even to see the blue tits.

July 2000

Ricky

I put the phone down gently but I was fuming. This was it? Summer? This really horrible, ugly, unwashed, bitch-grey day? I felt like smashing something with the sheer frustration that throbbed inside my brain. The Customs and Excise jackals had done their calculations and they reckoned that I owed them something in the region of a quarter of a million in back taxes, interest and penalties.

'Can you believe this fucking shit?' I ranted down the phone to Fass.

Fass thought he could bring it down to £190,000, but I was not to hold my breath because the cock-sucking bastards had too much on me. He was careful not to say, I told you so; but he didn't need to.

I swallowed my eighth aspirin that morning.

Fucking bastards.

I would have to sell three if not four of my restaurants to pay up. Sons of bitches. The restaurants were my blood, sweat and tears. The bastards fuck me up the arse, for what? To pass it on to some good-for-nothing, bed-wetting, glue-sniffing, thieving Albanian hiding out in a council flat, while pretending refugee status. Or to hand it down to some snivelling teenage single mother too lazy to get off her arse and get a fucking job. This morbid need to punish those who work and mollycoddle those who don't is the real reason why such a *beautiful* country is going to the fucking dogs.

I could feel the fury boiling in my stomach until I noticed that a spider had built a massive web just outside my window, almost covering all of it with its intricate thread. And inside me a funny note of joy. The dream was safe, the promise unbroken. Nothing could go wrong.

Nutan

I gave the postman a piece of jelly and coffee when he came upstairs with a letter from Nenek. He was always a nice cheerful face in the morning. He asked after Zeenat. I told him she was staying over at a friend's house. She often did that now. Stayed over at Anna's.

When he was gone I sat on the bed to read Nenek's letter. I read the enigmatic words twice and was no wiser. She told me not to worry about that mysterious headache that I had suffered that time Zeenat and I had fought. She said all the women in our family got it 'when our spines awakened'. And then she warned me that there was not too much time left, and I should take good care of my sister.

Was it her way of saying goodbye? Was she sick? Was she dying? I wrote back immediately wanting to know exactly what she meant by the awakening spine and the lack of time left. I posted the letter during break time. Zeenat did not want to come with me. She said she was tired. She must have been, for she pulled a chair up to face the plate shelves, crossed her arms on the third shelf and, resting her forehead on her hands, fell instantly to sleep.

Francesca

The telephone rang and I knew it was Ricky. I ran down the stairs but halted at the landing, my father had picked up the phone, and was speaking in a voice I had never heard before. 'Never call again.' Then he replaced the receiver very quietly. Oh, how much I had wanted to speak to him. I walked down the stairs and stood at the door. 'Who was it?'

My father looked at me, his face blank. 'Wrong number,' he said.

'Oh,' I said and went back upstairs.

I sat on my bed. He had called. People could change if they wanted something badly enough. Why did he call if he did not want us back?

I paced the bedroom. Nothing mattered without him. I had started to feel that I should not have come to my parents, and involved them in my business. If only I had friends to turn to. I should have just gone to a hotel. Ricky and I would have kissed and made up by now. I felt resentful towards my parents. Still, it was my fault they had turned against him. I was so confused I made the mistake of telling them everything. If I had not told them that part about the drugs, they could somehow have found it in their hearts to forgive him. He was the father of the children. But now, they stood in the way, unchangeable

And my impractical plan to go to Sicily and make olive oil. Who was I kidding? It was a silly idea. Of course it would never come to anything. I might as well give up now, and spare myself the humiliation of failure. Why, I didn't know the first thing about running a business, let alone sourcing the oil, pressing it and successfully marketing it.

All I knew how to do was shop. I didn't even know how to take care of my kids. This whole thing was mad. He was my husband, for God's sake. I needed him. The children needed him. I had never known or loved another. I didn't know how to carry on. I was like a fish out of water.

I had to find a way to set it right. I would call him. I sat in the darkness of my room waiting for the sound of my parents' footsteps on the stairs. I stood outside their door an hour later and heard my father snoring.

Carefully I crept downstairs and pressed the last caller button. My heart leaped to see the restaurant number come up. He did love me. He did want us. I took a deep breath, dialled 141 to withhold my number and phoned the restaurant. The manager answered, but before I could speak I heard Ricky in the background. He was laughing. A big jovial laugh. And I knew then. He was not suffering. He didn't care.

I put down the phone, and went to lie on my bed. Oh God. Give me my old life back.

Nutan

The streets were cold and deserted. It was that time after four but before six, when the coke was all gone and sleep couldn't be found in any bed. When you are craving for more even though you know that more will not bring a new high, or the old one back. The body had reached its inviolable plateau. All that was left to do was hunt down sleep, somewhere.

I guessed our room would be empty. Zeenat was hardly ever in any more. She slept over at Anna's house. Too often, I thought. There was something about that dirty girl's glowing eyes that made me nervous for Zeenat. Ever since we had that big argument, I was aware of Zeenat drifting away. Even while she was asleep, beside me, I sensed her moving steadily away. I felt she hid a secret and I was frightened of this terrible thing that could not be revealed even to me.

More and more I had started to feel that we should return to Bali. I realised that Zeenat was right. I had been infected by the cold strange air of this country. It was not good for us. England had turned us against each other. It was my fault. I had gone a little crazy, but I was all right now. I wanted us to return. To be as we were before. We had had our wonderful holiday and now we could go home. As I came up the stairs I saw that the light was on and I felt suddenly happy. Zeenat was in. Good, she was still awake. We could talk. She would be so happy to know I too wanted to return. I let myself into our room.

She was in.

Holding a needle.

She turned to look at me. This, then, was the terrible secret. But, Sita, you have stepped out of the magic circle. For the first time I saw the horrible pin-point pupils in her glowing eyes. Oh, oh, oh, I knew then where I had seen that glow before. Anna. Eyes as cunning as a cave fox, standing just out of reach. I recognised her too late. She was Kuni, the hunchback servant from Father's shadow play, standing behind my sister's shoulder urging, whispering, wreaking havoc. Did I not already suspect from her crafty face that she was a brilliant strategist? Working behind the scenes, luring Zeenat away from me.

All kinds of thoughts rushed through my head. So fast I felt faint. I had been so absorbed in my little discoveries I had not seen her making her own. My dumb shock irritated her. I saw it flash onto her face. She did not care that I knew. That shocked me even more.

'What are you doing?' My voice was barely a whisper, but carried all the horror in my heart.

'What does it look like?'

I opened my mouth to speak, to protest, but she raised a palm to me and counselled, 'Do not try to stop me. It is now a part of my life.'

She was neither remorseful nor ashamed. In fact she was fearless, triumphant. This was where the worried expression had gone to. I shook my head with disbelief, but there was more. She did something even more incredible. Slowly she lifted her hand, her movements as beautiful and graceful as a dancer's, and offered me the syringe. 'It is not like they say. It is the most beautiful thing, such a special flavour, like, . . . like blood,' she said and her eyes were shining. *Pretend you are me. Do what I do. Be me.*

Speechlessly I stared into her face. 'Oh Zeenat, what have you done?'

But she was not like a junkie at all; in fact she seemed exhilarated, powerful. How potent she had become! I stood hypnotised by her tremendous power. For the first time in our lives she was the one who had found the new experience. She wanted to lead the way. She did not walk into one of my scenes. She had created her own with a part in it even for me. In her hand she held my lines. Now she asked that I spoke them as the script demanded. In her play, the queen who walked slowly on the points of her toes towards her doom was noble beyond words. This time it was I who had to pretend to be her. Do what she did. Be her.

I remembered her as she was before. In the pink light of the tropical sunset. Graceful, eloquent and humble. A beautiful creature under the frangipani, knees gently bent, her body arching sideways, her hands lifted high above her head, her thumb and forefinger touching while her other fingers spread out in a courtly stylised movement. Now I saw that it was the gesture of a bird that spreads its wings ready to fly away. Look at her fly now. There is a wonderful line from a poem that touched me in some deep and secret place, but I did not know what it meant until that moment. *Am I dreaming you or are you dreaming me?*

Time stood still. Watching my sister across the room I suddenly felt the ancestors who throbbed in my blood. Puputan. Did I ever tell you that *puputan* means ending? A glorious ending. Arrayed in white and dripping with their best jewels my ancestors hurried onto the

Dutchmen's guns, never mind death. All or nothing.

All or nothing. If the only way to reach her was to take the needle into my body, and let her witness for herself how far she had drifted away . . . If she could stomach my destruction . . . I would dare her gun to show her that willing sacrifice for love and honour lives on. To shame her with her own horror. Only at that moment did I understand my father's shame. He was without honour because he had stood under my grandmother's dominance, too cowardly to rush into the waiting guns. 'To love is to maim,' his leather puppets cried mournfully again and again in their borrowed voices.

And what did the insane Rajah's daughter do?

She did an insane thing.

I took the first step towards her, and . . . reached for the needle. I thought she would be so horrified by the sacrifice she demanded that she would stop me, but instead she said soothingly, 'It's all right. I'll do it for you. All it is, is you put it on your skin and push it down. That's all. It's beautiful. You'll see for yourself how beautiful it is.'

In my head my father's voice sobbed in the broken voice of the betrayed old king. 'My beautiful queen, a tigress? How easily she accomplishes my ruin.'

It was bizarre. That Zeenat should wear my face, but no longer allow me to read her thoughts. With quick, sure hands she tied the opaque rubber tubing around my upper arm. Then she searched for a vein, beating the hollow inside my elbow. One, green and trusting, popped up under my skin. I watched numbly. Expertly she found the gateway into my body. She did not look at me. She pushed the needle in. *It hurt.* Blood rushed into the syringe. 'You have to do that,' she explained. I closed my eyes. Disbelieving what we were doing.

For a moment I saw us slumped defeated on my bed in that shabby, disgusting room, the curtains drawn to shut out the light of the street lamp. It was a horrible picture. If Nenek could see us. *It's all right. I'll do it for you. All it is, is you put it on your skin and push it down. That's all.*

My stomach heaved and I turned my head and vomited on the carpet. And then I was falling, not into a black unfamiliar abyss of degradation and horror, but upon a soft, warm cloud. It swirled up gently around me. No longer haunted by my sister's cunning eyes I sank into her lap. She was right. We, who emerged from the same belly and the same seed, must remain together. It was better than anything else I had tried and it really did have a very, very special flavour. Tomorrow was a dream. It was a good thing she had done to me.

'You're right. It's beautiful,' I murmured.

Bruce

The warm night had brought all the young things out, in their high heels and their sweet little skirts. They stood with us in the queue to get into the Blue Swallow. The doormen looked us over. They wanted glamorous beauties on their premises and they were happy to let Elizabeth in, but not Ricky.

'No jeans,' they said, their brute faces implacable.

'Let's go somewhere else,' Elizabeth suggested.

'Nah, I'll see you inside,' Ricky said, and wandered off down the street.

'He must have a spare pair of trousers in the restaurant,' Elizabeth guessed.

We had just ordered our drinks at the bar when I spotted Ricky.

'Hey,' he shouted, jean clad and waving.

'How did you get in?'

'Went to the club next door, gave the toilet attendant

twenty quid, and got him to smuggle me in through the back door.'

We laughed. 'I'm on a mission,' he said, scanning the place for dealers. I gave him a hundred quid, he added another hundred.

He slipped the stuff into my hand, and glancing around immediately began salivating over an Oriental chick at the bar. I looked over. Gorgeous hair and intriguing pout, but I refuse to fuck another Chinese bird. They just don't live up to all the hype. All the ones who have lain a while in my bed were cold.

'Got to get me some yellow,' Ricky shouted over the din and left on the pull. I passed one packet into Elizabeth's hand and we went our separate ways in search of the toilets.

On my way back I passed a stunning red-head in a sequinned bikini top. Naturally I looked, but when I turned to catch Elizabeth's eye, she was looking at me strangely.

'What's the matter?' I asked.

'Nothing. Let's go to China White. Maggie is there,' she said restlessly.

A bloke came up and, completely ignoring me, invited Elizabeth to dance. A sort of sickness poured into my gut. It wanted me to wrench the head off his ridiculous neck. I caught his face between my palms. Gently, you understand. And turning his surprised face towards me, smiled. A tiger's smile. Alarmed, he jerked his head free, stuttered something, and backed away. He was only a kid. Drunk as well. I watched him disappear into the crowd and felt hollow. She was not my woman. I had won a meaningless skirmish, but the battlefield was denied me.

When I looked at Elizabeth, she was considering me, her expression level. 'Subtle, aren't you?'

'Shall we go?' I asked brusquely. I didn't like the way I felt.

She nodded. 'Let's go get Ricky and the Chinese girl.'

Outside, the doormen glared at Ricky. He winked at them.

'Magic,' he taunted as we got into a waiting minicab.

'Human beings are pests,' Ricky suddenly declared. I twisted around in the passenger seat to look at him. Oh my God, he was already shit-faced.

'No, really. We are like big rats. I saw this programme once about this beautiful paradise island that the rats have almost completely destroyed. The little bastards have eaten everything, the animals, the plants, the birds, the flowers and the trees. Fucking everything. And when even the tree roots are gone, they will turn on each other, just the way we will. The rats ate an island, but we'll eat a whole planet. Think about it. We really are like rats. We give nothing to any other creature on this earth. We don't make honey, our milk is only for our own, our flesh, which is supposed to be sweet, we consider too precious to be eaten by another. We don't know how to make nests out of our saliva. Even after we are dead we won't allow our skin to be used for leather. We just know how to shit and fuck.'

'So what you saying, rats fuck a lot?' the Chinese bird asked.

'That's all they ever do, Bella,' Ricky said, laughing grotesquely, his hands slipping up her thigh.

I caught the driver checking Elizabeth out in the rear-view mirror. I turned around and she was looking out of the window, bored and unhappy. I looked at her beam-me-out-of-here expression, and started to feel uncharitable too. So when next the Oriental laughed her mean hard laugh, she looked to me like a yellow pillowcase of frogs.

July 2000

Ricky

At breakfast one morning my nose started gushing blood, but I didn't bother with a doctor. I knew the diagnosis. Stop taking drugs for a while. Let the walls recover. Stop taking drugs.

Yeah, right. I went into the kitchen and cooked myself some freebase.

If you have never tried it before, you gotta. It's that fucking good: but like all good things it costs an arm and a leg. Ha, ha, a restaurant, actually. It seemed I had picked up a habit that cost a couple of thousand a week.

'Sell a restaurant. That should keep you going for a long while,' someone recommended.

'Yeah, that's right. I sold four to pay off the VAT bastards, didn't I? Do I even need six? Hey, easy come, easy go.'

When my nose got better I wouldn't have to spend so much any more. Besides, I planned to stop soon. I planned get my shit together soon. Soon. Very soon.

Nutan

We met Anna outside Tesco. She looked cold and sick, and even skinnier than when she used to work at the cafe. She was holding two shopping bags bulging with whiskey bottles. I was mesmerised by her eyes. They were unreal, glowing green with a pin of black in the middle. Had we money, she wanted to know.

We nodded. 'Come on then,' she said, and headed for a phone booth.

'Have you got one of them things?' she asked into the receiver. 'Am I all right for five? Twenty minutes. The usual place. Cheers, mate.'

She sniffed and wiped her nose on her sleeve. We helped

283

her with her shopping bags across the road, and into the back alleyway. At the back door of an off-licence, she pushed her bony face into the padlocked grille gate and bawled in. A middle-aged man came.

'Ya all right?' she said.

He nodded silently and went back in to fetch a key. 'Just you,' he told her.

'Only be a minute,' she said, taking the bags off us and stepping into the dim interior. We stood outside.

'How many bottles?' he asked.

'Eight.'

He took them out of the plastic bags, and inspected them quickly making sure the seals were unbroken. From his pocket he produced a twenty-pound note for her. She came out and he locked the gate and went back in.

'Does he know they are stolen?'

'Obviously. Any one of them along this street will take hot stuff, but they're all right really. They never try to stiff you on the days they can see you are really sick and desperate. Selling in the pubs is the worst. People will try to rip you off bad, the more ill or desperate for Bobby you look.'

Bobby or Brown or Bobby Brown, slang for heroin.

'They know in the end you'll take anything.'

I looked at her that day, and thought to myself, you poor, poor creature. You will never have anything. No family, no children. Stealing. Getting taken for a ride by merciless strangers who see only a desperate junkie. We would never get like that. We would stop well before we got there. We were sensible. We would just stop before we got that far. We would know when to stop. It was nearly a week since I had my first hit, and I was completely without cravings. The trick was to do it infrequently, so our bodies never got used to the stuff. If we could handle the coke we could handle Bobby Brown too.

Anna took twenty pounds off us. A bag was ten pounds, she told us but she was going for the deal, five bags for thirty-five pounds. We waited at the bus stop. The guy was late, and she was beginning to panic. I stared at her with a mixture of fascination and disgust. Her nose was starting to run. She wiped it with the back of her hand. 'Fucking bastards. They are all the same, flying high on powder power.'

Powder power. That sense of power a dealer got, from the clawing desperation of his customers.

'Bastards. You tell them you're really sick, and you're standing outside their door, and they say, "Meet you in an hour." All they have to do is come down the stairs. They have us in their pockets. They become our doctors. If they don't give us our medicine we are ill. They just don't give a shit. They make you suffer for a whack.'

Whack, an injected shot of heroin.

She told us she had started sleeping with a sixty-year-old man who paid for most of her heroin. Her boyfriend, a dreadlocked geezer called Rizla, didn't care as long as he got some of her bag too.

The dealer came. Anna's hands were shaking with need by then. Her house was only around the block. Her footsteps were light and fast. We ran to keep up. The door to Anna's squat had been kicked down at some stage, and had since been nailed shut. So its only function was to bar entrance. To enter you had to push aside the boards covering the windows and climb in.

In the dry sour air of the living room five smack heads were huddled on the floor in a half-circle, around a blazing gas fire. It was the most unbelievable room ever. To believe its squalor you had to see it. There were needles, crack pipes, pieces of foil and spoons simply abandoned all over the floor. Take-away pizza boxes, children's toys, an assortment of dirty clothes and rubbish had been flung into the corners of the room. On a torn, badly stained sofa pushed up against a wall lay a comatose person. Against another wall was an incredibly dirty mattress with a twisted, crumpled, dark brown woollen blanket across it. Everything else, they told us, had been sold or stolen.

You opened cupboards in the kitchen, and they were full of more dirty needles, sheets of foil and blackened spoons. It was a horrible, horrible place yet it fascinated me. I stepped into it just to see, like a tourist would. I suppose the same way you have stepped into my world with so little persuasion. Even hell, because of the sheer abundance of naked bodies, can seem voluptuous when you are standing at the border.

That day is the only day I remember really seeing how every single person in that house was pale and drawn with prominent lacquered eyes. After that first day I could no longer see how ill and terrible they looked. Once you become one of them you cannot see it any more. Not in their eyes and not in yours.

Their acceptance of that impossible squalor should have alerted me, but it didn't. I should have wondered about this thing that had the ability to reduce human beings to such a state of degradation. I should have taken my sister's hand and left. I shouldn't have stayed, but I was young, foolish and trapped in my own fantastic adventure. Who could demand such obedience? Now I know. Now I know.

Then we didn't know what we were getting into. We were taking it to be sociable. In a little group. A gang. And if you didn't take it you couldn't belong. And the drug dealers, they look like normal people. They just had more money. We stayed overnight at the flat.

Get a spoon. Put the heroin in. Add citric acid, vitamin C powder, lemon juice or vinegar. If you use citric acid or vitamin C you have to mix a little water with it. With a lighter burn the bottom of the spoon until the liquid bubbles. Remove from fire. Drop a small bit of a cigarette butt or a bit of cotton wool into the liquid to act as a filter. Place the needle on the filter and draw the liquid up through it. Not using a filter causes a dirty hit. A bad hit can make you really, indescribably, ill. Always watch the bubbles. You don't want them in your arm. Look for a vein. Never inject directly into flesh. It really hurts. Causes a lump. An abscess that burns and stings horribly. You must always find a vein.

It was a disgusting thing to do. But we did it. You might ask why we didn't start by smoking. Not everybody can smoke. My sister couldn't. It made her puke. So much so she ended up vomiting blood.

Anis

It was late. I was drunk and fumbling with the keys in the door when I heard her call my name. I tried to swing around, but staggered backwards instead and nearly lost my footing. I dropped to one knee, and in the light of the street lamp met Zeenat. She was standing on the bottom step. For a moment my brain wouldn't get into gear. I blinked.

'What . . .' I said, and she said, 'Shhh . . .' and put her finger to her lips. Ah, secrets. But I had remembered her like a child.

Smiling softly she came up the steps and taking the keys from my hand, unlocked the door. She held it open for me. I lurched in, and watched in a daze as she shut the door, the click of its catch curiously determined, and yet echoing, hollow and dead in the shadowy hallway. She turned to look at me then, and though it hurt me to look into her eyes

I couldn't break away from her gaze. They were ferocious with purpose. She was different. Different from all the rest. She alone wanted to take. She alone hadn't learned to give. I saw it that night in her dazzling eyes.

August 2000

Anis

I was wrong about Zeenat. She had not come to take. In fact she had come to introduce me to a friend of hers. Someone I knew only from afar, but until then had managed to avoid. She has kept many a friend company far into the night, not willing to leave even in the cold morning light. Sometimes when I was very drunk at parties she would whisper, 'Quick, reach me your hand.' Her voice was sweet and from a distance she reminded me of Millais's Ophelia. An utterly pale and divine body lying half-submerged in water. Beautiful in sleep, but awake? I never knew what she would be like awake, you see.

Now I know.

'It's okay. It's not like what they tell you. It's all right. I'll do it for you. All it is, is you put it on your skin and push it down. That's all,' Zeenat told me.

Did not Krishna say to Arjuna on the battlefield, 'Whosoever offers to me with devotion a leaf, a flower, a fruit, or water, that offering of love, of the pure heart I accept.'

I accept. I accept.

So awakened the sleeping beauty, but I had spurned her for so long, her eyes had turned vindictive. Her lips twisted into a mean smile and her nails were brown and cruel. Instantly they curved deep into my flesh. How tight her grip was! She would have me until death do us part. You have no idea how determined she is. How she will stop at nothing. How she will torture my body with aches, pains, cramps, projectile vomiting, and keep me awake for months with twitching limbs, if I be so bold as to try to walk away from her.

But to tell you the truth I don't mind her cruel eyes and twisted lips for when I close my eyes, her breath is fragrant beyond words, and by and by even the curved brown nails in my flesh become exquisite. I knew what the Israelites cried out, in their beautiful language, when fed manna in the desert of sin: '*Man hu?*' What is this? I too cried when her pale mouth regurgitated her sweet liquid into mine. There are people in the know who say it is only your own blood she feeds you. Could be, but it is really delicious. I should open my eyes. Perhaps it was a mistake to close them in the first place.

Elizabeth

As soon as I walked into Ricky's flat and saw Maggie drunk and very white in dark glasses, I knew what had happened. Promises are cheap. Did I not already know that? Men like him were a dime a dozen, a hazard of her profession. She held her ringless hand up towards me and waved it around a little. 'Bloody cheapskate took it back. I should have listened to that old whore and sold the flipping thing, shouldn't I? But hey, this means it's time to rattle up a party.' She sounded hearty, but I knew her too well. Her heart was broken.

Afterwards we went back to her flat. She fed the cats, and the ants, then collapsed on her tattered sofa and flung away her sunglasses. I saw the purple shiner the bastard had given her then.

'I'm so sorry, Maggie,' I said, and she burst into tears. And there was just nothing I could do for her.

All the time she sobbed, 'I've been so stupid. He only wanted to be my pimp. He only wanted to use me.'

Bruce

I ended up in an awful way, high, and thinking it was all lies. There was a storm in my head when I rang her fancy Mayfair doorbell. In the obsidian number plate I saw how quickly wasted I had become. Was I already that fat? She opened the door wearing smoky blue, arms crossed, expression frosty, and one eyebrow raised.

'Followed you home one night,' I said, by way of explanation. I had to, to get her address. She never gave it out, didn't like me, or for that matter anyone else, inside the little love nest she shared with the Arab.

She eyed me with dislike. 'What do you want?'

'Invite me in, for God's sake. Where do you keep your heart?' I asked.

'In the fridge,' she replied, and leaving the door open, walked into the flat.

The woman was so coldly calculating it was almost admirable. I closed the door and for a moment had the unreal impression of strolling through the Egyptian rooms in Harrods. I cannot think of a more apt description for that Ali Baba's cave of treasure. Still, in all that vulgarity I did not see any physical evidence of him. Not a box of Havana cigars on the coffee table, or a white headdress hanging from a hook, or a hookah in sight, not even a small one.

I followed her into her kitchen. She opened the fridge and brought out a bottle of wine. Behind her was a painting of a man and a floating woman and I knew immediately that alone was hers. The rest belonged to him. That she had chosen, and then hung in the kitchen, out of sight.

'Like Chagall?' she asked.

'Never heard of the guy.' I did like the painting, though. There was something far away and unreachable about it. Like her, in a weird sort of way.

'I think he was the greatest Russian painter of all time. He painted like a doomed child. As if he believed in miracles.' She poured straw-coloured liquid into a glass and raised it to her lips. So no wine for me, then. Sometimes her deliberate rudeness made me want to smack her.

'Is there anything more civilised than the two words, white wine? Together they conjure up such an idea of grace and elegance, don't they?' she said, studying me from above the rim of her glass.

I looked at her blankly.

'You do know that you will never sleep with me, don't you?

That's all right with me. Sleep was not really what I had in mind. 'I wonder', I said reflectively, 'if God knew while he was painting your wings so beautiful, what a cruel butterfly you would turn out to be.'

From my pocket I fetched a rectangular velvet box, in it a black pearl bracelet. I didn't buy it. Paddy 'found' it and thought it might match her choker. I put it on the table, and pushed it a little in her direction. I saw her eyeing the box, but she did not reach for it. I was going to tell her that it was safe to open. It was from Paddy, but at that moment I recognised the music she was listening to and couldn't resist showing off. 'Vivaldi's Four Seasons, Winter,' I said.

'Autumn,' she corrected briefly, automatically. Then she walked around the kitchen counter to face me. Leaning a hip against the table edge she crossed her arms. Her face was expressionless. 'Let's see if we understand each other. You can't buy me,' she said.

'Why not? Doesn't the Arab?'

She began to laugh then. 'You're not in his league, *love*.

Three high street hairdressing salons?' she mocked contemptuously.

Even when she laughed so hatefully, I was mad for her. It made me vicious. 'You know what you remind me of? A bat. Yes, a bat, hanging upside down with a brain that turns everything right side up. Injecting antiseptic into the unsuspecting before drawing your pint of blood out.'

She looked at me without affection. 'And aren't ye a great little bastard?'

I walked to the fridge. 'Now I fucking need a glass of your civilised drink,' I said, and opened her fridge. The contents made her a stranger all over again. Fresh dates, exotic cuts of meat, blue cheeses, a tray of gooseberries, cucumber soup, and different foreign-looking food from places like Harrods or Fortnum and Mason. Where were the cheddar cheese, bacon and eggs? My eyes fell upon a small round container. Ahh, of course, caviar for the princess. My philistine tongue hated caviar, but I wanted to annoy her. I opened the container.

'Second drawer to the left,' she said.

Was that irritation I heard? Inside the drawer in a separate compartment all for itself was a pretty mother of pearl teaspoon. I helped myself to a teaspoon of her caviar.

'Good?' she asked sarcastically.

Actually, I don't know what I tried before, but her stuff was excellent. Little slippery salty explosions of taste as the eggs expired on my tongue. I took another spoonful. I knew a Russian word. Some punk had once tried to offload some dodgy caviar as the high-quality stuff to me. Ah yes, *malassol*, meaning, as the little thief explained so convincingly, 'little salt. Eggs of such high quality require the least amount of salt to ripen.'

'*Malassol . . . Beluga*,' I threw casually.

'Very impressive for an East End boy.'

'See, that's what you get with sweeping generalisations.

It's like saying all Englishmen keep their socks on in bed, or *all* Irish girls who can afford to live in Mayfair are prostitutes.'

She sighed wearily. 'Are you sure you wouldn't prefer to be somewhere else?'

'No, not at all. I am as happy as a pig in shit here,' I said, grinning nastily. You might call it a deep sense of alienation. I will simply call it, unmet needs. I simply couldn't stop. 'So when the Arab's in town, this is his love nest, then?'

She smiled, cruelly amused. 'Actually no, the Mullah has suites in the Ritz. It's too much trouble with four body-guards, outriders, and a servant who walks ahead perfuming the air he intends to breathe.'

I couldn't help the expression that crossed my face.

And it turned her mean. 'I go to him, an illicit pleasure, like black truffles, so rich-rotten that only a whiff is necessary, usually after the bespoke shoe maker has been,' she explained, grey eyes glittering with malice.

'Oh.' I stared at her in her distant world. Her cynical acceptance of a highly repulsive situation. The caviar in my mouth made me feel slightly sick. How could such an intelligent woman be content to be the expensive play-thing of a religious hypocrite? Unless, of course, she was irretrievably shallow . . . a sort of monogamous hooker. A well-trained nurse ministering feigned passion to a disgusting pig.

I had thought more of her.

Perhaps I had imagined the exchange more exciting, more reckless. Wilder, with a touch of danger possibly. Not this sterile 'come up and see me after the shoe maker has been', pact of abuse. Why did I still desire the scent of this strange woman's pillow in the morning? Or perhaps she was so deep her time was yet to come, or had passed. She did, after all, once tell me her heroine was Aspasia, apparently the most famous Greek hetaera; the word, she explained to me meant mistress, which naturally I took to mean whore. I began to hate her, him and myself.

The telephone rang, its sound muted.

I saw her jump, her eyes flying to the display panel. It said, International. A fine tension came into her body, and looking at me with guarded pleading eyes, she raised her forefinger to lightly touch her lips. In the shocked silence she turned slightly away from me, picked up the receiver and changed. Why, she spoke fluent Arabic.

'It was the potato famine. It taught us to adapt quickly or die,' she once said.

Who was this creature I had so carelessly fallen for? Watching that beautiful mouth speak that guttural language grieved my heart. I saw her again in that backless number of hers, the black one with the fish tail kick to the bottom. In my head, an olive-coloured hand, meaty, pampered and proprietorial, landed upon the small of her back, and having branded it, gently guided her away from me. And even though I knew she was only looking to help him spend some money, the scalding green liquid in the rusty pot inside me boiled over, blistering flesh. Raw with jealousy, I considered her. She had learned his language.

Laughing, a low sexy sound, she replaced the receiver with a soft click. Her unsmiling eyes found mine.

I flicked the coin of love. Throbbing hate kept its face on the other side. 'Is it sweet, the Arab's blood?' I bit out, my voice cold.

She did not have to consider the question. She responded with the speed of a snake's tongue. 'Much the same as yours, as I recall.'

I just gave up. What was the point?

'Want a line?' I said.

She nodded. 'Want some wine?'

I nodded, and returned the caviar to the fridge. It was a sad lost cause. Nothing but a head fuck. What else was left, but get too fucked to give a fuck. She blew past me like a gust of cold wind, but my yearning heart still ran after the heartless draught.

Nutan

Sometimes when we go to Anna's and she is out prostituting we sit in front of the fire and wait. When she comes back she takes all her drugs out of her pockets and then sits down and cries with self-disgust. And, still crying, she injects herself. Sometimes she feels so dirty she gets in the bath. Too often the drugs are so powerful she falls asleep while scrubbing herself. I feared the day she drowned in her bath.

One night she stopped breathing. God, she became so still. It was terrifying. Luckily there was a boy present who pushed at her chest and gave her mouth-to-mouth resuscitation. We rushed her to Emergency and they shot adrenaline into her arm. It washed the heroin out of her system and brought her around immediately, but it also plunged her into deep withdrawal. She came out absolutely furious and slapped the nurse.

'Fuck you, bitch. You took my buzz off. Do you know what I paid for that? That's forty quid down the drain,' she screamed. She was going mad. Absolutely mad. She could have died and she didn't care.

Bruce

Ricky was lunching alone when I found him. I went to sit beside him. He poured me a glass of red wine, put an empty plate in front of me and began heaping it with chunks of polenta and rabbit stewed in red wine. 'Eat, eat,' he invited.

'About Elizabeth and the Arab?' I began.

'Forget it,' he advised, tearing a piece of bread and using it to mop up the juices on his plate. 'It's a waste of time. It's like chucking sugar into the ocean and waiting for the waters to turn sweet. Hunt somewhere else, her thighs don't part. I tried for years before I gave up.'

'I believe I love her.'

He turned around to look at me incredulously. The piece of soaked bread stalled on its journey to his mouth. 'You believe . . .' Then he threw his head back energetically and laughed, his eyes closing with mirth. When at last he could bring himself to stop, he said, 'You mean you're desperate to fuck her?'

I felt slightly irritated. 'No, I *know* I love her,' I said, emphasising the words.

'Oh, that's different then, why didn't you say so before,' he said sarcastically. 'It's all crap, or greed, depending on how you look at it. It's hardly love when you fall for the most beautiful woman you've ever met, is it? For fuck's sake you don't even know the woman. What if she didn't look the way she did, huh? What if she wasn't such a goddess?' He stuffed the piece of bread in his mouth and began to chew. 'What happens to your love then?'

'Oh, fuck you. How am I supposed to answer this hypothetical question? She looks the way she looks, and I am in love with her, allright?'

'And how come I've never seen you with a girl that isn't drop-dead gorgeous? And how come your relationships never last?'

I looked at him. 'You arsehole, you told her that, didn't you?'

He grinned shiftily. 'Hey, she asked. What do you want me to do? Lie?'

'She asked?' I repeated.

He shrugged and rubbed his jaw. But this sudden interest

in Elizabeth's welfare didn't gel, and something Anis once said came to mind: the wolf worried that the sheep would get wet in the rain.

'Sorry, man, I didn't know you were interested when I told her,' he defended, but I could see he didn't give a shit.

He knew what he had done. He knew I wanted her from the first time I saw her. He just didn't want me to have her. Not even for one night.

'Ow, get off this shit, man. You don't have to dress it pretty. It answers just as well to the other name. You wouldn't have got her anyway. Elizabeth likes girls.'

'Oh, fuck off,' I said, and leaving the food and the wine untouched I walked off. He was shouting more smut, and laughing uproariously as I slammed out of the flat.

Nutan

I dragged my eyelids open, the taste of metal on my tongue. My skin itched. Anis said it was the poison from the drugs oxidising inside my body, my body trying to eliminate the poison. It was light outside, time to go to work again but I was still so tired. I shook Zeenat awake. I had to shake her for a long time before she would stir. 'It's time to go to work,' I said.

'I've handed in our notices,' she said groggily.

'What do you mean?'

'I'm going to be an artist's model for Anis. It's good money,' she mumbled with her eyes closed.

I fell backwards with relief, and sleep came to take me instantly.

Bruce

I took her to Luculus. Small, intimate and expensive. I was determined that it would be a good meal. A start in a new direction. She ordered oysters followed by the confit of duck. The French waiter was smarmily approving. 'Very good, madam.' He took the long menu off her, flirting with his eyes.

'I'll have the same,' I said.

She looked around at the other diners. Almost all of them older than her, discreet in manner and, judging by the dead fur in the coat room, all European. I poured the wine and we made small talk. Six oysters slid down my throat, but the conversation remained dismal. She was waiting. I couldn't put my finger on it, but it was as if she was expecting to be ambushed.

'So, Ricky tells me you are a lesbian,' I said casually.

She laughed and slid a tiny piece of buttered bread into her mouth. 'Lipstick, I'm afraid,' she confessed, her eyes twinkling. 'But why spoil a sweet little fantasy? Ricky really gets off on the idea. Two cute babes usefully whiling away their time with a little licking while waiting for the ultimate gratification from the great god himself.'

'But what about all those times he lures a naked girl into bed and you go in and close the door?'

'Yeah, I get into bed and offer them a line. Those girls will do anything for a line. They go out and say whatever he wants to hear. And he rewards them with more coke. And everybody is happy.'

'Why this elaborate charade?'

'I don't know. It's the Greta Garbo trick, isn't it? Available to all and possessed by none, sort of thing. Well, it keeps the guys running anyway.'

'So why shatter the illusion for me?'

'Because I don't want you running,' she replied carelessly, but the eyes over her wine glass were careful.

Our main course arrived. That last remark hurt. The duck was a little too salty.

'Why do you wear so much make-up, anyway? What else are you hiding?' I asked.

She looked up quickly at me. It was in her eyes. I had not failed her. This was the ambush she had been waiting for all night long. 'Why do you do it?' she asked softly.

I caught her unwary hand across the table. Her eyes were big with surprise. 'Look into my eyes.' I said to her. 'Are you behind my eyes? See yourself? Now, what do you see?'

Caught in the fierce gaze of my eyes some sort of awareness crept in, a dawning of some emotion, until suddenly her gaze shot away.

'What *did* you see?' I asked.

'That you recognised my name and my fiction, but that you do not know me.'

'So tell me. Who are you?'

'Who am I? Is that what you want to know?' She put her wine glass down, her expression strange. Then she reached down to her handbag and produced a small white bottle. She poured some of the white liquid onto her fingers and began to rub it into her face. All the time her eyes were locked on to mine. Make-up smeared, grey ran into pink and golden brown, and black mascara streaked down her cheeks. Then she picked up her napkin and began to rub it all away. Shocked, I stared at her. Barefaced, she returned the napkin to the table.

Not once had I taken my eyes off her, but I felt, like a touch on my skin, the avidly inquisitive, incredulous stares of all the other diners. Without her gold-brown mask she looked pale and exhausted. The skin on her lips so thin it was almost transparent. Why, she was defenceless and pitiful. I felt goose pimples rise on my forearms and an odd possessiveness filled my gut.

She waited unblinking. Wanting something from me.

'God, you're beautiful,' I whispered.

Then we were locked in a battle of wills. For interminable moments she hated me, or herself, and then she was violently pushing her chair back and leaving. The little restaurant had gone silent. My confusion complete, I could only stare stupidly at her striding back. What did she want me to say? That she was grotesque? The door opened and she was gone. Dumbly I saw her run and get into a black cab. I loved the woman. That was the truth.

I looked down at my duck and raised my hand slightly. Instantly a waiter stood at my elbow. I made the movement of writing. When the bill came I counted out some money and left it in the velvet book. She had revealed herself to me as if it was some test. And then behaved as if I had failed. The air outside was surprisingly cold.

Across the street a group of women were rolling out of Draycotts, their voices forced and loud in my bewildered ears. I stopped at the window of the art shop in front of Joseph. I just needed to think. In the window there was an old-fashioned painting of a basket of fruit, exact to every droplet of water. The lack of imagination left me cold. I had failed her test. I thought of her with smeared make-up. All the while expressionless and watching. Something important had just happened, but I did not know what it was.

Beside my reflection on the glass window another appeared. I turned to look at her. Ah, one of the happy girls from Draycotts. Her waiting friends milled about on the other side of the road.

'Hey, want to come to a party with us?' she asked. She was young and passably pretty.

'Why do you wear make-up?' I asked.

Surprised, but game, she hugged her arms to her slim body, shrugged and decided to be dishonest. 'Something to do, I guess.'

'Fair enough,' I said, nodding. I wished her good night and walked away. I was much further up the road when I heard her shout, 'Fucking weirdo.' I passed another restaurant. It looked warm inside. A cold wind rushed into my face. I wrapped my coat tighter against the wind. Anis had a beautiful poem.

> *Cold wind I beg of you,*
> *Touch her ever so lightly,*
> *Make her shiver slightly,*
> *Make her love me a little.*

Elizabeth

I woke up suddenly, afraid, and swiftly looked around me. No, everything in my bedroom was still cream and gold. And pristine. Everything was status quo. Not to worry. Nothing had changed. Yet. I got out of bed and pulled the heavy drapes away from the window. White light tipped into the room. I pulled at the knots on the shoulders of my nightgown and it softly whispered to my feet. Nude, I went to stand in front of a full-length mirror. In the clear light I stared at all of me. How many times had I stood exactly there? Simply staring. Sometimes disbelieving, other times shocked. At how intolerably ugly I was.

But this day this glance in the mirror was more horrendous than usual. I put on my dressing gown and went into my living room. It was a richly decorated room. Splendid in a vulgar sort of way. I suppose it was just not to my taste. To be perfectly crude, I'm just not into all that Arab shit. I simply hate it. I moved from room to room like a guest, unable to relax in the foreign grandeur and majesty.

I know why I did that. Because none of it was mine. None of it. It all belonged to him. A click of his hand, and poof, it could all disappear. That was the reason I watched my step. Day and night I was on guard. Had never put a foot wrong in five years. It had been easy until now. Now things were changing. Inside me, matter was shifting, breaking away, and colliding. New and unfamiliar appetites were beginning to solidify. I was suddenly beginning to yearn for objects out of my reach. . .

I never thought it would happen.

In the splendid vulgar mirror over the fireplace I saw my face, pale, frightened, wretched. I must not. I must not fall for that man. Not Bruce. He alone had the power to break me. I could not allow him any closer. His inappropriate love would spin to hate when he found out the lies I had told. All of me was an obscene lie. He loved a figment of his imagination.

But my heart refused good counsel. It craved his company and made excuses to be with him. And recently it had begun not only to miss him when he did not call but to cry bitterly whenever he walked away from me. Oh God, why him? Of all people, why did I have to fall for him? He was a shallow beast, worshipping at the temple of perfection. How could I have been so spectacularly stupid? To have given my heart away to one such as him?

For years I buried my secret, even changing cemeteries for fear of discovery by grave diggers, and now I turned a corner, and it bumped into me. 'Why, hello,' the sly thing greeted lazily, pretending to be harmless.

I stood in the kitchen. The marble cold under my feet. I gazed at the floating woman in the Chagall painting. 'Mother,' I whispered, 'what would you do if you were me, and love was at the gate?' And I thought I heard her speak inside my head. 'Invite him in. Say to him, "You who have come from the other side of the world, I honour you, and though I am poor and cannot offer you much, you may share all that I own because you are my friend."'

You are mistaken, Mother. Love is no friend. It will take all of me. Look what it did to you. And I saw my mother again, that morning when she had rocked my sister in her arms, singing her terrible song. 'Oh, na, na, na, na, Oh, na, na, na, na.' Until they had to forcibly wrench her burden away.

Bruce

After my dinner with Elizabeth I went to the Spider's Temple the next day and found Ricky and Elizabeth sitting together on the long sofa deep in conversation. For a moment the sight of both their blond heads so close together startled me. I knew they were not lovers, but even their closeness was a source of jealousy. I was jealous of Ricky. They turned to look at me and Ricky began laughing, his big stupid Italian laugh. He thought it was funny that I had the hots for Elizabeth.

I didn't smile.

He got up, kissed the top of Elizabeth's head, and left. Elizabeth stretched her legs out into the space that Ricky had vacated. I knew she did that so I could not sit beside her. I sat opposite. She smiled at me as if nothing had happened the night before.

'What were you talking about?'

'Ricky got thrown out of Spearmint Rhino last night,' she said.

'Why?'

'He got on the stage and licked the lap dancer's pole.'

'Fucking crazy bastard,' I said, and we laughed together.

When she laughed she was irresistible. I wanted to hold her. On the radio Robbie Williams and Nicole Kidman were singing that sweet little duet, 'Somethin' Stupid'. I went and turned the volume up and stood before her. 'Dance with me?'

I held my hand out, and after a moment of hesitation she put hers in mine. I pulled her up and spun her away from the sofas. I had learned my steps at the local social club, where my mother went for cheap booze and a dance some evenings. Elizabeth was a surprisingly accomplished dancer and we made a good team, our steps matching perfectly.

She whirled away, laughing. She was mesmerising. I pulled her close to me and caught a whiff of her perfume before we were off spinning together. She felt good. She felt good.

Her eyes were happy, her mouth slightly open, her voice a breathless laugh. The song was nearly over and Robbie and Nicole were repeating the last line again and again.

I love you
I love you

'I love you,' I said and she froze. It was true I loved her. I felt her body contract as if I had burnt her. We stared at each other silently. Suddenly there was a noise. Somebody was coming through the front door. The spell broke abruptly and she was moving out of my arms.

'I've got to go anyway,' she said.

I grabbed her hand. 'Did you hear what I said? I meant it.'

'Don't go and spoil it all. You will destroy what little I have left,' she warned.

'The greatest thing I ever learned was from some man called Guillarme Apollinaire.' I said. There was no expression in the light grey eyes. 'Listen to this,' I said, ' *"Come to the edge," he said. They said, "We are afraid,"*

"*Come to the edge,*" *he said. They came. He pushed them . . .*'

I saw her recoil with horror. She did not like my story.

'*And they flew,*' I said.

And she broke away from my hold, backing away, shaking her head.

'No,' she said, very clearly, and walked out of the flat.

Why not? Why not you and me, Elizabeth?

September 2000

Anis

That marvellous light is gone from Zeenat's eyes. Still I am filled with an unexpected tenderness. What a schemer!

Nutan

I went looking for Zeenat. Anis answered the door, but he stilled my greeting by resting his forefinger across his lips. I followed him into the living room that he used as a studio. It was a large empty room with many paintings lined up against the walls, some quite large. The floor was wooden and paint splattered. And in the middle of the room was a canvas on an easel, beside it, a table full of paints and a jug full of brushes. From tall, wide, bay windows, light, splendid white light streamed into the room. It finished the room in a rather remarkable way. It left no sheltered, covered spaces.

Half reclining on a low table illuminated by that peculiar light was Zeenat, disrobed. The scrutiny of bright light is essentially unforgiving and bitter, and that morning I saw it boring into her naked body, and in some inexplicable way harming her. She was leaning forward, her body raised from the ground, the muscles in her arms taut, resting on her whitened fingertips. Her long hair spilled to the other side of her. Unmoving, she spared me only the briefest of glances. She was doing it for us. For the money. I should have been grateful, embarrassed even, but I wasn't. All I could see was that strange glazed expression on her face, the muscle in her uncovered throat that quivered a little. I knew that look. She was high and I too wanted to be where she was. I needed some.

Utterly engrossed in his art Anis had already forgotten me. In their completely silent world I did not exist. For a while I stood at the door, invisible and uncertain, then I went into the kitchen. On a square table there was a pot of marmalade, a slab of butter in an open dish, and two unwashed plates. They had toast. I didn't know Zeenat had started having breakfast. We never had breakfast in Bali. There were coffee sediments in two mugs. I knew which one was Zeenat's. It was the one with the un-dissolved sugar at the bottom. We Balinese like our coffee very, very sweet.

The sink was full of dirty dishes. There was a small TV on a counter. It was on mute. Beautiful models strutted on a catwalk. There was something strange about their silent progress. Why would anyone watch Fashion TV, let alone without sound? I stood by the window looking out into a concreted space. It was full of dried leaves. A wall separated Anis's 'garden' from the road. Beyond the wall were people and cars. Inside the house they were breeding an unnatural stillness. Built a cocoon just for them.

None other may enter. Not even a twin sister.

Yet it was not tranquil, the silence. It was pregnant with waiting. What were they waiting for? I heard Anis walking away from his painting to get the buyer's perspective, and then returning to his creation, his shoes loud on the bare floor. Silence again. Something bothered me. I thought of my sister. That light. That unkind light had exposed her to my eye. Showed me something I should not have seen. Yet, I could not go back, erase what I had seen.

I stared out of the window, unseeing. That look on

Zeenat's face. Leaning on her fingertips, in that humiliating position with not a shred to cover her twisted body, her tender breasts exposed to the cruel light. It was almost a form of disrespect, abuse. Why, the people walking on the street could see her if they would only raise their heads a little.

My reality was shifting. My sister ignored my presence. Why did she let that sadistic selfish man degrade her in this way? To be bare and distorted into that position? As if an animal begging. She did it for the drugs. I knew she did.

I felt myself raging. He should not be allowed to do that to her. And then I caught a whiff of its odour. It was naked and raw. Jealousy. I stared at it. I was jealous of Anis. I must chain it to a wall. It taunted me, 'Go on, chain me. The walls may be different, but the chains are always the same. Breakable.'

We should never have come to this cold horrible country. It had changed us. I wanted to return but there was a sly, wheedling voice inside my head. *'Tusing jani, tusing ada de wasa.'* Not now. It is not an auspicious day.

Filled with dread I slipped into Anis's bedroom. It was why I had come in the first place. I knew where he kept his stash. I wanted some. Just a little. It hurt when I didn't take it. I was afraid Zeenat would know how much I had come to depend upon that drug. I was afraid lest she should know just how much I had begun to take when she was not looking.

Ah, Father, have you seen what you have done to us? You have turned us into your leather puppets. It is Sita, Father. She got lost in the jungle, and now Rawana has carried her away. Quickly, Father, pull our strings or we could die. Help her. Help us. Play with us. Make us dance again, puppet master.

Zeenat

I smelt my grandmother's clove cigarette. Smoky, warm. The smell was unique, lost, dead. A temptation to return. To ashes.

Anis

Balinese art makes use of the varying perspective in its conception. Different parts of the same picture appear to have been composed from a different viewpoint. So the wall is seen from the front, the flowers from above, the women washing in the river from the left and the birds on the trees from below.

Bruce

In the coat-check stand of a night club Ricky grabbed the girl in front of us. She was a bit unusual. Her hair was frizzy, her features thick and typically black, but her skin was whiter than mine, and her eyes small and blue. Coldly, blankly they stared at Ricky.

His voice warm, his eyes deep. 'Shall we fuck later, Bella?' he asked.

The small blue eyes looked Ricky up and down. 'Be frank, do,' she dismissed in an utterly snotty, upper-class accent and turned away.

'Does that ever work?' I asked Ricky.

He laughed. He didn't give a shit. 'Just keeping the technique sharp. I wasn't serious anyway. Watch me later.'

When I ended up at his flat in the early hours of the morning the music was loud, there were half a dozen people partying and the half-black, half-white girl sprawled on a sofa. She was wearing Ricky's bathrobe and smoking a joint. The small blue eyes watched me. I dropped into the sofa beside her. Sometimes I couldn't understand his success. He was callous, almost to the point of abusive, but all kinds of women responded to him. I couldn't understand how he did it. The odd one escaped his grasp, but hardly ever.

'I thought you weren't coming,' I said.

'Yeah, man.' The accent was so brilliantly Jamaican I wanted to laugh.

Ricky came out of the toilet, spotted me, grinned, and raised his eyebrows. From his belt he unhooked a set of keys. He dropped them in my lap. 'Elizabeth's in my bedroom. Some arsehole slipped something into her drink.'

'What?'

'Go for it, man. This might be the only way you get to fuck her.'

I snatched the keys, ran up the stairs and unlocked the door. It was dark inside. I closed the door quietly behind me. When my eyes got used to the dim illumination from the pub signage below the window, I saw her lying quietly on the bed, watching me. Relief flooded through me. I felt weak with it. Jesus, I had been frightened.

'Are you all right?' I asked softly. My weight made the cheap mattress give. She looked so small and vulnerable I wanted to cover her. I began to gather the sides of the duvet to wrap her with.

'Don't,' she whispered. 'Everything in here smells of sweat and sex. Just let me rest a while.'

'How do you feel?'

'All right now, but my arms and legs still feel a bit dead.'

'What happened?'

'Another shite who didn't trust the efficiency of his pick-up lines.'

I laughed weakly. ' Ahh, Elizabeth, Elizabeth. A lifetime

has passed since I tried that.' Can't you see how hard I've fallen for you?

'Lucky Ricky was there,' she said.

'Hmmm!' I lay down beside her. It was true I was a little drunk then, but I felt utterly peaceful lying in the dark beside her when her sharp tongue was dulled by an ugly drug. In the dark I began to wish.

Anis

My sister called.

My father was dead. I stood by the window. It was drizzling. The leaves were glossy green and the tree barks nearly black. A woman in a dark suit and very white legs ran across the street. I liked it when it rained in this grey gentle way. It made me feel safe inside my flat. He died of a massive heart attack. So quickly, my mother did not have time to react. Before she could bring the glass of milk he asked for, he was already dead.

I turned away from the window, closed my eyes and I saw him not humping some man, but sitting with me in the rain, back in Africa, watching a group of baboons twirling and prancing about, trying to catching the clouds of flying termites. Aaah, you should have seen the enchanting things. Almost poetic the way they danced in the drizzle, picking winged termites out of the air.

Zeenat came to stand beside me. I felt her, slight and uncertain. 'What is it?' she asked.

'My father is dead,' I told her.

'You will meet him in a field, in another world,' she consoled.

'That's what I'm afraid of,' I said wryly.

She took my face in her hands and turned it to meet hers. In that raw light she looked different. There was a pallor about her skin. And I had forgotten that her eyes wore specks of brown. They were glistening, large and translucent. Like vampires we haunted the nights, and hid during the day.

It occurred to me to paint her in the nasty grey light. I didn't want to go to the funeral, hold my mother's hand and lie to her about how sorry I was that her hypocrite husband was dead. I sat Zeenat by the window. Too many times I had painted her by night. Hours I painted. The light changed and twice Zeenat and I stopped to inject ourselves. Sometimes her eyes closed, as is her wont, but still I painted. The room darkened and even in the half-light I didn't want to stop. Until suddenly I remembered my father's 'not to be read until after my death' document.

I put down my brushes and, gently lifting that child out of the window seat, laid her in my bed. Carefully I covered her scarred arms.

At my father's house my sister opened the door. I was not close to her. She was married with children, but I had lost count how many. She looked at me silently, censoriously. She had assigned all the blame for the breakdown of the father and son bond on me. I was the selfish ungrateful brute in her melodrama.

I side-stepped her. The hall was full of groups of people talking in lowered voices. They all looked up to stare at the estranged son, famous and a little mad. My mother hugged me while I stood stiff and embarrassed in the flaccid envelop of her body. The creases of her body had begun to trap the musty smell of old age. I had to save her from that disgusting document.

I closed my father's study door behind me.

Ah, the predictable fool, he still kept the same password. I went through every file, but it seemed as if everything had been wiped clean. He could not have had the heart to destroy it, not completely. He must have had it on disk. I began to search. I was coldly, precisely, thorough. I looked everywhere. There was not a file I did not open, a folder I left unchecked, a book I did not open and flick through. I opened cabinets, up-ended drawers, looked behind pictures, even crawled underneath the desk to look for false compartments. Then I went a little crazy, took out a pen knife to the sofas. At first small cuts here and there then long great slashes. But nothing. I ripped up the carpets. Nothing. Was it possible?

That he destroyed it long ago. That he had never meant for us to see it after all. Perhaps I had judged him wrongly. Maybe he had never intended for us to know about his secret double life. Good. Let my mother and sister believe he was the perfect husband and father. Let them have their memory.

The door opened she stood framed in the open doorway. Old, fragile and draped in white. Then she closed the door and walked in, looking around the room desolately. It was all for nothing. She looked up at me and the piece of sari that covered her head dropped to her shoulder. How old she had become! Her hair was full of silver. Her eyes were pitiful.

What was she thinking? That I was looking for my father's last will and testament? That I wanted his money? She covered her face with her hands and shook her head from side to side like some dumb animal. I stared at her, mute. Her grief or reproach was beyond me. She did not know what I knew. Then she came forward and stood before me. Gently, gently, her old fingers skimmed my face, my eyebrows, my eyelids, down the bridge of my nose, to my lips, and up to my cheekbones. As if she was blind. As if she was savouring the moment, fiercely committing my face to memory for ever. But when her fingers found my collar bone so far out from my body a sigh escaped from a region deep inside her.

'Is this suffering the *dharma* of an artist, then?' she wondered quietly to herself. 'I know only the *dharma* of being a wife and a mother.'

And I saw the three of us, my mother, my sister who was only three or four then, and me sitting in our back garden, under the shade of a jackfruit tree. We were eating mangosteens out of a huge basket. How many hundreds we must have eaten during the season. It was my mother's favourite fruit.

She reached into the folds of her clothes and produced a computer disk. 'Is this what you are looking for?' she asked, her sunken eyes boring into mine.

I felt it then, my stomach sinking, my knees turning to jelly, the need to collapse. She put it in my hand and I gazed at it without understanding. When my confused eyes met hers, hers were not pitiful, but pitying. She knew. The *dharma* of a son is to behave in such a way that other people will look and exclaim enviously, 'What could this man have done in his past life to deserve such a wonderful son?' I had failed in my responsibility. Still her eyes were gentle. She nodded a few times, as if she understood, or forgave, and turned away to leave. She was already at the door and touching the doorknob.

'How long have you known?' I asked. My voice was hoarse, unfamiliar.

'Always,' she said, and covering her hair with her sari again, she opened the door and went out to join the other mourners. Her *dharma* was done.

Nutan

I never stopped loving my grandmother, but I went days and then weeks without even thinking about her. I felt guilty, I really did, but I couldn't help it. I was an addict. It got the better of me. *Is Bobby there? I'm really desperate for a bit.* I wished I could turn back the clock. I was so lonely. I hadn't washed properly in weeks, the water was too cold. And there was no food in the cupboard because I had stopped eating. I had lost two stone. I was disgusting. I hated myself. I wished I could simply lock myself indoors. Not see anyone. All I wanted to do was take drugs. I took it to go to sleep and I took it to wake up. *Ask the chemist for a pink pack of eight needles, will ya?*

I no longer greeted the postman in the mornings, but one day Nenek's letter couldn't just be slipped through the letterbox, it needed to be claimed with a signature. I was embarrassed to see the shocked expression on the postman's face. It was a long time since we had shared a mug of coffee and something sweet together. 'Are you all right, love?' he asked. I mumbled something, thanked him, and shut the door. Nenek had put a cinnamon root inside the letter. I closed my eyes and breathed in the scent. Oh! Nenek, you were right. You were so right. I unfolded the letter.

Nenek was frantic for a reply from either of us. I frowned, trying to remember the last time we had written. Had two whole months passed already? Nenek said that Father was planning to write to his relative to ask him to check on us. I jumped out of bed, rummaged around in my suitcase, found the number I was looking for, and ran all the way to a telephone box. I was panting so badly I had to stand outside the box to catch my breath again. Then I phoned the number our uncle had given us. My hands shook. His wife answered the phone.

I told her that if my father wrote worrying about us they were to ignore that letter. We were fine. She told me that Father had already written to my uncle four days ago. Quickly I assured her that we truly were fine. We had just gone away on holiday to Paris. She sounded relieved. I don't think my uncle needed such trouble in his life. I put the phone down. We had to be a lot more careful in future. If my uncle had come down . . .

I sat on my bed and wrote to Nenek. It was a long letter. I told her Zeenat and I had been in Paris for three weeks. I told her it was wonderful. I told her about the hundreds of statues everywhere, the beautiful old buildings, and the romantic bridges with their yellow lights. How we had been to all the art galleries and had stood amazed before the Eiffel Tower. In a gossipy tone I told her about the French men, their charm, and the elegance of the women. Oh, and did she know that the French hardly bathed. What was more, they liked eating raw oysters with a little bit of lemon juice squeezed on top. I told her I too had tasted one, and that it was absolutely disgusting. Very slimy, I said. And on and on, I told her about all the things I had only heard from Ricky's lips. As I wrote my lies I felt warm tears roll down my face.

When I was finished I stood in front of the mirror, a wreck, and watched me inject myself. I looked into my eyes shining like an oil-slicked pebble. Did I? Did I really hate myself that much? Why? What did I do to deserve it? Sticking a needle in my arm. It does hurt when you put a needle into your arm. They don't tell you that, do they? Strange. What will be next, cutting my own wrists? *Can you sort me out? I feel really ill.*

Ricky

There is a song my daughter used sing. It is called 'Ten Green Bottles'. I found new words for that song. I called it Ten Italian Restaurants. The new lyrics fit like a fucking dream.

I sold another. Had to. My finances were a bit of mess.

Fass had to retire. His other eye was giving up. I found an English accountant, but as I outlined the situation, his expression of polite attention took the road to repugnance. For that I have to take my hat off to Fass. Morality never bothered him. He had accomplished much without blinking an eyelid. Eventually, *il Inglese* straightened his back and stiffly made clear he wanted no part in the business of creative accounting. Pretentious sod.

I heard of a Chinese accountant in Soho, who was meant to be pretty good too. I got the number. Just had to find the time to call the bugger. Five Italian restaurants hanging on the wall. If one Italian restaurant should accidentally fall . . .

Francesca

I heard my mother say, 'Allora nowa deh flour.'

And the children asked, 'What, all of it?'

They were baking something for me that I couldn't eat. I closed my eyes and tried to shut out all their voices. Then I felt guilty. I was such a bad mother. I thought of myself, as a wolf in terrible pain, my limb trapped in an iron mangle, and bleeding profusely. Howling in agony, but snarling at anyone who approached to help. In a way, it was a kindness to abandon my children to my mother's care.

I had lost so much weight I could feel my ribs, but when I first saw how thin I had become I thought, well, it is almost worth the suffering. And then I slid into a heap on the bathroom floor, and cried, but so softly I don't think anyone heard.

If I went downstairs my children would cut their laughter, my mother would greet me with false cheer, and my father would pretend a smile. They did not want to see me suffer. When I left, I did not imagine it would hurt this way. I thought I was stronger. I was so enraged when I decided to leave him that it dulled my capacity to feel. But ever since then, the sense of loss inside my belly had grown unbearable. I could barely rouse myself to get out of bed. It was better in a dark room when I lay in one position.

The bedside clock said it was nearly lunchtime. I forced myself to get up. My hair was lank and dirty as I scraped it into a pony tail. Then I went downstairs. Before I opened the kitchen door I stuck a smile on my face. Their eyes watchful, the children climbed down from their high stools and came shyly towards me.

'We're making a chocolate cake for you,' they explained. I knew they wanted me to hold them, but instead they held themselves politely in front of me. Not sure if they should approach closer.

My mother wiped her hands with her apron, and picked up a book from the top of the fridge. She switched to Italian. 'Imula's daughter is a psychiatrist now and she recommended you read this.'

And I remembered what Ricky had said about my mother. It was when I criticised his mother as the kind of person who would build a library and instead of shelves full of books she would have panels painted with book spines and he had laughed mockingly and said, 'and yours would get someone else to stock her library for her.'

I took the book by Clarissa Pinkola Estés *Women Who Run With Wolves*. A coincidence. Had I not earlier likened myself to a wounded wolf?

'Go and read it and I'll bring you some coffee,' she said. And partly to get out of the cheerful atmosphere in the kitchen I took the book and left. Curling up in my father's favourite chair I began to read. My mother touched my shoulder and I realised I had not heard her enter. I was so mesmerised by the book. My mother placed the coffee on the table and went out, quietly closing the door. Now and again my mouth murmured, 'This is right. This is so right. Yes, of course . . .'

I learned many things about myself. I learned that I was a she-wolf, that my shadow was four-legged. Only no one had taught me to howl. Presently I came upon the story of a heartless man who put a dog into a cage wired to give electric shocks. He did this in the name of research. At first just the left side of the cage would give the dog an electric shock when it wandered over. The dog was quick to learn. It stayed on the right. Then the shocks came from the right, and the dog immediately moved. They changed the rules again. The dog returned to the right. It repositioned again and again. Then the entire cage became capable of giving it a shock. The dog learned that no matter where it was, it would receive a shock. So it sat in a place and accepted the shocks. And then the heartless man opened the cage door. Did you think that the dog ran out? You might have thought so, but I knew it wouldn't. I knew it would sit where it was, defeated.

The scientists term such behaviour 'learned helplessness'. That was what had happened to me. Paralysed with terrible pain I sat and gazed at the open door. But, no more. That instinctive decision to return home had been my starving soul's first attempt at impeccable judgement. I had been locked into a loveless marriage, and denied the soil of Sicily for so long that even the necessary thought of returning had become too formidable a consideration. Fed on a diet of broken promises, I had in turn become uncompromising to myself. I tore at my tongue, blinded my eyes, and cemented my ears, to be what I was not. To be what I should not be.

I had sold my dreams of bread made in a wooden trough.

Carefully I tiptoed up the stairs and locked myself in my old room. I did not want to be disturbed. Not yet. From the bottom of the wardrobe I pulled out the old wooden chest my grandmother had given me. When I opened it I fell into another world. Home-made corn dolls, pine cones, a blue and yellow marble, a few books, and a precious velvet dress. And underneath it all, my three 'Books Of Moments' tied with blue ribbon. My father had brought them back from England when I was a child. I untied the blue ribbon and opened the books. And saw row upon row of neat childish writing. My little dreams. A tear slipped down. I touched it. It was not sorrow. I promise it was not. It was just a moment of sadness for a thing lost.

I had abandoned them for Ricky.

I unscrewed the cap of a blue marker, and inside my book of Proud Moments, I wrote in bold writing: I LEFT MY HUSBAND.

Inside my book of Great Ideas: GOING HOME TO MAKE OLIVE OIL.

And in my book of Laughter: HA, HA, HE THOUGHT I WAS A DOG, BUT I'M *A* WOLF.

I held the books close to my chest. I knew it was going to be a long struggle, but it could be done. I could do it. When I went downstairs and opened the door of the living room, my children swung their faces away from the TV. I went on my knees and beckoned to them, and they scrambled to their feet and ran into my open arms. How desperately the little things clung to me. I must love them so much that they learned the confidence to move safely away. I had to allow them to grow strong, and teach them love. Ricky and I had wronged them.

I looked at my father. 'Papa, I need to buy some land in Sicily.'

And my father smiled. It was a slow smile, but in it glimmered a mine of satisfaction. 'The land has carried your name for a long time now,' he said. I smiled back through tears. Ah, Papa, you were ready for my moment of lucidity.

'Remember Toto?' he said. I nodded.

'His mother sold me some of the land that should have

been his. It is not huge, but it is enough. There is no well on it, but we can dig one for about £30,000 if you decide you need one. There is a nice-sized barn where Toto's family used to store their wheat before the war. In some places its walls are worn to rubble, but it is just perfect. You will work with your hands to put it right so it becomes a home for you and the children. Work will cure you, you'll see. I believe in you. Make your olive oil, my child.'

October 2000

Bruce

It was when Elizabeth and I went to Anis's home to drop some stuff off that he first explained the significance of the Buddha Touching Earth Mudra.

'May I?' Elizabeth asked. 'They're no good,' he dismissed but then changed his mind and nodded. She started looking at the canvases lined up to face the walls. She offered no comments until she came to a painting of a huge Buddha. 'Why are his hands not in the usual pose? I thought they were always resting in his lap,' she asked.

So Anis leaned back against a painting and told us the legend of Buddha's moment in the jaws of temptation. On the fifth week after Buddha had attained enlightenment, he was meditating under a Bodhi tree, when Mara, a dazzlingly beautiful *dakini*, temptress, came to lure him away from the righteous path. The celestial being, full of bright light and the rich fragrance of a thousand blooms, floated before him. To please her even the sun conspired to hide behind a black cloud. It became as if night. Seductively her glowing body danced before him, weaving her most intoxicating wiles, and promising pleasures indescribable. She threw a yellow hibiscus into his lap and invited him to make love to her.

But Buddha only reached his right hand to the earth, and called upon it, to bear witness that he had never been tempted, not even for the briefest moment. Such was the greatness of Buddha's will that the earth replied, shaking and trembling six times as proof that indeed at no time had he been distracted from his chosen path.

'Touching earth. What an extraordinary story,' Elizabeth murmured, gazing thoughtfully at the painting.

Anis

Where was the old passion? It was contrived and horrible when we tried. I loved her so much, but I was always so weary. Perhaps if I wasn't so weak, and she so fragile and ill. I lay in bed drowsy and felt afraid of losing her, and yet I could not think of anything else except the next dark, slow moving dream.

Nutan

I was sitting on Ricky's bed shooting up when he walked in. We stared at each other and for a few seconds his face went slack with shock and disbelief. But then his reaction became horribly aggressive, he strode forward and pulled the needle out. Blood squirted. He flung the syringe across the room, pulled me up and dragged me in front of the mirror.

'Look,' he said. 'Look at what you have become. A fucking junkie.'

And I saw myself through his disgusted eyes. For the first time I really saw myself. Oh, I looked terrible. My cheeks were sunken; my hair was matted. And my eyes!

'Get off this shit, or don't ever come back here,' he threatened in a sickened voice. I believed he meant every word. He flung me away from him. I fell to the ground and he looked down at me. There was only contempt in his long slow appraisal. He found me repulsive. It would not matter to him if I never came back. Then he turned around and left.

I wanted to cry, but more than that I wanted what still remained in the syringe. I remembered the awful face in mirror, but I needed the drug. I began to crawl towards it. Ricky came back into the room. Without a word he picked up the needle and left. Slowly I stood up. Filled with self-loathing I walked to the door. In the living room there were voices. Had they also seen what I saw in the mirror?

There was a comb somewhere. But I could not find it. I felt ashamed. I ran my fingers through my hair. My hands were shaking with horror. I had seen myself, you see. There was a tube of lipstick in one of the drawers. I began franti-cally looking for it. I was filled with the disgust I had seen in my lover's eyes. I found the lipstick, not mine, some other woman's. My hands were shaking so much I couldn't put it on. The disgust. It had unnerved me. I wanted to stop. I really did. You must believe me that I really hated myself at that moment. More than anything else in the world I wanted Zeenat and me to stop. Even before this I had begun to fear the violent mud we played in. I feared it had reached our waist. I feared any deeper and we could get stuck. We must stop. We were not yet too far along.

Ricky

Four Italian restaurants hanging on the wall.

Yeah, had to sell another. Hadn't been paying PAYE for a long time, had I? The penalties add up. They always catch you in the end. It's unfair but what can you do. I mean you've got to pay the most mercenary group of people alive. Chefs. You pay the little bastards fifty pounds a shift, and you would think that would be enough, wouldn't you? But no, you've still got to pay their national insurance and tax too. The Chinese accountant suggested doing what all his other Chinese customers do on a regular basis. Arrange for a fire in the restaurant that was most in need of refurbishment. Naturally make sure all the accounts are in the inferno. The insurance is usually a done deal.

My God, that guy was even more ruthless than Fass. I stared at him. It possibly dawned on him at that point that I was not his usual Chinese triad client. Unfazed, the black eyes suggested the second best solution. That I shred everything, and pretend I lost them in the back of a taxi on the way to my accountant. I nodded. More my cup of tea. I did it and he came up with an estimate of my figures. Much lower. Had money left over from the restaurant sale. I was thinking of stopping the free basing. I wanted Francesca and the kids back. We were a family. Those children needed me. They are my flesh and blood. I could stop whenever I wanted.

Nutan

I locked us in. We were going cold turkey. Anis had gone to the clinic, but both Zeenat and I had learned from Nenek to distrust hospitals. Even the smell of a hospital was fearful to us. Luckily Bruce had managed to obtain the medication used in the hospitals to lessen the withdrawal symptoms. They started immediately, the cramps, the pains, the jerking limbs, the sweats, and the cravings. Oh God, the cravings. To stop them we crammed more and more pills down our throats. They made our tongues lazy and sent our feet to sleep. Spittle dribbled from our slack mouths.

I remember Zeenat in slow motion resting her hand on my head. 'I'm sorry,' she slurred. 'If it was not for me you would not be here now.'

So difficult to keep my eyes open. 'Never mind, don't cry,' I mumbled.

Until suddenly, we realised we had taken too many pills. There were no more to dull the pains, or the intolerable cravings. We paced the small room like crazed animals, our eyes wild and desperate. Zeenat's fingers drummed surfaces nervously. Again and again her body jerked with violent convulsions. Mine too. It was ugly. It was completely uncontrollable.

Suddenly she turned to me, her eyes feverish in her agonised face, 'Shall we?'

'No,' I cried.

'Please, please.'

'No,' I said.

'Please. Just this once.' She started haphazardly pulling on her jacket. 'Look at me. I can't take it any more,' she wailed distractedly. She stood in front of me, grasping her stomach helplessly and without warning a fountain of vomit gushed out. Covered in her own sick, and still clutching her stomach she begged, 'Please, give me the door key.'

In a haze I saw her, but did not recognise her. Her blood-shot eyes blazing with terrible need, her mouth in a frenzy. She fell to her knees and pleaded piteously for the key. He was calling. The devil passion. He had taught us a language, fierce and captivating like the language of wild animals. He held her tighter. She had been with him longer. He made her suffer more. I shook my head. She swung around, moving crazily, desperately. A caged animal. Then she ran to the door and began to kick it. It made a great racket, but held fast.

'Give me the key,' she screamed at me.

Only I knew where it was hidden.

She ran to the window. She opened it and before I could lunge for her she had jumped out, and landed on the awning of the kebab shop. She was so thin it held her weight. I heard a ripping sound. She slipped down it on her back and landed on the pavement, like a cat on her hands and feet. She didn't even look up to see if I watched. She just lurched off down the street, limping badly. She had to have her fix. I watched her go until she turned the corner, unwashed, her jeans ripped, sick in her hair and clothes. With her gone there seemed to be no point in suffering. That is what an addict does. Looks for excuses.

I lurched for the door key. I was so ill and my hands trembled so much I almost did not open the door, and incredible as it seems now, I actually considered the exit Zeenat had taken. But finally the door opened and I stumbled down the stairs. I too needed my fix. I would have to take it on tick. Surely he would not refuse me in such a condition. Even inflated with powder power he would see that I was only the ghostly skin the snake leaves behind.

Bruce

Elizabeth, Maggie and I went to visit Anis. I was shocked to see that the wing he was in was more mental asylum than hospital. There were sounds of people crying, shouting and wailing in the background, and he was so dosed up on morphine he was lying on a bed, dribbling. When he saw us he tried to sit up, but couldn't. He looked awful.

'Walk me,' he garbled, eyes glazed.

I supported him into a sitting position. He was incredibly slight. His elbows dug sharply into my palms. I held him up and dragged him around the room. His legs were like lead. It was useless. So I carried him back to bed and he slumped sideways.

'This is terrible,' he mumbled.

Maggie started to cry.

'You're going to be fine,' I told him.

'Of course . . . it is all . . . weeeiirrrd . . . if you eat and drink . . . in Alice's Wonderland.' He tried to grin and dribbled saliva. Maggie rushed to wipe his mouth. She used her bare hand. I was startled by her instinctive compassion and my immediate revulsion.

'They should show these images on TV. Nobody would dare try this drug ever again,' Maggie said. There was a sob in her voice. I put my hand around her shoulder.

'Hey,' I said. 'This is a good thing. He will be better when this stage is over. No pain, no gain, right?'

She nodded but tears still shimmered in her eyes. She had a soft heart. I turned to look at Elizabeth. She was hugging herself with both hands and simply staring at Anis. We sat with him for a while, watching him fight to stay awake. Finally he gave in to sleep. Even in sleep his mouth groaned, his body jerked, and his legs kicked, sometimes so violently it jolted him out of his stupor. It was a horrible sight.

When we were outside, Elizabeth said we should go and see how the twins were getting on. They were doing it on their own because they had a thing about hospitals. They didn't trust them. Besides, their visas had run out, and they were terrified of being identified and deported. I thought the girls were on to a bad idea, but I got them some sedatives from a friend of a friend.

But when we got to their room, the door was wide open, the girls were gone, and the place looked like a bomb site. My fastidious eyes noted that even the mirror was vomit splattered. The smell was so sour and disgusting it made me retch.

Nutan

Zeenat and I became irritable and crabby. We snapped at each other. One day she accused me of taking money from her jeans pocket. 'I only took sixty pence for an iced bun,' I said, but she didn't believe me. In fact I had stolen the money. Only so I could get a bag.

We looked bad too. When Zeenat bent over to pick up her knickers the other day I saw all the bones in her spine sticking out. Sometimes I thought she looked at me with hate in her eyes. But then I thought it couldn't be. She loved me. If she didn't she wouldn't go out and get enough money for both of us. Without Anis I didn't know where she got it from. Had she become a thief? She loved me. I knew she did. It was just that jealous drug. It left room for no other love.

Bruce

It was four in the morning. Every single drop of coke was gone and Ricky had just scraped the top of the TV set to make one last line. He and Maggie were going crazy for some more. They started calling around, but no one had any, and if they had they were not selling. Then Ricky had an idea.

'Why don't we just crush up some sleeping pills and snort that?'

He had heard that it was a good high too. Maggie was all for it. At times like that, when Maggie got so desperate, her face deathly pale and dark rings around her frantic eyes, I began to see how nasty even cocaine could be. What really bothered me was that sore on the side of her wrist that she usually covered self-consciously with her other hand, but forgot about it when she was really high. It looked swollen, purple and disgusting. All the poison she put into her body gathered in that one hideous spot. Ricky had one too. A really bad one. On his arm.

I was tired and wanted to go home. I had a meeting at one

o'clock with the bank manager, and it was not good news he was waiting to impart. The account was light, problematically light, for some time now. I wanted to take Elizabeth home and then not snort, but swallow of couple of sleeping pills, set the alarm for twelve, and crash out until then. But Elizabeth wanted to wait a little for Maggie.

Ricky ran up the stairs and came back with a small handful of Rohypnol. We helped him crush them. Maggie had the first line and Ricky, greedy as ever, took a massive one. There was only a little left and Ricky offered it to Elizabeth, but she was not interested. She was a careful one. She refrained from taking things if she did not know exactly what effect they would have on her. I suppose she couldn't trust her secrets to new substances. She liked to be in control. She waited to see what it did to Ricky and Maggie first. Ricky snorted the last bit too.

It was Maggie who reacted first. She climbed on the coffee table, stood on her toes and stretched, as if she was a ballet dancer about to pirouette or leap off into the air. But she bent backwards and let herself free fall. Ricky moved quickly to catch her. He started laughing. 'You all right, Bella?' he asked. She looked deep into his eyes and smiled an odd crooked smile.

I felt Elizabeth stir beside me. Ricky set Maggie down and she slipped out of the circle of his arms and walked towards the window. She opened it and began to climb out. All of us rushed towards her. We pulled her back.

'What the fuck do you think you are doing?'

'I wanted to fly,' Maggie explained with shining eyes. She turned to me. 'Beth can, you know. She's done it before. There is nothing else like it, is there, Beth? Walking out of the window. The wind rushing towards you. Like a bird. Free.'

We dragged her back to the sofa. And suddenly Ricky started behaving funny; running his hands through his hair jerkily, and blinking rapidly. I knew that look. He was becoming hyper. Maggie moved towards him. He grabbed her and they started kissing ferociously, tongues, teeth, sucking sounds.

'Shall we go?' I said to Elizabeth.

But just as suddenly Ricky pushed Maggie away and began prowling around the flat. 'Let's do something. Let's do something. Let's have a party. No, an orgy,' he muttered. And then the guy said, 'Music anyone?' picked his guitar up and smashed it against the wall. It broke at the neck. Oh, oh, I looked for Elizabeth's eyes. They were wary.

Like a crazed animal Ricky paced. 'Hey, where's the coca? Let's go find some coca, huh. You got a phone?' He looked terrible.

Maggie took her top off, and fanned herself with her hands. 'God, it's boiling in here,' she said. I began to worry.

'Wow, I know what,' Ricky said, and all of sudden, he roughly yanked Elizabeth off the sofa and crushed her slender body into his. I felt sick.

'What will the spider woman say, my little Elizabeth, if you and I should fuck? Shall we? Right here. Right now. Shall we?'

'Stop it, Ricky,' Elizabeth said firmly, pushing at him with both hands, but he only tightened his hold.

'It's paradise. No snakes, remember,' he said, and catching the back of her neck in a steely grip, started kissing her. I mean really kissing her. I could see him trying to force her mouth open. Her struggles were puny. I took a step forward. 'Hey,' I said. But his other hand was already beginning to hitch her skirt up. I saw a flash of thigh.

And then I saw black. I rushed towards them. 'Hey, Ricky,' I shouted. His head came up and I threw him one. It caught him under the chin and knocked him out cold. He crashed to the floor on his back. Elizabeth squatted beside him.

'He was getting out of control,' I said by way of explanation. Elizabeth was silent.

Suddenly an eerie little voice called Maggie's name. And when we looked around we saw her crouched in the corner of the room calling her own name. It was a horrible creepy sound. 'Maaggieee, Maaaggieee.'

Elizabeth went to her. 'What's the matter, Maggie?' she asked softly.

'You don't understand. You never will.'

'Understand what?' I heard Elizabeth ask.

'Aw, forget it. Never mind. Just teach me to fly like you. I trust you. You're the only one I trust. You won't let me fall, will yer?' She pushed herself upright, looked at us hazily and mumbled, 'I feel dizzy. Help me, Beth, help me.'

'I'll wait with her until the drug wears off,' Elizabeth said to me, but I dared not leave her alone with Ricky. Just in case he woke up crazy.

'I'll wait with you.'

'Thank you,' Elizabeth said, and although her voice was choked up, her eyes did not rise to meet mine.

Anis

I went to pick Maggie up at her flat. She lived on the ninth floor of an ugly building block. So high up the wind howled around the building as if a storm was brewing. I suppose it felt a little like being in a lighthouse set perilously close to the edge of a precipice. Underneath us a sheer drop into a pounding sea.

The flat itself was a run-down dump, but made charming by the incredible volume of books Maggie owned. A veritable library was housed in her living room. Rows and rows of books on bookshelves, stacked into equal columns to hold aloft a piece of glass that served as her coffee table, and in tall piles to hold up old-fashioned brass candlesticks on either side of doors. They lined the walls and lay on every available surface. Her two cats, one tortoiseshell, another a petulant pure white, negotiated themselves around the miniature towers with familiar ease. I was surprised by the collection. There were books on poetry, history, art, philosophy and many works of the greatest writers.

She brought a small saucer of quartered persimmons.

'I didn't realise that you were into things that were not directly harmful to your health,' I said, sitting down on a disintegrating grey and white sofa and picking up a book about Freud. I opened it. 'So what's the story with him then?'

'They say he was a sexually repressed fraud who never cured a single patient. Now Jung, he is another story. More your type. He was a Tibetan lama in another life.'

'*You* believe in reincarnation?' I burst out.

'I'm a Catholic, Anis. I believe in Judgement Day.'

The tortoiseshell came to investigate. I stroked her head.

'Lilly's lovely, isn't she? Now Wellington's a vain, selfish nightmare. You are, aren't you?' she said, smiling fondly at Wellington. The white cat stared unblinking.

'Have you read all of this?'

'Yeah, and *The Wizard of Oz*.'

We both laughed.

'Here, take these,' she said and dumped into my hand a pile of beautifully bound books on philosophy.

'Oh!' I was surprised. 'Thanks. I'll read them and tell you what I think when I return them.'

'No, don't return them. I want you to have them. They're up your street. Just give me a minute, I'll get my shoes on.' I was touched. She began to put on her ballet shoes.

'Why do you wear ballet shoes all the time?'

'Och, Anis, ask another?'

'Okay, why do you take drugs?'

'I suppose I have an addictive personality and maybe I have a death wish.'

'Suicide?'

'And burn in hell for eternity? No, I'll wait. Besides, suicide takes courage.'

I stared at her. So she was not like an insect; wings, legs, eyes, everything made from the same building block, a sugar derivative. Here in the lighthouse she didn't seem to be built for the sole purpose of looking for more and more drugs. She became visible to my artist's eye, an amazing creature. Actually she was very beautiful in a wasted pale way. I asked her if she would sit for me.

'Why not?' she said, shrugging.

'Now?'

'OK,' she said.

I brought her back to mine.

'Will you let me paint you without the ballet shoes?' I asked.

For a moment she hesitated then I watched her take them off. Her feet were ghostly white, the edges pink and delicate. She wriggled her toes. For a second I forgot, and she was as pure as a child. I had an idea. I began to mix some colours while she padded around the room looking at paintings, her expression rapt. Slowly I was beginning to like her. I even liked her wandering around in her bare feet poking about my paintings. Zeenat was completely uninterested in my work. But Maggie had a good eye for technique. Always she pulled out the best ones to study a little closer.

Her eye found the unfinished one of Swathi, tucked far behind all the others. The one I had stopped painting the day her aunt called to say she was dead. Maggie dragged it out.

'Oh, Anis,' she whispered, her right hand going to cover her mouth. She squatted on the floor and stared at it. When

she turned around, her eyes were frightened, as if she knew
what my answer to her question would be. 'Where is
she now?'

'Dead,' I said shortly.

Maggie looked at me and then at the painting again.
'Why do you not finish her? She is cold and waiting. I smell
grief. Hers and yours.'

I felt her bare feet too close. Like a child she broke my
barriers.

'Shall we get started?' I said.

'Where do you want me?' she asked.

I went into my bedroom and deep in a disused drawer I
found the book I was looking for. I wiped its dusty cover
on the sides of my trousers and held it out to Maggie. 'Read
this while I paint you,' I instructed.

She took the book. '*Dharma*?' she asked.

'Duty,' I told her. "The duty of every living being is
sacred and not to be sneered at. Whether one is a teacher,
doctor, father, mother, leaf, animal, architect or courtesan
the concept remains equally valid.' I did not look up from
my canvas, but felt her gravely open the book to the page
with a book mark and lay it on her lap. She began to read.

'"The *dharma* of a courtesan is to receive money for
pleasure. It is her duty to paint coral lac-dye on her lips,
decorate her eyes with lampblack and rub saffron on her
breasts until they glow. Without love many tigers will enter
her cave and though their occupation be brief she must
treat them all equally as revered guests. At noon she may
rub perfume on her forehead and walk along the same
street as the man who had rode her like a horse the night
before, but in the strong light of day he may grimace with
disgust. Then it is the duty of the night horse to forgive."'

She stopped. I did not look at her but repeated an old
story my grandfather once told me.

'When the king of the ancient city of Takskashila asked

his royal astrologer why his city was suffering such a terrible drought, he was given an unexpected answer. He was told, "Celibacy is a poisonous serpent that Fertility will consider only from afar." The drought was caused by the spiritual heat produced by the relentless prayers of meditating ascetics gathered in the kingdom's forests. The solution was simple. "Invite courtesans from all over India. And as they go about their activities rain will fall." The king invited the courtesans and the rain came.'

I stopped and Maggie continued reading.

'Neither the bridal palanquin nor the rice shower will be hers to claim, but still the prostitute may take pride in the essential nature of her role, that even the great Goddess Durga Ma's celebration cannot start without some soil gleaned from her garden. And so they will come to her, high born and splendid, with garlands of jasmine wrapped around their left wrists. And her hands, red with henna, must reach for her anklets of bells. Again and again she must dance for them. Then perhaps the kind man intoxicated by her beautiful movements will call her a dancer.'

From where I stood I saw her glance at the ballet shoes she had discarded by the door. I saw the tears that ran down her face, but I could not allow her to stop there. I had an idea for painting. 'Go on.' I said. To see her heart and soul I had to offend.

'In times of yore she was a noble healer and a high priestess who earned money for the temple she lived in, she knew she shared the same *dharma* as the lotus. She must live in the slime, the lower parts of her body perpetually in contact with the impure, and yet not a drop of the filth or mud must taint her skin. Is it not so that the same mute mud that seeks her corruption mutely conceals her most vile secrets? Who dares question the purity of a lotus? Not the mud. Never the mud.'

Maggie's tears splashed onto the page of the open book. I should have gone to her then, comforted her, but I couldn't. With the light behind her, her tear drops sparkled and the brush in my hand grew a furious life of its own. I had failed in my *dharma* as a son, a lover, a brother, a friend. Only the duty of an artist was left to honour. To an artist's eye grief is natural and so beautiful, he cannot leave it be. I don't know how long I painted the courtesan's tears. It seemed she cried a river of tears.

Now it seems so perverse, but it was the most natural thing in the world that day. That she should cry so hopelessly for an impure lotus seemed right. That her poor heart was broken didn't seem to matter. I had to paint a courtesan's tears. The courtesan's punishment had to be captured on canvas. When I put down my brush I went to hold her.

'Shhh,' I said and just like that she stopped. For a long time I held her body curved into mine until she was familiar to me. Like a long-lost sister.

Bruce

'Hello Maggie,' I said, dropping down beside her on the couch. She was flicking through a fashion magazine, looking bored.

'Hello, Bruce,' she said.

'Where is everyone?' I asked casually.

'Elizabeth's baking a cake,' she said.

'What?'

'Yeah, surprising, isn't it? She likes baking.' She looked at me sideways. 'And babies.'

No point beating about the bush. 'How come Elizabeth refers to me as The Thinker?'

She swung her head around to face me and burst into a

huge grin. A Maggie grin, and I knew that no matter what she said, I wouldn't hold it against her.

'In some places in Ireland they always name you the opposite of what you are.'

'Oh, great,' I said.

'She doesn't mean it, you know?'

'Want to come out for a drink?'

'Okay,' she said, and shot up suddenly. Looking down at me she said, 'What you waiting for then?'

I took her to Ashley's bar. We drank companionably until even the one-word, pithy writers were incoherent with drink.

'I'm on a roll, keep it coming,' I shouted drunkenly.

'You know, people who have the greatest need for protection keep the fiercest guard dogs.'

'What're you trying to say?' See how drunk I was.

'Never mind that. Do yer love Beth?'

'I do,' I said solemnly.

'Will you promise me that you will marry her?'

'I will.'

She nodded slowly. 'Good man. Don't forget now. You've promised.'

'Will you make Elizabeth promise to marry me?'

'Don't you go worrying your pretty little head about that. Leave Beth to me. I'll sort her out. Now have you thought about doing it the African way where the bride and groom are so happy they dance up the aisle?'

'No, I'll take her to the church, I think.'

'She wants three babies.'

'Sounds about right to me.'

'There is something I have to tell you about Beth,' she said. I turned to look at her. She sounded almost sober suddenly.

'What is it?'

Then she looked away and said softly, mysteriously, 'No,

she'll tell you herself when the time is right. It's unimportant anyway. She thinks it is, but it isn't. You'll see for yourself.'

Ashley was turfing out the writers. 'Is it already closing time?'

'Yeah, man, it's four in the morning.'

We followed Ashley upstairs. In his back room he had more than forty varieties of whiskey. I tried them all and passed out on his sofa while Maggie and Ashley were still drinking and discussing gay rights.

Elizabeth

Anis brought a writer called Rani Manicka to the flat today. She had written one book and was looking for material for her second. She wore old jeans and a huge blue jumper. Very unglamorous . . . except for her shoes, silvery grey with tinges of pink. She caught me looking at them and grinned.

'Aren't they gorgeous?' she asked. 'I had them made specially. They're salmon skin. And I even have the matching gloves.'

'I read your book,' I said.

She appeared surprised. 'Did you like it?' she asked immediately with such unconcealed eagerness that it made her at once pathetic and strangely appealing. She wanted to hear that I liked it. I was sorry I brought it up.

'Well, I didn't quite get to finish it. It's a good book, but I like my reading slightly more complicated, less commercial.'

Suddenly she was looking at me anew, as if I had given her some detailed personal information. She smiled. 'Too commercial, huh?'

'Maybe . . .'

Unexpectedly she reached out to touch my hand. 'Surely

you have not the cold heart of a critic that must degrade all appeals to the emotions as commercialism. Will you respond only to calls to your intellect? We authors are a breed of people, shy and sensitive. Our insecurities make us turn away from the cruelties of the outside world and live in the pages we create. Would you have us only walk on barren soil and eat cold reason?'

That sort of threw me. Luckily Anis walked up to us with a large tumbler of whiskey for her. She was amazingly quickly drunk and, her little notebook abandoned, she started banging on about some Hampstead critic who had slagged off her book. She was spoiling my buzz and I wanted to tell her to shut up, but she did very generously throw four fifties into the coke kitty after all, and she was not even on it. So I told her, all critics were failed or aspiring novelists doing a slow burn on battered chairs, so who gave a shit what they thought anyway.

She nodded in slow motion. 'You know, you're a good person and I feel really sick,' she said, standing up unsteadily and looking quite ill. She reeled in the direction of the door. 'Got to get home.'

At this rate she would never get her story. She had not the stamina to catch us in our stride. Ricky looked on, an amused, slightly contemptuous expression on his face. Maggie accompanied her and Anis to the door. Maggie exchanged phone numbers with her. What could Maggie want with a writer who had absolutely no sense of fun? When I asked Maggie why she gave her number, she said, 'Felt sorry for her. How could someone like that write a believable story about sex, drugs and rock 'n' roll without some help?'

I passed her a rolled-up note. 'Yeah, whatever.'

The door opened and some Italian friends of Ricky came in, bearing a basket of fresh porcini mushrooms. They had picked them that evening in Windsor Great Park. Ricky was ecstatic. Immediately he began cooking a simple but divine dish of spaghetti and mushrooms. As we sat around the table eating, one of the Italians said, 'Now all we need is a couple of hookers.'

And Ricky looked up at Maggie and asked, 'Want to earn some money, Maggie?' Bitch that Haylee was, she laughed, and the Italians tittered half-hopefully. I was so furious I wanted to hit him, but I couldn't. No one must see the real Elizabeth. Maggie was looking blankly at Ricky, but I knew she was bleeding inside.

'Why don't you do it, Ricky? You're cunt enough,' I said, pushing back my chair.

'Ooo, claws,' Haylee trilled, and Ricky threw his head back and laughed. Taking Maggie by the hand I said, 'Come on, Maggie. We don't need to be here.'

As we left the flat, I heard Ricky's voice say something, and the rest of the group hooted and screamed.

Maggie was very quiet in the taxi on the way to Tramp. Although the Mullah was a member I never used his name to sign in because it would give him access to my movements. I knew easier ways. In the queue waiting to get in was a man in his late thirties or early forties. I walked up to him, and didn't bother to bat my eyelids or act coy. 'Will you sign us in?' I asked.

He smiled a big can't-believe-this-is-happening-to-me grin. 'For sure,' he said. He was American. Quite a nice guy. He got us in and bought us drinks, and even agreed to finance the drugs, but absolutely no one had stuff to sell. Not even the Italian waiters. I could see Maggie was getting really desperate and there was an Arab crowd sitting in the dining room that looked like they were on it, but theirs was a world too small. I couldn't risk it.

So we went back to Maggie's. She dumped herself on her sofa. The cats stretched and came to snuggle up to her.

Suddenly she jumped up, startling the cats and landed on the floor on her hands and knees.

'Look,' she said, and carefully began to lift little white bits from the carpet. Cocaine. Meticulously she gathered them into a line. 'Want some?' she asked, dividing the row.

'Yuck,' I said, 'I'm not having that. For God's sake Maggie there's cat fur in there.' But she didn't care. She snorted it anyway. I leaned back against the door and watched her spiriting away the dirty old crystals into her body feeling utterly miserable.

Anis

Maggie opened her front door and took me by the hand. 'Come, I want to show you something.' Her voice trembled a little. I don't know what I thought, but I let her lead me down a narrow hallway. She opened her bedroom door and said, 'Look.'

Every available space was hung with paintings. There must have been thirty or forty. All executed by the same person. The style was unmistakable.

'Like them?' I heard her ask in a frightened little-girl whisper. She released my hand and I moved closer to inspect them, but I felt as if I was in a dream. First impression: slightly other-worldly and humorous, but then, why this stunned excitement? Even the skin at the back my neck tingled. The paintings reached out, and touched something inside me. As if they had voices, invisible hands. Could everyone else not hear and see them? Was it really possible that this sorry vessel who sold her body daily contained such a dazzling gift?

Behind me I felt her waiting, tense and silent. Her work made me feel ashamed of my pathetic attempts to mock my father through my art. This girl painted from the heart. She didn't paint anger, she painted pain. She didn't bother with laughter she just mixed joy into her startling colours.

It was museum quality. You cannot imagine how incredible a find it was. A cheap two-bit hooker, untrained in the ways of paint, so effortlessly creating such astonishing masterpieces.

When at last I turned to look at Maggie, I found her watching me very carefully.

'Like them?' she repeated, very casually this time. She was preparing herself to be rejected.

So I said, 'You're not bad.' Why didn't I tell her how brilliantly, amazingly, fantastically talented she was? No, not because I was jealous, but because I was frightened. It was so good I wanted to do it properly. I wanted to surprise her. I wanted to secretly show her work to my dealer and get him to set up an exhibition. Make her a star. What was I afraid of? That not understanding the extent of her own genius she would rush out and snort the entire collection up her nose, getting ripped off into the bargain.

The breath she had been holding came out in a long shuddering sigh. Silently she walked to a picture of a very pale girl in an enchanted purple glade. The girl's body was half turned so you saw the most wonderful dragonfly wings sprouting from her back. There was a beautiful expression of innocence on the girl's face and immediately I knew that she was Maggie. Maggie carefully took down the picture. Gratitude shone in her clear blue eyes.

'Would you like to have it?' she asked. I held the picture and was unable to speak. It was too generous a present.

'I see shapes,' she explained. I looked at the wonderful light, the gay brushstrokes, the unspoilt craggy hanging cliff sweeping into a deep blue skyline, the wonderful innocence of the girl, and I couldn't help the direction of my thoughts.

How did such a beautiful child become a common prostitute?

I looked up at her and it was as if she had read my mind.

Hurt, she opened the door and ushered me out of her paradise.

Nutan

Got some heroin, but it was shit. How could people be so mean? Didn't they care when they caused suffering? It could be the drugs, but I felt as if we had fallen into a bad set somehow.

I couldn't be sure because I had stopped keeping track, but it seemed as if we were increasing the dose very fast. We were neither of us well. It was living in that dark, smelly room. Even the guys from the kebab shop got on my nerves. The other day one of them offered me money for sex. When I looked at him angrily he said, 'Oh sorry, I thought you were your sister.'

By mistake I had injected into flesh, and my hand was so swollen it hurt to move it. I detested dirt and yet I lay amongst unwashed sheets, helpless and useless all day long. I had not washed or bathed for a long time. I ought to have been ashamed, yet I lay there waiting for my sister, knowing she would always give me the bigger, better garland.

Zeenat

There were orange and russet leaves in the park. The days were shortening. On the pavements people hurried around me. I envied them. They were whole. Their coats kept them warm. Their cold did not come from inside. The biggest fire made no difference when the cold came from inside.

345

Ricky

I called my brother and told him I needed to buy another restaurant. Could he sell my inheritance? I needed £100,000. My brother was shocked into silence. I forgot. Land was never sold, only bought and hoarded down the generations.

'Buy me out then?' I offered.

But he said he had just planted his vineyards and wouldn't see any returns for two years. I asked if he could get something from the bank, if he could at least send me half. He said he'd try.

'How soon?' I asked, 'I wouldn't want to lose this deal.'

'A week,' he promised.

'All right then, send my love to Mamma and Papa. Don't let me lose this deal.'

The money, bless my brother, arrived in a week. I paid off two sets of bailiffs and then I began to party. But two weeks later I was in the shit again. So I sold my Rolex for five grand. A day later a letter arrived, something about the house being repossessed if a large sum, I forget the figure now, was not paid. They wanted me to contact them. They wanted to discuss the matter.

'*Va funculo*,' I said, and called a house removal firm. In the house was hundreds and thousands of pounds' worth of furniture. Give me a price for the whole lot. He eyed my unshaven face, and looked away from my gambler's eyes. The bastard rubbed his chin and said, 'Ten grand?' We settled on fifteen. The bank was welcome to their fucking house. I didn't need it anyway.

I stood in the middle of the empty house. For a moment there was a sense of loss, so painful, I felt my stomach sink. An echo of children's voices, a woman calling, '*A tavola*, dinner is ready.'

Fuck that. I didn't bother to lock the door or turn off the lights. On the way to the flat I called my dealer.

'How many?' he asked.

'Many,' I replied.

Anis

Such a terrible storm raged outside that the wind ran down the streets screaming. I stood at the window watching the needle-sharp drops of rain hammer at the glass. A fuse must have tripped and we had no electricity, but I simply couldn't be bothered to fumble around under the stairs. Zeenat had found some boxes of candles. She must have used them all because the place looked like a Gothic film set. Candlelight had turned Zeenat into an exotic stranger. I felt as if we were meeting for the first time over a flame in a pagan Balinese temple.

She sat on the floor with her knees together, and her calves folded underneath her. There was a flash of lightning, and I still remember that moment when she was illuminated by the bright white light. I stared at her, shocked. She was no longer the little brown bird I had started painting. She had become a fierce merciless bird of prey.

As I watched the mighty bird of prey, little Maggie took refuge in my head. Oh! Maggie, I'm so sorry I made you cry, but I saw you as a finished painting, and finished, you were beautiful beyond reason. But just you wait, I am planning such a surprise for you. You have no idea what a dream your life is about to become.

Nutan

I dreamt of myself dead, lying on a marble slab. I was cold, so cold and huddled around me were ghosts.

Ricky

When Elizabeth called to tell me that Maggie was dead, that she had fallen out of her ninth-storey flat, I was certain she had jumped. The crazy girl went looking for death.

And she found him under her window.

But then Elizabeth said, 'She must have been on the Rohypnol, and trying to fly.'

Of course, she was right. The spider's love. It made paradise dangerous. Was it a little warning? A request for more?

I still don't remember a thing from that night. I remember helping to hold back Maggie when she wanted to fly, but afterwards it is a complete blank. To think I smashed my guitar to bits, and cannot remember doing it. Worse, they told me I fell on my chin and knocked myself out.

Elizabeth

In the quiet of the night, the news of Maggie's death affected me strangely. In a way it exhilarated me, she was gone where there was no need. Had I not seen death's face and secretly wished for his blow? Even though my sister reminded me that it was a cold and dark place, it still held its attractions.

In another way, I mourned her with an anguish suitable for a mother who clutches the lifeless body of her most golden child. And sweet Jesus, help me, but I missed her like a child baying for its dead mother.

I remembered the night when that rat had dumped her, and she'd shown me the bleeding wound in her heart.

Why did she wear her thorns of abuse so patiently? Will you do her memory the honour of listening? I promise her story is not a long one. She was born to a street prostitute.

They lived in a grubby one-bedroom flat that was cold even in summer. Her mother traded in the back streets, careful not to get into the cars of men with blank eyes. Sometimes she grew careless and returned with bruises, but she survived.

Then the women in the street began to protest, and she had to bring the men home. And Maggie saw all the squalid men who trooped up the stairs and heard the dirty sounds they made.

Maggie was seven when her mother came upon Klaus, her pimp, gently running his hands up her daughter's legs while she sat, reading aloud for him. When he was gone she said, 'Do not let him touch you ever again.' But life went on as before. Maggie slept on the sofa and they on the bed.

One night Maggie opened her eyes and saw him standing over her. His face was in darkness, but she smelt him, strange and musky. She wanted to scream for her mother, but she could not. She lay paralysed on the sofa. From her mouth came only the tiniest whimpers, half-muffled and half-eaten by the strange musky smell.

Suddenly her mother was at the doorway. She had waited two years for such a moment. She shot him in the back, and he collapsed on top of Maggie. Her mother dragged her out from under the dead weight and sat to wait until the good people came to take her away. There was a grandmother living alone in Ireland, but she was considered crazy and unable to care for the child. Never mind, the state took over.

Sometimes Maggie wrote to her mother in prison. Her mother told her she had no regrets. She would do it all again in an instant. Maggie thought that was true love. I don't. I think her mother made the worst mistake of her life. She didn't save her daughter. She cast the child upon a path filthy with the feet of the depraved. They fed upon her.

So she would not refuse to wear her crown of thorns they lied about her worth.

I sometimes think of Maggie's mother. Sitting in her prison cell, fed, clothed, sheltered, and safe rereading her daughter's lies with a contented heart. There was no one to tell her that her greatest act of sacrifice had been for nothing.

Anis

I was devastated by the news of Maggie's death. It was so sudden, so unexpected that it didn't seem real, couldn't be real. I looked at my half-finished painting of the courtesan's tears, and began to doubt everything: her quick, easy laughter, that first sitting when I had made her weep, the treasures hanging in her shabby flat. Oh, what a waste.

But even worse was the feeling that I was responsible, guilty. That day in her flat I should have told her how fantastic her work was. How heartless and presumptuous I had been not to have freed her from her nightmare that very day. She might have given up the prostitution and probably even the drugs. At the very least she could have sold a painting and not had to sniff powdered sleeping pills. I could have changed everything.

I wrestled with guilt and was taken captive. Oh, but he was hard. He allowed no moment of rest. 'You fool, you fool,' he snarled. 'You had her life in your hand.'

I was strangely drawn to the trappings of Maggie's life: her apartment, her books, her knowledge. I asked Elizabeth for the spare keys. The yellow and black police tapes had been taken down. It was evening when I opened the door and was suddenly back at the edge of the precipice, exhilarated by a sense that I could discover something of great importance.

Was she my mirror? Were the things I detested most about her exactly the beasts I tried to suppress, but knew lived undisclosed inside me? Was not her need for oblivion mine too? Even the dead moths my grandmother swept off the veranda brought envious thoughts. They were free. No ugly secrets to keep.

Her books were everywhere: Freud here, Nietzsche there, Voltaire on the window sill, and Shakespeare by the book-case. I opened the window she had fallen from and a cold gust of wind swept in. Loose papers flew from a table top. I left the window slightly ajar, and switched on the electric, log-effect fire. Very quickly the little place was warm and cosy. I imagined her sitting by the fire in a nightdress, her feet up on the faded footstool and the tortoiseshell cat asleep on her knees. One hand buried in the cat's fur and an open book in the other. The flames of the fire lit up her engrossed face. I thought I felt her presence then.

The real reason I had come was to see that unfinished painting, the secret one she had once alluded to. I crept into her bedroom, and was amazed again. Exactly forty-one paintings whispered like ghosts to me. I returned the painting of the purple glade she had given me to its original place, and simply sat on the bed, savouring the moment of being completely surrounded by sheer beauty. She thought in shapes. Glorious courageous shapes.

I searched, in the drawers and cupboards, moving through the glamorous stoles and gowns, until finally I touched the roughness of canvas. What secrets could the dead tell me? I took it out and gasped. A golden boy smiled sweetly. A quarter of his face was still unfinished in a flat reddish wash, but in his child's hands was an unforgettable sight in white and orange. The saddest cat I had ever seen in all my life hunched pitifully in those hands. Its old haggard face hung from scrawny shoulders, and its strangely human eyes were half-closed pits of suffering. Yet

351

it was the most beautiful thing I had ever seen. Its emotional content electrified me. The beautiful child was fading, but the sorry cat lived.

Remember when I told you about the language of art? That cat was as much Maggie as the flayed skin on the Sistine Chapel is Michelangelo. Simply entitled 'Boy and Cat' it distinguished my 'Courtesan's Tears' as an infinitely inferior piece of work. In the reddish glow of Maggie's lamp 'Boy and Cat' lived as the artist had intended. For ever. How I wanted it for myself. And why not? If I exchanged the purple glade painting for this one . . . After all, its monetary value was far less so I would hardly be cheating the beneficiaries of Maggie's estate.

I went back down to the car to fetch my canvas, easel and paints. I sat at the dining table and began to make sketches; the hair, the arms, the legs, the ballet shoes but not the face. The face I could not do. There was a photograph of her on a side table. I stared at it for a long time. It had been taken in a night club. It was not a bad photograph, but something eluded me. As if the real Maggie was hiding. I put the sketches down and went to stare out of the window. Below were lights, cars, people.

The wind whipped my hair. On that day she too must have climbed this ledge. I found myself climbing out of the window and balancing on the ledge. I stood then as she must have . . . on the edge of discovery. Damn Ricky, for bringing the Rohypnol into her life. She was a Catholic. She would never have jumped. 'I have not the courage,' she had said. And I believed her. Violent death must have taken her by the ankles.

I stood on one foot. Did I have the courage? A strong gust of wind buffeted me, and I very nearly lost my balance. Immediately my hands, my legs and brain clung to survival, and I climbed back in, shaking. She had jumped but I had not the courage.

I felt cold, so I closed the window, and climbed into her bed. The pillow smelt of perfume, something delicate and flowery. I switched off the bedside lamp and lay awake for hours. Expecting her to return. Sometime during the early hours I dozed off and saw her squatting on a bed of dried leaves; the moon on her face. Her hands were buried under the crackling leaves, and a wonderful mad smile was on her face. 'Listen to the earth,' she whispered, 'munching all we have buried today.'

I awakened to sunlight slanting on the paintings. The effect was fabulous, but I was startled when I sat up, and mistook my reflection in a mirror for a stranger. What an odd girl Maggie was. She met a mirror upon waking. It was crooked. I went to straighten it and, behind it, found Maggie's diary.

I opened the handsome, leather-bound volume, and the first thing my eyes fell upon was:

I bid you come to Maggie MacFadden's funeral.

The diary snapped shut. What was that fear? Suddenly I was an intruder in Maggie's home. The beautiful paintings grew hostile eyes. I had no permission to read Maggie's thoughts. I phoned Elizabeth. The silence was so complete that I thought the line had dropped, but then she uttered a sound that sounded like a strangled sigh and said, 'I'll be there in half an hour. Wait for me.'

I took the diary to the kitchen and sat on a chair to wait for her. On the window sill black ants surrounded a blob of jam. I watched them disappear into a hole in the wall. The buzzer rang. I let Elizabeth in.

She looked at me carefully. 'I brought some breakfast,' she said, moving past me, and into the kitchen. Her hair was white in the morning light. She was undoubtedly very beautiful, but I had never wanted to capture her image, hers was a beauty too cold and hard. Behold, the way she made Bruce suffer. She opened a window. I hadn't noticed until then the stale smell left behind by the cats.

She turned around and smiled at me. I did not smile back.

From paper bags, she extracted croissants and two Styrofoam cups of coffee, and from her handbag, little packs of butter and strawberry jam.

'Sugar?'

I nodded. She tipped a sachet of sugar into one of the cups. Then she opened a cupboard and brought out plates and knives. And in that sunny silence, we sat down to our first breakfast together. She began buttering a croissant. I did the same. They were still warm.

I felt comfortable with her. As if we were intimate friends. A very peculiar sensation, considering I disliked the woman. When we finished she brushed the crumbs from our plates onto the window sill. She and the ants were old friends. I held up the diary.

She looked down at her hands. 'When the bud is young it clings tightly to the tree, but when it has bloomed its best, it falls willingly into any outstretched hand. Maggie said goodbye to you when she gave you her painting of the purple glade. It was the most precious thing she owned. She said she was once brave and happy in that place.' Elizabeth considered me, unsmiling now. 'She also told me that she gave you some of her most treasured books to read.' She looked at the diary in my hand. 'But that is not one of them.'

I stared at her. What was she saying? Maggie knew she was going to die? That Maggie jumped? That Maggie did the unCatholic thing? That little Maggie had the courage I didn't?

'But, she told me she was a Catholic . . .'

'Ah, Anis, although Maggie claimed to admire the works of Nietzsche, the only thing of his she ever quoted was the trite "the last Christian died on the cross".'

'But what about the Rohypnol?'

'What about it? Didn't she know exactly what effect it had on her?'

354

Suddenly I felt betrayed. Maggie had sold out. She was a genius and she had not fulfilled her *dharma*.

Then Elizabeth told me about a recurring nightmare that had plagued Maggie for the last two years of her life. Sometimes even four times a week, and always in full colour. In it she was trapped in a public toilet. There was excrement everywhere in that toilet, the floor under her feet, the walls, the sinks, the mirrors, and even the ceiling was covered with it. Sometimes in her desperate efforts to get out she accidentally touched it. Then her mother appeared. And she too was brown and glistening. In her outstretched hand she held a peeled apple quarter for Maggie to eat. The disgust Maggie suffered was so acute that she always woke up gasping and wretched.

The Maggie I knew was in the rear-view mirror, and receding fast. 'Do you know what's in this diary?' I asked, holding it up.

'No, but I am sure there are many things in there that are not for our eyes. I think we should burn it, for Maggie.'

No one could tell you too much, could they, I thought as I looked at Elizabeth's closed, secretive face. Slowly I pushed the book towards her. She removed the leather binding and we burnt it in the kitchen sink. A few pages at a time. Afterwards we walked away from the charming piles of old books, the sad brilliant paintings, and the wind howling tirelessly outside.

As we walked to my car I suddenly knew why, for all my trying, my pencil had not encountered Maggie's face. It was because I had refused to see her, to really see her. I had tried to gloss over the unpalatable bits, and put my own unworthy interpretation upon her motives.

She was a prostitute, and that thought filled me with disgust. Prostitutes' bodies I thought of as toxic septic tanks. Everyday excessive amounts of semen, uncontrollable compulsions, and vile sexual perversions were flushed into them. And association with them could only pollute. Although I had tried to pretend otherwise, I had judged her a species different from me. Even her genius had not kept her precious. Hence she had refused me her face last night. She had recognised me for the hypocrite I was. How right she was not to trust me.

Strange, how I learned compassion in a dead woman's kitchen. Laughable, that it was cold, hard Elizabeth who taught it. Had I misunderstood all the messengers God had sent me? I had still not learned to cherish a memory. I, who possessed the most beautiful memories of Maggie. I had nearly destroyed something precious. Again.

I returned to find Zeenat in my bed.

The scenery changed, but the devastation was the same. I stroked her hair tenderly. It was unwashed. There was something else I had noticed. Her skin had turned silent. That delicate scent of crushed flowers that her skin used to utter was gone. Inside the vermilion petals of this lotus slept a wretched cobra. If I did not wake him, would he slide away while I slept?

'I love you,' I whispered sadly.

She did not open her eyes, but her mouth curved into a vague smile. 'I've saved some for you,' she mumbled.

After terrible responsibility, irresponsibility.

'Thank you,' I said.

Bruce

I took Elizabeth out to lunch to talk about Maggie. I had promised Maggie things. Promises I wanted to keep. We had just ordered drinks when her mobile rang. She stood up, walked away from me, and answered it in Arabic. When she came back she was in a hurry to leave.

'Sure, go,' I said coldly, raging with jealousy.

'Sorry,' she said, and hurried out. I watched her get into a black cab.

'Will that be a meal for one then, sir?' a voice inquired.

'No, that will be a meal for none.'

I put some money on the table and drove to Elizabeth's apartment block. I parked some way down the street and waited. About one hour later a white stretch limo pulled up at the entrance to her building. Five minutes later she was at the door. Her hair had been swept into a smooth chignon and she was wearing a long white dress with a diamanté collar. As she came down the steps she lifted her dress slightly, and I saw that she wore flat white sandals. No doubt the bastard was short and fat to boot. A huge man leaped out of the passenger seat to install her in the back. The long car drove off. I felt sick to my gut. It was money.

She did it for the money.

Yet, I had never seen her flush. She held expense accounts in expensive shops, but never ready cash. The Arab was cunning. Luxuries while you remain mine. When I thought about it, I could afford the greedy bitch. At a stretch. I thought of her in the Ritz hotel. Going up to a suite of rooms in her inappropriate evening dress. What was the matter with him anyway? Did he not know that European women did not wear wedding dresses and veils at lunchtime? Everybody at the Ritz would know what she was there for. They would snigger and say, 'Here comes the whore.'

I waited. Three hours, I waited.

When the limo pulled up I experienced a rush in my stomach. The huge man leaped out of the passenger seat, opened and closed her door for her. She did not look at or thank him. The elegant chignon was gone. Her hair was back to its usual shoulder-length bob. I waited for while before I rang her bell.

'Yes,' she said.

'I need to see you,' I said.

'Not now, Bruce. Maybe I'll see you at Ricky's tomorrow. Goodbye.'

'Wait,' I said. 'What did you eat?'

I stared at the black mouth of the intercom.

'Lamb, Irish lamb,' she said finally, tiredly.

'You don't have to do this. Marry me.' I had never intended to say that. By the shocked silence coming out of the intercom, neither had she expected to hear it. Next, I made it worse. 'I promised Maggie I would,' I said. Lame, but it was the truth. It was what I wanted. I wanted to grow old with her. The silence continued.

'You can't afford me, Bruce,' she said harshly.

'What? You want to be a fucking hooker all your life?' I burst out.

'I am what you say I am. What does that make you?' she asked frostily and, apparently not needing an answer, turned the intercom off. I kept my finger on the buzzer until the doorman loomed on the other side of the door, behind the protection of wood and glass.

'Is everything all right, sir?'

Pompous prat. 'Yes, everything is just fine,' I said, and strode off.

Elizabeth

There was a little girl I used to watch from across the road. When it stopped raining she came out in her wellies. First she was careful to avoid the puddles, but it was no time before she was stepping into them. When that was no longer satisfactory she started stamping in the water, splashing her clothes gleefully. But even that was not enough. She took her wellies off and filled them with rain water. I watched her enviously, her immense pleasure in being naughty. Her knowledge of defiance. It was great and wonderful. Once, I wore wellies too. Once when I was child and knew the value of deliberate defiance. Before I sold myself.

Bruce

I was a bit depressed. The Arab got the better of me. I spent the night with Ricky and a Filipino prostitute. We had polished off a couple of bottles of brandy, the coke was nearly gone, and Ricky was getting edgy. He wanted to go out and get some more, and although I didn't want any more I gave him some money. Maggie dying so suddenly had soured everything. I was sitting there on default setting. More and more I felt sordid, by association. When he left, I leaned back and closed my eyes, but I was so exhausted I must have fallen asleep because I opened my eyes to Haylee blowing gently into my ear. For a second I thought I was in a dream. After all I had tried in the beginning to bed her, and it was definitely a no-go area.

'Hello,' the jam pot purred.

'What are you doing here?' I asked blearily, blinking at my watch. It was nearly five. Ricky must have 'forgotten' to come back with the stuff.

'Just got back from a party. Thought someone might be awake here.' She glanced at the Filipino prostitute, still out cold from all that drink.

'No, there's no coke around. Ricky disappeared more than two hours ago to get more. He obviously found another party.'

'Oh well, let's just get drunk then.' She poured us both two large measures of brandy. Put one glass into my hand, and settled herself opposite me.

'Want some really juicy gossip?'

'Okay.'

'Ricky slept with Zeenat.'

'What?'

'Yep, she ran out of here in tears. You know that shit she does now, I bet you, it's the guilt. That's what you get for cheating on your own sister.'

'Does Nutan know?'

'Don't think so.' Her voice died to a whisper. 'No one knows. Just you and me.'

Anis

I picked Maggie's grandmother out of the crowd immediately. She was a nervous, pink, other-worldly woman in a little red hat. Perhaps I had seen her ghost smiling from one of Maggie's paintings. She clutched a battered handbag to her midriff.

'Hello, Helen. I am Anis.'

'Oh,' startled pale blue eyes regarded me.

I guided her out of the airport. We did not speak.

After she had identified the body, she came out blinking. 'There was not a mark on her,' she said wonderingly. 'You're not her man, are you?'

Ah, that. 'No, I'm just a friend.'

'Oh, well that's good.'

Her granddaughter was dead but at least she had taste when it came to men.

'Would you like some lunch?' I asked.

'No, no, thank you. I have to get back.'

'Right now?'

'Aye, I've made a pan of raspberry jam and it needs bottling. Besides, the foxes need feeding.'

'There is still that collection of Maggie's paintings. I dare say it is worth quite a lot of money. Would you like to have a look at it?'

She shuddered. 'No, no, you have them,' she said.

'No, you don't understand. They are worth a good few hundred thousand pounds.'

Her eyes widened with surprise. She bit her lower lip, and then licked it uncertainly. 'Well, perhaps you would be kind enough to sell them for me, then.'

How naive she must have been to trust a stranger in such a matter. What if Ricky had come to pick her up?

'Of course I will.' I could do better than that.

'Thank you.' She smiled a small lost smile that made me want to comfort her.

'It was an accident,' I said.

'Oh, yes, yes. Of course.' She looked at me kindly with those puzzled, pale eyes. She did not understand life. It did not touch her cheeks gently as it passed, but spun her round and round crying, 'Catch me if you can.' I thought of my own grandmother. People thought Helen was mad, but she could speak to the foxes.

'She screamed all day long when she was a . . .' Helen stopped abruptly, frowning. 'No, wait. It was my daughter who did that. Maggie was the sweetest child you ever saw. Oh, how could I have forgotten?' she lamented in a small forlorn voice. Her mouth trembled, large teardrops gathered at the edges of her pale eyelashes, and ran down her neglected cheeks. 'I gave too much to her mother. There was not enough left for Maggie.'

Then suddenly the tears stopped. 'Did you know what she did for a living?'

I didn't take my eyes off the road. 'She was a dancer, but she should have been an artist. She painted like a dream.'

'I've read all about it, you know, the psychopathology of prostitution. They blame it on an unconscious desire to revenge neglect.'

My eyes left the road. She didn't look so small and abandoned any more.

'When she was young she used to take all her clothes off
and stand at the window facing the street. Funny isn't it,
how I didn't pick it up then.'

I dropped Helen off, and telephoned my art dealer. I told
him I had found a most fabulous painter. That she painted
the way I dreamed of painting.

'Fantastic,' he said, 'when can I meet her?'

Then I told him she was a dead prostitute.

The bastard smacked his lips and said, 'Oh, how I do love
you.'

Nutan

We became furtive and sneaky, and the doses were larger
and more frequent. We hid from each other when it was
obvious to both of us what the other was doing. Never
again would we be so joyously innocent, as we had been
once before.

Sometimes I waited for her to drop off to sleep and when
I was sure she was sleeping I tiptoed out of the room. But
once as I was opening the door her head shot around.

'Where are you going?' she demanded, in a high and
peevish voice.

'Just for a walk,' I lied. She considered me for a bit
longer, frozen in my tracks, a criminal. She must have
known I was lying, but she lay her head back down like a
beaten dog, and went back to sleep.

I crept out. Unashamed and filled with animal cunning I
bought some from the dealer around the block, except as
usual there was not enough to share. I couldn't take it back
to the room. So I locked myself in a toilet at Victoria train
station.

The relief . . . oh, the relief . . . it was so immense I could not stop. Dose after dose. A few times, someone tried the door, and I cried out weakly, 'Occupied.' I forgot about my sister. She was waiting in the room, too sick to come out. Fuck her. She could get her own. When I stood up I felt so light-headed I had to sit down again. My jeans were wet. The floor was wet with piss. I hated myself. God, how I hated myself.

Anna would say I was 'a proper smack head.'

Zeenat

I remembered when we danced, and showered flowers upon the crowd squatting in a circle around us. We did it under a starry sky and a full moon. The swaying palms were our amphitheatre. Stone lamps dotted the paths to our stage. In the skyline was the dim outline of the temple's thatch roof. It was beautiful, perhaps more so than if it had been performed on a stage. Overhead a flock of pigeons circled, the whistles and flutes attached to their necks and feet making delightful, tinkling music. Crouched between the legs of children, cats with greedy violet eyes watched the birds in the sky. How fleeting and far away the memory was. It was another world. We were different then. We sang as we bathed in the river.

Ricky

I telephoned my brother. Told him I had been offered a share in another restaurant, a hundred and fifty seats this time. He was impressed by my empire. 'Is that the twelfth restaurant now?

'*Si, si*, why don't you invest some money too? It's a

fantastic deal. You have to spend to make. Do you want in?'

'Well, it's a bit hard at the moment,' he hesitated. 'You know we just replanted the vineyards . . .'

'Well, re-mortgage your house then. This is too good an opportunity to let go. You see there is a wonderful system in this country. Investors have precedence over creditors. So even if things went badly wrong you would be first to get your money back.'

'Are you sure?'

'Absolutely. Guaranteed. You just can't lose.'

'Well, if you think . . .'

'I do. When can you send the money?'

'Couple of weeks, but first I have to. . .'

'Yes, yes, ask our cousin who works at the Banca Di Creditor Cooperativo Del Nisseno to process it as soon as possible. Hurry,' I tell him. 'You don't want to lose the deal.'

He wished me luck. By the way, did he see Francesca and the children?

Sometimes. They lived on a farm not far away. He had heard that Francesca had made agreements with different farmers to buy up their olive crop every other year. This way she had a constant supply and they enough for their own needs. He said she had installed on her land some fancy pressing equipment from Tuscany, and had started bottling her own olive oil. She never ever came to visit Mamma, but from his tractor on his way to the land he saw the children. They looked brown and happy, their legs sticking out of almond trees, running without a care in the olive groves.

I promised myself then that I *would* get my shit together, stop the coca, and bring those kids and Francesca back. Soon, very soon. I could stop any time I wanted.

Bruce

My father was in the last stages of cancer. It wasn't a shock. We knew he was dying slowly, so I was rather startled by the hollow feeling inside me. The old lion had become precious. I rang Elizabeth's bell. She listened to me while I rambled on about being six years old, and climbing a ladder up a cupboard to get to my father's stash. A single well-thumbed black and white girlie magazine. Only one photograph had remained vivid through the years: a blonde girl, spread-eagled in a barn, straw sticking to her body. Tears came into my eyes to think of him poring over those pages. How innocent his forbidden pleasures had been.

'Come to think of it, she looked a little bit like you,' I said.

Escaped silver strands of hair curved at the sides of her neck. I shifted, and rested my head on her chest. A silver filament brushed my cheek, and I moved my head to the left and found her lips. I think she might have struggled a little in my arms, but she was so warm, and I wanted her so badly, it was a soothing resistance. And then she stopped, and kissed me back. It was beautiful. I couldn't believe it. My hands went to pull at the shirt tucked into her jeans. Without warning she froze. It stopped me in my tracks. Her eyes were shaken.

'No,' she said harshly.

I pulled myself away. '*What?*'

'Sorry, I started on the vodka at lunchtime,' she said very coldly, but her face looked white, shocked.

'What the fuck is the matter with you?' I snarled.

'Sorry, it was a mistake.'

'What is it with you? It's not Lent, so you can't be doing penance,' I shouted.

'Just go. Please.' This time her voice shook badly.

I was savage. I wanted to smash her. Break her down to

pieces. Make her beg for mercy. Yet, I loved her. Her eyes were oil patches in my path. No matter how carefully I tried to walk on by, I slipped and fell every time.

'Don't fucking worry, I am.' I looked at her. At the white face. 'You're either a first class mercenary bitch, or the biggest coward I've come across. Either way you look at it, it's a poor show, Lizzie.' Her hands were clasped tightly, the knuckles pale. 'Ricky was right. Chasing you is like throwing sugar into the ocean, a bloody waste of time. And you know what else? I give up.' I spoke really softly. I didn't even slam the door behind me or bother to wait for the lift. I ran down the stairs.

I should have been livid, but the rage was gone as quickly as it had come, and I felt crushed. Shit. What a fucking mess. Even my finances were in a terrible state. I had been neglecting my shops and they were going down the drain. Things had changed after Maggie died. I needed to get my life back together, or lose everything. First I needed a holiday in the sun, get my head straight, walk along a beach by myself, eat foreign food, and maybe fuck a few strangers.

I felt awful. I went to see Paddy. He was stretched out underneath his wreck.

'Hey, Paddy,' I called.

'What you doing here?' His head came out from the side. Took one look at my face, and he was commiserating regretfully, 'They make hares of us all.'

I felt so bad at that point I wanted to bawl.

'What say you, we shoot some pool and drink the new day in?' he offered, smiling lopsidedly.

I think we drank for a long time. I told Paddy about my dad, and the blonde girl in a barn, hay stuck to her body, but we never spoke about Elizabeth, not once, this beautiful woman who had refused my love. We changed pubs so many times I have forgotten our trail, the anonymous seats we sat upon, the taste of the drinks we swallowed, the stained urinals we pissed in, the freshly wiped tables I rested my elbow on while wishing to weep.

Was this love? Was this what everyone was so excited about? This appalling ache that gnawed endlessly in your gut no matter how drunk or high you got.

A young girl came to flirt with both of us at the last pub we went to. By then it was quite obvious our attempt at being merry was a complete disaster.

'Do you think I'm pretty?' she asked coyly.

Do yourself a favour and take a guess sweetheart, I wanted to say. She was pretty enough, but she was no Ice Queen. My Ice Queen was melting like a Dali painting.

'You have her,' I said to Paddy, and stood up to leave.

'Stay, we'll both have her,' Paddy said.

'No,' I said, 'I haven't got the heart for it.'

November 2000

Ricky

The manager at Villa Ricci, irritating sod, had picked up a
new habit of locking away the till drawer at night. He told
the waiters it was because he was bored of coming in every
morning and finding it completely clean, from when I had
raided it the night before. I don't know who pressed his
panic button. It wasn't like I didn't leave him a note asking
him to use his money first on something, just until the day's
takings started coming in.

Bruce

I went away to the Bahamas. There were neon-lit places a-
plenty, where the night life was kicking, but I wasn't
interested. I kept myself to myself lying in the sun by the
pool. On the first day a beautiful girl in a green bikini
came to occupy the lounger two away from mine. She had
one of those bodies you rarely find any more, big breasts,
tiny waist and flaring hips. Something about the way she
looked at me reminded me of Elizabeth. I lay back, closed
my eyes and was glad she had not smiled, because I didn't
want her. I was through running after skirt. Fuck them
all. They could keep their cheap black market coquetry.

I couldn't sleep nights, so I walked down to the beach and
lay in a little depression in the sand listening to the distant
sound of boat engines, and the water lapping against the

shore. It was about the time of the full moon, so sea came very close to the beach, and waves sounded full and thick.

In the soft dark I closed my eyes and a secret door opened. Elizabeth walked through it and we danced to Robbie Williams and Nicole Kidman singing 'Something Stupid'. But in the end it was always the same. I grew angry with her. I really didn't get her. There was a point when I was sure she had been just as keen. Sometimes I pondered the thing Maggie had said, 'There is something I have to tell you about Beth.'

Just before dawn the lights in the dining rooms of the hotel would come on, and I would pick myself up and start walking towards them. As I got nearer I heard the clanking of cutlery; tables being laid for breakfast. It comforted me that sound – there were other people awake and going about their business. Life went on.

Once a group of Australian revellers invited me to join their 'barbi'. They swigged strong booze, consumed yards of sausages and economy packs of hamburgers bought from a local supermarket and proceeded to get stoned senseless. Someone held out an expertly rolled joint, but I had to decline. Weed did my head in. There were Sheilas there for the taking, but they were big boned, and not to my taste. Anyway, I didn't have any rubber on me, and I was damned if I was going to sleep with one of them without protection. I knew them of old. They were just like every other teenage backpacker, fucking their way around the globe. I felt old and decrepit in their company. I left them to their party and returned to my little depression in the sand.

When I got back from my holiday I went to work, putting the business back to where it was before I took my eye off it. It was nothing that couldn't be fixed. As my father said, 'The sweat on your face will feed you.'

He died, by the way. Quietly. Only my mother cried, and

then only a little. What do I still remember of him? Crouching at his nearly transparent feet, clipping his toenails because he was too feeble? Ah yes, of course, his eyes. I think I'll always remember them. His cold flinty eyes, closed.

I had decided not to go back to the Spider's Temple. It was tainted by Maggie's death. Once Ricky left a message on my answer machine, looking for more stuff, and sounding strung out and Haylee called to invite me to a party. I didn't return their calls. And that was that.

Sometimes late at night, on my way back from a club, I drove by Mayfair, but I never saw her; in clubs I looked for platinum heads, but never encountered hers. Once I went to the entrance door of her apartment block and stood staring at the buzzer until that pompous maggot of a security guard came to inquire, 'Everything all right, sir?' Other times, especially if I had had a drink, I longed to look into the grey, grey eyes of my cat, but I was damned if I was going to keep chasing her and getting nowhere. Some things you had to let go.

I went out with the boys and got stinking a few times, but mostly I just worked, and by and by, I began to recover. I thought about her less and less. Then I began sleeping with other girls. It was just sex, but it was a start. Although there were times that I closed my eyes and pretended it was her, in my hands, in my mouth, so close, so close.

Nutan

I dreamed of my sister. I was in a strange dark place, a limestone cave perhaps, where a woman dressed in black was bent over a pot. 'Look what I have prepared for your sweet sister,' she howled, and howling, laughed. When I sat up suddenly, distressed and confused, I saw Zeenat standing at the end of my bed watching me. I blinked with shock. She looked terrible. Unwashed and uncared for. I had not realised how fast my sister had declined. I called her name at the same time that she called her own. It was then that I realised the awful truth.

In the night my sister had moved the mirror. I was looking at my own reflection. Like a hunted animal I stared at my squatting reflection. How repulsive, and yet how fascinating. The dark circles, the slicked eyes, the skin so strangely close to the bone. Look at me. Half human, half beast. But my eyes grew ashamed and slid away. The mirror is a dangerous thing. It is sincere in the company of the insincere.

My sister was already out to score. No make-up or nail varnish, before breakfast, before brushing her teeth. She threw her hair into a band, and rushed out in the direction of Victoria station. There were sores on my legs. I rubbed them absently, wondering when she would return. Outside it was freezing cold, but I would have to brave it if she didn't return soon. I too, needed it, before breakfast, and before brushing my teeth. I looked for a cigarette. The first puff usually made my head spin but it stopped my hands from shaking. I fell back on the bed, and tried to find some warmth between the thin blankets. From beneath stale stained sheets I observed our living conditions.

Our room was foul beyond all belief. Food was rotting under the beds, the carpet was caked in dirt, and the walls discoloured and vomit splattered. Soiled clothes littered the room, and the wash basin was cracked and dirty. There were blood stains in and around it. How curious, that it should not disgust me.

But dirt had simply stopped bothering me. I knew there was a rat somewhere in our room. He had changed addresses from the kebab shop downstairs. It was the food in the take-away boxes we discarded on the floor. Something was rotting too. A monstrous smell pervaded the whole room. I looked at my watch. I knew where she was. I pretended I didn't. I pretended to believe that she was shoplifting, but I knew where the money came from.

I had no more feelings for others. I pretended to care just to increase the odds of getting more out of them. *Got anything, man?*

The thoughts, how heavy they lay in my head. I sat up and held my head in my hands. Oh, where was she? I heard a sound on the stairs and leaped out of bed. The Goddess with the elixir of forgetfulness was at the door. The door opened. There she was. Unwashed and uncared for. Why, we looked exactly alike.

Anis

The physiological effect of heroin on love and desire is to destroy both. If another person exists it is only as a partner in the endless business of procurement. By the same token, eating, drinking and mating are for animals. Life with its unnecessary complications and base cravings becomes a nuisance. Look at them, their fists full of dusty earth.

We relinquish the desire for everything in exchange for just one clawing need, one monstrous joy. We are content with hollow cheeks, wintry hopeless smiles, and bones that protrude. We hardly eat. We think it all splendid. We are desperate only to move from one splendid sleep to another.

Bruce

I received an invite to Maggie MacFadden's art exhibition, and although I knew Elizabeth would be there, I couldn't keep myself from going. I tried to blend into the groups of civilised people sipping cheap warm champagne. From afar

I spotted Anis and the twins. You couldn't tell so much with Anis, because he looked well in a black suit and a dress shirt, but the twins were rakes, with matchstick arms and legs.

And then Elizabeth stepped up to them. She was dressed very simply in black, and I thought that she had never looked more beautiful, or more unreachable. Anis said something in her ear, and I saw her rest her hand on his sleeve, and nod. It was a gentle intimate gesture. So she kept in touch with him, then. They had become close. Anis and the twins moved on, and I saw Elizabeth's eyes scan the room quickly. For me? Alone, she looked helpless and childlike.

I still loved her. Just one look and all the progress I had made receded. I made a step towards her. People changed. Maybe she had. But just then a man approached her, and her beautiful grey eyes turned to him. In them I recognised the same cold expression with which she had once held me at bay. I left my glass at the reception desk and left. Nothing had changed in the honey trap. I was a fool.

Ricky

Fuck, I got such a good price for the restaurant, £90,000. Selling restaurants was getting to be a habit. But it was just so easy. Give one up and suddenly you're all right. I had a few debts to settle, but the rest was all for *moi*. The money would keep me going for a long, long time. I was still okay. I had two on the wall and I wasn't selling any more.

Nutan

I began to notice that my face took on a sickly yellow hue as the afternoon wore on. It wasn't so with Zeenat. Probably because she painted hers. Every afternoon. I sat on the bed and watched her. I suppose the bright red lipstick helped too.

Zeenat

Make-up. It hides everything, fear, pride, shame, jealousy. Everything.

Anis

I was horribly tired and hungry, but even the thought of food had made me nauseous all day. It was not yet completely night when I thought perhaps I could, after all, manage a bowl of mussels in white wine at Spago. I had just turned the corner by Barclays bank when this waif popped out of nowhere. Tangled hair and dark circles under crazed eyes. Junkie, I thought. Surprising. It was a good area.

'Blow job for a tenner,' she offered nervously.

I quickened my pace. She did not follow, but suddenly my feet came to a dead stop. I stood there blank and numb and she ran after me.

'We can go into the alleyway,' she urged. Her eyes moved rapidly, and her hands, black with dirt, twitched.

I pulled a twenty-pound note out of my wallet. She must not touch me. I had to give it in such a way that our skin did not touch. She snatched the note from my hand and scuttled away on her skinny legs. There was a cold claw in my stomach. I staggered two steps back, and leaned again the low wall of someone's garden. Sweat appeared on my forehead. People went past. None of them knew. *That she touched me.* Her skin was freezing cold. Why did I allow her to contaminate me?

She was the future.

Nutan

I can't laugh or smile any more. I feel jealous of people with normal lives. Look at them, taking money out of cash machines, paying for things with credit cards, pushing shopping trolleys full of food, or standing at the bus stop waiting to go home to a proper family.

They were clean. *They were not waiting for the next hit.*

I was numb when she beat me, again and again. Her face twisted and twitched cruelly, yet I did not even feel the blows. Now, I think they must have been weak blows she drizzled on me. Poor thing, she was too ill. I remember collapsing to the ground.

She yanked me by the hair. 'Don't,' she warned, 'spy on me.' How angry her smiling face had become. Then she threw a packet at me. My hands were still around my head, when I heard the sound of her heels disappearing around the corner. I went limp and flat inside. But I didn't need to spy on her. I knew. I had always known. I cooked it in a spoon with a lighter, and right there inserted it into my body. I slumped against the wall, in the dirt. Of course I knew what she was doing.

Anis

On the fifteenth day of the month a woman's head and hair have great sexual energy. Running one's fingers through her hair or carefully trickling water or oil on her head will spread the energy to the rest of her body. I touched Zeenat's lips.

Aaah, such scarlet lips.

I still remember when a sudden flash of red used to startle you.

Zeenat, Zeenat. What do you say, we start again, hmm?

Nutan

My sister looks dirty and grey, yet men give her money.

Anis

I sat in the kitchen watching Fashion TV without the distraction of sound, satisfied by the sure, elegant progress of bodies in their prime. The female model has advanced her walk over the years. Once the fashion was an exaggerated sway of the hips, the way a man in drag might, now it was a more sexless, high-stepping gait. Like camels on sand. The doorbell rang. Ricky came into the hallway, large and meaty. He reeked of stale tobacco.

'You all right, Bello?' His voice was too loud. 'Fuck, it's hot in here.'

Hurriedly I ushered him into the kitchen, and closed the door.

'*Mama mia*, look at those *putanas*. Are they chewing gum up their arses or what,' he said. I looked at the beautiful images moving on the screen. Fuck him. He ruined everything.

'Need some money?' I asked.

He raked a hand through greasy yellow hair. The confident devil-may-care, lazy mouth opened. 'Yeah,' it admitted. 'Just until the money from Italy arrives,' it lied.

We both knew the routine. He followed me into the studio and moved to the middle of the room while I closed the door. I took out my cheque book. From the corner of my eyes I saw him move towards a painting of Zeenat. The room was silent except for the scratching of my pen. I signed the cheque.

'I didn't know you painted Nutan.' There was something contemptuous buried in his voice.

'That's Zeenat,' I said.

His eyes rushed to meet mine. A look, sly and bitchy, crossed his face. He pretended to laugh, as if that ugly moment on his face had not happened. As if I did not know his secret. As if we were still talking about Nutan. He threw his hands up into the air, and mocked, 'Hey, I'm not jealous.'

I looked at him, and I realised that I truly detested him. He was soulless. There was something irredeemably ugly inside him. Good and beauty in all its forms irritated and bored him. He wanted to damage; destroy indiscriminately. He did it on purpose.

I handed him the cheque. He made sure it was signed and filled in correctly. So the dealer would accept it first time around.

I wanted him gone, so I refrained from saying anything, but the next time, when the blood was colder in my veins, I would tell him that my funds had dried up. I hadn't sold a painting for a very long time and I was reduced to living off my grandfather's trust fund. I led the way to the front door.

'*Ciao*,' he said gaily.

In the kitchen the procession of stunning girls continued,

but my mood was ruined and I could not concentrate on the light moving across their bodies.

Quietly I opened the bedroom door.

Zeenat was asleep. I knew why Ricky did not recognise her on my canvas. She was not as I painted her. I lifted the blanket and looked at the huddled form. She was horribly, horribly thin, a gently breathing skeleton. I slumped on the edge of the bed and dropped my head into my hands. I stayed hunched and defeated until a wordless frozen hand entered my shirt.

She was always cold.

Even when the heating was turned up to full blast, her skin was icy. Even her breath was cold. I could not understand it. The freezing fingers moved deeper into my shirt. Her palm settled on my chest. It was a shock to my system, but I let her.

Even though I knew what I must surely find waiting on my bed, numbly I turned to meet those eyes.

Ricky

Sat up all night in the kitchen cooking up freebase.

December 2000

Elizabeth

From the taxi, I caught a glimpse of Zeenat sitting at the window of a café. Opposite her was that writer, Rani Manicka.

Zeenat

'Call me Rani,' she said, opening a beautiful hexagonal silver box intricately engraved with flowers and leaves. It reminded me of the precious heirlooms Father had surrendered to arrange our fall.

'It's an Indian antique. People carried their betel chew accessories in it,' she explained. Now she used it as a handbag. She brought a box of cigarettes out of it and offered them to me. Warm smoke filled my lungs.

She had promised me two hundred pounds for my story, but she said that if I made it good, it was worth another two hundred. I looked into her eyes. They were shining with curiosity. She switched on her tape recorder. 'Ready? And remember if it gets too difficult you may switch to Balinese. I'll get it translated later.' I needed the money so I made it as good as I could.

I was born in a rice garden. Everywhere you looked my ancestors had hand cut terraces into the mountain slopes. Throughout the year the mountain changed as if wearing different costumes. First it was as green as a sour apple, and then it blossomed, a delicate blue, and finally it swayed golden in the sun. But I liked it best when the terraces were flooded with water and, like mirror mosaics, reflected the blue sky. Then they were full of ducks eating fresh-water snails.

At the edges of the paddy fields little boys on fully grown water buffalo would gallop fearlessly past, as we held up long poles smeared with sticky sap to catch dragonflies. We must have eaten them by the hundreds, fried in coconut oil, and when we were thirsty, we reached for sweet green coconuts.

Under an enormous flame tree stood the shrine of the Dewi Sri, our Rice Goddess. In November, when the tree was profuse with brilliant red flowers, it was the most beautiful place in the entire village. I wish you could have seen that vast carpet of red. The Rice Goddess is so loved that even at harvest time the women will shield her from the alarming sight of long knives. Instead they conceal small blades called *ani-ani* in their hands, and cut the rice ear by ear. I have sat in the bamboo groves when the fields were radiantly gold, and heard the Rice Goddess sing her beautiful rustling songs amongst the stalks heavy with seed. In the evening when all the Gods have climbed the giant stairs of our hill-slope terraces, and returned to their abode, the women go to the little bamboo houses and reclaim the food they offered that morning. For Gods feast only on scent.

The plants will be gold and pregnant at this time of the year. Here it is cold. So cold. There is no balance. There is not one temple filled with incense to invite the Gods in. No one thought to leave a smouldering coconut husk out for the demons. So the demons went to live inside the houses. On pitch-black nights in Bali men light dried banana stems, and swing the strangely beautiful resinous flame with its shower of golden sparks in great circles to keep away malignant spirits. But even at midnight I never feared the English night outside my door. There were always street-lamps to pour blue light on the streets and evil lived indoors anyway.

Smeared with sin and shivering in my own sweat I walked among the dead souls of the city. The only thing that kept me warm was heroin. It was a mistake to leave the Rice Goddess, her fields, and the gentle sound of chuckling in the waterways. I once knew a little girl who sat with her slippers in her hand by the well. Her hair was always long and messy but she was always smiling. I think my sister loved me then.

Nutan thought me generous because I alone shouldered the responsibility of providing the smack. So she did not have to become a filthy flower like me, and could lie, neither sleeping nor awake on our dirty bed. She thought I had sacrificed myself for her, but she didn't know that it was guilt that prompted me. It was the same reason I had given her the longer garland, the bigger kite, and the best bit of the cake. Racked with guilt at my greed I punished myself by offering her the thing I had wanted.

I often wished failure upon her, but when failure did pounce on her head I felt terrible. So I would try to compensate for it by giving her things: affection, encour-agement, anything she wanted . . .

She didn't understand, knew not of that ruthlessly competitive streak inside me that needed her to sometimes fail. Younger siblings are like the tail of an animal; having grown up in the shadow of its head they appear subservient, but secretly, they are always seeking to under-mine the arrogance of the head. Will I ever forgive myself for ministering that first shot?

Why did I give my sister the smack?

Perhaps at that moment when she looked at me from her higher, purer place I simply couldn't bear it. I had to have her with me, where I was. We always had only each other. Ibu had eyes solely for Father, Father was blinded by his passion for Nenek, and Nenek loved Ibu to the exclusion of all. So you see we had only each other. Or maybe it was even simpler than that. Maybe I was like the head hunters that Nenek used to tell us about. It was never enough to kill a stranger. The head must have a name before it can be shrunk and hung on a wall. Only then was revenge sweet. I was always jealous of her. Of that special light she carried inside her, the one I did not. It was the reason Ricky wanted her and not me.

Why did I have sex with Ricky?

Has she never told you? What is hers is mine, and what is mine, hers. No, of course not, I am just being facetious. The truth is I do not know why. I could say he forced himself on me, but the deed was done long before his flesh entered mine. He only fulfilled a lush dream I had. I do not even know why I want him, still. In fact in Bali we would say Ricky has the character of a *tunggak semi,* flower stem, conceited, arrogant and selfish. Every Balinese is taught to detest all lack of refinement in behaviour, appearance or feelings. And to be coarse is synonymous with bad, even evil, but I found him irresistible. To think I betrayed my sister for that black tongue. I can't understand my flash of madness.

I betrayed her and, to forget, I rushed to Anna's and stuck a needle into my arm. It was my escape. It transported me to a soft place. This place of colossal calm, it does not really exist, but when I am there, I become so unconnected to my own body, that I am unable even to call for assistance. All the moments without heroin do not count. They are intervals when I am not even a person, just a desperate animal driven beyond all reason to find the next dose. There is a point you arrive at when depravity becomes a comfort. Its foul smell a source of familiarity. Slowly you begin to want to see that hateful gleam in each other's eyes.

Anis is generous, and not just with money or drugs. He has a generosity of spirit. I remember him always as he was the first time we met, unshaven and in a black turtle-neck sweater. It was Elizabeth who said, 'To meet a character like Anis you have to look inside an Ernest Hemingway novel.' She was right. He is generous in the noblest way, forgiving like a child. He never keeps a grudge and he loves me dearly, but I play him false. Poor Anis. Treacherous Zeenat. Only the pig's skin and bones are offered to the *buta kala* spirits, but all of a dog is for the spirits. He thinks I am a pig, but I am a dog. All has been offered.

He does not know how little this body of mine costs to possess. If he came upon it at the right hour of the night on the right street corner. Or perhaps he does . . . Perhaps he does know, but it is his nature to forgive, to love anyway. I like to think a character in a Hemingway book fell in love with me.

Nenek used to say that human beings record every sin they do, in their brain, their tongues, and unbeknownst to them in the lines of their palms. She used to pick up our palms, and carefully study the faintly formed outlines, as if from the curves alone she could tell our sins. Whenever we had done wrong, we squirmed in her grip.

It would be impossible for me to show her my palms any more.

I looked into the mirror the other day and saw a funny thing. I saw in my eyes, half extinguished, but still burning, a gleam very much like my grandmother's. The same dark eyes, and the same wicked decadence that inbreeding brings to a face. And all those years ago my mother must have seen it when she ran her fingers over our eyes, noses and mouths, and lied. *It is a good thing that both of you were given your father's face.* Poor Ibu.

I always knew about Nenek and Father. It was not because I once heard her referred to as *madu*, honey, a term that really means a kept woman. No, I knew because of my mother's eyes, the way they used to watch Father whenever Nenek was around. She had taken away Nenek's man, only to find it was not enough. Ungrateful wretch, you cry? No, because Father never relinquished his love for Nenek. Nenek owned everything Ibu wanted. Astonishing beauty, power, feet, my sister and me. If we awakened in the night, frightened, she would never allow us to get into Ibu's bed. I know she did it to protect my sick mother, but unwittingly she cut my mother off.

Have I said enough to earn the extra two hundred pounds?

No, but nearly, you say. Do I fear death?

No, I never wish for death. Not even when I am on the back seat of a stranger's car, and his stale breath is in my face. Neither do I need death to end it all. Day and night, the impulse, the all-consuming craving, is for more and more heroin. And I like the danger, and the duplicity that goes with scoring too.

Is this enough? Is it worth four hundred pounds yet? If it's not, just give me two. I'll tell you the rest another day. I've got to go soon. Someone's waiting for me.

If this is really the last question. Tell you about Anis?

In Bali it is the woman's work to shake the rice grains in a wide round basket. The action removes the dirt and husks. They fly away into the wind. In the same way opposition and conflict separates the pure and beautiful from the coarse and polluted. Anis is the only good thing that has come from my time in the wide round basket. He is a *dewa* in disguise.

Of course it is clear that I should return as soon as possible to Nenek so she could cure me of my affliction as I have seen her do for others. She gave them herbs that made their vomit rush out of them in a large curve. You have a special word for it.

Ah, projectile. What a pretty sound. . .

Nenek will also cure Anis. And then we will be happy. There is a word they use in my country. It is called *enten*, it means waking up momentarily, and then falling back to sleep. It is what we believe life is. A fleeting moment of being awake. I, the maker, and you, the beholder, must see my moments when I am an addict or a prostitute only as offerings to time. They all pass. No need for remorse or self-loathing.

I will be cured and I will be happy. I will meet the Goddess of Death in the cemetery by the curve of the river, but only when Anis and I have seen our grandchildren.

I closed my mouth and looked meaningfully at the door. The good writer switched off her tape recorder, and held out a wad of notes, too thick to be two hundred pounds. My story had earned four hundred pounds. I left her staring out of the window. I had to go and get Nutan. Already I could imagine her pleased face. We would go together to Anna's. There was much celebrating to be done. It was Christmas in two days' time.

Nutan

We were all slouched in the dark staring blankly at the telly. Sometimes I think that was why it took so long for us to realise that she had turned blue. That something was wrong with her.

I remember seeing Zeenat put a needle in her arm, and I can even remember seeing her eyes roll back, as she slowly slid to the floor. Quickly, quickly, I too must have the needle. The warm blanket. Look how softly she fell into hers. How gently it caught her. Me too. The rest of them were lying back watching Snakehead fill up a syringe. He caught my eye. Yes, my turn now.

He shot up and, stepping over Zeenat's slumped body,

came to inject me. He knew I was too high to do the job properly. I don't know how long I sat there, deliciously warm, staring at the telly, but suddenly there was movement, half hurried, half languorous. I turned my head, reluctantly.

And there was Anis – where did he come from? – bending over . . . Zeenat.

'For God's sake, Anna, help me get her into the recovery position,' he shouted, his voice strangely shrill and panic-stricken.

'Switch on a fucking light, someone.'

'Fuck it, the bulb is gone.'

'Come on, help me, someone.'

'Hold her, hold her up.'

Through half-closed eyes I saw them turn her on her side, and shake her.

'Come on, Zeenat, breathe, please,' Anis begged.

It's funny how Zeenat once described heroin. Brown eye-shadow. Sometimes the other addicts will try to sell you bits of brown eye-shadow they have stolen from Boots. It was Anna who first warned us about it. 'Fucking nightmare if you inject it,' she said.

My limbs were large and heavy. I tried to reach out my hand to touch her, but it was cast in bronze. Hey, I wanted to say, I know what's wrong with her. She's done this once before, taken too much, but she can be brought around. Please don't take her to a doctor. They could take her away from me. But I couldn't get my tongue to work. The four hundred pounds that writer gave Zeenat. We had spent it all.

Someone found a torch. They shone it in her face. Her lips were deep blue. Everybody started screaming at the same time. I became frightened then. I had warned that girl, 'If anyone gives you the bread of death do not eat it.' Anna began to slap her, but Anis pushed her away roughly, and tried to give her mouth-to-mouth resuscitation. But nothing.

'Jesus, she's still not breathing.' I heard Anis's disbelieving cry.

'For fuck's sake, can we call a fucking ambulance now?' Anna screamed.

I could tell by the way Zeenat's eyes had rolled all the way up, leaving them completely white, that this time it was different. I was paralysed, my tongue too stiff even to scream. Later, I would look for her later. She was temporarily lost to me, but no doubt she would resurface.

Tears were pouring down Anis's face. He cradled her body, wailing, 'No, no, not again, please no . . .'

Anna was white, but for her mouth, which was a black hole, 'Oh fuck no, no fucking way.'

A boy I did not know very well was simply staring at me, his eyes blank, and his mouth moving soundlessly.

Snakehead was slowly backing out of the room. I knew what he was thinking – the addict's logic – there is no point in everybody getting caught with the corpse.

Then I was gone. Off on a cloud.

Ricky

It was Christmas, I was all alone in the kitchen and it was not a turkey dinner I was roasting. I was getting worse and worse. Oh, the paranoia!

Bruce

My sister and I decided that, for Mother's first Christmas without Dad, I would spend Christmas Day with Mum, and she would do Boxing Day. Mother roasted a huge turkey. Far too big for the two of us. We sat to eat in silence. Afterwards we exchanged presents. A little gold bracelet for her and a sweater for me. I fixed the bracelet on her arm. It looked pretty even on her thin liver-spotted hand.

'Now you,' she said. 'Try on your new sweater.' It was too tight.

'Never mind,' I said, 'I'll take it to the store and get it changed.' And with that my mother's lips began to tremble. Suddenly she was sobbing into a handkerchief.

'Do you know,' she said, 'your father always wanted me to wear very high heels, but I wouldn't. I thought it was too tarty. I worried about what the ladies up the street would say. I realise now it was a mistake. I should have worn them. At least once, to please him.'

'Ah Mum, don't cry,' I said gently. 'He saw you in them. In fact I'm even willing to swear they were six-inch heels.' Her eyes were blurred with tears. I said, 'I know because when a man loves a woman she comes into his dreams, doing all the things he wants her to.'

Nutan

When I woke up, I knew instantly, she was gone. It had never occurred to me that she would leave me behind. We did everything together. Again and again, that moment of her departure, a blackness inside my mouth, my eyes in soot.

And my body, oh God, how intolerably it ached. Every action was agony. Even my skin rasped hellishly against my clothes. It was too painful to endure. I needed a shot badly. Anis was still at the police station. I was so bad my eyes wouldn't focus properly. One dose. I just needed one dose, that's all, and I would be fine, but I had no money. I was so desperate I couldn't wait one moment longer. With Zeenat gone I had to find my own stuff. I had only one thing of value left.

But it is very precious. Your mother made it for you.

Yeah, but I could get another when I go back to Bali. They are easy enough to get.

It took her many, many months to make it. Don't you remember she said it is for your wedding?

I'll get another.

It is irreplaceable. Your mother is dead.

It is only a piece of cloth. I have other things that belonged to her.

At the bottom of my suitcase I found it.

Your mother made it especially for you.

Piss off and leave me alone. It's only a piece of cloth.

I stuffed it into a plastic bag and rushed off to the bottom of the road. It was lunchtime, and somebody in the pub was bound to want it. I thought I could maybe sell it for fifty pounds. It was easily worth a hundred. I had seen them being sold for hundreds of pounds in the tourist boutiques in Seminyak. Inside the pub it was dark and cool. My nose was running badly. There was a woman in a nice skirt. Surely she would be interested. I went up to her.

'Would you like to buy a traditional gold-embroidered cloth from Bali?'

My nose ran all the more. I wiped it with the back of my hand. I saw that she had seen that all was not well with me. Maybe she even thought my nervous quick smile meant I had stolen my brocade.

'Show us then,' she said.

I took the cloth out. Even in the darkened room its fine workmanship shone precious and exquisite. Her eyes flashed. My nose was running. I really needed a shot in a hurry. She took the cloth in her hand and examined it carefully for flaws. She could find none. She looked up. And her eyes . . . I will never forget her eyes. How careful they were. How greedy.

'How much?' she asked.

'Fifty pounds,' I said.

'Tenner,' she said.

I looked at her incredulously. 'It's worth hundreds. It's brand new.'

'It's off the back of a lorry,' she said, laughing contemptuously. Her companion grinned.

'My mother made it,' I told her.

She looked at me blankly.

'Give me twenty,' I begged.

'Sorry, I've only got ten pounds.' The bitch was not sorry. I looked around the room hoping there was another woman I could approach, but only men occupied the other pub stools. And I simply didn't have the time to go around to the other pubs.

'Give me the money, then.'

She opened her wallet. It was full of money. She pulled out a ten-pound note and held it out to me. As I rushed out I heard her companion congratulate her on her 'bargain.'

Ibu made it for me. I wanted to go back in there and throw her lousy tenner in her face, but I needed my fix. I really did. It was only a piece of cloth. Maybe later, when they released Anis, I could go to him. He was bound to have some.

Ricky

The chef jumped me today. His cheque bounced. Twice. RDPR had made the jump to RD. Yeah great, join the queue, dickhead. The suppliers are all COD now. Fucking rats. The linen guy won't deliver. Little piece of chicken shit. All these years he made money out of me and now, at the first hint of trouble, he bails out. Fuck him. When I have sorted my shit out I'll make sure he doesn't get a penny from me again.

One of the restaurants is in the shit, losing money hand over fist. Went there last night. Fucking hell even the alcohol there smelt as if it was losing money. It's bad at the moment. It's fucking bad.

Nutan

I went back to our room, wet, dirty, and faint with cold. I must have walked in the rain. I don't remember. Midway up the stairs I heard voices in our room. I didn't know what to think. I was so confused. Perhaps it was the police, but when I stood at the doorway, I saw the owners of the kebab shop downstairs, our landlords. Until they noticed me they were cursing and swearing and going through our things.

'What are you doing?' I asked. My voice was feeble and frightened.

They jumped guiltily, and then they went red with anger. 'Look at the state of this room,' one of them screeched. He was the one who tried to offer me money for sex. 'Don't think I don't know what's been going on here.' And with the toe of his shoe he pointed towards a syringe.

'Fucking junkies,' he shouted hysterically. 'Where is the rent?'

I stared at him blankly. 'My sister died yesterday,' I told him.

Unconsciously he took a step back, as if my news could taint him. Yes, the one you used to pay for sex, I wanted to say, but I was too tired. There was silence. Only the traffic outside was relentless. But he didn't care. I suppose one could hardly blame him.

'If you can't pay your rent now you have to leave.'

'What about the deposit, my things?'

'Deposit? What deposit?' he sneered. 'Look at the state of

the fucking room. Who is going to pay for all this damage? Get out. Get out now.'

I turned around and started walking down the stairs. I didn't know what to do. She was dead. I had nothing left. There was only one thing to do. Get a shot.

'Here,' the man shouted and two passports flew past me. I picked them up, and stumbled away. I had nothing left but the old jumper and jeans on my back. But very soon I would need another hit. So I stole some whiskey from Sainsbury's and sold it at the off licence. I bought two bags of brown, nicked a spoon out of a café, a lemon from a greengrocer, went around the corner, and shot up in the back of a church compound. In fact, it was a cemetery.

The dead in England are quiet and peaceful in their place in the ground. I must have lain on the grass over someone's grave for a good few hours. Just didn't know what to do. Where to go. Thought I was going mad. Anis was probably still detained at the police station. It was getting dark and cold. So cold I began to shiver wildly. Never before had I felt so abandoned.

I got up and made my way to Anis's home. The house was in darkness. I broke a window and entered. I hadn't eaten since Zeenat and I shared a tub of Muller rice. I found his stash straight away. I shot up, and the unbearable feelings went away. But I had to keep shooting up or bang, they would all be there. Insufferable, insurmountable. You see, she was dead. I never imagined it could happen. I never thought she could leave me.

I should have slapped her across the face, so hard the needle flew out of her hand, that day when she offered me her own death. I cursed myself again and again. I betrayed her first. I left her alone in the room, while I went out to get drunk and high with Ricky and my new-found friends. She, who had never done me any wrong.

I knew why she did it. All our lives they saw us as one.

Dressed us exactly the same. Twin girls. She tried to be an individual. Tried so hard. Now it was too late to claim her as my own.

I thought about suicide when I saw my face in the bathroom mirror. I saw myself dying. Blue in the mouth. Not breathing. By witnessing her death I was haunted by my own. I would relive that moment for ever. Always it would seem logical to follow. I even dreamed of shooting up that fatal dose and waiting. I had never understood loneliness. Alone, I was without symmetry. Ugly. Just one. Who was I?

Nenek had known. 'Dream of Ibu,' she told Zeenat. 'Dream of Ibu.' She should not be surprised then when I break my news to her.

Ricky

It got to a situation where everybody was looking for me. For money. It got so bad my staff pretended I was not the owner. The owner never came in. I would be standing at the bar drinking coffee, and my staff would be telling men in suits, 'No, he never comes in any more. I think he might be in Italy.' And I wouldn't even bother to turn around to look. One day I walked into the restaurant and this beautiful woman called out, '*Ciao,* Ricky.' I acted on instinct. I smiled at her. She smiled back seductively.

'*Si,* Bella,' I said.

And two men in polyester suits at a table by the window stood up, and served me with my summons. She left with them. Without her smile her face was bitch hard.

Nutan

It was still dark when I woke up. I knew I had been robbed but I did not know what they had taken. Where was I? My chest was thick and congested with foreboding. Long beautiful bay windows? Oh, Anis's home. I was safe then. Perhaps it was only a nightmare. I could not remember. I tried to remember. Everything was a blank.

Was it another warning dream about my sister?

I dreamed . . . I dreamed, the unthinkable . . . Oh, no . . . frantically I began to pray to the spirits.

> 'Oh, Powerful spirits I welcomed you to my
>   home.
> If I have harmed you, forgive me, be kind.
> Accept my offerings, oh powerful ones.

I was Nenek, alone through the howling night, begging, tears rolling down my face. It was only a dream. If I implored hard enough like my grandmother did all those years ago . . . Did she not, with the help of the spirits, keep Ibu alive for years? That was what I would do too. I would command the spirits.

> Do not take what is not yours.
> Do not show your wrath.
> Oh you, leave me the child.
> Consent that she lives another day.
> Do not call her name, at night,
> NOT TONIGHT.'

I heard a sound in the living room. I opened the door and crept along the passageway. My footsteps were silent. What was the shadow that followed me? The living room was dimly lit. I stood at the doorway, shivering, terrified. In the light from the little Chinese lantern, Anis was slumped on the floor, staring at a blank canvas. He turned to look at me.

Oh God, no, look what the devil spirits did to his face. His mouth was torn and his eyes were black holes of horror. What was it? Why was I filled with fear? 'Zeenat,' I whispered.

It did not say anything, that mask of suffering.

He picked up a needle by his side, and held it out to me. There was a sob in my throat as I stumbled towards him. 'Hurry, I am falling.'

I snatched at the needle, but my hands were shaking so much, I could not find a vein. Anis took it from me, and gently, tenderly with infinite care put it upon my skin, and pushed. *It's all right. I'll do it for you. All it is, is you put it on your skin and push it down. That's all.*

Anis

I came upon Nutan today sitting in my kitchen with her wrists cut. She was simply watching her blood flowing into a puddle on the floor.

'No, no, don't,' I cried, kneeling by her, pressing the wounds together.

'You don't understand,' she said. 'I was feeding the spirits. They are hungry and unhappy.'

I was so surprised I released her bleeding hands for a moment. In my ears my grandmother's voice whispered, 'Do you hear it? It is the earth wanting blood and bones.' Perhaps blood spilling to earth is a forgotten knowledge. Perhaps, deafened by the roar of progress, we cannot hear this murmur. Otherwise why would every ancient civilisation pay for their continued survival with human sacrifice?

It stands to reason. The earth must eat too, I thought, as I bandaged her wrists.

Nutan

A man strolled slowly towards the screen. More men, all in black, appeared in the background and came forward to disappear into nothing. It was an Issey Miyake fashion show, shot in a car park, or maybe a storeroom. The effect was ghostly and eerie. Why did Anis watch it without the sound?

I touched the doorframe, it creaked, and Anis turned to look at me.

'I dreamed of her,' I said. 'I dreamed that I said, "Don't".' I put my hand out and took the shot in my arm.

' "I, too, thought it was you that should have died," she said, as I lay dying.'

I knelt at his feet and touched his face. My hands moved to the open throat of his shirt, and my fingers slid in. We could stop and sleep halfway.

'What marks has she left on you? Show them to me.'

'Don't,' he said harshly. 'Don't taint what is left.'

I felt confused and dirty. I just wanted to be where she had been.

Catch her perfume. Smell her a little. She was so real she hadn't faded with death. Anis explained that time would fade her. Help rub the sharp edges down.

Elizabeth

I went to visit Anis. There was nothing in his fridge but sour milk, mouldy cheese, and something so gone I could hardly bear the stench. I had guessed as much and brought my own ingredients. I made ham and cabbage stew, and we sat on the floor to eat it. He pushed his fork around a bit, but I sat and waited until he cleaned his plate. Then he excused himself and went into his bedroom, while I stood at the window, trying not to imagine what he was obviously doing in his bedroom. When he came back he looked normal. I smiled at him, but he did not smile back.

He went to the stereo and the room filled with the big beautiful sounds of Mussorgsky's 'Night on Bare Mountain'. He gestured that I should return to the cushions where we had sat to eat. His face unreadable, he took my hand and kissed my palm gently. 'Thank you,' he said. Then he began talking. A few times he broke off to go to the bedroom, and sometimes his eyelids fluttered down, but he would force them open, and talk some more.

And into my heart came distress for a little boy who had stolen a squalid secret, and then burdened himself with it to protect his mother. All those years of needless guilt. She had known all along. How we hurt the people we are meant to love! I felt angry at this unknown woman who had allowed her son to become a trespasser in her home. But that little boy, still alive and suffering, looked sadly into my eyes, and told me his mother was not to be faulted. She had fulfilled her *dharma* impeccably. She had been a good wife. What about her duty as a mother, I wanted to ask.

'I stand accused as a vampire,' he said bitterly. His mouth twisted. 'I find nice girls in dark places and suck out their life. A Picasso minus the genius.' He laughed without humour. 'I could so easily be that horrible spider Ricky worships, crawling along, black and hideous. Luring these beautiful women into my web, persuading them to take their clothes off, and somehow destroying them. Swathi, Maggie and now Zeenat . . .'

'How can you say that?' I cried. 'Swathi was dying when

you met her. If anything, you made her last days mean-ingful. To be the muse of a great artist is a special gift. So seductive a compliment that she even fell in love with you. Is it your fault that you could not return her feelings? And Maggie, do you know what she said about you? She said she let you paint her because you painted souls. You were the first person she met who had the ability to see through corrupted flesh. And for the first time she found herself beautiful in a man's eyes. That's why she gave you her painting. Not even I own a painting of hers. She did it to say thank you. You cannot blame yourself, not when you were planning the most marvellous surprise for her. It's not your fault that she simply couldn't wait. I loved her, and I don't blame you.'

'Look at me,' I said. He looked up, his eyes swimming with enormous survivor guilt. He was too sensitive. Not meant for this harsh world. 'And as for Zeenat, I won't allow you to bear blame for her. Have you forgotten it was she who brought the first bruise to your arm? And when you tried to get clean, it was she who led you this way again, wasn't it? She's gone. You must let go of her.'

One side of his mouth lifted as if to smile. 'You don't understand,' he whispered. 'I can't.'

Nutan

My sister said, 'I've got some stuff. Come back to the old room where we used to live, and we'll take it together.' I woke up, and began to dress. And then it hit me. But you're dead.

I had to leave Anis's house and take my sister away from the cold room where they kept her body. I had to place her poor head in my mother's lap. It was where she belonged. I should never have brought her to this poisonous world. We

398

were safe in our little island. I had to return to stand again before my grandmother's eyes.

While flowers will be scattered into her coffin, Father, that distant stranger, who had agreed to endanger his daughters to punish a lover, will sing in the archaic Javanese tongue, that peculiar whinnying tone that he usually reserved for the most high-born of his puppets. In a highly exaggerated voice he will say what he said at my mother's funeral, 'We will wait for her to be reborn on earth. Perhaps she will be my great-grandchild.'

Somewhere behind my eyelids a storm was brewing. In the end, you see, I am not like my high-born father. I am like my grandmother, the taste of earth still on my tongue, unable to pretend a lack of passion. Death I can rejoice in but what about the absence until then? What will I do with the unbearable absence, when I will awaken in the dead of night, and crave for her flesh beside me?

What a blind careless python I was! I accidentally swallowed a giant creature called grief. I don't know how many years it will take, but leave me alone while I digest my meal. I am no different from you now. I too am unutterably alone.

Anis

There was no moon in the sky. I could not sleep again. It was my conscience clawing. Where was the next step? The one I stood on was unbearable and I needed to move on. I don't know why I never had dreams of that moment when she lay dead in my arms, but God knows I saw it often enough in my waking hours. I know it is often enough that you read it in the newspapers, child finds parent dead from an overdose, or the other way around. But how can anything you read at your breakfast table, cluttered with warm toast, jam, butter, honey, and the goodness of fresh milk, come anywhere towards expressing the horror of watching someone wrenched away from an overdose.

History is a banshee in a sackcloth, a mad glare and a bony pointing finger. She has seen my profit. Although it was not I who went to look for the newspaper men. They came like a pack of wolves when they heard there had been a dead body in Anis Ramji's arms. As a result my paintings began to fetch more, startlingly more. Perhaps it was something to do with the rising value of a dead painter's paintings. They were making the logical conclusion about my future. And here and there women have begun to find my surly melancholy attractive.

Still the dead do not condemn me. She always comes in a moment of blushing happiness. '*Wastan titiang 'e Zeenat.*' My name is Zeenat. She asks for '*gambar titiang,*' my painting. But would you believe me if I said that sometimes I awoke to her fragrance?

Ricky

There was a little scam I was running. I was selling shares in my restaurant to my manager and Chef. No one knew, but the restaurant was about to be included on the list of assets when the VAT men finally declared me bankrupt. It would happen in a matter of days.

The fools carried around worthless papers, talking loudly about the fantastic changes they would make, and softly about what a loser I was. I humoured them. Poor sods. It must have taken them a long time to raise twenty thousand each.

The manager I didn't feel bad about. He stole the money from me anyway.

The old Chef. Yeah, that was sad, but what could you

do? The guy had been with me from the first day, served me well enough, was well past fifty, and I was taking his hard-earned pension money, but in a way I had no choice. I could not offer a share to the manager and not to Franco. He was my camouflage. Who could imagine I would deliberately cheat old Franco? The whole thing would have fallen apart if I didn't offer it to my Chef first. My manager would have suspected foul play.

But they were all only excuses. The simple truth was I needed my Chef's money. I was sinking. I had to clutch onto anything. It was my Chef who gave me his cheque first. Not even his shining grateful eyes could make me feel bad. I needed the money. I took the cheque to Paolo and he cashed it for me immediately. It seemed like such a lot. I thought it would last for quite a long time, but it went quickly.

January 2001

Ricky

How much will you give for a gold Rolls Royce?

Five grand! Fuck you, man. It's only three years old. Mint condition.

Come on, stop standing on my balls, you know you're going to sell it for at least triple that.

Oh fuck it, can you come by for the damn thing today?

Yeah, but what time can you get here by? I'm in a hurry.

Nutan

I followed Elizabeth's instructions to the dot, and rang her doorbell at 1 a.m. sharp. But I waited in the cold a long time before she answered.

'Come up,' she invited.

A man trying to hide his face stepped out of the lift. Still, I think I recognised his clean, good looks. He was famous. I thought I had seen him on the telly. Elizabeth opened her door, and I stared at her in shock.

'What happened to you?' I asked.

'It was an accident,' she said through swollen lips. Carefully, wincing, she eased herself onto a pure white sofa. 'The only good thing about Mr M is he always leaves half a bag of strong stuff. It's on the table in the kitchen. Fetch it, would you?'

We sat on the sofa and finished the coke. It was 3 a.m. when she looked at me and said, 'Last one's for you.'

'Here,' she said, and gave me an envelope full of money. 'Take her back, back to Bali.'

Strange the way life works out. Elizabeth was the last person I would have thought to turn to for help. She always seemed so unfriendly. Yet, she was a hero. To procure Zeenat's air fare back to our island, Elizabeth had done something that was utterly repugnant to her. I didn't know what to say.

I fell to my knees and opened my mouth to thank her, but she stopped me with a raised hand and a cold voice. 'Go home now. I must wash, and sleep, and heal again. Next week the Mullah will return. I did not do it for you. I did it for Zeenat.'

Why she desired no human warmth was a mystery. She obviously had a warm heart, but purposely gave the impression that she was cold and unfeeling.

Confused, I turned to leave, and she said, 'Wait, wait a minute. Why don't you leave the money here? Let me make the arrangements for you.' I looked into her eyes. They were direct and honest. She was right, of course. I couldn't be trusted. 'Will fifty pounds be enough for you until tomorrow?' she asked.

I nodded.

Outside, I was suddenly overcome by my loss. The blow that had killed my sister had slashed me too. A death mist was collecting in the air.

I took the night bus to Vauxhall. A woman wearing a leather jacket came to sit on the seat in front of me. The smell of it made me feel sick. Quickly I moved seats. At the entrance of a run-down block of council flats, I pressed the button that said 77. I had to press it three more times before a barely coherent voice answered.

'Can I come up,' I asked.

The buzzer sounded and I pushed open the door. I had to forget. Tomorrow was soon enough to remember.

Bruce

At 3.30 a.m. I got a text message on my mobile from Haylee.

> Get 2 Elizabeth.
> She is raising
> Money 4 Nutan

Even though I knew what the message really meant, my heart was in my throat at the prospect of seeing Elizabeth again. I also knew that if Haylee sent that message, it was because I would be too late. But maybe, maybe even Haylee could recognise true love, and desire for it to succeed. Maybe I still had time. Even so I rang her bell, already sad. Why couldn't she have just asked me?

For some time I could only stare at the busted lip, something inside me broke.

'Haylee sent me on a crazy rescue mission,' I said. Even I heard the trembling in my voice.

'Too late,' she said cheerfully. 'Nutan must have told her. But hey, full marks to Haylee for trying.'

I went into her bedroom, and got a blanket. Carefully I wrapped her poor thin body in it. I felt like crying. She defeated me at every turn.

'It's not as bad as it looks. You're a man. You know how it works. No penetration, so no harm done, right?' she joked through bruised lips. She was tough.

'Why?' I asked, shocked.

'I had to do it. I owed her one. I didn't care enough to slap her in the face when I first found out about the smack.'

'Why didn't you just ask me for the money?'

'I think I was probably saving you for something bigger.' She laughed weakly.

'Oh, Elizabeth.'

'Why do you keep coming back? I've tried so hard to push you away. God, to think I even took all my make-up off in a restaurant to show you how truly haggard I could look.'

I stared at her incredulously. '*That* was why you took your make-up off? You thought you could put me off?'

'Now that you put it like that, it does seem a little crazy . . .'

'A little? . . .'

'Everything is a lie, Bruce. I hid the past away thinking it would die in the dark, and all it has become is old and bad-tempered. Shine your light a little over here and you will see it very much alive and now malicious.'

She told me everything then; the brother the sea took, the changeling who desired the city even if the inhabitants were dead, and the men who came to grasp her so hard they left bruises in the shape of their fingers on her arms.

It was almost more than I imagined. To be this close. To hear these intimate details. Even with her shiny lip, she was beautiful. Her light grey eyes not hard and cold, but moist and tender. I know it's such a cliche, but I loved this approachable, touchable person so much it hurt. I started dreading the moment when she would regain her icy composure and slip back into her ironic self.

'Want to hear one more confession?'

'What?' I asked. I could take it.

'I don't like taking coke.'

'*What?*'

'It's true. From the first moment I see it, a little hill, white and bad, I begin dreading the moment when it will all be gone, and I, locked into that horrible downward spiral, raiding cash machines, knocking on strangers' homes at five in the morning. Filled with a black despair that only another line can cure.'

'Want to give up?'

'Yeah.'

'Me too,' I said.

'Are you serious?'

'Yes, Maggie's death changed everything. For the first time, I saw Ricky's temple for what it really is; a filthy horrible place full of sad lost people. Nobody there is happy. They scream with laughter, but they are all dead inside. You have to be if you are worshipping in a spider's temple.'

'Are you really sure?' she asked.

'Absolutely. Can't remember when I last took a line. Are you?'

'Never been surer of anything in my life,' she replied, her voice strong and certain.

'I really love you,' I said softly.

'Do you? Do you really?' Her tone was sad, so sad.

'Yes, yes, I *really* do,' I sighed. Why did she find it so hard to believe that I truly loved her?

'Well, if you're absolutely sure,' she said, moving away from me. When she turned around, her bearing was erect and proud, her eyes grey diamonds once more. And then with an unkind twist to her swollen lips, she taunted, 'Is this the perfection you waited so long to possess?' She untied her robe and let it fall to the ground. She was naked underneath.

I stared transfixed. There was a roaring in my ears.

Time slowed down and I heard myself say, 'Oh God!'

Anis

I stared resentfully at the blank canvas in my living room. It was waiting for me, but I was waiting for the moment I would be able to bear the smell of paint again. I wanted to paint her blue, but I was bleeding red. It streamed out of me, unstoppable, the way greed gushes out of a gambler's eyes when the wheel begins to turn. There was no release from the terrible torment. It obliterated everything.

I watched the sun come up. Pale yellow beams making squares of light on the paint-stained wooden floor. Watching it, I remembered my grandfather, sitting straight-backed and cross-legged on just such a patch of sunlight in his house on the hill. He sat for hours throwing his breath out of his chest, his being vibrating in the sound currents of '*Om*'. His face, ageless with such enviable calm.

'Emotional feeling obstructs clarity,' he used to say, reaching for the conch filled with turmeric water that he kept on the sunny window sill. 'Meditate, Anis, meditate for deeper peace. Without detachment there can never be silence. Concentrate your gaze and perception on the spiritual eye in your forehead, and wait for whatever response comes to you.'

Crawling towards the square of sunlight I experienced compassion for my father. For surely his soul must have despaired for the endless lies, the paralysing guilt, and the unforgiving son.

Beast he may have been, but he was still a creature of nature. He should have read philosophy. Aristotle would have shown him to look between cowardice and rashness for the golden mean, courage. I recalled him from the last time we met, when he had ground the inside of cheek against his clenched teeth, when my disgust had vanquished him.

My mother told me that when I was three years old I

loved my father so much that I demanded to be the first one he cuddled when he got home from work. And if it happened that he didn't I ran outside and urinated on his shoes as punishment. Even then, my love was cruel and demanding. Who was I to be ashamed of him? I closed my eyes.

'You are that.'

Who?

'The unknown knower. Be still, you are that.'

On the patch of sunlight it was easy to assume the corpse pose my grandfather had taught me.

Bruce

We stared at each other. Had hours passed? My eyes hurt, but hers were brilliant with pain. So this was the 'unimportant' thing that Maggie had almost told me when we were getting drunk at Ashley's. I remembered another snatch of conversation from the past.

Don't you like being so perfectly beautiful?

Don't you know how natural it is for a human being to ruin what is perfect?

Although I had never let my eyes wander away from hers, I had seen it. All of it. Then unable to stop myself, my eyes travelled across the tight pink of scarred flesh. Somewhere from the tips of her breasts to her groin she was horrendously burnt.

'No plastic surgeon can ever mend me,' she whispered.

Numbly my body moved towards hers and my fingers reached out to touch the scars with disbelief. As if it could be just another trick she had pulled to keep me away. She flinched. It was not a trick. I lay my palm flat on her stomach and with meticulous care walked my fingers through the smooth bits, the uneven ridges, the whitish parts, that pink section. I explored all as she stood unmoving. And it was all repulsive. Oh! Cruel, cruel fate . . . I who worshipped perfection.

'Fire?'

'Acid.'

'Of course,' I said as if it was the appropriate answer. That such a great beauty should conceal such a shocking imperfection.

'The Arab?'

'The Arab,' she said.

'Why?'

'When one intends hardly to use a possession one must be sure it remains unused by others. After all he never lays eyes on it. He has use for me only as if I was a boy.'

'Ah.' What was this strange calm? She was unexpectedly hideous . . . and I who worshipped perfection . . .

God, what a bombshell!

My knees gave way.

'Sorry,' I said, and buried my face in her scarred stomach. My tears startled me. Why, I hadn't cried since I was a boy. I thought of us dancing, our steps matching so perfectly it was as if we had danced together for years, but then Ricky's taunting voice filled my head. *It's hardly love when you fall for the most beautiful woman you've ever met, is it? For fuck's sake you don't even know the woman. What if she didn't look the way she did, huh? What if she wasn't such a goddess? What happens to your love then?'*

What a spiteful joke fate played on me.

Her perfect hands cradled my head. The skin soft, un-scarred. Poor Elizabeth.

'Hush,' she comforted.

It made me cry harder.

Then her stroking stilled and she said, very, very softly, 'Run . . . run, Bruce, run now.'

I smelt her fear as I stood up to look into her beautiful

eyes. I picked up the fallen robe and gently arranged it around her shoulders.

'I thought I loved you . . .'

One unconquered tear escaped and rolled down her cheek. I reached out to brush it away.

'. . . but now, I know for sure. I love you, Elizabeth. Don't you know you are more than this face or this body? I love you more now than I ever did.'

An involuntary sob, huge and savage, escaped from her mouth.

'If on some evening I should find your words are only lies . . .'

My fingers went up to stop her mouth. 'Hush.'

And my mouth found hers in our first real kiss. This one I didn't have to steal. Gently. Her mouth was busted. Our faces wet, it was sad and sweet. Not the earth-shatteringly passionate kiss I had dreamed about, but I wouldn't exchange that sad sweet kiss for anything in the world.

'When I was young, my mother read *The Velveteen Rabbit* for my bedtime story, but I could never understand what the skin horse meant when he explained to the rabbit how a toy became real to a child. He said it didn't happen all at once. He said it could take a long time, and usually by the time the toy became real it could be hairless, eyeless, loose in the joints and shabby, but because it had become real, it would never be ugly, except to the people who didn't understand. And once it had become real it could never again become unreal. He said being real lasts for always. Today, for the first time I understand what the skin horse meant. Hairless, eyeless, loose in the joints or skinless, you are real to me. For always.'

'My joy, my grief, my hope, my love.'

'Don't cry, please don't cry. You'll see. My love will last, for ever. And afterwards I'll learn to love you some more,' I promised. 'When did you first know you loved me?'

'When you opened my fridge and helped yourself to the caviar.'

'*That long?* And you let me suffer all this time.'

She pulled away. 'We have to leave this place,' she said, and led me into the bedroom. I sat on her bed. Ahh, goose down. It gives in to body weight without fuss. Could it be true that she was mine? Was she really mine? She dressed quickly, and then extracted a battered suitcase from the back of the wardrobe.

'You were already packed?' I asked, amazed.

'My hands dared what my heart did not.'

'Are you taking nothing else? The expensive clothes, the furs, the jewellery . . .'

She looked around her slowly and pointing at different things said, 'That is his. That is his. And that. That too . . . oh yes, this is mine.' And she plucked a candle out of an elaborate gold and ebony candelabra. Smiling, she walked towards me. And then she remembered her painting.

And we went to stand under her Chagall. Her fingers stroked the floating figures farewell. When she came towards me her eyes were misty. We left the evidence of the drugs for the Arab's men. He would understand. She was fallen. We shut the door and put the key through the letter-box. I took the suitcase from her hand, and she kept the candle in hers. We walked down the stairs together and I saw all the unconnected moments as a beautifully crafted plan.

Nutan

The airport looked vast and cold. When last I had been there, it was with such excitement, such a sense of adventure. Now it promised an unbearable ordeal. Fifteen hours without a shot. I didn't know exactly that I could survive, but I had a bag for before I checked in, and another for when my luggage was returned. There was Valium from Bruce for the flight.

'Is that all of your luggage, Madam?'

'Yes,' I said. The only things of importance I had were the spoon and citric acid. I needed them until I laid my head in my grandmother's lap. Surely she would forgive me and cure me as I had seen her do to others many times before. It was an unpleasant treatment but it worked.

I asked Anis if he wanted the syrup of forgetfulness for his pain. My grandmother could arrange for it. He looked at me without expression. 'No,' he said. 'Her memory is too precious to give up.'

I waited until the last moment before injecting myself in the toilet. And then I made my way through passport control, hand luggage check, and down the long grey lanes to Gate 33. The woman who took my boarding pass gave me a funny look. I should have felt ashamed, but the drug was kind. It supported me. I slumped into a seat and nodded off. A man in a uniform woke me up.

'Boarding now. Are you sick?' he asked, but he must have known.

I made to it my seat and collapsed into it.

Now let me tell you a secret? Something I have never told anyone else . . . I may disgust you, but I am past caring. First let me tell you what Anis told me. He said that when he was a boy he read in one of his father's old books that a Persian called Ludovico Di Varthema had travelled to Java in the sixteenth century and found cannibalism rife. The Javanese were eating the sick, the old and the infirm. They would take their no longer useful parents and their sick siblings to the marketplace to be sold as food, and with that money they bought the old, sick and infirm of another family. When the shocked Ludovico protested, they shook their heads in exasperation and cried, 'Oh, you poor

Persians, why do you leave such charming flesh to be eaten by the worms?'

The night that Ibu died Nenek cut a tiny piece of flesh from the back of my mother's neck and ate it. No, she did not eat it because it was charming flesh. She ate it to keep my mother's magic in her body.

I knew that she'd done it but only now I understood why. For the very reason a man who finds a diamond will always seek to keep it. She wanted to keep her daughter's essence. I knew she would consume a piece of my sister too. And I would join her because I am not my father's high-born daughter. My real ancestors are the Bali Agas. We do not believe Father when he says rebirth is the frustration of death.

'*Rarisang*,' my grandmother will tell me. 'Do your duty.'

But first I must sleep. And when I wake up the ordeal will begin.

Stay close to me.

Fear nothing, do not flee.

Francesca

I glanced up at the clock over the stone fireplace. *Madonna*, it was five already. I stood up and stretched. Three hours had passed since the children left to spend the night at their Nonna Delgado's home. How quickly time had flown while I was caught up writing labels with lavender ink, and painstakingly tying each bottle with undyed string. The fire was dying out, so I put a few more logs onto it, and stood back to admire the table lined with row upon row of bottles. Francesca's Extra Virgin Olive Oil.

I hurried down a cold narrow corridor. My plan was to install proper heating next year. I selected a pretty green dress from the bedroom cupboard, and headed for the small bathroom. I closed the door, hung the dress on a hook, and switched on a small electric heater. Sitting on the edge of the bath, I warmed my hands over the hot air. They were no longer the beautifully manicured, soft hands of Francesca Delgado. They were the honest, callused hands of Francesca Sabella.

In the mirror, my face looked back, fuller and softer, with lips returned to their normal size. Thinking of how they were then made me shake my head in wonder. It seemed now like the most grotesque aberration to have slavishly followed the examples of other unhappy women. My skin was still fashionably brown but not because I had lain for half an hour on a sun bed, but because the sun was my clock. As its first rays touched the sky I awakened, and until it fell out of the sky I worked on the land.

Even my hair was no longer a straight precise curtain. It was full of soft, sun-streaked unruly curls. Once an award-winning hairdresser had seen me as beautiful in my natural state. He had cut as little as possible, and then coloured it with the streaks that the sun naturally made. I had hated it then, but I was different then.

When the room was warmer, I filled the sink with water, and undressed. My breasts were no longer pretty cones, but long swathes of flesh. I did not dislike them. They had fed three souls. It was right that they should look generous and fertile. A little lower, my belly swelled smooth and round. Still lower, broadening hips led down to thighs big with muscles gained from squatting to gather olives. I ran rough hands on my skin.

How easily I had become pear-shaped! But I could not find it in my heart to mourn the loss of that marble-like perfection I once was. This here was the body of a woman. A powerful joyful woman who had reclaimed her own life. This body felt everything. Once, I walked, spoke, talked and laughed, and you could never have guessed that I did it blindly, without feeling anything. Without admitting to my absolute poverty. In my abundant curves lay the blessings of my ancestors, my mother, my grandmother, and her mother before her. And because its ways must surely belong to my daughters one day, I had to teach them to claim its beauty too.

I had found a role for myself. I was happy being the mender of things broken, the protector of my children, the nourisher of the soil, the keeper of memories old and forgotten, and the creator of goodness in a bottle.

When the bathroom was nice and warm, I washed myself in the freezing water, and stepped into my dress. I draped a thick maroon shawl around me, and misted some perfume in my hair. In a cupboard under the sink I found my make-up bag. Because I no longer awakened in the middle of the night to look at the time, or feel the empty space beside me, I had no use for foundations, concealers and serums. Not even blusher was necessary. A touch of lipstick, a coat of mascara, and I was ready.

I went back into the living room, and peered into the darkening day. And I saw him coming down the hill, clutching a bunch of wild flowers in his hands. He was nothing like Ricky. He was quiet and serious, and he was waiting for my divorce to be final to marry me. Quickly I dabbed a little cream into my palms and rubbed them together. Then I locked the door behind me. There was a time when I would have left it unlocked, but even Ravanusa had changed. There were hypodermic needles stuck into the barks of olive trees. It broke my heart to see those poor trees. I carried a wooden box for collecting the needles now. Even this cold grey light would soon fade. I began to walk towards the waving man, curious to know what was next.

Nutan

I left her at the airport and took a taxi home. I was too weak and sick to make the necessary arrangements. The bumpy trip up into the mountains is a painful blur now, but I remember sitting in the car, and looking out in shock. It was the most incredible thing, but nothing, absolutely nothing had changed. I don't know what I expected but not that complete indifference to my sister's destruction. It was like being in a time warp. How incredible that this world should exist completely separate from the other. Had one whole year really passed?

It began to drizzle. A boy sheltered on the crumbling stone steps of a temple square, a velvet hibiscus tucked behind his right ear, and one hand languidly fondling a white fighting cock. Once in a while the fabulous bird snatched a morsel of food from his mouth. Did Ricky even exist? And Anis? If they did, they were fast vanishing.

Then the car stopped, and I fell out. Numbly I walked along the wall of our compound; clusters of pale green mangoes hanging over the wall were just starting to yellow. I entered our gates, the niches, as ever, filled with offerings. I don't know why I did it, but I hid behind the *aling aling*, and peeped into our compound. Perhaps I was frightened, or wanted to put off that moment of reunion, I don't know. I shan't forget it, though. That first unobserved glance at Nenek and Father.

My father was squatting by the cockerel cages, his hair not in its usual knot but loose on his back. Behind his ear he wore neither a red hibiscus, nor his customary black and yellow orchid. In his arms he held his favourite white cockerel. But his face . . .

Oh God, if you could have seen his face. It was as if I had been gone not just over a year, but fifty, or a hundred. The flesh was gone from his face. His skin sagged from his

416

cheekbones to his jowls, and gathered in tiny folds all around his mouth. His eyes were sunk deep into his face. His chin and nose appeared to have moved closer to each other, and he looked like one of his leather puppets.

I knew immediately which one.

The slain head-hunter warrior's father. I remembered him still, anguished and broken, in the flickering light. 'You have eaten the flesh of my son and so have become my son,' he whispered, in my father's voice.

I moved my eyes and saw Nenek sitting on the wooden steps of her living compartment, smoking a cigarette. She was exactly as I had seen her in my dreams, a hundred years old, but unfaded and glorious. Rocking me in her ancient arms and wiping away my tears.

There was a stillness about her. She was waiting for me. She knew I was coming though I had not told her. I was too frightened. I could not yet say to her, 'My sister is gone.'

I slipped past the *aling aling*, and it was the insane Rajah who first turned to look at his daughter. And what did the insane man do?

He bawled like a child. I had never seen him sob like that, not even when my mother died. The beautiful bird clasped against his chest forgotten, his nose ran and saliva dripped from his gaping mouth. For a moment I was mesmerised by his grief. I had not thought it possible. He who was so distant and cool. But then I realised that I felt nothing. My shrivelled heart blamed him. It was he who had brought the shimmering fox home, endangered his own daughters for a lover's glance.

I turned away from his grief, and stumbled into my grandmother's arms. Kneeling at her feet I buried my face in her lap. The scent of her. Oh, the scent of her. How it pained my heart. She lifted my head up.

She touched my shrunken face.

'From the day you were born, I knew this moment would

come. I tried. How I tried to still the hand of fate. But all my magic and all my power was for nothing. Did you know that I once glimpsed him, your yellow-haired murderer? Yes, fortune sent him. He came to this island, to this village. You and Zeenat were only children then, but even then he tried to touch you. I snatched you away, and thought I had made a difference, changed the future, but no . . . You went seeking him, didn't you? But you are not to blame. It was your fate. It was meant to be. Destiny is not written in sand, but carved in marble.'

She smiled a slow, sad smile. 'Never mind, I will cure you. I know how to make it better.'

And then she laid her hand on my forehead, and I was comforted by the cool sure feel of it. But calm brought clarity, and suddenly I was face to face with what had always lived unspoken, and dimly understood, in the deepest region of my heart. I remembered the one time Nenek had looked at me with futile eyes. It was the reason why only I, and never my sister, had glimpsed pale snake. Why he had come to visit me in London, the reason for my mysterious headache, and cryptic words – the awakening spine . . . my inheritance . . .

I was her heir.

The successor.

She looked into my eyes, and said, 'In a dream I tracked you down and saw you, not frail, injured, or guilty, but courageous, and shining bright. Under your feet the ground swelled, and on your glorious head sat the crown of a legendary *balian*. Your fame will be such that people from the four corners of the world will come to see you. You are the keeper of far more knowledge than I have ever been given. Do not run, and do not fear the future. I have seen it, and it is wonderful.' And because she spoke the truth, her voice was strong and sure.

Ricky

I knew it was over, even before I walked into the flat. The desertion was absolute. All the laughing people had disappeared as if into thin air. The air smelt stale and horrible. I had never noticed the tattered curtains, the cigarette burns in the sofa, or how disgusting the shag pile carpet had become. It was a nice flat once, with electric blue carpets, and geometric shapes on the curtains. In my greed I transferred the flat back to my name and played about with the equity in it.

It was possible the bank could move in on the flat tomorrow. But today it was still mine. I could still sell the TV. Perhaps Paulo would take it for fifty quid. That was a gram. Or I could throw in the stereo, and maybe the microwave, and ask a hundred for the whole lot. And that was two grams. As I sat there plotting my next hundred quid I had a thought. An idea. I went to the TV, and prised it open with a screwdriver. Lo and behold, in the crevice between the joints of the casing was enough coke to make a giant line. For years, bits of powder had been falling through the crack waiting for just this day.

Carefully, I collected the powder. Some of it was so old it was brown, and probably disgusting to you. But to me it was gorgeous. I have never been one easily revolted. Once when I was young, I forgot a pork chop in my desk on a Friday and when I returned after the weekend and opened my desk there were maggots writhing everywhere. The boy sitting next to me ran out of the classroom screaming, but I felt nothing. I sat at the desk of the boy who had run out screaming. It is the way I was made.

Pathetic, but there was not a note in my wallet to roll up. But it was okay. I found an old straw in the kitchen. I snorted it quickly, and fell back into the divan, sighing.

Ah, what the hell. It was worth it.

Fuck them all. I don't need them, anyway.

'Clouds are thoughts. Commit them to memory,' Maggie used to say. Silly girl. Flew out of a window. The spider love, crazy black widow, wove a fucking serpent into paradise.

Did I ever tell you about the time Haylee took her sweater off for me?

'*O la Madonna*,' I said.

She smiled. 'Wait, I'm not finished,' she said, and turning around, wriggled out of her jeans. And I couldn't help it. I had to bite it. Her arse was that beautiful. *Che bella?* Was it yesterday? It feels like yesterday.

And Francesca. What a child she was, alone in an empty field, big blue dragonflies darting about her. Flinging margherita petals with such determination.

'He loves me, he loves me not.' Oh, those beautiful, beautiful years. Where are they?

Now she is a producer of high-quality olive oil. I always thought of her like a child. Never thought she could make it on her own in the big bad world. No hard feelings, eh, Francesca?

I remember her laughing in Bali. She was so happy then. The memories are like gentle waves, rolling one after the other.

But I am afraid of the ones yonder, the big powerful ones. They are black and angry. Soon they will be upon me, but no worries, the drug will be taking effect any time now. Numbing the mouth, and blocking the waves.

Hey, where are you going? Come back. I'm not finished with my story. I'll rise from the ashes yet, you'll see. The Spider Goddess is still weaving. It's creepy, but she still has surprises in her busy jaws. Cruel ones. Beauties I will catch struggling in her web.

I may or may not hand their unwary souls over to her. She waits slyly outside my door, whispering, 'Death is nothing.' So that I feel obliged to be generous. It is worthless, human life. Listen, hang around, and I will let you decide their tiny fates. Come on, stay.

You don't want girls. Okay, forget the girls. I've got more.

I'll take you to Soho. I'll show you the sons of bitches gobbling up their crafty pleasures. Don't look askance. I'll make you weep, yet. It's a bad world out there.

Stay. Don't go. Need I remind you of the Corsican witch? 'He will grow to be a phenomenon,' she said.

I am not finished. From nothing to nothing. You're wrong. I will be rich again, and you'll come back then, won't you? To steal an ounce, take a pound. All the beautiful women will return, shaking their tight little arses, rubbing their disillusioned thighs together, and opening their voracious mouths, spiteful even in sleep. As Bruce described it, their currency is sex. Their cheap little purses are full with it. And they know the exact value of each chip they hold.

Have I ever told you about Morocco? No, not the place, the girl. Almost indigo, with a body as hard and shiny as polished wood. It must have been my Moor ancestors whispering in my blood, craving for the touch of black skin. In the reddish lights of the Stork club I wanted her.

It is true what they say about black girls.

Once you've had one the others pale slightly. Not only, if chemically untreated, is their hair like a cashmere cap, and their skin softer than any other race, but in the dark they smell of musk and sex. And of course, there is the way they respond. *Dio bono*, they fuck like animals. They don't need to get drunk first to be horny, and they don't wake up in the morning with excuses. 'I don't usually do this sort of thing . . .' Unashamed of their sexuality they go out for the night looking for honest satisfaction, a toothbrush tucked into a little purse. That's why they make unforgettable lovers.

And blond men are a magnet to them. Her smile floated in the dark.

'Do you come here often?' she asked.

'No, not really.'

I took her home. She had waist-length extensions in her hair and an arse to die for, high on her back, and tight with muscles. Moving closer, and mingled in the perfume, I encountered the musk. Not unpleasant, but sinfully strong. She peeled her white dress off. I grabbed her, and heard a tearing sound. Her underwear was in my hand.

She crossed her arms. 'You bastard,' she scolded. 'That cost me two hundred pounds.' She said this with an utterly straight face.

Brazen hussy. I looked at that cheap scrap of polyester and lace that my mother would have haggled down to five pairs for the price of 3,000 lira, the equivalent of about five pounds. I grinned at the hustle. She was testing her currency on an unknown connection.

Italians catch birds by throwing seeds on their balconies in the expectation that the dining birds will get too heavy to fly away. I had never tried it before, but I had always thought it sounded like a good way. Give a little, take everything.

'Okay, I'll pay for it,' I said, and she came towards me, fit as an athlete. And here is the truth. She didn't stiff me. It was the best two hundred I ever spent. Hunger is no fun. After all she ate two hundred pounds worth of seeds.

Me, I loved all the birds that came to rest on my balcony.

I could take the contempt in their eyes. It was their shield. How else could they cope with their contamination, the daily betrayal of themselves? I agree with the most sordid and admirable character created by the great man Mario Puzo. 'You have to feel sorry for the girls, they're working. I'm playing.'

Come on. Stay a while. What can it harm? I'll cook some

pasta. Penne Arrabiatta, okay with you? It'll be night soon anyway, and we'll light some candles. There may be no electricity. I am a magician. In the candlelight I'll weave my magic, marvellous magic. You will be swept off your feet. I promise you, you've not heard it all before. It's going to be good, really good. She's not finished, the Spider Goddess. I've still got a few surprises left up my sleeves. This can't be the end.

Come, you will not sit with inverted glass. We'll get drunk on the forbidden together. Wait a while.

Please?

Don't go . . .

Hey. . .

Ah well, catch you next time.

15 January 2004

My dearest Nutan,

Oh, you won't believe who I saw today. I know I wrote to you only a couple of days ago, but I absolutely need to talk this one through now. I almost can't believe it happened. At first, he just looked like a tramp foraging in a bin outside the tube station, but suddenly there was something familiar about him. He had a greying reddish beard, but the hair that escaped from his multi-coloured Rastafarian hat, although dirty, was blond. He wore a ripped, mud-streaked leather jacket, and as I came closer I heard him muttering to himself, 'Mad, mad, mad.'

I began walking towards him. He had found a discarded sandwich, and with blackened hands was prising it open. He peered at the contents, and then he brought it closer to his face, and smelt it. And I gasped. It can't be, my shocked brain whispered. Impossible. But good God, it was. He looked up suddenly and our eyes met.

Blue eyes looked at me. There was nothing in them. Then he started smiling.

'Do I know you?' he asked.

It was my hair. He has never seen its natural colour, or cut so close to my head. I shook my head, instinctively knowing not to speak.

'Got any change to spare?' he asked. He sounded lucid. Then he was as I remembered him. But as I looked, a sarcastic smile was spreading over his face, and I realised I had been gaping at him. I fumbled around in my purse and

found a ten-pound note. He snatched at it. I turned away and hurried towards the station entrance. Some part of me was hurting, but I could not offer my hand. He was too dangerous. He damaged everything he touched.

I had a vision of him recuperating in my spare room. His hands slowly creeping out from under the blanket to catch my children by their tiny necks. In his grasp, they decayed. But all the while he was asleep, and without knowledge of his murderous hand. I thought of my husband, my babies, and the home I had made. They were far too precious a blessing to risk.

Some perverse part of me wanted to hide behind a pillar and watch him. There is a perverse pleasure to be gained from the spectacular fall of another. But I feared him too much. I know you said that because there is no truth he adores enough to give his soul to, he could never be truly dangerous. And that worst atrocities in history have never been done by the faithless, or the small-time swindlers. But still . . . even in a Rastafarian hat, and rummaging through rubbish, rising from the soles of his torn shoes was an exciting dangerous mist.

As I melted into the crowd I heard him shout out, 'You can hide, but you can't run. The spider is swinging. Lazy in the wind. Waiting for you, Elizabeth.'

I froze. Of course, he knew it was me. Ricky and I are soul mates, fused together in some inexplicable way. Once a source of comfort, but now a fear in my heart for we both lit incense and worshipped at the Spider's altar. Both of us bringing tasty morsels for her to eat. She accepted the gifts we brought to her web, but she drew from us too. Then we gave willingly, but it is a long time now since I have stopped craving the poisoned bribes she dangles as bait.

I have protection now. I go to church. I lead a clean simple life, and I have forgotten the taste of a line of coke, vodka at six in the morning, and the hand of a man I detest on my body. She will never catch me swinging in the wind. Travelling down the escalator, with the warm air from the tunnels blowing at me, I sensed Ricky's gaze. He was still searching. I did warn him that he would never find his soothing nightmare, but he did not believe me.

Lots of love,
Elizabeth

10 April 2004

Dear sweet Nutan,

Bruce and I just returned from Anis's new exhibition. It is late, the babies are fast asleep, and Bruce is in bed, but I simply had to write, and tell you about my night. Oh Nutan, it was absolutely wonderful. He is a true genius. Remember how he used sensuality to express contempt, and without a shred of kindness? Well, no more.

People were glancing sideways to see if others were responding with the same emotions they were experiencing. He was always an excellent craftsman, but his sorrows have taught him true wisdom. And true wisdom has given him clarity of vision. Every brush stroke was so right, and he reached out with so much dignity that it brought tears to my eyes.

He was wearing a beige Nehru suit. He appeared spiritual, as if he has found a higher meaning. Don't get me wrong, he still feeds his arms. Once he said to me, 'An addict mistakes his pain for his pleasure. It is a special place, my prison. The door is wide open, the walls are made of cinnamon bread, and the chains are rings of almond cake. I will always be an addict, Elizabeth. Until you read in the newspapers that I am gone with an overdose.' He has found his own solace for his is the despair in the human condition.

The star piece of the night was a beautiful painting simply

titled 'Swathi'. A sad woman with slightly parted lips. As if she was caught as she began speech. Anis said that that one he painted to repay a debt.

He has painted us all. A gallery of broken people. You will see for yourself when you come at Christmas time. There was Maggie, fresh and lively in a green glade with white flowers. Butterflies sitting on her hands and a Mona Lisa smile on her face. She knows something we don't. It is a grand and frightening painting. She always wanted death.

There is one of you. It reminded me of a wild animal that is accidentally domesticated, but returns to its natural wildness. Your eyes are glowing and far-seeing. They have seen the hunter's traps. Under the skin of your arms networks of alert, powerful muscles are waiting to spring away, your body remembers, your bones know. This time you are ready. This time you will not be knocked senseless, or captured. And if you lose, it will only be some fur, a little skin. Only your mouth is sad. It made me sad to see you through Anis's eyes.

But best of all is a strange painting of Zeenat dancing in a temple. Her nails are long and golden, her clothes are beautiful, and on her head is a gold headdress. Her face is serene, but her eyes are not downcast, or shy. They are lifted up, and blazing with a strange light. I know it describes an unreal fantasy, a dead end, yet it is impossible to refuse the consequences of his longing, the illusion that in some mysterious way, she is alive. To pretend that he still meets her in some secret place where she dances for him. Otherwise how could he paint with such detailed accuracy? Not from memory.

Bruce wanted to buy it for you, but Anis was not selling.

It was distant and desolate, his smile. 'This one's mine,' he said.

Then that writer Rani Manicka arrived, and Anis left to greet her. I think she and Anis are together. I saw him brush his thumb along her cheek, and she smiled a slow secret smile.

She was wearing long gloves so I couldn't see for needle tracks, but I am quite certain she has picked up Anis's habit. There were lines beside her mouth and she looked aged, and without sparkle even while she laughed. I knew instantly what was gone, her moment of innocence. Once her face was open and curious, now it is closed and secretive. Her eyes glittered nervously like a cat in the dark.

I found her standing under the painting of Zeenat. 'It was I who paid for her death, you know,' she said, sadly. Then she told me she had stopped writing the book on us. It seemed wrong to profit from Zeenat's death. I could not offer her any solace. We talked a little about you, and I promised to send her regards to you.

'Please do,' she said, and adjusting the tops of her gloves, moved on. It makes me sad to know that there was a time she had to give you a tape recorder to carry while you were out scoring, so she could hear the lingo of the drug addicts' world. I wish now that Maggie had never gone after her the first time she came to Ricky's.

There was also a painting of Ricky with tears tattooed under one eye. He looked like a God or an avenging angel. I did not tell Anis about the episode featuring the Rastafarian hat, and the dustbin. His good heart might try to find Ricky, rehabilitate him, but Ricky will only laugh and destroy Anis. Bruce, Anis has painted playfully. 'Even silver-backed gorillas have to laugh at bubbles,' he said to me.

There is one of me, too. Irish child. From afar, it did not seem like me, but up close, I had to protect myself from my own suffering. I actually heard my mother's voice in my head, singing an old Celtic song. On a dark background he has revealed me with platinum hair and such torment. Only now do I know what true genius does. It takes you by the *hand up an unused creaking staircase into the gloom of a forgotten attic. There are horrid cobwebs that long to cling to your skin in this attic, but even in the dark he navigates you past them. Then without warning he becomes that fairy-tale matchstick girl who lights her last match and whispers in your ear, 'See.'*

In the flickering flame you come face to face with a lost truth. His artist's eye knew me before I knew him. He catches us all in the lies we sell.

Haylee holds a bunch of grapes in her hand, and her porcelain face looks out to the world with that sideways glance that makes men go crazy, but her mouth! What he did to her mouth! It looks like a swollen wound. Yet it is a tremendous painting. The spontaneous allure in the big blue eyes and the too-ripe mouth.

In a white leather pants suit she stood for a long time in front of the painting. I thought she was furious, but she turned to Anis, and said, 'What a clever boy you are! But what's with the crazy mouth?' Then she looked out from under her eyelashes, put her lips together and pushed them out in a perfect pout. Eyes shining, the old fun Haylee said, 'I've got some. Want a line?'

It was a strange moment of déjà vu. *'I've got some. Want a line?' Oh, the thrill that used to race through me when someone said that. Anis was the first to react. He picked up his wine glass, kissed her on her forehead, and wandered off with the advice, 'Be a good girl.' She offered him the wrong poison.*

'Shall we?' Haylee asked. 'For old times' sake?'

I looked at Bruce. What I saw in his eyes he saw in mine. The same question.

'Shall we?' I asked. For a moment we just looked at each other, and then I nodded, and so did he. Together we turned to face Haylee. She was beautiful Mara come to tempt us. A dakini in white leather.

'Thanks, but we're all right, Haylee,' Bruce said.

For a quick second there was need in the temptress's bright blue eyes to corrupt, to taint what she could not have, but then she winked suddenly and said, 'All the more for me then,' and slipped away.

I looked up at Bruce. 'Did you really feel it?' I asked.

'What? The earth shaking six times when I touched it, because I really, really *wasn't* tempted? Yes I really, really felt it.'

And he put his arms around me, and together we laughed.

Oh, I just looked at the time, and it is already three o'clock. I can't believe I have been rambling on for so long. Better go to bed. I've got a long day tomorrow. But before I go, I must tell you that after a whole year of religiously consuming your *jamu* pills I finally got a reaction. Bruce pounced on me in the middle of the night growling, 'What's this fucking perfume you're wearing? It's driving me crazy.' Not bad after three years of marriage, huh? Oh, and remember that powdered root you sent for Bruce's birthday? Well, it's picked up a bit of a reputation at the gym. Send some more. We could make some money here. Looking forward to seeing you soon. Give my best regards to Nenek, and Bruce sends love.

Big kiss,
Elizabeth

11 May 2004

Dear Rani,

I followed a temple procession this morning, a row of deeply pious womenfolk in square-necked lace blouses, balancing tall coronets of offerings, the sound of their feet awakening clouds of dust. In the cool mountain air we went past the wondrous flame tree, down the lanes between *the gold and green rice fields, into the village, and past the giant Waringin tree. It is still growing, languid but without restraint. Dripping aerial roots that grow into trunks.*

I am amazed by it. One single tree becoming a dream-like forest full of parasite ferns and liana. Not long ago its growing limbs trapped, then strangled and eventually broke an old stone demon in its path. Amid fears that it planned to swallow the entire square, the banjar, *council of elders, cross-legged, sat facing each other, and discussed the matter for hours. Finally they decided to do nothing.*

The tree had been there for hundreds of years, the skirt of yellow our ancestors tied around its waist signified it as sacred. Better to desire ruin than clip its holy roots. Yes, ridiculous I know, but it is a Balinese eccentricity. We do not take care of our things. We are charmed by decline and the new life that impermanence encourages. We accept the wisdom that decay brings. As white ants must devour wood, and the rainy season must rot paper, it is right that the years must grind man to dust . . .

Higher up the winding mountain path, ancient tribes-women moved in single file on their way to the marketplace. They are pig traders. Cradling the creatures as if they were babies, the women comforted their crying by allowing the young animals to suckle their dry breasts.

We carried our fragrant flowers to the furthest end of the village, by a red brick wall, past lanterns, up stone steps to the temple of Siwa, the Destroyer God. We went through a high door into the last and most sacred temple enclosure. In the inner temple we carefully replaced the remains of the previous day's gifts with even more offerings of fresh yellow rice, cakes and fruit. As clay braziers poured out sandalwood smoke I knelt, sat on my heels with my hands in a begging position, and prayed for you.

I write for two reasons. First, to enclose Elizabeth's last two letters. I think they should be in your book. (Kindly return them when you are finished. Even the faintest traces of Elizabeth are precious to me.) Second, because my grandmother – remember that woman you named 'remarkable' when I told you about her – has two glasses of advice to offer.

She is wise and I hope you'll drink deeply of her words. She asked if you could find a way to title your book, Touching Earth. This, she says, because the earth seeks to bless your book. And the other message is: 'Shed no tears if you have bled. It was only corrupt blood. Put your lamp down now, and fetch your pen with pride, for your innocent glance dared embrace beauty, even in her shame and filth. And there she is, beautiful again, in the opulence of a lover's brow even as he turns away for ever, sleeping on a stomach disfigured irreparably, in the richness of a body grown away from perfect, in the discarded brushes of a prostitute, and, while you are shedding tears for your unsheltered head, in the stars that shine upon you.'

I am also sending some roots. There are separate instructions for each one. Follow them carefully. They are only for you. Anyone can fall but everyone can rise again. Come back to Bali . . . just as I saw you at the beginning.

Nutan